I0720708

PRINT EDITION

Shelf Life: The book of better endings © 2019 by
Mirror World Publishing and Rob Gregson
Edited by: Justine Dowsett
Cover Designed by: Justine Dowsett

Published by Mirror World Publishing in July 2019

Mirror World Publishing
Windsor, Ontario
www.mirrorworldpublishing.com
info@mirrorworldpublishing.com

ISBN: 978-1-987976-55-7

Shelf Life

The book of better endings

By Rob Gregson

To those who love an open door.

1. Death and Taxis

Knock, knock.

A gloved knuckle struck the café window. It was the merest tap, but coming so unexpectedly and so close to her ear, it might as well have been an air horn. Finn's wrist responded with a jolt that sent a hot slop of cappuccino leaping for the sanctuary of her lap.

"Dah!" Snatching up a napkin, she pressed it to her jeans, glancing aside as it began its transformation from a pristine white to a sad and soggy beige.

Outside, a tall figure in a smart winter coat waved a greeting. It was directed at Chrissie, her sister. The attentions of sane, attractive, eligible men always were.

"Is that Tony?" Across the table, her mum gave Chrissie a nudge.

"Yup. That's him." A grin lit her face, though whether it was prompted by the new arrival or the spectacle of Finn's quietly steaming trousers, it was impossible to say. Perhaps a little of both. She turned her smile upon her friend. "You coming in?"

Her question was partly spoken, partly mimed; her lips made comically exaggerated movements.

Tony shook his head, pointed along the street, and mouthed something that was lost to the noise of the café. The place wasn't busy, but the baristas were showing off their determinedly buoyant personalities to two punters at the till. By way of accompaniment, a Miles Davis album contended with the mechanical snarl of an ice blender.

"He's nice, Tony, don't you think?" Her mum watched the young man leave, seeing him off with a coquettish wave of her own.

Chrissie shrugged. "He's alright." She'd always had her pick of admirers. That they went out of their way to grin at her through coffee shop windows was something she took entirely for granted - like oxygen or perfect cheekbones.

Her mum adopted an expression of casual innocence. "He's from your office, isn't he?" She took a keen and constant interest in their respective romances, despite Finn's continuing failure to deliver anything worthy of discussion. Keeping her bookshop afloat was demanding all her focus right now and it left scant time for men. A brief smooch at a midsummer barbecue was about the sum of her contributions to that particular topic, and now it was approaching Christmas.

"He worked at the last place." Chrissie took a sip of her coolly unspilled espresso.

"Oh, I see." Her mum gave a rueful nod.

"Mm. He got a bit funny after I got the promotion."

Finn leaned back and dabbed at the damp, chocolate-stained patch on her leg. Here sat her two dearest people in the world, but the discussion was taking a predictable turn. They'd do their best to include her, but this was very much Chrissie's story.

Since leaving university, Finn had grown used to performing this minor supporting role. Her sister was only a year older, but she led by far the more interesting life - all centred on a bright and breathless fast-track career in financial journalism. While Finn could only regale her family with tales of imaginative window displays and the rising damp along the back wall, Chrissie's anecdotes were of foreign capitals, famous moguls, and hastily-arranged interviews in airport departure lounges. Different lives for different temperaments.

Once, long enough ago for its title to have faded from memory, Finn had read a book about a man who seemed forever fated to live an unremarkable life. Some unspecified, epoch-making change was evidently unfolding right across his city but, at every turn, the most trivial events would always conspire to lead him the other way. She saw a lot of herself in that: an ill-fitting extra; a bit-part player in someone else's tale.

"So what about your new place, Chrissie?" Her mum's eyes twinkled. "Anyone interesting there?" They both knew what she was really asking; the desire for grandchildren was never far from her mind.

Chrissie smiled over her cup. "They're *all* interesting, Mum. I work with all sorts of amazing people."

Her mum pursed her lips and turned to Finn in mock annoyance. "Does she tell you anything, Cathy? She doesn't tell me a thing."

Finn shook her head. "Not a peep. I think she's secretly working for MI5."

"Nothing she does would surprise me." Her mum returned to her interrogation. "Come on, Chris. You fly off to all these places, you meet all these celebrities..."

"They're not celebrities. They're just business people."

"Oh, you know what I mean. You're hardly in the country these days. Your old mum just wants to know what's going on in your life."

Finn flashed her sister a conspiratorial smile and looked away. To her final breath, their mother would always proclaim an equal pride in both her daughters, but there was no hiding the fact that one of them prompted much more interesting conversation. Chrissie played things down, never pretended to be anything more than she was, but her burgeoning career and her growing absences from home inevitably put her centre stage whenever the three of them got together. By contrast, Finn was the dependable stay-at-home sister who saw her mum at least twice a week - and that was fine with her. She wouldn't swap places.

Now, as the talk turned to chance meetings in the snowy streets of Manhattan, Finn let her gaze drift through the window into the Great British drizzle beyond.

There was nothing wrong with staying here and being who she was. Her old university tutors might have frowned to see a promising student immersing herself in the vulgar world of retail, but literature was still a big part of her life. In an odd and unforeseen sort of way, she was still doing what she loved.

And who needed ice skating in Central Park when they could have all this? Finn stretched out her legs and did her best to luxuriate in the early Yuletide ambience. Who could say no to the warmth of good conversation? To the cheery parp of a passing black cab? To the Lowryesque figures who passed by the window, hunched and bent beneath their umbrellas?

Well, okay, maybe that was stretching things. Ideally, she'd be doing much better business in a smarter part of town - some place where legitimate customers outnumbered the drunks; where kebab-disposal wasn't regarded as the chief purpose of her shop doorway. For just a while at least, it might be nice to be somewhere interesting; somewhere a bit more encouraging of a passion for art and literature.

As though to illustrate her point, a white van mounted the kerb outside and juddered to a stop. A thin, dangerous-looking yob flung open the door and advanced with aggressive gestures towards someone just beyond her view.

"Cathy."

Finn looked back. Her mother and sister were looking at her expectantly.

"Mm?"

"Take a photo, would you, sweetie?" Waggling her phone, her mum leaned towards Chrissie, wearing the sort of smile one might instinctively associate with an abuse of medication. "She'll be off again at the end of the week; we've got to capture her while we still can."

"Oh, right. Yeah." Finn took the phone and fiddled with the zoom. "You ready? Say... *titular*."

The two of them grinned. "Titu..."

Bang.

The sound was abrupt and momentarily stunning; loud enough to rattle the window in its frame.

Outside, the young thug was pointing a pistol. It fired again.

"Shit!" Chrissie spun in her seat.

Finn tensed, barely processing what she was witnessing. As she did, her camera-phone produced a brilliant white flash.

The shooter was striding back to the van's open door when the bright burst drew his attention. He looked across at the café window and, for a moment, he met Finn's gaze. Two unreadable eyes narrowed; then the driver's arm was tugging at his sleeve and drawing him inside.

Wordless and white, Finn watched the vehicle speed away. From behind her came agitated shouts and the sounds of chair legs scraping tiles. She could only stare. The flash had been an unlucky accident - she'd been pointing the phone in a different direction altogether - but that wasn't really the point. The gunman might easily have formed a very different impression.

Outside on the pavement, someone screamed.

The longer Finn drove, the more she felt a strangeness settling. The city had a sullen cast. The moments passed, close and weighted, like the quiet, bated minutes before a storm.

Movements in doorways, the cars that drew up alongside her - everything appeared differently now, though it wasn't a transformation any camera would detect. It was she who was altered. Her world was impressing itself upon her in the age-old language of the hunt and, within her, some ancient survival instinct was responding.

Brake lights flared, snaking back through the dark and drizzle of the early evening. Checking her mirrors, she clasped the wheel tight - angry at being forced to leave like this; angrier still at how the experience was shaping her.

Outside, the world of the everyday rolled to a halt, all fancy falling away. Streets looked hard; the parks and the riverbanks unwelcoming. They offered no comfort now. The sentiments she'd attached to them were hers, not theirs; no more lasting or reciprocated than tattered poems pinned to the bark of a tree. The gingham-striped lawns wouldn't miss her. Shops would still trade, rocks would still grow smooth in the river. Her little exodus would go unnoticed.

Ahead, the stabbing reds dulled, distancing themselves as the line of vehicles moved on.

She glanced at her fuel gauge and saw the needle drooping to the quarter mark. What remained would take her well clear of the city. That would do. There would be plenty of opportunities to fill up somewhere on her long drive north.

Normality: that was all she wanted. Living like this felt surreal; somehow ridiculous. Gangland killings and criminal investigations were the province of dark-browed action heroes, not a woman like her. She ran a bookshop. She listened to *You and Yours* on Radio 4. She had a goldfish. Everything she owned and enjoyed declared her rightful place amongst the ordinary. Even now, in the midst of her flight, a pair of old running shoes sat in the footwell behind her, muddy and loosely wrapped in an Asda bag-for-life.

But normality had become elusive. Fear and unreality had suddenly intruded into her life, and all just because she'd chosen the wrong seat by a café window. Those few short seconds had been enough to overturn everything.

Yesterday had seemed endless but, in the early evening, an earnest-looking detective inspector had recommended she take herself *far away* for a while. His presence, his very title had seemed absurd - like something that belonged on the other side of a television screen - but still she'd taken it for sound advice.

So here she was, just twenty-four hours later, fleeing organised criminals in a green Fiat Panda; abandoning her flat, her friends, and her business in exchange for a period of safe anonymity somewhere in the Pentland Hills.

First though, she had to make things safe. Her mum and Chrissie had seen nothing of the killer, but who could say what he'd seen? His eyes had met hers - that she knew - but would he recognise her again? Had he seen enough to track her down? Had he noticed she'd had company?

Probably not. Real life was messy and hurried. All-knowing super-villains were the stuff of cheap fiction. But then, the formidable D.I. Holland had considered the risk serious enough to express his concern, and if there was indeed a credible threat to her, then it might also extend to those closest to her. She wouldn't rest easy in her Scottish bolthole knowing there was still an address book on her shop counter listing the whereabouts of all her family and friends.

Turning at the next junction, she saw the unlit frontage of her little bookshop, its darkness conspicuous amongst the bright facades of the newsagents and the betting shops around it.

Stopping the car, she slipped out and remote-locked the door as she stepped up onto the kerb. Another key set the metal shutters rising.

She scanned the street as the grey panels wound noisily into their housing. Few pedestrians were abroad - a scattering of early-leaving office workers making for bus stops and the taxi rank; nothing untoward. Seconds later, she was turning on the lights.

She knew that last bit wasn't textbook. Experienced international spies would probably use night-vision goggles or something, but that wasn't the sort of kit that most young booksellers had lying about in their handbags. Besides, she needed to see clearly if she was going to find what she'd come for. The quicker she found it, the quicker she could be away.

She hurried to her counter, expecting the rattle of glass that would tell her the door had settled shut behind her. Instead, there came a man's voice, jovial and strong.

"Hello there. Good evening."

For an instant she froze, then forced herself to turn.

The voice fitted the man. He was tall, well-dressed, and spreading into the roundedness of late middle age. A three-piece suit and gleaming brogues spoke of better neighbourhoods than this.

"Can I help you?" She smiled her shopkeeper's smile; an ordinary response to mask a mind contemplating extraordinary possibilities.

He returned a salesman's grin. "Miss Finn? The proprietor?"

It was a familiar overture. She saw a lot of speculative calls to the shop; offers of anything from public liability insurance to supermarket surplus.

"Yeah, hi." She turned away, feeling vainly for the precious notebook. "And you are?"

"Oh, I'm sorry. My name's Marcus. I'm a personal injury consultant."

Terrific: an ambulance-chaser. She turned back to face him. "Oh right. So that's… what? A sort of paralegal thing?"

The man chuckled, shook his head and reached into his jacket.

"You know, it's funny," he said. "A lot of people make that mistake."

He was still smiling as he took out a pistol, pointed it at her chest, and fired.

2. The Postman

Scowling at the downpour, Hitch angled the hand-written page to catch the strobing lights of a carrier drone that passed overhead. Cold blue washed the page for an instant and moved on.

It was the right place. He snapped shut the address book and considered the tenement opposite. A vertical chessboard of barred windows and soot-black brick, it stood with its lower third rooted in the night. There were no streetlights in the neighbourhood; no fixtures of any kind that hadn't been carried off by scavengers. Down here, it was just a deep sea of shadows and violence. Somewhere around the fifteenth floor, the streaming glass and ductwork reflected the colours of the city - a pointillist scatter of neon, sodium, and fires run wild - but he'd see none of those tonight. He wasn't going to rise that far.

Standing in his dripping doorway, he pocketed the book and peered hard into the rain. It was futile. In this light and weather, his chances of spotting a carefully-concealed watchman were about as lofty as a beetle's bum. An entire marching band might be taking a quiet breather just yards away and he'd never know it.

On the other hand, mistrust was a long-established habit, one that had served him well. Futile or not, it was an animal instinct; something that kicked in whenever he broke cover, and with one last job to do, it was time to move.

Clutching his coat tight around his throat, he probed his way across the road and felt water running into his hair and shoes. Silently, he cursed. The incessant rain was one of the many things he hated about this place. Cold, dark and sodden: why would anyone choose to make it their home? If it was just to show how tough and dangerous you were, then really you were trying too hard. People never ceased to disappoint him.

Approaching the building, he thumbed a card in his pocket. The door answered with a sullen clunk. It was heavy - checkerplate sheets bolted to wood - but it opened smoothly when he pushed. Stepping inside, he swung it shut, then squinted as the strip lights blinked and buzzed in reluctant procession up the stairwell.

His impression of the place didn't improve much with illumination. Give or take a few broken bottles, the little hall was empty: just the stairs, a single metal door and the inevitable aroma of other people's piss. Halfway up the door, a no-nonsense padlock underlined the sentiment of its single terse instruction: *Keep Out.*

So - eight floors and no lift. Well, that was just super.

Hitch had been fitter once. In his younger days he could tear about and scurry up trees with the best of them. Now, too much booze and too much fast food meant that eight flights of concrete steps could very nearly kill him. By level four, his lungs were tight, his calves were cramping and his eyes were stinging with sweat. By level six, his heart was hammering on his ribs like an angry neighbour and his mind was beginning to fixate on all the many inventive horrors he might one day inflict upon the building's maintenance manager. He completed the final ascent without actually vomiting but by the time he reached the door of room 801, he was far from the living embodiment of youthful vim.

He retained just enough wit and energy to pause and look about him. A thin, disdainful-looking cat regarded him from the flickering light of the passage. Hitch stared back at it for a long moment and, after an exchange of dark looks, concluded he could probably take it in a fair fight. The cat seemed to agree. After an ostentatious stretch, it turned and padded away.

Breathing hard, but feeling that he'd made his point, Hitch watched it go - its slow retreat revealed in zoetrope motion by the irregular winking of the lights. It wasn't nice here. The passage smelled damp. The wallpaper curled at the corners like pencil shavings. Lacking only a taped outline of a human figure upon the floor, it looked the kind of place where forensic scientists might spend a lot of time.

Shaking his head, he inhaled deeply, turned to the door and rapped out the three-two-four tattoo that announced him as a friend.

Footsteps. A second or two later, the peephole flickered.

"Oh God. It's you." It was a woman's voice. It lacked joy.

Hands thrust deep in his coat pockets, Hitch gazed at the unblinking circle of glass and said nothing. Gusting sheets of rain lashed the stairwell windows behind him - a fitting fanfare - but only silence and inactivity ensued.

Several uneventful moments later, he began to wonder about his tactics. He'd hoped that standing there rock-still might make him look a little bit cool or mysterious, but now the thought occurred to him that she might just have walked away. Cats were one thing, but he wasn't sure how long he could keep trying to outstare a door.

At last, however, there came a series of metallic scrapes and scratchings, the squeal of unoiled hinges and a widening rectangle of orange light.

A cheerless face looked back at him. "I suppose you want to come in."

"Hallie?" He followed her into an atmosphere that was ripe with cheese, garlic, and resentment. "I thought it was you. What are you doing in a dung-hole like this?"

"Shut the door."

Hitch bolted it shut and reset the small electronic jammer pressed against the frame. "Nice to see you, too." He turned to find her glaring at him, her arms folded tightly across her chest. He tried to remember what he might have done to deserve such a greeting and conceded that, whatever it was, it would only be the tip of a very ugly iceberg. As such, it was undoubtedly one of those problems best addressed through a policy of careful and continued avoidance.

He nodded to her couch and a box of half-finished pizza. "You got any spare?"

She blinked slowly. "I'm saving it for the dog."

Hitch glanced around. The apartment was tiny. The living area afforded just enough room for a TV, a shabby rug, and the couch itself, which looked like it had been lifted from the set of a fire safety commercial. The windows were partly veiled by broken plastic blinds and, to one side, three sheets of laminated plywood masqueraded as a breakfast bar. Beyond them stood a selection of firetrap appliances and a rusting sink.

He looked back at her. "You don't have a dog."

"I might get one."

He shook his head. "What are you *doing* here, Hallie? You hate it here."

"I didn't say that."

"You didn't have to." He pointed his palms at the ceiling. "I mean, look at this place. You're not a student; it's unnatural."

She gave him a weary look. "I'm *working*, Hitch. It's what we do, remember?" Returning to her place on the sofa, she put her legs up on the only other seat and gathered the pizza to her chest.

"This isn't working, it's hiding." He wandered into the kitchenette and was disappointed to find only two straight rows of bottled water set out under the worktop. Apparently, the only thing in here that was even vaguely alcoholic was himself. "And why here of all places? It's awful. It smells like the inside of a shoe."

"Why d'you think? The Watch got wind of your last little adventure; this was the next safe house on the list."

Hitch squatted by a doorless cupboard and grimaced at a well-ordered array of health foods. "Safe? Have you *been* outside?"

"No."

"No. Well there you are." Seeing that she was now making a point of refusing to look at him, he quietly slipped a packet of hazelnuts into his pocket.

"The package is in the bathroom," she said. "The address too. You'd best be getting off."

He looked up sharply. "You expecting someone?"

Blithely, she shook her head.

"Oh. I see. Humour. So you're still dabbling with that, then?"

She looked pained; tired. "Look, just *go away*, Hitch. I've tried so hard to be kind, to be understanding, but..."

Three sharp electronic beeps interrupted her.

"*Shit!* Is that you?" She yanked up her sleeve and examined the reader on her wrist.

Hitch did the same. "Ah. Yeah." He offered a sheepish smile.

Feeling her sudden ferocity all but searing his skin, he hit a pair of buttons on the little device and leapt to his feet, dropping the room into silence.

Everything ceased. Her angry glare was now fixed on the point where he'd been crouching. Outside, caught in the light of the window, raindrops hung motionless in the night, gleaming like opals upon a cloth.

With no choice but to leave her locked in her instant of wordless fury, he hurried from the kitchenette and looked again at his reader. It showed the first ripples of a gate appearing around the apartment door.

Tapping in an address, he took four quick strides towards the room's only other exit, then stopped as a familiar pang all but overwhelmed him. Seconds were precious at times like these but, really, there were just some things a guy had to do. Returning to his friend on the sofa, he bent forward and laid a hand softly on the back of her head. "Sorry, sweetheart," he said.

Then, snatching up her last remaining pizza slice, he ran for the bathroom as quickly as he could.

3. A Hundred Questions

ilence. Only the beginnings of the pistol's muffled report reached Finn's ears and then all sound abruptly ceased. The bookshop's organic murmurings, the noise from the road outside; all of it vanished at once.

So - death was silence. Well, that was one mystery solved.

She'd blinked at the instant her visitor had fired - an instinctive, pathetically ineffectual response - and she'd held her breath. Now, as she let it out, she heard the movement of the air. Against the perfect stillness, the sound was startling.

She opened an eye.

The scene hadn't changed, but it was stopped; a frozen moment. An orange-grey floret of smoke bloomed from the killer's gun, but it hung there, quiet and harmless, like a sculpted thing planted in the barrel. Beyond it, still visible, the stranger's incongruous smile.

She opened the other eye.

"Thirty seconds. Go."

Her whole body flinched. The voice - a woman's, crisp and businesslike - had come from her left, from the cupboard under her stairs, and that didn't make sense at all.

The cupboard door vanished, bright light spilled into the shop and a tall, silhouetted figure ducked through the frame.

"Cathy Finn?" A darkly-uniformed man strode towards her, one muscular arm outstretched. Behind him, another figure was emerging.

"Who the hell are you? What's happening?" She glanced back to the still-motionless assassin.

"My name's Reed." He stopped short, but offered her his hand. "Please come with me; we'll get you somewhere safe."

Behind him, two similarly-outfitted colleagues hauled in a silver, kayak-sized tube that couldn't possibly have fitted inside her cupboard. She vaguely recalled something about special forces teams breaking through walls to rescue hostages, but she felt sure that had to involve explosives or something. She didn't remember anything at all about kayaks.

"What is all this? Who are you?"

"Police. Now please, there isn't much time."

"*Twenty-five seconds.*" The woman's voice came from a communicator on his shoulder.

Finn stepped towards him, feeling a strange wrench, as though she were willing herself awake from an unpleasant dream. There was a wrongness to it, an unnaturalness, but for all that, the strange tide of experience was already sweeping her up. Perhaps only the sheer unreality of it was driving her on. Questions were hurling themselves at her like hail against a windscreen but, with no time for deliberation, she found herself relying once again on that primitive instinct for survival. Some bizarre clock was ticking and it seemed she had to choose quickly between an assassin's bullet and a rescue that could be neither real nor possible.

She took Reed's hand but then stopped as she registered the lettering on his bullet-proof jacket. "*SWAT?* What the hell? That can't be..."

"Look, I'm sorry." His face was conciliatory, but his grip was strong. "We are the good guys, I promise you. I'll explain later, but we've got to get you out. Please. Come with me."

He pulled gently on her hand, urging her towards a cupboard that ought rightfully to contain only an electricity meter, a box of till rolls, and a smiley-faced vacuum cleaner. Instead, she was snatching glimpses of a brightly lit room with a white tiled floor.

"Twenty seconds."

She didn't move. A thought had struck her.

"Tell me something, Mr. Reed." She swallowed. "Am I dead?"

Grinning, he shook his head. "No, no. It's kind of crazy, but it's nothing like that."

She felt another tug on her arm. This time she went with it, craning her neck to watch Reed's associates lifting the metal tube upright.

"Fifteen seconds."

"Probably best not to watch this," he said. "It can be a bit unsettling."

Finn looked back at her assassin. "What are you going to do to him?"

"To him? Nothing. Come on."

She stopped again. "Nothing? Then what are you doing? What is that?"

At a touch from one of the operatives, a panel in the tube swung open. The other reached in.

"Ten seconds."

"Come on," said Reed. "It's better we explain in there."

Feeling his other hand on her shoulder, Finn allowed herself to be guided backwards towards the door, still watching the bizarre scene playing out in her ordinary little shop. Hurriedly, Reed's two colleagues fussed inside the tube and brought out what had to be a mannequin. It was dressed exactly as she was - jeans and a grey hoodie beneath a long woollen coat. The hair, too, looked precisely the same colour and cut.

"Wh..." Her question was interrupted by a dull white flash. The scene closed on her in an instant. Now only a plain, door-shaped slab of alabaster filled her view. It was set - fixed and frameless - into a stone wall in one corner of a bright, echo-filled room. Instead of damp, ragged grey carpet, her feet found marble tiles.

"Just come back a bit, please." Reed guided her a few steps away from what surely still had to be her cupboard door. "They'll be coming through in a second."

Finn looked at him, dazed and in need of something solid on which to fasten her thoughts. The room - which by all logic really ought to be filling the entirety of Mr.Mahmud's newsagents - was about the size of her living room and looked to be empty, save for a single wooden door in the opposite corner. In the absence of furniture, fixtures, or even one or two fundamental laws of physics, she had little choice but to begin her re-evaluation with Reed.

She guessed he was in his late twenties. Tall and strongly built, close-cropped hair, good looking. No accent she recognised; not American and certainly no SWAT team specialist.

He nodded to the alabaster rectangle as he shrugged off his protective vest. "Here they come."

The stone didn't change its appearance as his two companions passed through. Nor did it seem to hinder the now-empty silver tube which they set down beside them.

"Hello, Miss Finn." The nearest sent her a grin. "Glad to have you with us."

"There'll be somebody here in a moment to explain," said Reed. "It's going to seem weird, I know, but… well, trust me: this is a good place to be." He began to turn away.

"Oh, no." Finn grabbed his arm. "No, no, no. You don't do the 'mysterious stranger' act and then just disappear. What just happened? Where am I? What *is* this?"

Dropping his jacket against the wall, he rubbed his scalp. "I'm sorry, but we've got other people here to answer questions like that. People a lot better at it than me." He glanced at the door, his voice hardening a little. "And they should've been here by now."

Finn released him with a sniff. "Yeah, well they're late. You're all I've got."

"Hey, Reed." The youngest of the three looked up from packing his kit into the tube. "We've gotta go. Three more of these before lunch."

Reed nodded. "I know; I'll catch you up. If you see anyone from Reception…"

The other rolled his eyes. "Yeah. *If.*"

Reed watched his friends manoeuvre their strange capsule through the door. Then, noting Finn's glare, he took a breath. "Okay, look. Um... You *are* in a safe place, so please don't be alarmed. It's, ah... natural that you'll be feeling a sense of disorientation at this time but..."

"No, no, stop, stop." She waved impatiently. "Just... just forget all the rehearsed stuff. *Talk* to me. Your friend just said 'lunch' but it's coming up to five. Where am I? What is this?"

Reed glanced again at the door. "It's... complicated."

"No kidding. Help me, here, Reed. What we just did - none of it makes sense. Am I dead? Am I dreaming? I mean, give me *something.*"

He looked away, his eyes unable to settle. "I'm sorry. Just remember: I'm not good at this."

"I'll remember anything you want so long as you get to the bloody point."

"Okay, well... Did you ever read any sci-fi?"

She pulled a face. "I've seen *Star Wars*. I used to watch a bit of *Stargate* when I was little."

"Okay. That one was about gates to different worlds, wasn't it?"

"Uh huh." She was pretty sure she didn't like the direction this conversation was heading.

"Well, think of..." He stopped at the sound of the door opening. A matronly, olive-skinned woman hurried in, a folding stool tucked under each arm.

"Oh, thank the gods for that." Reed seemed almost to deflate. "Cathy Finn, I'd like to introduce my friend Cariola. She's *very* late, but I know you'll get on fine."

"Late and ridiculously busy," muttered Cariola through a smile.

Reed looked back. "Um, Miss Finn, it was good to meet you, but now I've really got to get going." He nodded her a small bow.

Finn responded with her flattest, most baffled look. "Okay. Right... Well goodbye then, Mr. Reed. Thanks a lot for... whatever this is."

He offered an apologetic smile. "Got to run."

Cariola caught his eye as he made to leave. "You're doing *Resolution's Brink* next, aren't you?"

"Yeah, and now I'm running out of time to kit up."

"Well I'm sorry, but you know how things are."

"*And* they messed up the outfits again." He picked up his SWAT vest and strode to the door. "This is getting out of control."

Cariola smiled thinly. "I know that, Joe, and I'm trying to do my job here, sweetie, so perhaps we could save the complaints until later, eh?"

Giving a quiet snort, Reed offered Finn a final wave and was gone.

"Now then, Cathy." Setting down the stools, Cariola gave her the most reassuring of smiles. "I'm sure you've got a hundred questions."

4. Cucumber and Lettuce

At barely three feet high, the door was a lot smaller than Hitch remembered it. Arched and made from brightly painted timbers, it was attached to the tree with shiny brass hinges that gleamed even in the darkness of the hollow oak. It took only a moment to poke at the latch with his foot and push it aside. Shuffling out took considerably longer.

He rose into a warm, softly dappled glade - the sort of place where you wouldn't be at all surprised to find an aristocratic fox strolling about with a walking stick and a monocle. A gentle breeze soughed through the ferns. Birds chirruped high in the branches. Bees hummed softly as they wove themselves amongst quietly wafting fans of sunlight.

Squinting at the brightness and the sheer saccharine ghastliness of it all, Hitch stretched his neck and wondered again why his hangovers insisted on pursuing him across every threshold. It was an annoyance that came as no surprise - just another sticky dollop from the dung cart of inconvenience that life seemed intent on unloading on him.

Closing the little door with his heel, he took stock of his surroundings. He knew the setting well enough, but it was a long time since he'd come to it this way. Three different cities lay behind him, as did a battlefield, a Regency manor house, a submarine, and a castle. He'd moved as quickly as discretion would allow and now, if only for a while, he felt confident that he'd shaken off his pursuers. Their fathomless obsession with his affairs had torn a ragged hole in his plans for the day, but that happened sometimes; he was nothing if not adaptable and now he saw an opportunity to set things back on track.

Approached by one of the countless paths that seamed the harlequin fields of the valley, the farm lay only a little way down the hill, not far beyond the edge of the wood. A remote cluster of golden buildings and rose-grown walls, it was one of the safer places to trade: quiet, lots of doors and little danger of bumping into any unsuspecting locals. That last point was especially important. In all the worlds, there was no one more chatty or inquisitive than country folk, and with some seriously determined watchers on his tail, an encounter with some chirpy, basket-carrying gobshite could very well mean disaster.

Tucking his newfound package into a poacher's pocket, he started walking.

He heard the children long before he saw them. They spoke with a cheery confidence that made his jaw clamp up tight.

"I say, Hettie, Mummy really does make some super sandwiches." Through gaps in the hedge flashed glimpses of a young boy lounging in the grass beside a large wicker hamper. His shirt and shorts were bright enough to induce a migraine. "Mine's ham and cheese; what's yours?"

Still no more than a flicker of white lost amongst the hawthorn, the sister laughed. "Cucumber and lettuce - just the thing for a warm summer's afternoon!"

"Ha! *Rather!* D'you know, I think..." The boy paused, sat erect and then spoke in an altogether different tone. "Good heavens, look at that! What a queer-looking chap! I don't like the look of him one bit!"

There was a rustle of fabric. "Gosh, Peter - nor do I. He's awfully scruffy and secretive-looking. I shouldn't be at all surprised if he were a vagrant or a burglar!"

"Well, I'm not afraid of *him,*" exclaimed the brother. "Let's run over there and frighten him away!"

Whooping loudly, the two children raced across the paddock and flung themselves upon the gate.

"I say! You!" cried Hettie, waving an accusatory sandwich. "What are you doing by our farm?"

Huddled into his heavy coat, Hitch shambled closer before turning upon them a red and baleful eye. "It's *me,* you prissy bum nuggets. Now get down off that gate; I'm in a hurry."

Peter stared. "Postie? Is that you?"

Hettie glanced quickly about before hopping off her perch. "Crikey. Look at you Hitch, you look dreadful."

He chewed on a hazelnut. "It's a new look. What d'you think?"

"You're hungover, aren't you?" Peter stepped back as Hitch opened the gate.

"What can I say? I'm weak."

Hettie rolled her eyes. "Oh, what's the matter *now?*"

"Oh, you're too young to understand. Life's very..." Hitch waved as though batting flies from his face. "Complicated. Complicated and disappointing. Don't ever grow up - it's rubbish."

"Grow up?" Peter rolled his eyes. "Us? Chance would be a fine thing."

Setting the gate shut, Hitch shook his head. "No, no. You say that but you'd hate it. It gets so messy. There are relationships and obligations and..." He winced. "Expectations. There are always lots and lots of expectations."

"You're a frightful mess, Postie." Hettie gave him a despairing look. "You really should try to buck yourself up, you know."

"Yes. Thank you. It's a fine idea and I'm sure I'll give it all the consideration it deserves." A strong self image was an important asset to a man and though he was now failing an impromptu appraisal by a ten-year old girl, Hitch was determined not to let it bother him. "In the meantime, I've got a business to run."

Peter glanced back to the farmhouse. "The usual?"

Hitch nodded.

Hettie regarded him dubiously. "And what have you got for us?"

Peter's face brightened. "Any porn?"

Hitch blinked. "What? *No.* Of course not. I'm not giving you porn. You're eight years old."

A sulky frown worked itself across the boy's face. "Yes. Eight years old *forever...*"

"Don't be revolting, Peter." Hettie shook her head. "So what *have* you got for us, Postie?"

"Any smokes?" The boy offered a hopeful smile, but retreated into silence when he noticed his sister's darkening scowl.

Hitch fished in a back trouser pocket and produced a small rectangle of plastic.

"Is that for the PlayStation?" Peter edged forward, enthusiasm defeating a naively attempted poker face.

"Oh, I do hope it's not another racing game." Hettie's shoulders sagged, but the gesture was exaggerated; a haggler's gambit, nothing more.

Hitch shrugged. "The box had a picture on it; sweaty men with swords and big guns. I think it had the word *Slayer* in the title. If you're not interested..."

Peter glanced hopefully at his sister, who gave a wry grimace before nodding her assent. "Two pounds three ounces?" she said.

Hitch attempted a calculation but quickly gave up. "Is that...?"

"A kilo," said Hettie, turning towards the house. "The usual."

5. Ian Pea

Deep down, Finn knew her best chance of making sense of things lay in having a rational discussion. However, in the face of so much nonsense, getting angry was proving a far more instinctive and satisfying choice.

She banged a fist on the stone doorway that refused to let her home. "So I *am* dead. Reed didn't save me at all. This is some god-awful afterlife."

There was the squeak of a stool on marble as Cariola rose to stand beside her. "No, Cathy. You're alive and well. I told you; you were *extracted*."

Finn had wanted to like Cariola. She'd saved her, after all - if 'saved' was really the proper word - but it wasn't happening. Finn needed answers and Cariola was evidently new to her role - new, and by no means a natural. She'd spent the first few minutes of their meeting in a state of some perplexity, shuffling a thick wad of papers, gabbling through a series of standard statements and launching strange questions at her, seemingly at random. Whatever documents they were, she'd clearly brought the wrong set and, so far as Finn could tell, she'd quickly had to resort to improvisation.

Finally, however, and with no logical preamble, she'd got to the gist of things. And as gists went, this one really wasn't good.

"*Extracted*," said Finn. "Okay, but you're still saying that in the eyes of everyone I've ever cared about, I've just been shot and killed."

"Yes, dear." Cariola offered her a supportive smile. "I'm sorry. But if you'll just let me go through a couple more pages, I'm sure..."

"*Killed*! As in 'never going back.' As in 'never seeing my family again.'"

Cariola leafed nervously through some more pages. "Well, I don't know; if Chrissie or your mother face the same fate you did, then we'll extract them too."

"I don't *want* them extracted! I want to warn them. There's a killer out there!" She began pacing, wide-eyed. "If I can't wake up and tell them, they could be next."

"I promise you, Cathy, they'll be fine..."

Returning to the intransigent doorway, Finn directed upon her the sort of expression usually reserved for over-eager traffic wardens. "You can't know that. I *have* to go back - and you've no right to stop me. This... this is an abduction." She waited for a moment to see whether the implicit threat of legal action was going to have any effect. It didn't seem to be working, so by way of consoling herself she muttered something rude and incoherent. It was at times like this - not that there had actually been very many times like this - that she wished she'd studied law instead of literature.

"I'm sorry, Cathy, it can't be done. That isn't how it works." Cariola ventured an ill-advised pat on her arm, treading that fine line between condescension and getting a good kicking. Happily oblivious to Finn's faltering self-restraint, she raised her eyebrows and produced the kind of placid smile that might normally accompany an explanation of how to operate a spoon. "You were *shot*, Cathy. That's the reality in the world you've just some from. A man walked into your shop, he took out a pistol, and he shot you three times in the chest. People don't come back from that."

Wondering whether now would be an appropriate time to start pulling out handfuls of hair, Finn slapped the stone again. "But you *stopped* him. I don't know how, but Reed and the others, they came in and stopped everything; they took me out of the path of the bullet."

At Cariola's silence, Finn felt a cold dread creeping about her. She remembered the insistent countdown, and what she'd taken to be a mannequin. She was beginning to suspect what it all meant.

"They put a *corpse* there in my place?"

The counsellor nodded. "A sort of mindless clone. We call them *shades*. But we're getting a bit ahead of ourselves; it's really all a lot clearer if we go through the checklist."

"Bugger the buggering checklist." The counsellor had already taken her name, her date of birth, and a raft of other particulars, and after that it had just got stupid. Whether as a sick private joke or some strange experiment in surrealism, she'd then asked her to list the names of the current Prime Minister and the US President, what year she believed it to be and the season's best selling single. When she'd asked her to hum it into a recorder, Finn had nearly punched her. Since then, their relationship had barely improved.

"I'm sorry," said Cariola, "but they're all just standard questions."

"*Planet of origin* is a standard question?"

Cariola looked at her feet. "No, I told you: that was the wrong section. I'm sorry about that."

"In what possible circumstances could that ever be in the right section?"

Cariola fidgeted. "It isn't important. I just need to make sure we have a proper understanding of who you really are."

Finn glared. "Look, if it gets me out of this prison cell and back on my way home, I don't care if you tell people I'm the Archangel Gabriel."

The counsellor's brow folded itself into deep corrugations. "But just to be clear, you aren't saying you actually *are* the Arc..."

Finn stared. "No, *of course* I'm not the Archangel bloody Gabriel! I'm Cathy Finn, I'm twenty-four years old, and if you don't let me go, I'm going to have to start punching people."

Cariola shuffled her papers. "Yes, well I'm sure we can fill in the rest as we go."

"Go?" Instinctively, Finn edged closer to her wall, to the shop where she belonged. "No, no, no. I've got people who need me. I'm only going one place, and that's home."

Cariola studied the floor again. "Cathy, I've told you. We can save people - extract them - but it's beyond our power to change their fate as others see it."

Finn folded her arms. "No, you didn't."

"What?"

"You didn't say that. You never said anything like it."

"Didn't I?" Cariola glanced back at her papers and frowned.

"No. You said 'genre' and 'diegesis' a lot, but..."

"Yes. Sorry. That bit was for office use only. I shouldn't have..."

Finn tried another approach. "Look, you're obviously busy. Why not just open this door and leave me to it? You can forget all about it and I'll take my chances on the other side."

Cariola shook her head and rolled up her bundle of forms. "I'm sorry, sweetie. These doors only ever open once. Whatever was supposed to happen on the other side, that still has to happen. That has to be what people in your world see. In the reality you've come from, Cathy Finn's story ended in her bookshop."

Finn couldn't bring herself to imagine her mum's reaction. Instead, she put her faith in logic and what she still hoped was an obvious truth. "Right. Okay. Except that it *didn't* end, did it?"

"No, dear, but you saw what was going to happen. You couldn't go back now. In your world, there *is* no life to go back to."

"*My* world? *My* reality?" Finn found herself treading a crumbling path between despair and defiance - twin chasms, each a giddying descent into madness. "You keep talking as though we're... Where *are* we?"

At this, the counsellor produced a happier smile. "It's called New Tybet. Believe me, Cathy, this is *such* a wondrous place you've found. People like you and me have been coming here for generations."

People like you and me. Finn doubted there were many classifications into which she and Cariola would both comfortably fit. Beyond *vertebrates* and perhaps *mammals*, the taxonomic options seemed to dwindle very quickly. Still, there seemed little point in inviting another argument or maintaining her assault on a wall of cold stone. Instead, with a plan of sorts stirring, she looked at the other door, at the one comprehensible thing she'd seen since being hauled from her shop.

"I won't believe it," she said. "Not until I see it."

"No, of course." Cariola followed the direction of her gaze. "But that's fine. It's a lot to take in. When you feel ready, I'll take you to the reception meeting. You can get your bearings there. Then, after the presentation, everything else is really up to you."

Finn snorted. "I haven't been ready for any of this. I don't know what the word even means."

Cariola smiled. "I suppose it means not so shocked that you can't step through that door with an open mind."

"Mm. Reed talked about science fiction; different worlds..."

The counsellor raised an eyebrow. "Oh, did he now?"

"Yeah. So what did he mean? What are we talking? Klingons? Little grey saucer men?"

Cariola grinned. "There's a little bit of everything, Cathy, but you'll integrate at whatever pace you choose."

"Right. Sure. And it's *Finn*, by the way."

"Sorry?"

"Finn. Only Mum and Chrissie call me Cathy."

"Sorry. Finn, it is."

Finn nodded to the door. "Well then, I suppose we should get on with it, shouldn't we?"

Nodding happily, Cariola led her to the door and opened it without comment or ceremony. With a gesture, she invited her through.

On the other side, there was still no sign of Mr. Mahmud or his newsagents. Instead, in a tiny control room, half a dozen techie types huddled with their backs to her, all fussing over papers, pads, and computers. The nearest screen showed the room she'd just vacated. The next showed the interior of her bookshop, still glowing innocent and ordinary behind a bright, bold-faced caption: *A Young Wolf's Cry*.

The operative closest to her glanced her way and flickered a distracted smile. Then, perhaps catching the intent of Cariola's warning frown, she gave a little flinch and tapped the glass. It faded for a moment, then displayed a high, helicopter's view of an icy fjord. Another caption appeared: *Hvergelmir: the Three Roots Trilogy*.

"What's all...?" Finn stopped abruptly as a door in the right hand wall yielded to a pair of bearded Vikings. Each was trying to wrestle himself into a heavy fur coat.

The first paused when he saw her. "Frightfully sorry," he said. "Thought you'd finished."

Behind him, in a bright passage extending off to the right, a crowd of orderlies gathered. Several propped up large silver tubes; some consulted notes; others stood talking by wheeled costume rails. None remarked upon her miraculous appearance, nor even cut short their discussions. They certainly didn't look like they belonged in some futuristic spaceport; more the backstage corridors of a busy London theatre.

"Other door," smiled Cariola.

Stepping over Reed's discarded SWAT vest, Finn followed her guide to the room's only other exit - a featureless white panel in the corner of the opposite wall. It slid open at her approach - *USS Enterprise-style* but without the satisfying *pssshht* - and revealed a great torrent of people. They were all immersed in animated debate and walking the same way, left to right, along a broad, white-lit corridor. Their numbers made it sound like a stampede.

"They're off to the welcome meeting," explained Cariola. "Don't worry; most of them will be feeling just like you."

Doubting that very much, Finn scanned the faces of the passers-by. There wasn't a phaser, a pointy ear, or a tinfoil trouser to be seen - just scores of ordinary-looking people in varying stages of bafflement and distress. There were no obvious uniforms or identification cards amongst them - nothing that clearly distinguished the counsellors from the new arrivals. Were it not for the presence of the occasional bloodstained battledress, they could have come straight off the escalators of any shopping centre in the country.

"Shall we?" Cariola gestured to the right, inviting a leap into the turbulent river of humanity.

Finn nodded and stepped forward.

Placing a hand on her forearm, Cariola stuck by her as closely as she could, and for exactly twenty-six paces Finn remained meek and impassive, following the herd towards the reception meeting and all the answers that supposedly awaited. As she went, silently counting her strides, she noted the doors that punctuated the walls of the great passageway and checked the illuminated signs above them. Each bore some new and cryptic legend: *'The Quantum Gatemaster'* neighboured *'Volpone's Niece'* and, on the opposite wall, *'Hamlet (131c)'* gave way to *'Plimsolls and Paraquat.'* If there was a pattern or a logic to it, then it lay beyond her ability to see it.

At step number twenty-seven, Finn saw what she'd been looking for. The words *'Resolution's Brink'* glowed quietly above yet another aseptic-looking exit. She smiled to herself. She didn't know what lay beyond the door, but according to Cariola's parting exchange with Reed, he had been headed there next. Now, at last, she had an idea of what to do.

In the chaos of the corridor, with jostling figures to every side, it was an easy matter to let slip Cariola's hand and allow a fellow crowd member to filter in between them. Rather than attempt an immediate dash, she glanced at her counsellor, offered her a reassuring smile, and stayed level with her for another four, five, six, seven paces. Then, anticipating another eddy in the mass, she ducked back and allowed a great scrum of soot-mired colliers to pass. Their burly forms and loud debate afforded all the cover she needed. In the next moment, she was turning aside and heading for the wall.

A small part of her felt bad about the betrayal - Cariola was doing her best - but weighed against the risks to Finn's family, the balance was only ever going to tilt one way. When she reached the side, she began inching her way against the heavy press of bodies and didn't once look back.

The return was harder than she'd expected, as were many of the knees and elbows that connected with her. She soon gave up counting her steps; paces counted for little when all she could do was shuffle sideways along the wall. Amidst all the smiles and muttered apologies, she doubted she could have kept track anyway. Instead, she pressed on, peering upward until she saw the word *'Brink'* glowing white and welcoming above her head.

Looking down, she found a plain panel. No fingerprint pad or retinal scanner challenged her, not even a lock or a slot for a key card; just a recessed square of metal and the instruction 'push'.

She pushed.

The door opened into another control room, the mirror image of the one she'd left, and all but one of its occupants were gazing intently at a large central screen.

"Yes?" The face that challenged her belonged to a young man. He sat on the end of a console, absently tapping at the face of something resembling a smartphone on a wrist-strap.

"I'm looking for Reed," said Finn. "There's been a mix up on his next outfit."

The man snorted but looked unsurprised. "Cuh. It's a mess, isn't it?"

Finn raised her eyebrows. "Tell me about it."

"Bloody Ian Pea."

"Yeah," agreed Finn, wondering if she'd just heard that right. "So, Reed; is he, er...?"

"Nah, you'll have to wait." His eyes flicked to the main monitor. "He's just gone in."

"Oh right, the, um..." Finn looked past him and blinked.

On the screen, suspended above a field of stars and blackness, a slender tube of steel and fissured glass connected the great grey bulkheads of two starships. Within it, clad in an armoured suit of copper and blue, a helmeted figure hung by the airlock door. He clawed weakly at a sparking access panel as yellow warning beacons strobed through the rapidly venting air.

Beyond him, deep into the lightless distance, warring vessels flared and slowly splintered, blossoming upon the darkness like petals of silver, blue and white.

A buzzer sounded in the control room and the scene froze. One of the technicians tapped his headset and spoke above the hubbub of the room.

"Thirty seconds. Go. Quick as you can, Mr. Reed."

Reed burst from the seal at the far end of the docking tube dressed in a NASA-style spacesuit. Grasping a side rail, he propelled himself smartly towards his target. Behind him on a long webbing leash trailed a weightless, kayak-sized canister and an exact but lifeless simulacrum of the struggling man.

Reed's voice crackled over the control room speakers. "Commander Tomkyn. Please come this way. I can help you."

Abruptly, the other figure ceased his scrabbling and turned, rotating smoothly in the zero gravity. A mirrored visor concealed his face. His breathing came in ragged bursts but his hand beckoned weakly.

Reed pulled himself closer. "Commander: I need you to take my arm."

Tomkyn took the rail and straightened. "Ah, but to what purpose, winchman?" His words, suddenly strong and clear, had a mocking tone. "That I may return with you to your miraculous land of cedar and honey-dew?"

In the control room, the lead technician flashed a look of alarm. "Twenty seconds. What's happening, Mr. Reed? Is he delirious?"

Reed ignored the question. "Commander, I can get you out of here, but we need to hurry."

"A kind offer, but one that I must respectfully decline." Tomkyn bent to withdraw something from a thigh pocket. "You see, I've devised a little extraction of my own."

In the control room, the technicians' worried chatter erupted into panic as he levelled a chunky-looking sidearm at his rescuer. Reed yanked on the tether, perhaps hoping the silver canister might somehow deflect the blast, but it was too late. In the same instant he was rocked by a bright, concussive pulse of energy that shattered windows and sent him drifting, limp and silent, out into the void.

6. Slippery

You really couldn't beat a good apocalypse: loud and chaotic with everyone's attention directed elsewhere.

Strolling beneath red and roiling clouds, Hitch espied an ageing businessman cowering by the steaming wreckage of an executive saloon. The brain-boiling din had masked his approach so he announced himself by rapping cheerfully upon the man's shoulder.

Still clinging to his briefcase, the other spun his head and pointed to the blazing sky. "Aaaaagh!" he said.

"Yes." Hitch had to shout to be heard above the cacophony of thunder and civilisational collapse. "But the thing is, I need a door. One with a proper frame that isn't all bent and broken. Have you seen any?"

The suit paused, blinked at him and then flung his arm at another patch of sky. "Aaaaagh!" he insisted.

"No, right, I understand. The meteors *are* bad." He stopped. Peering over the man's dust-rimed hairpiece, he glimpsed a security van. It wasn't in pristine condition: it stood on four burning tyres and its front end was buried deep in a boutique store window but, crucially, its heavy metal side door was intact. That would do very well.

"It's all right," he grinned. "Never mind. Have a nice day." Wafting the man a wave, Hitch started to make his way through the concertinaed remains of the city traffic.

As he approached, the van door gave a little wobble, its surface distorting like rippling oil. This coincided with a sharp buzz from the reader on his wrist.

"Ah... fudge trumpets." Hitch ducked beside a shattered four-by-four and pushed up his sleeve. Before he could do anything, the air abruptly stilled. The clouds ceased their churning; tumbling rubble paused in its dust-trailed descent. Within the instant, silence had swallowed up the world.

Damn it. They'd got the drop on him. Now he couldn't stop them getting through.

Through the crazed glass of the windows, Hitch watched as the ripples bulged and a shabbily dressed figure flowed effortlessly through the van's metal skin. Tall, bull-necked, and built like an SUV, he consulted his reader before lifting dark eyes to scan the ruined cityscape.

Keeping low, Hitch turned and threaded his way back through the labyrinth of abandoned vehicles. There had to be a...

There. He saw it. Across the junction, a subway sign and a wide, descending stairway, ringed by time-stopped travellers who'd somehow survived the aftershocks.

Another fierce buzz from his reader. A second gate was opening to his left.

Hitch scowled. Two watchmen and from two different directions: that was new. He wasn't sure what he could have done to draw that level of attention, but someone was certainly trying hard to send him a message. It couldn't be good. Messages from people with that sort of clout were seldom the sort to be accompanied by a seductive wink and a small chocolate assortment. This looked like another file for the 'evade and forget' folder.

"You! Stop!" SUV-Man had seen him. Like the detonations that only moments ago had been resounding through the crumbling canyons of the city, his voice was a thing of power; it was used to being heard and obeyed. And that was reason enough to run away.

"There!" The second watchman pointed at him from a fire escape landing high to his left.

Hitch hurried on, wishing he were faster, or fitter or - better yet - just an awful lot further away. Situations like this always favoured the action hero and that very definitely wasn't him. Action heroes moved well. They were fast and they could do that cool-looking knee-slide thing that got them across car bonnets in just fractions of a second. He couldn't do that. Springy athleticism was something he'd left behind in another life. Now, whatever speed he could muster was achieved through an inelegant combination of lurches, jumps, staggers, and collisions - a painful form of locomotion that saw him crashing through the gridlock like an poorly controlled Pac-Man.

Fortunately, SUV-Man was no faster. Wide like a mattress in a mackintosh, he was more hampered than most by the vehicular maze and, against walls of smouldering metal, his strength afforded him no edge at all.

Panting at the top of the subway steps, Hitch glanced back. The behemoth was only seconds behind him and his leaner colleague was now down off the metal ladders and approaching at a sprint. He was shouting something.

Keep moving. Whatever it was, it couldn't be good.

His reader buzzed yet again, an angry bee trapped beneath his sleeve.

Three? What the hell? No one had ever sent three watchmen after anyone. That was beyond unsporting.

As he landed at the foot of the stairs he saw it: a lift shaft doorway, yawning open but with its frame intact. Beyond it, splayed steel cables and palls of thick smoke promised only a painful demonstration of some of Newton's better known laws, but that was of little concern to him. Some laws were there to be broken.

With the destination already locked, he hit his reader at precisely the same moment that a third watchman popped through the wavering door of a janitorial cupboard. Dressed in a cleaner's garb, she started towards him, but her movement lacked conviction. She could see she was too late.

A wobbly film of light smeared itself across the open lift shaft door and Hitch hurled himself through it.

A strong, warm wind caught the dust from the cobbles and spun it into the night air. Firelight lent colour to this fleeting creature of straw and ash, giving it the appearance of something Abyssal, something swift and frantic and compelled to seek the flames.

An instant later, two sailors ran by hauling a wooden ladder, their turbulent wakes dispelling it. They spared Hitch no glance as he stepped from the doorway - merely shouted warnings to their fellow night-walkers as they sped on into the noisy city.

The buildings here were tightly packed - a fatal flaw on a night like this - but that was exactly why he'd chosen it. Lots of doors and lots of noise.

To his left, officers cried harsh commands; elsewhere, people argued, wept or traded earnest warnings. Gusts from the east bore the scent of wood smoke and calamity. High above, the spire of Old St Paul's reflected the dancing colours of the hearth.

It had been inadvertent, but in his quest for speed and seclusion, he'd found himself doing the classics tonight: the Sack of Ilium, 55 Central Park West, Dol Guldur and now this. All around him, the Great Fire raged, but it wasn't going to distract him. He tapped his reader, eyed the doorway opposite and ran on.

Three more thresholds brought him home, or at least the nearest thing to it: a basement flat in a seventies-set depiction of Chelsea that few had ever read. Obscure novels were a massive headache for Administration but they had their advantages. Here, so long as you avoided the merchant bank and the car chase that occurred at precisely seventy fifty-seven every evening, it was the quietest retreat imaginable.

He checked the plant pot as he descended the iron stairs. Behind the glass, the leering sun-face pointed to the right, which meant no unexpected guests had called. Beyond it, his reflection eyed him warily from the window. It looked unimpressed, but then it often did. And what did a mere reflection know, anyway? He chose to ignore it.

The door clicked open when he thumbed his card and familiar smells hurried out to greet him like eager pets: leather, tobacco, stale food. He followed them in.

"I'm home," he announced loudly. "It's been a hard day and I must have wine."

"I'm with someone." Fiona's voice came from her bedroom. The door was shut, which came as little surprise. She murmured a few words to her unseen companion, then added: "You left a crate of something in your room."

"Ah yes. What rare genius. So I did." Hitch shambled along the hall, then called back over his shoulder. "Did you find a buyer?"

"Hitch, I'm *with* someone. Shut up and go away."

"Right. Yes. Going away now. By all means continue with your... um." He shrugged off his coat and launched it at an empty hook on the hallway wall. It hit its target, pendulumed once in each direction, and then dropped to the floor behind Fiona's bicycle. He awarded it no more than a disdainful snort before prising open his door.

He'd be the first to admit that his room wasn't tidy but, like him, it was designed more for function than for show. The function in question was storage and, in this respect, it did its job very well. Stacked chests and boxes, books and anti-grav pallets filled most of its volume and, indeed, more than half his bed. Only the paths from door to mattress and from mattress to basin lay largely free from stock.

He paused when his eye fell upon the basin, the mirror, and his rusting razor.

You really should try to buck yourself up, you know. That was rich. What did a couple of over-privileged country kids know about the challenges of real life and adulthood?

Pursing his lips, he gave the sleeve of his sweater an experimental sniff.

A short while later and wearing a rather fetching ensemble from his flip-flops-and-dressing-gown collection, he crossed the hall to the bathroom. He'd eschewed the Glingue and the Moloko Plus in favour of a dry plum wine that he'd picked up from a weird elf creature somewhere. It was surprisingly good and he wondered whether the location might come back to him. There had been ridiculously big trees - he remembered that much.

He used the bottle to push aside the door.

His visits to the shower were invariably brief but they adhered to a familiar routine. Today, however, rather than the smells of soap and pine-fresh deodorant, his nose encountered the cold, hard barrel of a pistol. Beyond it, a determined-looking brow.

"Ah." Hitch uncrossed his eyes and tried to focus. "Hello, Boorman. Welcome."

"Got you, you slippery bastard."

Hitch leaned back, away from the barrel. "Yes. Well that would certainly seem to be... um." He paused. Behind him, several pairs of footsteps approached from the hallway. New shadows gathered round his feet.

"Sorry," called Fiona, distantly. "But you wouldn't believe the reward they were offering."

Hitch turned his head. "Really? How much?"

"Shut up and get dressed," said Boorman. "Winchester wants to see you."

"Winchester?" Hitch faced the gun again. "Oh. The top brass. Well that's very flattering, of course, but I'm sure I can't be nearly important enough to..."

"We've lost three extraction teams." The goon's jaw tightened. "She thinks a man of your *talents* might be able to figure out why."

"Oh. I see. Well then, I suppose a refusal would be churlish." Hitch slipped off his dressing gown and hung it on the end of the watchman's weapon. "And given her status and everything, I suppose I really ought to smarten myself up."

So saying, he pushed aside the shower curtain and stepped into the cubicle, taking his bottle with him.

7. You are Here

"Cathy, no one is angry with you for running away." A red-eyed Cariola offered another unconvincing smile. She'd been averaging about three a minute and they must have been wandering these corridors for nearly a quarter of an hour.

"No, sure. Hence all the liberty and everything." Grimly, Finn gestured to their little entourage: three men who'd joined her as soon as she'd left the control room. Two behind and one ahead, shepherding her along with a bored, unsympathetic glumness that hinted at roles in some sort of secret service; roles they evidently didn't enjoy.

The two tailing her made an odd pair. One was large and stone-faced, and looked like he'd been specially bred to block doors. The other was smaller and scruffier and seemingly fascinated by Finn. Whenever she turned around, she'd find him starting at her with an unnervingly steady, heavy-lidded gaze. Concerned that he might be attempting some sort of Jedi mind trick, she adopted the most obvious defence she could: she stopped turning around to look at him.

Ahead, their leader was a little more than a scowl in a leather jacket; dark eyes, thick, v-shaped eyebrows and a beard that would have required its own pat-down search had it ever attempted to pass through an international airport. With grunts, sighs, and unhappy murmurs, he dealt with the succession of security doors that barred their way, providing endless codes, swipe-cards, and verbal responses. Thus far, he'd spoken into a voice recognition device, put his hands into a fingerprint reader, and set his eye to a wall-mounted laser scanner. He hadn't yet dropped his pants and plonked his cheeks onto a photocopier but it seemed only a matter of time.

Now, padding down yet another passageway, Finn was reminded of that dreadful time in school when she'd been led to the secretary's office, there to await news of her dad's operation. Then, as now, she'd felt a keen sense of powerlessness and unknowing. But while the school office had a window that afforded a view of a cherry tree and the blue tits that flitted between the feeders, this place seemed to have no outside walls at all. By her own reckoning, she was now thoroughly entombed in a secure section of the complex, probably some considerable distance underground. Coming here had involved a maze of passageways, lifts, and stairwells. Whatever this place was, it was big. It made a city hospital look like a cushion fort.

The more they pressed on, the more Finn found herself objecting to this summons; to this blind assumption that she'd willingly defer to some as yet unseen authority. Whoever sat waiting to pass judgement on her, she was pretty sure she hadn't voted for them. Under the circumstances, Finn decided that delicacy and decorum could go boil their heads.

She looked sideways at Cariola. "They think I had something to do with that attack on Reed, don't they?"

Her companion's chin wobbled. "Oh no, no; I'm sure..."

"I mean, you can see their point: I've only been here five minutes. I duck out of your meeting, I follow Reed into a control room and the next thing you know, bang! Some sneaky scumbag shoots him with a ray gun."

Cariola looked away. Her shoulders gave an involuntary twitch. A stifled sob followed.

Finn sighed. "Oh, God. That was tactless. I'm sorry. You were friends."

"Ahh."

"What?"

"Ahh." The counsellor sent her a bitter look. "We *are* friends. Joe Reed's not dead, he's been captured. You said so yourself; you said the man who shot him followed him out of that tube thing and then sealed him into his own capsule."

"Yeah, no, of course. I didn't mean..." Finn took a breath. "I'm sure he'll be fine. He's seemed like a capable guy. I mean, that's why I wanted to find him again, really: I thought he could help me get home to Mum; help me warn her."

Glancing back, she saw the heavy-lidded man still staring at her. He popped a nut in his mouth and slowly chewed it.

"Oh, but to be drifting in the dark like that, all helpless..." Cariola began to wail.

"Oh, come on, now. Hush." Finn took her hand. "You've got all these doors and all this technology. I mean - you can stop *time*, for goodness sake. I'm sure someone can go in again and grab him."

"I told you; doors like that only open once." Cariola produced an unpleasant, liquid-sounding sniff. "They'd have to find a different door."

"Well, there was a door in his big silver canister thing. Couldn't they use that?"

"What?" Cariola gave her a sharp look: anxiety flecked with a reviving optimism.

The nut-chewing Jedi leaned in. "No good. It's non-diegetic. Interesting thinking, though; very creative."

"I'm sorry?" Finn found she resented his intrusion and his condescension in roughly equal measure. "Who are you anyway? What are you talking about?"

He flashed her an airy smile. "The extraction capsule. It's non-diegetic. Not part of the original narrative." He cocked his head as a thought seemed to strike him. "You look familiar. Tell me, did we ever...?"

"Enough," said the enormous guard beside him. "Prisoners aren't allowed to gossip."

Stung by his terminology, but determined to make a show of ignoring him, Finn turned to Cariola with a question, but discovered the counsellor was still wholly committed to the sobbing thing. She gave her a quiet pat instead.

Abruptly, their unhappy little column came to a halt before yet another door. It was attended by a stern-faced official. Like everyone else Finn had seen, he wore no uniform as such, although in his case it looked like he badly wanted one. He'd chosen the darkest, smartest, most functional clothing he could find, complete with leather elbow patches and a many-pouched belt that would have made a superhero proud. A badge, a tie, and a frankly effete-looking cap completed the ensemble - the overall impression falling somewhere between leather fetishist and shopping mall security guard.

Superintendent Scowl flashed him a card and muttered something about going to see Winchester. In reply, Patches nodded approval of his travel plans and tapped something into a device on his arm.

"And you must be Cathy Finn," he said, stooping to look up into the festival of snot and tears that was Cariola's unhappy face.

Finn raised a finger. "Um, no. That would be me."

Patches blinked. "You're Cathy Finn and *she's* your counsellor?"

Finn nodded.

He glanced again at the emotional wreck beside her. "You sure?"

"Pretty much. It's been an unusual day."

"Uh huh." He frowned at his device, entered a few details and waved them all through.

"Right here," said Scowl, gesturing to an unremarkable side door a few paces ahead.

Pausing only to remove a handkerchief and to produce a loud fanfare of forcibly ejected mucus, Cariola slid open the door. Thus heralded, Finn stepped into a small, empty, clinical-looking waiting room.

She followed her counsellor to a row of hard, shiny plastic seats; chairs that said very clearly that visitors weren't meant to get comfortable. Captain Grumpy vanished through one of the room's other doors, while his rectangular companion stuck to what he was best at and wedged himself firmly into the doorway through which they'd come. Meanwhile, with a kind of inevitability, Obi Wan with the hazelnut habit chose to sit immediately opposite her. He started staring again.

"What was all that rubbish about original narratives?" she asked, carefully resting her gaze on the bridge of his nose rather than the eyes themselves. On a day like this, you couldn't be too careful.

Obi frowned. "They didn't cover that in your reception meeting?"

"I never went to any reception meeting."

The scruffy nut-eater blinked at last. "Seriously? Wow. So you really are new to all this, aren't you?"

"I got here about an hour ago." Finn narrowed her eyes. "So is this my interrogation, now? Have we started?"

Stretching, he laced his hands behind his head. "An *hour*. To get scooped, to ditch matron, to track down a winch and scam your way into an NDE control room. That's fast work."

Finn leaned forward and adjusted her gaze to *heavy disdain*. "I'm sorry, but this language you're using - it's just gibberish, isn't it?"

He gave her another appraising look. "Interesting..."

Abruptly, a side door opened to reveal an improbably large nose that jutted out behind it at approximately waist height. At least, Finn hoped it was a nose. She was a little relieved when a hirsute face followed it into the room and glowered across at her heavy-lidded inquisitor. "Your name Hitch?" he said.

Still chewing, Hitch gave a slow but emphatic nod, placed his hands on his knees, and rose from his chair with a theatrical groan.

As he moved, the hulking guard at the door stepped forward.

Finn felt her limbs tightening. "What's going on? What are we doing?"

"We?" Hitch tilted his head towards his escort. "Oh, I'm sorry. Boorman's not for you. He's here for me, aren't you, honey-bun?"

Muttering dangerously and clenching whatever he had that might be clenched, Boorman followed the other men through the door. All at once, Finn and Cariola were alone.

"Oh." Finn's brain attempted a quick reassessment. "So I'm really not a prisoner, then?"

Cariola sniffed noisily. "No, I told you; they'll just want to ask you some questions about what you saw."

"Oh." She shifted her weight on the fiercely unyielding chair. "Right. So can I... is it alright if I walk about a bit? My bum's going numb."

"Of course." The counsellor swallowed and pointed to the door beside her. "They said there's a drinks machine in there if you want anything."

"Oh. Okay." Finn was still pretty sure she was asleep or in some kind of bullet-induced coma but, nevertheless, the prospect of a warm drink did have its attractions. "So I can go through?"

Cariola dabbed her eyes with a sleeve and stood. The door opened without klaxon or complaint when she swiped her pass-card across it. Beyond lay an unoccupied room no bigger than the one they'd just left.

Lacking only some insipid motivational posters, it put Finn in mind of the boardroom of a not-very-successful small business. The promised drinks machine grumbled quietly in the near corner and a polished table stood in the middle between two rows of padded chairs. They looked considerably more inviting than those in the waiting room, which appeared to have been designed for no other purpose than to make whatever followed the waiting feel like a very welcome relief. Finn was about to indulge a whim to try one of them when she saw something on the opposite wall that made her stop.

More arresting than the chairs, the table or the drinks - which, admittedly, weren't very arresting at all - was a large framed picture. It showed a huge white dome that rose upon the outskirts of a great city of glass and stone and steel. Built to a scale that would send an Olympic stadium into therapy, it comprised a perfectly hemispherical hub, together with six arms - each perhaps two hundred metres long - which radiated across the landscape at precise angular intervals. Rising at least four storeys high and dotted with windows and cantilevered terraces, they reached out into the leafy suburbs, dividing a large part of the metropolis into great wedges of parkland, pathways and bright scatterings of water.

Abounding with lakes, greenery, elegant spires, and what looked suspiciously like a busy spaceport, the image appeared to be an artist's rendering of a particularly improbable City of Tomorrow - and Finn would have taken it as such were it not for one small label. A strand of bright cotton connected it to a red dot on an unremarkable point on the dome roughly seven floors up.

On the label were just three words: *You are here.*

"No."

"What?"

"No. I won't do it."

From the head of the control centre conference table, Winchester gave Hitch a tired look. "I haven't asked you to do anything yet."

Hitch rose from between his two minders, wandered to the far end of the table and took possession of a bowl of mixed nuts. "No. But you're going to, aren't you?" He waved a pecan at her. "And then there will be hardship and peril and... and *escapades* probably. I wish to put on record that I don't do those things any more. Someone write that down."

Flanked by members of her senior team and high-ranking representatives of at least three other departments, Winchester pursed her lips. She was about to speak when an aide approached her with a pad and a mimed request for a signature. Having supplied it, she regarded Hitch again and sighed. "I brought you here because we're in trouble, Hitch. People are getting hurt."

Hitch nodded. "You see? Didn't I just say? Hardship and peril."

"Hitch, I know you like people to think of you as this..." She gestured at his clothes. "Well, whatever *this* is, but I can't believe you're completely unfazed by someone killing off your former colleagues. You *did* this job once; you know the risks winchmen take."

"I do. And 'risks' is another word I've never liked."

A deep voice cut in. "You're missing the point. We aren't here appealing to your altruism." Hector was Winchester's second in command, a time-served professional with the scars and the icy gaze to prove it. His words had the timbre of an elephant tramping over deep gravel and though he was clearly reining himself in for now, there was no mistaking the threat implicit in his tone.

Hitch gave a sombre nod. "You know, you're right. I do miss the point sometimes. Never really been the perceptive sort, you see. Certainly not the kind of person you'd want to send out on any important mi..."

Hector rose slowly from his chair. Hitch swallowed the remains of his nut.

"Someone is killing our winch teams. Just let that sink in for a minute." The old man had eyes that could etch glass. As they roamed over him, Hitch suddenly understood why he was rumoured to have been a were-bear in his former life.

After a long and uncomfortable pause, Hector said: "The situation is unprecedented. Someone is deliberately sabotaging our extractions, and we don't know who or how. Whoever is doing this is implanting himself in other narratives with the specific intention of trapping or killing our people. I'm sure you're *perceptive* enough to realise that it jeopardises our whole operation."

"Mm." Hitch tried hard to convey an impression of things being taken with all possible seriousness.

"In short," resumed Winchester, "we need to find out what this saboteur is doing, and why. We need to know how far the threat extends. Until we know that, I can't risk sending any more teams into untested narratives. We'll have to suspend extractions in everything but the classics." She dropped her gaze to the table. "It means that for the first time in decades, pretty much everything we do here is going to come to a halt."

Hitch nodded again. "Well, that's obviously very regrettable..."

"You may be many things," rumbled Hector, "but you aren't stupid. You know what we're saying. We need information and we need your help. We've got people out there trying to pull things back - closing the field research centres and organising rescues - but our teams aren't trained to infiltrate the Unaware. It pains me to say it, and it's clearly an oxymoron, but you're the best man for the job."

"Infiltrate the Un..." Hitch sent his eyes wide in a show of indignation.

"Oh spare us the theatrics, please." With a glance, Hector summoned an assistant - a painfully trendy youth who came wafting up to the table beneath what had to be the most annoying haircut in this or any other world. He had with him a large plastic box. Hitch's coat lay on top of it.

Hitch assumed an affronted air. "I am certainly *not* the best man for the job. Anyone who knows me will tell you I'm barely a man at all."

Hector lifted the coat and laid it across the table. "We know *exactly* what you are, 'Hitch'." Some people retained certain special powers from their previous life. One of Hector's seemed to be the ability to put inverted commas around words without having to use his fingers.

Hitch looked away. "Oh, well I wouldn't believe every..."

"Since leaving our employment four years ago, you've struck out on your own with... well, let's be charitable and call it *modest* success. You're known to your clients as 'The Postman', you deal in contraband, and you've broken just about every non-interference directive that exists." One of Hector's smug minions slid him a document, which he perused for a moment. "Your list of misdemeanours might almost impress a lesser man. Take this, for example: at the Castle of Zenda in nineteenth century Europe, you did knowingly deliver a party consignment of Jägermeister, Pot Noodle, prophylactics, and ibuprofen to the supposedly incarcerated King Rudolf of Ruritania. That was one of your recent ventures, was it not?"

Hitch shrugged.

"And let's see: taking and publishing digital video images of the birth of Aphrodite; supplying one Abraham Van Helsing with a laptop computer and seasons one to seven of *Buffy the Vampire Slayer*; launching an unprovoked assault on an enchanted goose and, most recently, supplying proscribed technologies to minors."

Hitch shook his head. "They aren't *minors*, they're Recurrents, like all the rest of them. Those two have been doing these little kid roles for decades. They're as Aware as you or me."

"Hm." Hector rooted in the box. "And for what reward, Mr. Postman? Some rough booze, a handful of coins and a box or two of cheap biscuits?"

Hitch bristled. "Hey now, don't mock the power of the digestive. That's some of the best product in all the worlds. There are places out there where people would..." It dawned on him that a number of eyebrows were rising in his direction and it might be best if he were to stop talking.

"The point is this." Hector smiled. "You're a pathetic small time crook and a disappointment to just about everyone who's ever suffered the woe of knowing you. You've wasted what abilities you had, you're living in squalor, and now that we've got you, there's only one way you're ever going to get out and that's by helping us."

Hitch chewed another nut. "Well, I'm still not doing it."

"Ah, but you are." Hector had something up his sleeve. He was enjoying this far too much. "Because when I said we know exactly what you are, I really meant it... *'Hitch.'*" This time, when he said his name, he somehow contrived to put it in inverted commas and italicise it.

Hitch resolved to brazen it out. "I'm sorry, Hector; I don't know what you mean."

"I think," said Winchester, "what my colleague here is trying to say is that we'd be most grateful if you would lend us your valuable time and assistance." She smiled thinly. "And we'd especially appreciate it if you'd be *quick* about it."

Hitch felt his eyelid twitch. Her emphasis had been very deliberate; there could be no misconstruing her intent. She *knew,* damn it. That meant she had him tail-up over a barrel.

Something in his own expression - or perhaps the sudden slump of his shoulders - seemed to tell Winchester that she'd won. She didn't gloat, despite the fact that Hector clearly wanted to; she just straightened her papers and gestured for one of her aides to take Hitch's effects somewhere suitably remote. Then, knitting her fingers, she looked him once again in the eye. "So we understand one another, Mr. Postman?"

Hitch looked at the table. He didn't thrive on attention. "I'm not going to be any sort of hero. I don't fight, I won't shoot people, and I don't put myself in harm's way."

"Oh, we understand that," said Hector. "Like I said; we know *all* about you." He used his superpowers again.

"It would be a quiet, investigative role," agreed Winchester. "Something well suited to your talents."

Hitch sniffed. "And I want all my stuff back."

"And you'll have it." She nodded to her assistants. "Every last crumb."

"And my coat, my card, and my reader."

"Of course."

"And when this is all over, I want you people off my back for good."

Hector leaned over the table. "Don't push your luck, Postie."

Winchester rose from her seat. "I think we're finished here. Hector will give you a thorough briefing and then I want you to assemble a team to support you. In view of our current problems, I'd advise you to use people you can trust." She sent him a rueful look. "People I probably wouldn't."

8. Silas

They said it was a kind of rebirth, being extracted; that you could reinvent yourself and start afresh.

That was rubbish. In his first life, Jay had been a boring, do-nothing student; a hanger-on; someone who laughed at the other kids' jokes and offered none of his own. Just a low-achieving minor character with no back-story and no good lines; a guy who'd only really ever existed to be the serial killer's Victim Number One.

In those early days after extraction, the possibilities of his new life had seemed dizzying and endless. He'd entered a whole new world where no one would judge him, belittle him or call him Nippledick. When they'd told him he could even choose a new body if he wished, he'd jumped at the chance; soon he was strutting about all lean and muscle-bound, hoping that everyone would admire him and treat him differently.

They'd said his character would change, too; that his past life was just the product of an author who no longer had any power over him. *Wait and see*, they'd said; *your real self will soon show through.*

And so he'd waited for this bright butterfly personality to emerge. He kept up his hopes, killing time while he watched for signs of the transformation, but no new energy suffused him. The weeks became seasons and the seasons became years, and still he found himself unchanged. He just got slower and less motivated until eventually a sad truth dawned: that while all people were free to be their true selves, some people's true selves were just dull, limp, and forgettable.

His imposing stature had sagged. For lack of use, his muscles had shrunk like fallen soufflés and his fondly imagined future as a heroic winch or some high society gigolo faded away like paint on a sun-bleached fence. At heart, he was still a nobody and, weighed down by a sense of fatalism, he soon gravitated towards the office desk that became his natural home. There, he'd made an unremarkable existence for himself and, in time, he caught a couple of lucky breaks: he somehow found work as a junior researcher in Ethics and Policy and then - more through happenstance than action - he got himself promoted. In all the chaos of the last year, the problems of understaffing had greatly worsened and, as a result, he'd earned himself a posting, here to this god-forsaken pit and a facility that was *supposed* to be both secret and impregnable.

Now though, every conceivable aspect of the operation had gone wrong. For the first time in any history, native characters had discovered a research station. It was as shocking as it was unprecedented and it broke the most fundamental rule of non-engagement. However, with the enemy quite literally hammering at the door, he and his colleagues had seen no option but to take the emergency exit and run.

The others had escaped. They'd made it to the ruins of the pump room, where the gate lay hidden in a doorway by the ancient engine. He hadn't been so lucky. With an inevitability reminiscent of his former life, he'd tripped on his way across the compound - on a twisted length of steel reinforcement bar that he could have sworn rose up at him as he ran. The noise drew the attention of his pursuers, weapons were pointed and now, incredibly, he was their captive.

It seemed he was once again destined to play the role of victim.

"What's this?" asked the leader as Jay tried to rise from his knees. He'd been thrown down by a couple of sneering heavies and, with his hands tied behind him, he'd fallen clumsily at the head man's feet. Now, all he could see of him was the base of a freshly looted swivel chair and a pair of studded boots that he'd only previously seen through the glass of a video monitor.

"A spy," said the henchman. Back in the station, they'd nicknamed him Bunty - a name thrown about with all the casual irony of people who never expected to feel his calloused hands about their necks. Until today, the man had just been a curiosity; a bug under Jay's microscope. Now, the boot that shoved him back into the dust felt very heavy and very real indeed.

"We hang spies, do we not?" Alfred, the leader, sounded distracted. For him, homicide was an everyday chore - no more troubling than deleting spam. Jay had personally witnessed thirteen of his kills, each of which he'd meticulously logged and annotated for the benefit of future extraction teams.

"Aye, sire, we do."

"And has the wretch aught to say afore we off him?"

The pressure between Jay's shoulders abated and slowly he lifted his head. He swallowed, opened his mouth and at once felt his jaw trembling. Interaction with diegetic characters was absolutely forbidden; that was the researcher's golden rule. It was fixed; immutable; drummed into every new recruit from the very first day of training. Today, however, it conflicted with another important priority, which was to say, continuing to live. On balance, he decided it was a rule that probably only really applied to those who hadn't already been caught and threatened with the gallows.

Bunty sniffed. "It seems not, sire."

"No. Please." Even to Jay's ears, his voice sounded feeble and inconsequential; a bird chittering on a walrus beach.

"You wish to live?" Alfred turned a pale blue eye upon him and frowned as if surprised. "But observe: your lumpen form, your draggled countenance. You crouch, a tremulous miscarriage of a man. 'Twould be a kindness to kill you."

Jay shook his head, dimly aware that the madman's eccentric dialect was the reason his bosses had set up the station in the first place. But to a man facing a dozen blades and pointed rifles, the obsessions of a few old philologists now seemed the most distant and unimportant of concerns. "I have information," he heard himself saying. "Don't kill me. I'll tell you anything."

Alfred shrugged. "Death is not the worst that can happen to men." He turned to his minions and nodded slowly. "So said Plato."

Another voice cut in. "The other spies have fled, sire. Their watch-post is empty, yet filled with curiosities of marvellous design. The wretch might tell us of them."

Jay flinched as a small data-logger clattered on the concrete beside him, shedding fragments as it bounced.

"Trinkets. Trifles. Bagatelle." Alfred rose from his new throne. "We are men of wisdom; let others seek the counsel of frighted fellows."

"Sire?"

The chief dismissed him with a wave. "No more of this. String him up and gut him."

"No. Wait. Please." Even to Jay's ears, these sounded like the pleadings of an irredeemable loser, but what else could he do? Strong fists clasped about his arms and hauled him to his feet. An instant later, he was being dragged towards the wreckage of a pylon.

Eyes darting, he wondered at what point a feeble man should struggle. Start too early and you only risked antagonising your captors. Leave it too late and, well...

Bunty spun him round and thrust him by the throat against a grey metal upright. He gagged at the pressure and felt barbed wire pierce the skin of his shoulder. Someone else was readying a noose.

On reflection, that probably meant he'd left it too late.

As the men worked at his gallows, he glanced across to the other side of the steep-sloping valley, to the ruins of the dam complex where Alfred had established his brutal reign. A fire-blasted generator building was his stronghold; the corpses strung from the wires his warning to aspirant usurpers. Figures were already returning there, crossing the great curving wall with their spoils from the research station.

From his own side - a high hill of hardy scrub and yellow earth - a pair of cables still ran down to the remains of the pylon and then on, across the chasm, to the powerhouse. From there, more wires made a weary pilgrimage down the valley to his left, dipping between the masts in the direction of the burned city and the setting sun.

Bunty stood back and grinned. A leather-clad accomplice stepped up beside him, in his hands a length of steel cable fashioned into a garrotte.

Jay was struggling to conjure some suitably spiteful last words when a sudden, terrible detonation concussed his chest and ears.

From the dam wall, a ragged spire of dust and debris launched itself thirty metres into the air, hurling out slabs and spears of concrete as it went. Beneath it, a great grey spout of seething water leapt out into the valley like a fulmar taking wing.

Cries cut through the turmoil as fist-sized shards of masonry came raining down, striking heads, the pump room roof and the great metal fretwork above him.

"Stations!" came the cry. Here and in the main compound across the gorge, men scattered, taking up weapons as they found their way to foxholes, trenches, and towers.

"Report!" Alfred strode to the near end of the dam.

The smoke drifted to reveal a four metre hole in the crest and parapet of the wall. Through it, the lake was emptying itself in a mad tumult of noise and churning water. Upstream, a slow drift sucked mud and branches from the banks. Nearer to the breech, floating mats of logs and plastic detritus crowded in a hurried press, eager to launch themselves into the empty air.

Above Jay's head, seemingly unnoticed by anyone, a wavering thrum began to build. The wires were singing.

While other men surveyed the dam or the hillside approaches, Jay turned his head up to the side. A silhouetted figure was descending the wire at speed, hanging one-handed from a wheeled contraption set upon the cable.

An instant later, when it seemed he must impale himself on the jagged limbs of the pylon, the figure released his hold. He dropped, rolled smoothly and rose into a fierce kick that sent Bunty sprawling into the dust.

Alfred whirled. The newcomer was already facing him, standing at a distance of half a dozen paces, his right hand aiming a pistol squarely at his head. His left clutched what appeared to be the handle of a joystick.

Alfred spat, threw wide his arms, and raised his voice above the bellowing flood. "Hah! And who is this bringer of deluge and dissolution? This latter-day Burnet come to o'erturn the Earth?"

Around the compound, narrow eyes trained weapons upon the stranger. Bunty rose wheezing from the dirt and advanced upon him with a snarl.

"Stay your men," shouted the stranger, raising his left hand. "None need die today."

Alfred gave a casual shrug. "No, but such things happen. What said Plato? *What is purification, but the separation of soul from body?*"

The stranger smiled, his bright eyes scanning the faces around him. "If it's purification they seek, I have sure means to deliver it." He raised his clasped hand higher. "A device of rare invention. One such lay in yonder sundered wall. One still greater lies here beneath our feet."

Jay's eyes tracked downward to the ground, following the gaze of other men.

Careless of the levelled pistol, Alfred took a slow and deliberate step towards the wild-haired intruder. "*You*, a vagabond trickster, press me for a bargain?" Slowly, he shook his shaggy grey head. "I take no joy in barter. The worst form of inequality is to try to make unequal things equal. Did not the great man say so?"

The other looked him coldly in the eye. "So you cite Aristotle now. For myself, I study more contemporary thinkers."

Alfred wafted a hand. "Words are naught but sounds and mischief." He gestured to the complex behind him. "The measure of a man is what he does with power. Behold *my* accomplishments. Should I then fear the chattering fool that comes to me with words of *rare devices?*" He kicked contemptuously at the ground. "You prattle like a child at play; I have about me eighty men and rifles. What have you but words?"

The stranger smiled and looked about him. "Oh, but words will oftentimes suffice. What else keeps your rifles silent? Only the fear of what must follow should this little apparatus but touch the ground."

"A fine hypothesis," said Alfred, taking another pace forward. "But here is my own: you stall and stumble, having taken scant account of the mettle of desperate men. This is a hard, hard world that lies about, and every soul here lives only for the now. We fear not death, for it accompanies us like our very shadows. 'Twas Socrates who said the unexamined life is not worth living, and this we hold as truth. We build, we conquer and we do not fear. We live in deeds, not years."

The stranger offered an ironic bow. "Another fine theory. Loquacious, unquestionably, but expressed with passion, which must count for something."

"Then let me condense it to the abstract." Alfred stepped closer still, and now the two men were just two long strides apart. "You offer naught but fanciful deceit. When you die here, as you surely must, your precious trinket shall lie as lifeless and inconsequential as yourself." He smiled again. "That is *my* hypothesis, my miscalculating friend, so tell me: have you words enough to refute it?"

The stranger nodded once. "Aye, though they be borrowed from a poet. I refute it thus."

So saying, he tossed the device in a low arc between Alfred and Bunty. The henchman sprang to catch it while his leader's hand went to the revolver at his belt.

His faculties speeded by adrenaline, Jay watched as the stranger's pistol flared. A brief spray of crimson burst from the back of Alfred's head and then the weapon swung and fired again. Bunty was still in mid-fall but now his head rocked back as a bullet caught him beneath the jaw. By the time he hit the ground, the stranger was turning towards the pylon and aiming another shot that sent a gunman falling from the pump room roof.

"It's a trick; there's no..." Another man's warning was cut short by a white flash. The grenade produced no great explosion, only a blinding brightness that burned the stranger's silhouette into the backs of Jay's eyes. Next came the sensation of being grasped by the arm.

"My name's Silas," said the shape as he propelled him away from the pylon. "I'm here to get you to the gate."

"But how..." A loud whining ricochet sounded close by his ear.

"Run!" cried Silas. There was a blur of ill-defined movement and his pistol barked again.

Quite right, thought Jay. *Run now; questions later.* It seemed a sensible way of prioritising things.

Somewhere above his head, bullets tore the air and cracked against concrete. Harsh fragments stung his forehead, then a firm shove at his back sent him tumbling through a doorway. Half-blind and with his hands still firmly tied, he tried rolling to minimise the impact, but still he crashed into something heavy that rang like a gong when he hit it with his knees. A moment later there was a tortured shriek of metal as his new guardian shouldered shut the old steel door.

Jay blinked furiously in the newly fallen darkness.

"There's no lock," said Silas. Outside, bullets sang against the door.

"In the next room," said Jay. "There's a bolt."

"The gate's sequestered?"

Jay nodded. What little light filtered through long cracks in the ceiling was enough to make out Silas' outline as he hurried over and guided him between rusting pipes and rubble. Seconds later, they were both inside the engine room. Silas pushed hard against the heavy plane of rusting steel, which swung to with a squeal and a jolt.

From somewhere in his jacket, Silas produced a thin torch and stuck it between Jay's teeth. "Point it this way. I need to see the - ah." Using both hands, he grabbed the heavy bolt and slid it home. "Okay, that should give us enough time."

Jay slumped back against the heavy casing of the engine. "I don't understand," he said, his lips contorting around the unfamiliar intrusion. "Who are you? You talked like one of them but you know about the gate."

"It's complicated." Silas took back his torch. "Look, they'll have explosives - we can't stay. D'you know the code?"

"It's alphanumeric. Lyceum 627. But really, who are you?"

"Oh, nothing special; let's just say a poet disappointed and turned critic."

"What? What does that mean?"

An explosion from beyond the door dislodged grit and dust from the ceiling. It was followed by angry shouts and a loud clatter of gunfire. The first door had fallen.

Jay shifted uncomfortably. Why wasn't Silas entering the key code? Why wasn't he untying him? "You *can't* be from New Tybet," he said. "What are you doing here?"

Silas snorted. "That's a more difficult question than you know."

"And you killed diegetics. That's... That's..." Jay threw out his elbows. Under the circumstances, it was the only emphatic gesture he could manage.

Silas flashed a manic grin. "Yeah. All sacrificed to liberty's wild riot."

Jay stared. "But that's against every..." He stopped. Those familiar 'victim' vibes were returning. "Who are you?" he asked again.

Without further explanation, Silas rapped three times upon the metal door. "Joshua. Are you there?"

The reply came immediately. "Aye, friend, I am, and we have irrevocable advantage. Those loyal to Alfred are dead, captive or they make themselves fugitive. The field is ours. We stand ready to follow you."

"Thank you, Joshua. Fine work." Silas slid the bolt open.

Jay swallowed. "It was *you*, wasn't it? You told them about the research station."

"Very good," said Silas, swinging open the door. A crowd of Alfred's former soldiers were waiting to meet him.

Jay pressed himself back into the darkness. "What are you doing? What's going on?"

"Oh, you haven't heard?" Smiling dangerously, Silas reloaded his pistol. "They say all hell's breaking loose."

9. New Tybet

"So there's no such thing as reality." Finn eyed Cariola across the top of a cup of coffee so bad it could only have existed in a work of fiction. It was a surprising revelation, even by the standards of what was proving to be a decidedly unusual day. "You're telling me all worlds are just stories; even this one?"

Cariola nodded. "Everyone thinks their world is the only real one, but that's just natural." She'd composed herself since hearing that a team of volunteers was working on a plan to find and rescue Reed. Now, sitting in the still-empty meeting room, she seemed to be reflecting on Finn's desertion. "But you know, Cathy, things would be making a lot more sense if you'd attended the welcome meeting like you were supposed to."

Finn shrugged and took another masochistic sip. "Yeah, well I said I was sorry, but I'm not going to lie to you; I'm not planning to stay. My mum's in danger; my sister too. First chance I get, I'm going back to warn them." Finn's was a family that had been forced to deal with one unexpected bereavement; she sure as hell wasn't going to inflict another on them.

Cariola looked away. They were getting nowhere now, both entrenched in their positions. Barring a few carols at Christmas and perhaps an impromptu football match in no man's land, their relationship looked unlikely to improve. In other circumstances, their floundering friendship might have bothered Finn but it didn't today; at any level that mattered, she didn't really believe she was there at all.

To start with, handsome rescuers didn't just appear from cupboard doorways every time things got nasty. Millions died every year - many of them in places that were nowhere near under-stairs storage - and to imagine they all somehow ended up here was plainly silly.

And then there was the matter of fairness. She'd spent more than two decades living an ordinary life - going to school, studying at university, doing crappy jobs, tidying the flat. She must have vacuumed literally miles of carpet in her lifetime; it was unthinkable that it was all down to the imaginings of some obsessive-compulsive author with a weird thing about housework. To have put in all that effort only to get shot by a man dressed like an accountant - well, it lacked poetry.

All of which led her to conclude that this was some weird lucid dream. It had happened before; finding herself in situations so bizarre that even her sleeping brain had been forced to accept their unreality. But that had always been fun. On realising that the world around her was her own creation, her dream self had lost no time in exercise her godlike powers and before long, she'd be indulging herself in some quiet fun time with a young Johnny Depp, or flying naked around her local shopping centre. One time, it had been a mixture of both.

This time, though, any sense of control had flown. Perhaps dreams were inherently different when they were the result of blood loss and trauma. In any event, it looked like Cariola was just the first in a series of peculiar challenges her unconscious self had laid out for her. It was a game she had no choice but to play.

At least she could see how it was supposed to begin. Behind the counsellor stood a sliding glass door shaded by a metal-slatted shutter. Slow, subtle changes in the light hinted that it led out onto a balcony, but a chunky metal slot told her she'd need some sort of security pass to get through. So that was it: level one of the game was to get hold of Cariola's swipe-card.

Currently, it lay at the end of the table, beside her plastic coffee cup. This would take some manoeuvring.

Finn nodded casually towards the shutter. "So everyone here originally died in some other story." It was half a question and half a test. She watched Cariola's reaction carefully, hoping some small glance or gesture might confirm that there was indeed a world awaiting just beyond the glass.

The response was inconclusive. Cariola merely raised her cup, thought better of it and put it down again. "Not everyone," she said. "There was already a whole world here when the story started. But four hundred years of extractions has turned it into a bit of a melting pot."

Finn stood to consider the aerial photo. "So what changed?" She tapped the frame. "How did all this get started?"

Her question was met with a snort. "The Origin myths. Oh, there's a lot of nonsense talked about the She-Wolf, believe me. A cunning wizard who somehow took control of her own narrative? I think it's a lot of nonsense. You get all the power of creation and what do you do with it? Just build a few magic gates and then vanish?" She rolled her eyes as though she thought Finn could have heard nothing more outlandish all day.

Finn wondered if she was being tested. "Magic?" She was careful to look suitably dubious.

Cariola gave a straight-faced nod. "No one understands it, of course. People are always studying the Core but I think that's mainly for the research grants. The system works; that's all we know and all that really matters. It found your story, the same way it found mine and everyone else's."

"It found your story..." Finn blinked. Maybe it was her personality, but she'd sort of assumed that Cariola had always belonged to this mad, incomprehensible bureaucracy. "So you were also, um..."

Cariola looked down at the table and put a finger to her throat. "It was strangling when my turn came. Joe Reed came through at the very moment the executioner's cord was pulling about my neck."

"Oh, *Reed* saved you. That explains how you two..."

"Mm. That was three years ago now. It took me the longest time to accept that I could never go back." She lapsed into a thoughtful silence, then seemed to gather herself. She fumbled in a back pocket and produced a small glassy slab. "Anyway, we're not here to talk about me. I meant to give you this."

Finn stared. "Is that my phone?" She couldn't remember losing it; she'd assumed she'd left it in her car.

"A copy." Cariola slid it down the table. "You'll find the battery life's a lot better..."

"Thanks. It couldn't have been any worse."

"... and they've added a brochure. A city guide for new arrivals."

Finn picked it up. If it was a copy, then it was a damned good one. Even the scratches were the same. The only discernible difference was the addition of a detachable wrist strap. She looked up, eyebrows raised. "Think I can get a signal?"

Cariola shook her head. "Not the sort you mean. But try it." Her eyes narrowed a fraction. "You might find it's better at answering questions than I am."

Ignoring that, Finn felt the first inklings of a plan. It was simple enough, but if it was going to work, then she had to keep her chaperone's attention on the phone. Feigning the sort of intent technical interest most often exhibited by fashion-conscious teens, she slid a finger across the glass, stirring it into brightness and life.

The background image was the same as on her old phone's display and large digital numerals spelled out the time. It seemed to be running about seven hours behind GMT. Everything about it looked familiar, with one small exception: the word *auto* was blinking in the bottom right hand corner. Finn turned it to Cariola. "What's this?"

Cariola peered over. "*Auto* just means it will look the way people expect it to look. If you decide you want to settle on another world, then..."

"*Another* world?" Finn heard the note of horror in her own voice. One world of separation was more than enough.

"Mm." Cariola knitted her fingers. "You see, this is only really a stopping-off point for most people. Usually, they like to settle down somewhere more familiar - in your case, perhaps another twenty-first century Earth."

"*Another* one? Just how many are there?" Finn began fiddling with her phone again.

"Oh, lots and lots." Absently, Cariola sipped her coffee, then winced and quietly spat it back. "You see there are basically two kinds of worlds. There are *Unaware* worlds - the places where we all start; where people have no idea about the existence of other narratives. And then there are places like this - *Aware* worlds - where the secret's out and émigrés like us can carry on with their lives."

Finn nodded, though she was barely listening. Most of the phone's controls were identical to her own and, while her face had been producing expressions of sage comprehension, her fingers had surreptitiously been setting a new security code that locked down the screen.

After a moment, she glanced down and set her features into a theatrical frown. "Oh," she said. "*Signal interference*. What does that mean?"

Cariola craned her neck but Finn angled the screen away. "Oh, and now it says I'm locked out. Why's that? Did I do something wrong?"

Leaving her card on the table, Cariola rose from her seat. Finn handed her the phone.

"That's odd," said the counsellor, tapping uselessly at the display. "I haven't seen that before."

Finn gestured to the door to the waiting room. "Maybe it's because my real phone's in the room next door. Maybe it's intefer..."

Cariola look up sharply. "What? You can't possibly have your phone here. Technologies like that don't pass through the gates."

Finn shrugged. "Mine did. It's in my coat."

"That..." Glancing at the door, Cariola did a nervous little dance. "No, but that's..."

Finn held out her hands. "Go and see for yourself."

She winced. "I'm not really supposed to leave you on your own."

"Oh, for goodness... It's only there. I'll even hold the door open."

"Well yes, I suppose..." From this side, the door required no swipe-card so Cariola only had to turn the handle and step through into the empty waiting room. Finn's coat was still folded on her chair.

"Inside pocket," said Finn.

"I'll just bring the whole coat," said Cariola, crossing the room. Seems a bit rude to go rooting around in..."

Click. Finn closed the door. She heard the lock engage.

"Cathy," called Cariola. "The door, sweetie; you let it shut."

Finn gently waggled the handle, though only enough to make a convincing noise. "Sorry. So what do I do now? The handle won't move."

"Of course it will. Just..."

Finn ignored the rest. She snatched up the swipe-card and crossed quickly to the metal slot. A red light beside it blinked green when she pressed it to the scanner. An instant later, she was sliding open the door.

"Cathy!" Cariola sounded more agitated. "Slide my card under the door, would you?"

"Card?" Finn pushed against the shutter as she called back. "I don't see it; hang on, let me look."

She didn't hear the reply. The metal slats swung open to admit a bright blast of light, hot and dazzling as an Aegean sun. Shielding her eyes, she stepped out onto a narrow, glass-sided platform and gripped the handrail, just as her mind attempted to get a grip on this new reality.

Below and around her lay a wonderland of architecture and technology. Slender skyscrapers rose from lawns and boulevards while bridges of fantastical design spanned a river that flowed into a wide and glittering bay. Between here and that turquoise sea lay all manner of buildings, spires and plazas, bustling streets and green-fringed lakes where the sails of pleasure craft filled themselves with a warm onshore breeze. Above them all, flecking the air with flashes of gold and silver, skyborne vehicles drifted between the towers like gnats among the stalks of a summer meadow. The picture on the wall hadn't lied; the city was like *Futurama* with landscaping.

And then there was the sheer scale of the place. The city was *big*. Capital city big. Metropolitan mayor big. Science fiction big.

The same eclectic mixture of sun-bright glass and parkland stretched out for miles along the coast, the colours hazing into the distance, turning to faint pastels themed upon purple, grey, and blue.

This wasn't a city you could overlook. You couldn't excise it from history or maps, nor hide it from the gaze of passing satellites. No one could keep a secret like this. If it existed at all, then this had to be someplace new.

Behind her, Finn heard the inner door sweep open. Bustling and acrimony quickly followed.

"Cathy Finn." Heavy with disappointment, Cariola's tone was the sort often employed by harassed primary school teachers. "Come away from that window at once. You aren't supposed to see the city until after you've read the guide."

"Oh, she's a *sneaky* one, isn't she?" A man's voice joined Cariola's. There was a note of approval in it. "Well that settles it; my mind's made up."

Finn turned.

Leaning against the inside door frame stood the man they'd called Hitch. He nodded at her phone. "You're quite right, you know; you don't want to bother with the marketing rubbish. There's only one real way to get to know a place."

"Do you mind?" Cariola set her hands on her hips. "I'm grateful for your help with the door, Mr. Hitch, but this lady needs to have her induction."

"No she doesn't." Hitch rummaged in his hair as though he suspected it of hiding something.

"She does. I'm just going..."

Finn stepped back into the room. "Actually, the *lady* can speak for herself. What d'you want?"

Hitch detached himself from the door and slouched across to the table. He was followed by the security gimp, Boorman, and another man she didn't recognise. He eyed the drinks machine. "How's the coffee?"

"Lovely," said Finn. "Take my advice: get a nice big one."

Cariola placed herself between them. "What *do* you want, Mr. Hitch? I'm trying to help Miss Finn settle in."

Hitch peered round the side of the counsellor's head. "Oh, don't worry about that. I'd say she's settling in just fine. I mean, who else d'you know who's managed to land themselves a job on their very first day here?"

10. Life Story

"Whaddawewant?"
"Migrants out!"
"Whennerwewannit?"
"Neeaaaaoow!"

A leather-skinned lizard-man marched past with a placard. At least half the words on it were defamatory and misspelled. Part of a large, vociferous rabble, he stomped along in the company of some burly dwarves, half a dozen blue-complexioned extraterrestrials, and the seemingly ubiquitous herd of shaven-headed yobs.

Sitting in a sunny pavement café beneath tall trees and slender towers of glass, Finn sipped at a cup of very pleasant tea. It was infinitely more palatable than the evil concoction served up by the machine in the meeting room, but she was still struggling to enjoy it. What was annoying her was the realisation that even when she'd been bundled off to an entirely different planet, she still couldn't escape the presence of shouty, gormless bigots.

She watched the tail end of the mob drift away, leaving discarded bottles and large-font newspapers in its wake. After a moment, she turned to face her fellow diners. "So what was all that about?"

Cariola sighed and rolled her eyes, making it look momentarily as if she were having an orgasm. When her expression settled, it implied very firmly that she didn't involve herself in matters of politics.

"Ian Pea," said Hitch from around one end of a hotdog.

The watchman beside him frowned, but said nothing.

"Who's Ian Pea?" said Finn.

Hitch snorted and looked defiantly at his chunky minder. "Oh, just a sad, witless old winnet. Completely out of touch. Nobody likes him."

The watchman cleared his throat. "*E and P* stands for Ethics and Policy. It's the part of the Bureau that says who we can and can't help."

Hitch took another bite. "Well, that's the *official* line. But really..." He shook his head.

"Okay, enough," said Finn. "Let's cut to the chase, shall we? What's actually going on?" In the last hour she'd walked among giants and watched wizards conjuring fire. She'd seen space elevators strung from slender filaments that pricked the warm afternoon sky. She'd witnessed just what a vast and dazzling place this was, and she'd even found somewhere that made a half decent cup of tea. All in all, it was a convincing display of obvious unreality but she saw absolutely no reason why that should stop her from immersing herself in it. The sooner she did, the sooner she'd understand it, and the sooner she'd be able to escape.

Hitch leaned back in his chair and gestured towards the slowly diminishing noise. "Did you see that tall woman in the crowd?"

Finn nodded. "The one on the stilts?"

He shook his head. "Long legs; not stilts. Anyway, that's not the point. The point is this: I know her. I extracted her myself a few years ago. Now, here she is demanding we don't let anyone else in."

"Not everyone's like that," said Cariola quietly.

"Maybe not," said Hitch, "but there are getting to be more and more like her every day. It's a mess. E&P keeps changing its policies, the Ops teams are getting more and more stretched, and the more lives they save, the more people like that go around getting angry about it."

"But pretty much everybody came from another world, didn't they?" Finn glanced at Cariola. "That's what you said; it's all a big melting pot; nearly everyone here has either been rescued or they're descended from people who were."

Cariola looked glumly at the table. "That's right."

Finn shrugged. "Okay. So? Some people are hypocrites. What's new?"

"Nothing's new." Hitch took another mouthful. "I just thought you should see the sort of people we're being asked to help. I don't want you coming with me and taking any risks because you've gone all delusional about them. A lot of them really aren't worth the trouble, believe me."

Finn sipped her tea. "You really are quite the altruist, aren't you?"

"In my experience, humanity is a very disappointing race."

"I see. And where did all this vast wealth of experience come from? What was your story before you came here?"

Cariola cleared her throat. "Um, Cathy dear, that's not usually considered a very polite question."

"Isn't it? Oh."

Hitch narrowed his eyes. "Yeah. Some people come here with very dark histories; pasts that are best forgotten. A new name and a new face... they're important to a lot of people. A chance to make a clean start."

Finn sniffed. "Well, that seems a bit unfair. I mean you all know *my* story."

"Ah, but that's professional interest." Hitch quietly wafted away a burp. "Travelling around has been getting a lot more dangerous recently. I needed to know who you really were."

Finn shuffled uncomfortably. "So... how much *did* you find out?"

Hitch tapped a device protruding from his sleeve. "Oh, your whole life story. It's all here - cradle to grave."

Finn gazed at the screen, then her eyes went wide.

"My *whole* life? Was Dad in there?" She reached for his arm. "Did you get him out, too?"

"What?" Flinching, Hitch sat back. "No, no. It's um... No."

Finn turned to Cariola. "My dad *died.* If you extracted me, then you must..."

Cariola shook her head. "I'm really sorry, Cathy, but it's the way your story was written. A lot of your early life is only told in flashback. Your father never makes a direct appearance in the narrative."

Finn found her fists tightening.

"Look," said Hitch. "Basically, it starts with you getting shot. The rest of it's about Chrissie catching up with the killer and..."

"Alright, that's enough." The watchman put a firm hand across Hitch's wrist. "You know the rules."

With his free hand, Hitch brought a glass of wine to his lips. "Huh. And you know what they say about *rules,* don't you, Duggan? They're for the governance of wise men and the... No wait. They're for the... Well, they're stupid, anyway. I don't like them."

Finn found herself clenching her teaspoon like a weapon. "Catching up with the killer... and *what*? What do you know about my family?"

Cariola reached for her hand. "Cathy, it isn't..."

"It's Finn!" She slammed the spoon into the table, putting a ninety degree bend in it and sending Cariola's hand shooting back to the safety of her lap. A few neighbouring diners glanced her way, but Finn was beyond caring. She eyed her three companions in turn, speaking through gritted teeth. "Tell me what's happening to them. Tell me *now."*

Ignoring the obvious disapproval of his watchman, Hitch gazed blithely into his glass. "Well, I didn't download the full manuscript, but I made some notes. It starts with you driving to your shop. Some fat guy kills you and then your sister spends the next thirty-odd chapters tracking down all the members of the gang."

Finn blinked. "You're saying all this like it's already happened."

"It has. The story's been on the system for a few years now but there's a long waiting list; extractions take a lot of organising."

"But all this just happened today."

"For you it did."

Finn rubbed her temples. "But they're alright? Mum and Chrissie. They're both okay?"

"Yeah, yeah. Your mum's fine and your sister gets off with some young detective bloke at the end."

"Oh. Right." Finn's brain staggered round in a spiral. She badly wanted to ask how much they seemed to be missing her but she resisted; to voice the question would be the first step towards accepting the finality of her situation. She wasn't conceding anything yet. Instead, she focused on something else that had been bothering her. "So, hang on. I wasn't even the main character?"

Hitch shrugged. "Very few people are."

"Oh." Finn looked down at her untouched sandwich and decided that when she woke up from all this, she was going to devote a lot more effort to being interesting.

"Disappointed?" Hitch turned his eyes to the boulevard, where a troop of brightly clad jugglers whooped and jingled by.

"No." Finn tried to keep her voice flat but what came out sounded decidedly sulky.

"Well, never mind. Now you get to go on a life-threatening adventure. That'll be fun."

"But no one's forcing you to go," added Cariola. "You're under no obligation at all."

"No, no." Hitch waved his glass. "By all means stay here and be... um..." He didn't actually vocalise the word *boring* but his meaning was clear.

"Oh no, I'll definitely go, but why d'you want me?" Finn took a bite of her sandwich. "You don't know anything about me."

"I liked your style: ditching nanny and going after Reed. Most people just go with the herd."

Cariola frowned.

The watchman snorted. "Yeah. Right. D'you want the truth, Miss Finn? They told him only to work with his closest friends; people he could really trust." He flashed his charge a disdainful grin. "You don't *have* any friends, do you, Hitch? You've pissed on so many people's chips, you've got nobody left."

Hitch sighed. "Duggan, I save my clever one-liners for those with the keen wit to appreciate them. That being the case, sod off."

Chewing on her sandwich, Finn studied the troublesome Hitch. He didn't look like anyone dangerous or important; if his face looked like it belonged anywhere, it was probably an inside page of a charity newsletter. But then, who knew what great talents he really hid? They must have had some reason for choosing him.

When his little delegation had first burst in on her in the meeting room, they'd given her a brief explanation of what they wanted from her: to confirm she wasn't traumatised, to understand how and where their security protocols had failed, and - if she were willing, to assist Hitch in investigating some recent acts of sabotage. The last had sounded like a late addendum to their plans. She'd disbelieved it, of course, just as she was still more than a little sceptical even now. She'd thought it some ruse to winkle out of her whatever secrets they thought she might be hiding, but as time went on and increasing numbers of officials seemed to be backing the story, she began to wonder if they might be serious.

She didn't think for a moment that she'd actually be able to help, but if they were desperate enough to suggest it, then she was certainly desperate enough to accept. If nothing else, it meant freedom from the endless white walls of the great dome.

There was, of course, another, better reason for agreeing to it. If this Hitch guy lived up to his reputation - if he really was some super-genius navigator of the gates - then she could think of no one better suited to helping her get back home to her family.

11. Bad Signs

Standing at the northern edge of the village, the cottage was set a yard back from the road. A low stone wall shielded its little garden from the dust kicked up by passing hooves, and in that small enclosure, bees and hoverflies busily attended a tangled riot of blooms. Half the building's facade was embraced by ivy and, above it, the overhanging thatch sheltered an irregular array of swallows' nests. It was unassuming but beautiful; a place that spoke of life and energy - all of nature's busy commerce.

He knocked.

The village was quiet, baking beneath the sun of a long summer's afternoon; only the hum of the insects broke the stifled silence. He stepped closer to the door and felt its warmth reflecting back at him. There might have come a sound from within but the walls of the cottage were thick; it was always hard to be certain what might be happening inside.

He waited. It pained him that it took so long a time for its tenant to appear. He had good days and bad days. Today's long delay did not augur well.

At length, the door handle and hinges squeaked in quiet harmony, and from the shadows of the interior a face appeared. Round, pale, and overhung by dark, limply curling hair, it lacked definition - *a mere carcase* he'd once called it, though that of course was unfair. When he spoke, those same loose, passive features became suddenly animated; suffused with warmth, welcome and a youthfulness that could so easily be overlooked.

Hazel eyes glittered with recognition. "Silas! Oh, you've come!"

He smiled and nodded his respects. "My great friend! I trust my visit does not inconvenience you?"

"Inconvenience? But of course not! Come in, come in."

"Thank you." He stepped inside and began their usual exchange. "So, how have you been keeping?"

His host ushered him into the parlour to the left. There, the sunlight came green and golden through the little sash window, but the bright wedge of colour that pressed itself into the floor only accentuated the deeply shadowed corners of the room. His friend shook his head. "Not so well as I should like. You know how it is."

Silas nodded his sympathy and looked momentarily away. "Of course." He raised his eyes again. "Is there anything I can do to help?"

"Did you visit Bridgwater?"

Silas smiled. "I did. I spoke to our friend the doctor. I procured some supplies."

"Oh, you're a blessing, Silas. I'm really so thankful for you."

He handed his young host a paper parcel and, responding to his silent invitation, seated himself by the fireplace. "You don't mind, then, if I stay a little while? I shouldn't be imposing upon you?"

"Not in the least, old friend." His host grinned. "But you do have the most regrettable timing. Had you come sooner, you might have met Will and his new visitors. They called upon me before noon; they've not been gone above an hour."

"Ah, regrettable indeed."

A frown worked itself above those clever, enigmatic eyes. "It's a curious thing, Silas. I don't recall you and I ever having met in the company of others." The frown became a twinkle. "My friends might easily believe you a creature of my own imagining."

"Hah! Next time perhaps."

"Quite so. Well..." Gesturing to the small, wrapped parcel, his friend inclined his head towards the hallway door. "Would you mind if I...?"

"No, no. Quite right." Silas waved him away and waited. From the next room came assorted shufflings and the familiar clink of silver against glass. He turned his head and called into the empty doorway. "I was thinking again about our game."

"Our game?"

"Our *Hypotheticals*. If you like, I thought I might present you with another."

A shining tray and two glasses preceded the young man's bright smile into the room. "Oh, by all means. Your last was a most absorbing challenge: conjuring ships and cities amongst the stars. I thought upon it all evening; I scribbled notes long into the night."

"Ah, then I'm very pleased to have been of service." Silas relieved his host of one of the drinks and then produced an envelope from his bag. "This next posits a very different sort of world - one at war with itself. I was wondering: would you like me to set the scene?"

Finn wasn't equipped for the weather, which held all the heat and scent of a Mediterranean summer. Walking with Hitch across a busy concourse, she now wore only her t-shirt and jeans, but still she kept her coat and hoodie slung over her clasped arms. They were as cumbersome as they were inappropriate, but they represented her last connection with the real world. She wasn't about to give them up.

To her right, wooded parkland sloped down to a broad lake and, beyond it, a tall, turreted castle that could have been lifted straight from a Florida theme park. To its left, greying into the distance, the masts and towers of the city spaceport glittered in the sun. Lacking only a pink dirigible towing a banner saying 'welcome to your unconscious', the scene offered nearly all the confirmation her coma theory demanded.

Behind her, following at a discreet distance, Cariola and Duggan made an unconvincing couple. With one hand kept meaningfully in his pocket, the watchman was eyeing Hitch as though he were a hyena left to stand guard over a hen house.

The airy surroundings struck Finn as a fitting place to get things into the open. She nudged the arm of her scruffy companion. "So... you're a smuggler, then."

Hitch's brow became a washboard of indignation. "*No*. I'm not a *smuggler*." He dropped his voice and angled his head toward her. "I'm just someone who, you know, occasionally... smuggles things."

"I see."

He scowled. "No you don't. You're being all judgy. You're making wild and baseless assumptions."

"Am I? Oh well then, I apologise." She allowed a second or two to pass. "So why the career change? Was it the money?"

Hitch snorted. "No."

"Well then, why?"

"Oh, I don't know." He shrugged. "Because I didn't fit. Because maybe this isn't the heaven they like to pretend it is."

Finn shook her head. "No. Too vague and mysterious. Come on; what's the real..?"

Hitch pointed to a bright structure ahead. "Hey, look. We're here. E&P Central. Where it all happens."

Finn squinted. Ringed by flower beds and stone plinths proclaiming this to be *The Joint Faculty Research and Publishing Centre*, the building was very nearly an architectural masterpiece. A hexagonal tower of polished marble and mirrored glass, it rose some thirty storeys from the wide limestone plaza. Tall and shining, it was a symphony of bold geometries - the stark uniformity of its panes and planes broken by countless silver canopies that gave shade to its gleaming windows. Light rays gambolled upon their surfaces like giddy lambs at play and sent prisms fanning out across the concourse. But for all that, Finn couldn't quite escape a nagging doubt about the design.

"We call it the cheese grater," said Hitch.

"Ah." Finn nodded. That was it.

If anyone else had noticed the similarity, they were keeping politely quiet about it. Most other pedestrians seemed to be much more preoccupied by a large, milling crowd of protesters that had gathered round the entrance.

Initially, she'd assumed it was another foreigner-bashing demo but as she approached, she sensed something different about it. It was composed mainly of teenage girls and gaunt youths in unseasonably long coats. Even from some distance Finn thought she could hear some odd expressions mixed in amongst the chanted slogans.

"D'you get a lot of these?" she asked.

Hitch nodded. "There's a rota. But you're lucky; it's just the ERU today."

"The ERU...?"

Hitch sniffed. "Equal Rights for the Undead."

"The *undead?*"

"You know - vampires and zombies and stuff."

"I know what it means. But what..."

Hitch wafted his hand. "Just another special interest group. There are loads of them, all demanding something different."

"From E&P?"

"Yeah. They keep changing the rules about who they can extract. It was just the protagonist types to begin with - feisty heroines and the guys with the muscles and the good chins. But someone decided they were being elitist, so they started pulling minor characters, too."

"Characters like me."

Hitch nodded at the building. "You can thank them later."

Finn frowned. "But zombies? They aren't..."

"I know, I know, but that's what Policy is all about. They do enjoy their ethical debates. I mean, are bad guys really bad guys, or are they just innocent pawns doing their authors' bidding? It's that whole 'free will' question. They love all that."

"But zombies?" Finn had never liked horror movies. Zombies especially freaked her out.

"What can I say?" Hitch sniffed. "They're trendy. Zombies, vampires and shifters - there've been so many of them lately, people thought there was a fault in the Core. But no, apparently not; it's all anyone out there seems to want to write about. I don't know what's going on out in the realer worlds, but there must be no-brainers and blood-munchers shambling about all over the place."

"All over the place?" Finn felt the blood draining from her cheeks, doubtless looking for somewhere to hide. "Here? I mean... They haven't actually *extracted* any, have they?"

Hitch shrugged. "Dunno. They do trials from time to time. They've been discussing something with *Give Trolls a Chance*, and the werewolf pilot worked like a charm."

"*Werewolves?* Really?"

"Yeah, but that one was easy; they just packed them off to a planet with no moons."

"Oh. Okay. But just coming back to the zombies for a minute..."

"I don't think so. Probably too risky - you know; that whole 'one bite and you're brainless' thing." He glanced around the plaza and sighed. "Not that you'd notice if some of this lot got turned."

"Well, that's, um..."

"It's the computer characters that are giving people the big headaches just now."

"Oh?"

"Yeah. E&P love *that* little dilemma. People are building their careers on it. I mean, you've got these little digital people who keep getting themselves killed but then they can just get resurrected at the touch of a button. D'you bother extracting someone like that? Who's to say? It's a tricky moral question, apparently. We're all supposed to care very deeply about it."

"Has anyone tried?"

"Once. They pulled some weird little bouncy guy but he just ran around head butting things and demanding gold coins off people. Bit of a disaster really."

Finn narrowed her eyes. "You're winding me up, aren't you?"

Hitch smiled and looked away.

"You know, I don't know if I can trust a word you say."

Hitch pulled a face. "The consensus on that would probably be no."

"I'm going to talk to Duggan instead."

"Oh God, no. Don't do that. He's the most boring man that ever lived."

"I want to know where we're going - and why."

"I told you. We need a good cable."

"Yes. Hence the blank face and wanting to talk to Duggan. You might enjoy sounding all strange and enigmatic but be honest: it's not very helpful, is it?"

Hitch rolled his eyes like a truculent twelve year-old. "Okay, look, when you were extracted, there was the team that pulled you and then there was another team back in the control room."

"Yeah, computer types; I saw them."

"Uh huh. Well, one of them was a cable. You know - like an air-sea rescue team. You've got the winchman and the cable operator. The winch goes down to pick you up but it's the cable who controls things and pulls you out."

"Alright, but what does the... Oh." Finn was stopped in mid question by a sallow young couple and a long cotton banner, which they held out across her path. The message had been daubed in red and black and they'd spelled 'vampire' with a 'y'. It wasn't a good sign.

"Equal rights for nightwalkers," demanded the woman. Judging by her manner, she seemed to hold Finn personally responsible for whatever grave injustice aggrieved her.

"Oh, okay..." Finn smiled and pointed to the main entrance. "D'you mind if we, um..."

"Extractions now!" shouted the male. He raised the banner to eye level and gave it an earnest jiggle.

"Right, well, um..." Finn stopped. There seemed little point in continuing. To the great consternation of the protestors, Hitch had begun grabbing handfuls of their banner and bundling them to his chest.

"Hey!" cried the girl. "Get off. That's ours! You can't do that!"

"You're quite right," said Hitch, still gathering up the material. "This falls well outside the boundaries of acceptable social behaviour. But consider two things: one, I'm in a hurry. Two, I have a large and very aggressive minder behind me. You, on the other hand... don't."

The two protestors glanced at each other and then at Duggan who was striding towards them with eyebrows that met in the middle.

Hitch handed them their ball of fabric and smiled.

Hurriedly, the couple sidled away.

"So, like I said: here we are." Hitch swept an inviting hand in the direction of the main entrance.

Finn wrinkled her nose. "Agreeing to come with you was a big mistake, wasn't it?"

12. Liberty

"Woah. Them bailiffs look proper 'andy. Where've they come from, then?"

Sitting in the midst of a baying, twenty thousand-strong crowd, Viktor leaned in close, though he still had to shout to be heard. "They're ogres."

"Ogres?" The spider-web tattoo on Jones' face wrinkled as he shot him an incredulous look. It was the first time in more than twenty minutes that he'd taken his eyes off the bloody floor of the arena.

"Not originally, of course. They're just the bodies they asked for when they got pulled."

"What? You mean... Could I 'ave asked to be an ogre?" Jones' crestfallen look lasted only for a moment; it brightened quickly when he saw that the morning's contest was resuming. It was his first time in the amphitheatre and he seemed astonished by everything about it: its size, the great mirrored wall, the savage tumult of the crowd.

They were gathered to watch the leadership trials and the sudden-death electoral system that was as visceral as its name was apt. In the dawn round alone there had been two beheadings, three disembowellings and an impalement. Now they were onto the transferable vote stage and they'd just witnessed Schilling of the Western Elders failing to secure his nomination. Accordingly, and notwithstanding all his kicks and protestations, the two bailiffs had dragged him from the circle and bound him to one of the basalt columns at the base of the Bare Wall. Like the other failed candidates, he was cursing and writhing in a hopeless attempt to free himself.

"So what's the deal with them columns, then?" Jones wafted his club in the captives' direction. "I don't get it."

Viktor's one eye twinkled. It was a cunning conceit, always much appreciated by spectators. He enjoyed explaining it to newbies. "Take another look back there," he said.

Casting his gaze over his shoulder, Jones squinted at the great parabola of polished haematite that formed the Mirror Wall. "Yeah, so?"

"Now look at the other end; those flags on the top of the wall."

Jones did as he was asked. "Yeah? I still don't get it."

"The first one's where the sun comes over."

"Right..."

Viktor sniffed. Jones wasn't the brightest of folk but, to be fair, that wasn't really a problem in a place like this. Cleverness only bred mistrust. The lad could handle himself in a fight and that was enough. He gestured back at the Mirror Wall. "Where you came from - did you never take a magnifying glass and burn stuff?"

"What, like insects and that?"

"Yeah."

Jones's web widened as he grinned. "Aye. I did."

Viktor nodded at the columns. "Well, when the sun comes over the first flag, just keep your eye on that column on the right."

"Huh?"

Victor pointed at the battered wretch hanging from it. "He's your first insect, right there."

Jones looked back at the great mirror and realisation brightened his features like a slowly rising sun. "Oh, wicked," he said, squirming in his seat. "When? 'ow soon?"

"Oh, it'll be a few minutes yet, but don't worry; you won't miss it. It's not quick. Or pretty."

Now with heightened enthusiasm, Jones returned his attention to Consul Johns who, at the arena's centre, was once again preparing to speak. Around him, five places at the circle were taken; only one remained to be filled.

Slowly, the clamour subsided into the white noise of individual debates.

"Next," cried the consul, raising his cudgel, "Barabas of the Red Pelt contends with Olaf, chosen champion of the Dolorous Mai..."

"No. Enough." A male voice seemed to emanate from everywhere at once. Loud and without the merest hint of distortion, it sounded from the stones on which they sat, from the walls around them, perhaps even from the sky itself.

"So, who's this then?" In the absence of anywhere more specific to point his thumb, Jones jerked it upwards. "What's this bit about?"

Viktor chewed the inside of his cheek. "Dunno. This is new."

"Oh." Jones turned back, smiling expectantly.

A sense of bated unease grew amongst the crowd. The Trials were often violent affairs and none had yet ended without at least a little bloodshed amongst the onlookers. Traditionally, though, the fights were localised, usually jeered and judged by those for whom they were just another part of the day's spectacle. Now, however, every hand held a weapon and wary looks flashed all about.

"What is *this*?" cried Consul Johns, striding theatrically about his circle. "Who dares intrude upon our long-honoured tradition?"

"A spirit of divinest liberty," answered the voice. "They call me Silas."

From the masses over to the right there came a loud murmuring. Viktor rose to his feet, following the direction of their gaze, but all those in front of him were doing likewise. Scores of heads, necks and flint-head spears now obscured his view, though for a fleeting instant, he discerned a wild-haired figure walking towards the Circle of the Select.

"Down!" roared Chieftain Redridge from a little way behind him. "Take your seats, damn you or I'll have your heads."

When Viktor regained his view, the stranger had crossed halfway across the sand. The two hulking bailiffs barred his way. Both held stone clubs the size of dugout canoes and they seemed more than happy at the prospect of using them.

"Stay your hands," said Silas, his voice still strangely amplified. "End this motiveless malignity. You fret and squabble over meagre nothings."

"Motives and what?" said Jones. "What's 'e goin' on about?"

Viktor ignored him, electing instead to stare. The ogres approached the stranger, but stopped as he pulled a gleaming longsword from the folds of his cloak.

The tiered rows of spectators produced a deep, collective gasp. No one here had seen a metal blade in years. The planet was a prison for unreformed thieves and killers; the worst that a million fictions could produce. Set in the arse-end of nowhere, beyond the reach of starships, gods or magic, it was designed to keep its inmates forever locked in stone-aged isolation. What scant fuels there were would not sustain the necessary temperatures for smelting and the hard, unyielding bedrock lurked just metres beneath the sandy earth. The Mirror Wall contained the only metal most of them would ever see - left by whomever had created the place as a sneering taunt at their inability to work it. Now though, apparently careless of its value, the stranger sank the shining weapon into the sand.

"Step away from that!" Consul Johns strode forward, clearly conscious that the five Select were also edging towards it, and that the two huge bailiffs were looking increasingly inquisitive.

Silas held out his arms. "But I would speak to you of ambition and poetic faith."

"Get back! Now!"

Silas made a slow, elaborate bow and backed away from his sword.

Jones shook Viktor's arm. "Bloody hell. Just think: if one o' them ogres gets that sword..."

"I know, I know. Shush."

Down below, Consul Johns stood closest to the weapon, but the others were converging upon it too - initially at a slow walk that hinted at simple curiosity, then at a more hurried pace as each saw his fellows doing the same.

Edging backwards, Consul Johns raised a hand to speak. "People of..."

He said no more. An instant later, he was bulldozed to the ground by the first ogre, then trampled flat by the second. Others ran over him, too, as, one by one, the greatest, bravest leaders on the planet hurled themselves into a wriggling scrum.

Seconds later, the melee burst into panicked shards. From its midst, one of the muscle-bound bailiffs rose up with the sword in one hand and his former colleague's head in the other.

"Mine!" bellowed the victorious ogre. "Now let's..."

It was a bad day for syntax. Like the unfortunate consul, he didn't finish his sentence. Instead, he and most of the Select were annihilated by a single, broad blast of blue-white light. Lasting only a moment, it erupted from something small and innocuous in Silas' hand and punched a trim hole in the side wall of the amphitheatre. Between hand and wall lay several pairs of smoking, disembodied boots.

"The point I wish to make," said Silas, in the moment of absolute silence that followed, "concerns ambition. Success is dependent only upon the heights to which one aspires."

Leaving the crowd to mull on this, he strode over to the one surviving clan leader and helped him to his feet - though around him there were plenty of others to choose.

At this distance, Viktor couldn't tell who the other was. It might have been Kristatos but, if so, he was now half an arm short.

"What do you want?" said the newly truncated fellow. The voice, somehow amplified by his proximity to the tooled-up newcomer, confirmed Viktor's identification.

"I wish you all to follow me."

"And why would we do that?"

Silas pushed back the sleeve of his shirt to reveal something shiny. It looked like a reader. He held up his arm and turned slowly, exhibiting it to the crowd.

"You ask me why?" There was a smiling lilt to his voice. "Because I have the pass codes to the gates."

13. First Contact

"Thank you everyone." Sitting at the head of the table, Winchester closed her folder and sent her gaze flitting between the sombre faces of her departmental heads. "I think that's everything for now. I'm sorry to have spoiled your plans for the day, but I'm sure you appreciate the gravity of what we're facing."

Low murmurs of assent accompanied much pushing back of chairs and a slow migration towards the doors. Small clusters of directors formed at intervals beside the conference table and broke into muted discussions.

"Hector." She spoke quietly, keeping her head down. "Clear the room as soon as you can, please, and then have a word with your teams to update them. I'll be back to you within the hour."

Wordlessly, her second raised his ursine frame and moved towards the nearest gathering of frowns.

Now, inclining her head to the left, she addressed her security chief. "Max, would you please stay on for a moment or two? We need to consider our public line on this."

"Of course, Helen."

"Thank you." Winchester took a breath, then raised a finger to summon her PR.

"Ma'am?" As ever, the young woman stepped to her side without once removing her eyes or busy fingertips from the tablet on her wrist.

"Pauline, this Radio Vapid thing..."

"Radio *Rapid*, ma'am."

"Right. Yes. We'd scheduled an interview, hadn't we?"

"That's right. The five forty-five slot."

"Ah, well then, we'll have to postpone it, I'm afraid."

Pauline frowned and tapped at her screen. "Right. Well, we can probably move it to six-thirty, after the sports round-up, but..."

"No, no. We need more time. Besides, I'd much rather make a formal announcement through one of the serious news channels."

Pauline's face assumed the expression of someone who'd just been asked to drop kick a koala; surprise and distaste merged into an unlovely scowl. "But that's *factual* programming, ma'am."

Winchester blinked. "Yes. I'm aware of that, and that's why I think it the proper vehicle."

"But it's *factual,* ma'am. It does news and analysis." Had it also done bestiality and necrophilia, her face could not have registered any more revulsion.

Pauline was supposed to be the very best in her field, but Winchester once again found herself wondering why she always seemed to end up having to explain the basics of communication to her. "Yes," she said. "And that's what we need. We're dealing with some very serious matters and people are naturally concerned. We need to let them know what's going on before the rumours turn into something worse."

Her assistant nodded. "Oh, quite right, ma'am; absolutely."

"And since the emphasis will be on facts and information, I want a hard news channel and a proper interview. I don't want to be given a quick twenty-second slot between the adverts and some stupid celebrity phone prank."

Pauline shifted uncomfortably and poked at her screen. "But, ma'am, the audience figures on NTN are terrible. It's factual, you see; no one listens to it. If you want real audience reach then you've got to tap into the *Rapid* demographic. That's why we'd lined up the interview with Larry Spangles."

"Pauline. I do not want to make this announcement in the company of a man who sounds like a children's party entertainer."

"But ma'am, *Spanner's Spot* is the biggest early evening show there is. And Larry's brilliant - his ratings are through the roof." Pauline angled her wrist to show her a brightly illuminated bar chart.

"Pauline, Larry Spangles is not brilliant. I've met him. He's a dribbling, witless old pervert who surrounds himself with sycophants. He's only popular because he fills his studio with giggling simpletons. They're all paid to laugh at his quips and whoop every time he raises a flag."

Pauline smiled as if at some private joke. "Yes, ma'am, I know. There are net cameras in the studio. But that's what people like. If you want to talk to New Tybet, then you need to be talking to Larry."

Max, who had been attending patiently with fingers pressed against his lips, gave a polite cough. "If I may, Helen, I'll deal with this Spangles fellow. It touches on security concerns, after all. It'll buy you some time to devise a formal statement."

Winchester nodded slowly. "Thank you, Max. That would be a great help. Pauline - let these Vapid people know about the new arrangements, would you?"

"*Rapid*," muttered the PR manager, giving a frowny little twitch. "Yes ma'am."

"Thank you, Pauline. I'll be back to you shortly."

Max watched the young woman bustle out. Hector had performed his duties and now they were alone in the conference room. "I sometimes think you enjoy goading her," he said.

"Oh, it's not her, really." Winchester shook her head. "It's the fact that she's right. The sky itself could be on fire and most people would still rather listen to celebrity gossip than trouble themselves to wonder what's going on."

Max pursed his lips. "And what actually is going on, Helen? What are you going to tell them?"

Winchester took a deep breath. "Ah, well that's the question, isn't it? As you've probably gathered, there's rather more to it than just the disappearances."

"I'd heard whispers."

She looked him in the eye. "Do you remember a little while back, when we were researching the She-Wolf trail?"

"The Origin myths. I do."

"Well, I sent a few people to investigate, but you know how hard-pressed we've been; we turned up very little." She lowered her voice. "Anyway, the thing is, I think someone else has been doing the same thing."

Max narrowed his eyes. "An insider?"

"It would have to be. Some of these supposedly sabotaged tales... I've had people look into them and it looks like they were edited before they were added to the system."

"Edited?" Max dropped his eyes to the table. "But besides us there are only, what, three or four people with the access to do that?"

Winchester nodded. "Four. And I think at least one of them has been conducting their own investigations. What's really worrying me is that they might now be further ahead than we are."

"What makes you say that?"

"We investigated the recent attacks. Two of the narratives were on our possible She-Wolf list. There were strong signs that someone had got there ahead of our researchers."

Max lowered his voice. "So, what d'you think? Someone's discovered something about the Origin myths and now they're trying to stop us from finding it ourselves?"

"I honestly don't know. That might only be a best case scenario."

"*Best?* How could it be worse?"

Winchester chewed her lip. "It could be worse if someone has already cracked the legend's secret."

"What? You think someone might already be communicating with a narrative power?" Max shook his head. "No. Impossible. If someone had breached the Core, we'd know of it. Such a thing couldn't happen - not without some sort of sign or shockwaves."

"We might already be seeing them." Winchester ran a hand through her hair. "Publicly, I'm leading with the sabotage theory, but my great worry is that we're seeing the first indications of a higher intervention; an author-level power who knows about the gates and what we do here."

Max looked pained. "No. I can't believe that. I don't even know how we could test for such a thing."

"Well, think about it, Max. We've never been able to see into the Core. We don't know the provenance of the narratives we enter; we've never had a mechanism to do it. They just come to us by a magic that, quite frankly, no one understands. We send our people in there quite blindly; who's to say that some of these narratives haven't been written solely for the purpose of entrapping us?"

Max stayed quiet, ruminating. Winchester stared at the table for a few seconds and let the words settle. Speaking her worst fears aloud had not brought her the relief she'd hoped.

"So who else knows of this?" asked Max at length.

"I've not been so explicit with anyone else, but I've quietly been stepping up our research."

"Into the Origin legends?"

"That and one or two other areas. But it's difficult; when one's own departmental heads are under suspicion, things must all be done very quietly. I'm just using single operatives for now."

"I see." Max massaged his forehead. "So what do you need from me?"

"I need things locking down - any traffic must be considered a risk now. And I need your watchmen to be especially vigilant."

"Very well, but I can't really brief them on this, can I? Not properly."

"No, clearly not. There must be no panic, and if the risks are as grave as I fear... well, the consequences could be too terrible to conceive. Genocide, genre-mining, the most horrific forms of exploitation... anything, literally anything, becomes possible. It could all descend into the direst form of chaos."

Max nodded. "Liberty's wild riot..."

Winchester glanced sideways. "I'm sorry?"

"Just an expression." Max flashed her a strange smile and pushed back his unruly hair. "Well, listen, Helen; maybe I can help. I've been doing some digging of my own and I think there are one or two things you need to see. I wonder, could you spare a few minutes to come with me?"

"Come on, come on." Doctor Rowan gestured at her ragged blouse and the deep cleft between her bosoms, which glowered resentfully back at her like the eye of Sauron. "It's bad enough I have to dress like this; for heaven's sake let's get this place cleared."

Her lab was now a studio set - *Hammer House of Horror* blended with something from the sweatier, squelchier end of the internet. In the oily, holographic lantern light, straw and drunkards lay strewn upon on the floor while improbably lithe wenches paraded about with trays of roasted meats. Further out, hunched in shadowed corners, heavily cowled technicians masqueraded as assassins and tried to drink from their flagons without getting their hoods all soggy.

Closer to the mirrored glass of the projector screens, the illusion rather dissipated. Builders hurried out with stepladders and harassed expressions. A trio of barbarians sat by the bar checking their microphones.

"Ten seconds, everyone." The voice of one of her grad students sounded crisply through the speakers. "We have a connection. All systems are live and running."

"Right," said Rowan, grimly adjusting her décolletage. It wasn't just three months' work that were riding on this; now the whole board of directors seemed to be taking a close interest. It was just a shame that the most ambitious endeavour of her career required her to dress like a medieval harlot.

Seeing her team looking anxiously at her, she balled her fists. "Come on. Let's hold it together this time. Whatever else happens, keep that connection going; let's keep them talking as long as we can."

"Five seconds."

She took a deep breath. At the far end of the set, the tavern doorway was beginning to glow.

She still got a thrill from watching avatars form. Even in the midst of a momentous experiment like this, it was exciting; always a revelation. Initially, twelve lines of light formed a two metre cube, but this quickly deformed and shrank as though being crushed into shape under an immense pressure. The planes of the cube fractured into ever smaller polygons that evolved shape, texture and eventually even colour.

"Doctor Rowan!" She winced as an excited voice shrilled through her earpiece. *"We've got two of them!"*

She was right. Two figures now stood in the doorway: one thin and pale, one fat and flushed - both looking as though they'd been selected from opposite ends of some peculiar line-up of the aesthetically-challenged. By some strange quirk of the VR software, they appeared to be wearing two different outfits at once - one crudely rendered, the other finely detailed. Pallor-Man, for example, wore semi-transparent plate mail over a t-shirt proclaiming the onset of winter. Paunch sported a pixelated wizard's hat and cloak, beneath which could be seen a tatty sweatshirt. It was emblazoned with tomato sauce stains and the words *'Engineers do it in...'* Whatever the final line of this witty quip, it was tucked illegibly into the young man's jeans.

God's gonads; if these really were representative of higher level beings, it was little wonder things were such a mess.

After a moment, the two avatars seemed to gather themselves. Paunch held out a hand and turned it under his gaze. His lips moved but something in the system was amiss. All that came out was a crackle and a few broken vowels.

Rowan glared back at the projector screen, though now it showed only stone walls and torch-lit rain framed in glassless windows. Silently, she mouthed her instruction. *Sort it out. Now.*

Pallor-Man was tapping the side of his head. Maybe the fault lay at his end.

Suddenly, the sound broke through, perfectly modulated.

"Jez," he said. "No, I got it now. It's working, man."

His companion looked slowly around. "Frack me, bro'; look at this."

The other glanced up, still tapping his temple. "Mm. Yeah."

"Just 'yeah'?" Jez took a step towards the wooden bar - in reality no more than a couple of filing cabinets overlaid with planks and some clever holographics. "Seriously, Neil? You ever seen rendering like this?"

Neil shrugged. "Meh. The *Oculus* eng..."

Jez snorted. "Ah, bollocks. This is way beyond *Oculus*. I mean look at it - all the..."

"Em, hello," said Doctor Rowan, stepping forward. "Can I get you anything?" Not exactly words to echo down the halls of history, but they were a start.

Jez peered closely at her, gave her forehead an experimental poke and then nudged his friend. "Ah, yes. Um. Hail and well met, old crone. I am the Great Wizard Jean-Luc Targaryan and this is my companion, Lord Riddick McNeil."

Old crone? Bloody charming. And all this being recorded, too. Rowan forced a broad smile. "Oh, well, you're very welc..."

"We are weary travellers," announced the dread wizard, raising his chins. "We have... um, travelled many a dusty league this day, and are in sore need of ale and lodgings."

"Verily," added Neil, leaning in. "And forsooth."

Rowan continued to smile. "Right. Um. Well, that's nice. I'm sure we can sort you out with something. Would you like to take a seat at the bar? Perhaps you can tell me a bit about yourselves; how you got here; where you came from?"

"Ah, the journey," said Jez/Jean-Luc. "Danger and intrigue at every turn. Happily, the goblin hordes were no match for my powerful spellcraft and my good friend's steel."

"It's a plus five vorpal sword," explained Neil. "I got it from the Lich King's treasure vault. Phil's thief was on, like, minus two hit points or something and all our NPCs were already dead, but we still managed to take it out. It was awesome."

"Oi, frack-wit," muttered Jez. "Stay in character, yeah?"

"Oh yeah, yeah, right." Neil pointed at her cleavage. "But it's weird. It's like... she looks so real."

His friend stroked an imaginary beard. "Well, anyway, we come on a mighty quest. We have heard tell of an ancient evil that lurks betwixt the Black Mountains and the Forest of Souls. Know ye aught of this, old woman?"

"Em, no I'm sorry," she said. "But perhaps we could talk ab..."

Neil cut in. "Yeah, Jez; I think you might need to give 'em some money, dude; buy them a few drinks or something. Get a bit of trust going, yeah?"

"Yeah, but I don't know the inventory commands," said Jez. "This system's all new."

Rowan cleared her throat. "Well, shall I start by booking you a room?" Speaking with deliberate emphasis, she gestured theatrically to the door behind the bar. "I will now ask the maid to bring in some ink and parchment."

She cursed herself. Here was a real chance of putting a pen in the hand of an author-level intelligence - a history-making first - and yet she hadn't thought to put a single quill anywhere on set. Now it all depended on her assistant getting the hint. Where was she?

A moment passed, then Abby pushed through, one hand supporting a wooden tray that already contained more sloshing liquid than the tankards sitting upon it. The other clutched what was clearly a pencil. However, there was little chance of anyone noticing the anachronism; as she entered, a glitch in the system caused the whole scene to flicker. For a long and awkward moment, they were all very obviously standing in a brightly lit laboratory, surrounded by cameras, mirrors and cheap cardboard props. The scene reasserted itself but it left the avatars looking nervous and confused.

"Dude, what just happened?" The portly wizard glanced about him with a rather less than intrepid expression.

"No, no. It was nothing," said Doctor Rowan. "Probably just a flash of lightning or something. We get that sometimes, don't we, everyone?"

"Oh, sure. Yeah. Absolutely." From around the tavern, three barbarians and an assortment of unconvincing assassins chirped a hasty chorus of agreement.

"No, seriously." The great warrior O'Neil took a step back, his face even more ashen than before. "What the actual frack is going on?"

"Doctor Rowan," chirped an anxious voice in her ear. *"I'm terribly sorry but some people have just come into the control room. They're saying they have to see you at once."*

She lowered her chin to her microphone. "Don't be ridiculous. They'll have to wait."

"They say it's very urgent, Doctor."

"I don't care if they're bleeding from their ears. They'll..." She stopped. The avatars were still talking. Amazingly, she hadn't yet lost them.

"Oh, hang on," said Jez. "I get it. This is a beta-test, innit? Maybe this is like a showreel or something."

"Or like a holo-deck," said Neil. "Maybe we're on a starship or something?"

"Computer," said Jez firmly, "Load new simulation: *Kobayashi Maru*."

The scene stayed resolutely medieval.

"Worth a try," he said.

"Doctor Rowan, I'm sorry but there's a man here who..." The voice in her ear became faint. The feed disintegrated into a painful staccato of scrapings and pops.

"Ah, hello Doctor Rowan," said a man's voice. *"Sorry to bother you. I'm afraid I must talk to you at once. Life, death, imminent misfortune - all that sort of thing."*

Rowan turned away from the precious avatars. She'd given up all pretence. This was an absolute calamity. "Sir, you are ruining my experiment. Be silent this instant or I'll call security."

"I've got security here with me."

"What?"

"Never mind. I'm coming down." More wince-making scrapes and shuffling noises erupted in her ear.

When she turned back, the pasty O'Neil was pointing at her in alarm. "I heard that," he said. "She said this was an *experiment.* Oh God. Are we being abducted?"

His friend pulled a face. "Dude, chill. It's a VR simulation, yeah?"

Neil shook his head. "I don't like it. It's too real. Something weird's going on."

Rowan held up her hands. "No, no, really, boys; it's all fine. I just wanted to have a chat. I promise you: you're perfectly safe."

She was contradicted by a loud crash from immediately behind the projector wall.

"Sorry," said a man. "Who ordered these extra large anal probes?"

"What?" The warrior and the wizard looked past Doctor Rowan in wide-eyed alarm.

"Just kidding." Waving an identity card around him like a fan, the scruffy intruder materialised on set by walking straight through a holographic staircase.

Three panicked undergraduate barbarians looked to her for guidance. Their rehearsals had covered nothing like this.

"Abby - for facts' sake keep our guests entertained," said Rowan, marching towards whomever had just ruined months of preparation. "And you! Get the *hell* out of my lab!"

"Oh, so you're Doctor Rowan." Smiling, he held out a hand. "Hi. My name's Hitch. I'm just... ow, ow, ow!"

A summer of self-defence classes had taught her one or two useful things about wrist locks. Briskly, she marched him off the set.

14. Faustus

"Who the hell d'you think you are? Have you any idea how much damage you've done?" Standing at the back row of the observation deck, Doctor Rowan emphasised every other syllable with a fierce poke at Hitch's chest.

"I told you," said Hitch, flinching. "This is important official business. I've come for Johnny Faustus."

Finn turned away and left them to it. She'd been stupid to imagine that the shambling fraudster could ever have helped her get home. Perhaps there were others better placed to do that - people who worked in big laboratories, perhaps; people who had teams of clipboard-wielding assistants at their disposal.

Rowan looked to be a capable woman; she made an interesting candidate. That said, her work did seem to require some very peculiar facilities. This observation room, for example, was dark, stuffy and laid out like a mini cinema - the sort of special-interest establishment usually patronised by men with long raincoats and unhappy lives. Thick black carpet lined its walls and the floor sloped down to a great glass wall overlooking the laboratory-studio. An aisle bisected half a dozen short rows of folding seats. At the bottom stood an intently scribbling researcher.

With Duggan and Cariola still waiting somewhere outside, Finn decided to join him.

"How's it going?" she asked.

The young man glanced sideways. "Badly." There was more than a hint of accusation in his tone.

"Oh, yes. Sorry about him. But what are you actually doing?"

He returned his attention to the lab. "Avatar research. This should be incredibly exciting, but it's falling apart. Your friend's just ruined it."

Finn rested her forehead against the glass. "I'm not sure he's really my friend, to be honest; more of a travel pass, I think. But forget about him; what's avatar research about?"

A gleam came into the young man's eye. "Avatars are amazing. And Doctor Rowan's a genius. Those two guys down there, they might *look* like you and me..."

Finn raised an eyebrow. "You think?"

"...but they're actually a physical manifestation of a level one intelligence."

"I'm sorry? A level one...?"

Clearly unable to help himself, the researcher turned, slipping into full evangelism mode. "They're from the level *up*," he said, his eyes dancing. "They could very well share one of the same worlds as the authors who created us."

Finn pulled a face. "But they're just nerds. I get people like that in my shop all the time."

"No. No, they're not. They're nerds from a higher order of being. A higher level of reality." He grinned maniacally. "Don't you see? This is hard proof of the Many Narratives Theory. It's going to be bigger than the Large Concept Collider and the Drabble Narrascope combined."

Finn pointed at the two role-players. "*They* are a higher order of being?"

Below them, the brave adventurers were muttering quietly in a huddle, declining repeated offers of holographic drinks from equally holographic serving wenches.

"Back in their home world, they're playing a virtual reality game. It creates a fiction they can inhabit and control." He threw up his hands. "And we've tapped into it! It's genius; incredible, really. Real people immersed in a fictional narrative: a bridge between our realities. Doctor Rowan's found a way of actually *communicating* with them."

Finn gave him a worried look. She'd seen that expression before - usually on people who wore sandwich boards in public and shouted a lot about the end of the world. She was about to ask why communicating with a couple of socially inept young fantasists was so very important when, unexpectedly, she arrived at an answer of her own.

"Wait, you're saying these guys are from the real world?"

The researcher winced. "Well, *real*; it's a subjective concept..."

Finn put a hand against the glass. Suddenly, the discussion was taking on a new significance. "But you're telling me they're from the world where all these stories get written?"

"Well, *one* world where *some* of our stories get written; we can't assume there's only the one."

"I see. Right." Finn's pulse quickened but, gathering herself, she assumed the calmest expression she could. "Well, I've got to say, it looks like you might be losing them."

Below her, progress on set was painful to watch. Without Rowan, the researchers, in their wigs and clichéd costumes, were too overawed to engage their baffled guests in any proper conversation. The hooded thieves shifted nervously in their respective corners, and though the three barbarians exchanged urgent nods and nudges, all seemed rooted to their stools. Only the barmaid was attempting to talk, but the two visitors - clearly no suave socialites themselves - had retreated to the main doorway and were shunning her efforts to thrust a pencil into their hands.

"We're struggling with the language barrier," admitted the researcher.

Finn frowned. "What language barrier?"

"All this forsooth and zounds stuff; they switch back and forth. There's no pattern or logic to it. We can't figure it out at all"

"Oh that." Finn smiled. "It's just Ancient Geek. It's easy."

The young man stared at her. "Really? You can speak it?"

"Oh, it's not hard. I told you, kids in the shop talk like that all the time."

"Really?" His eyes widened further. "Oh, then your expertise could be invaluable to us. You must talk to Doctor Rowan the moment she's finished with your, um... colleague."

"Happy to." Finn stepped away from the glass. "First though, d'you mind me asking? Is there a ladies' toilet anywhere close by?"

Finn stepped onto the set wondering whether she should have tried to steal a lab coat. That was what spies and feisty reporters always seemed to do in situations like this. However, given that half the people behind the holo-projectors were students dressed in jeans and t-shirts, she wasn't sure what good a lab coat would actually have done her. Nevertheless, it felt somehow wrong not to be making the effort.

She'd got by Duggan easily enough - he was only interested in stopping Hitch from doing anything too reprehensible - but Cariola had been more of a challenge. Finn had only prevented her from following her to the toilet by gesticulating vaguely towards her nether regions and murmuring something about being a while.

Now, having passed herself off as a language expert to the two students in the control room, she'd made it to the laboratory. She just hoped she'd get there before the two avatars tired of the social awkwardness and pulled their own plugs.

"Through here?" Catching the eye of a technician, she indicated a gap between the projector stanchions. When he nodded, she stepped into a fantasy role-player's dream.

From the observation deck, which took in the whole of the lab, the area within the projector screens had looked like nothing very special - an everyday studio set overhung by lighting gantries, cameras and wiring. From the inside, however, it was a wholly immersive experience; now she was standing in a tightly enclosed three dimensional tavern, her eyes utterly convinced of the reality of it all.

She had no time to marvel at it, though. Knowing that her subterfuge would be discovered all too soon, she put on a bright smile and headed directly for the two role-players.

"Hi," she said. "Or should I say 'greetings fellow travellers'?"

The pale one shrank behind his friend. The other frowned at her.

"Eh?" he said.

Finn gestured at the room. "Clever, isn't it? All this? I've never seen graphics like it."

The wizard narrowed his eyes. "Who are you?"

"I'm a games tester. Hi. My name's Finn."

"But you're a girl."

"Mm. Well, a woman, really."

"What, a *real* one?" He looked, if anything, even more confused.

"Yup. I'm testing the remote login." Finn was slightly embarrassed to discover how easily she could slip into the role. An internet connection and a few too-quiet afternoons in the bookshop had given her a passing familiarity with online gaming. Evidently, that was all it took.

"So, you into fantasy, then?" The pale friend craned his neck around the wizard.

Finn shrugged. "Fantasy, sci-fi. Any alternate reality stuff."

"Oh. That's cool. Um... I'm Neil." He gave her a little wave. "I write a bit of fantasy myself, actually."

"Really?"

"Yeah. Nothing published yet, but..."

"No, no, but that's still good." Finn smiled but knew her time must be running out. From beyond the screens, several anxious-sounding conversations were gathering in volume. She took her phone from her back pocket. "Look, I don't suppose you could do me a favour, could you?"

"Sure," said the wizard. "I'm Jez, by the way. Hey, is that the new MyPhone?"

"Mm. My sister bought it for me."

"Awesome, aren't they?"

"Yeah, they're great. But listen..."

Jez frowned. "So how come you've got it rendering in the game?"

"Um. Dunno." This was about as far as her bluff would take her. "But listen, I need you to do something. Can one of you give me your phone number?"

"Oh sure, yeah. You bet." The two adventurers spoke at once.

"Okay, great. Neil? What's yours?"

"Um. It's 07751..." He leaned in to mutter the remaining digits, evidently concerned that any number of crazies might be listening in.

"Okay, thanks. Now I need you to take down this number, okay?" Finn showed them her phone screen and her mum's home number. "You got it?"

"Yeah," said Jez, "but it says 'Mum'. What's that about?"

"Um, yeah. That's right." Finn glanced over her shoulder to see Doctor Rowan striding towards her with a Boudican frown. "Look, just call her, okay? Tell her I'm fine. I wasn't murdered, understand?"

"*What?*"

"Tell her I'm on a witness protection programme. Cathy Finn, okay? Tell her..." She paused as firm hands grabbed her arm. "The body wasn't mine. Tell her... tell her it was me, not Chrissie who lost Bagpuss down the well. She'll know what it means. Tell her..."

Whether the two avatars understood or were ever likely to help her, she couldn't tell. Apologising profusely to her visitors, Doctor Rowan got a stronger hold on her and, aided by one of her technicians, she dragged her smartly away.

A short while later, another fierce argument ensued.

"Oh no. No, no, no." Recognising the face in his doorway, the tall technician leapt from his seat and backed away between the desks, dragging a pair of swivel chairs with him to cover his retreat. "No. Whatever it is, the answer's definitely no. Absolutely not."

"Cathy Finn," said Hitch, beaming, "I'd like you to meet our new cable, Johnny Faustus."

"Hello," said Finn.

With a very angry Doctor Rowan signing forms in the corridor outside, Finn was now on her very best behaviour. Employing many surprisingly creative profanities, the good doctor had spelled out to her the utter folly of her recent attempt to send a message home, and clearly now regarded her as at least an equal nuisance to Hitch. Taking all that into consideration, Finn would probably have to wait quite a while before asking her for any favours.

The young man aimed a finger at Hitch. "One: my name's not Johnny Faustus. Two: I'm nobody's cable, least of all yours."

Hitch angled his head towards Finn. "Excuse his rudeness. I think he's still sulking about a little investment project I invited him to..."

"*Invited!*" Indignant eyes bulged. "It was blackmail, that's what it was. And it wasn't a project either; it was basically a heist."

"Well," said Hitch, "the point is, you were disappointed. I'd be the first to admit that it didn't work out quite as well as we'd hoped."

The man who wasn't called Johnny Faustus glared. "No, it didn't, really, did it? I get jumped on by a great truck-load of watchers, you shoot off like a startled rat, and they toss me out of Gate Control faster than you can say bleedin' stitch-up. And I didn't even know we'd been doing anything wrong."

Hitch gestured at the gleaming lab. "Well you're working again now, aren't you? And, hey, look at this place; things seem to have worked out nicely. You might say..."

Not-Johnny picked up a coffee mug and brandished it in a way that suggested he'd never been very good at sports at school. "I swear to God, Hitch, if you say you did me a favour, I'll..."

"No, no, no." Hitch held up his hands. "I'm just saying you're doing all right for yourself. People obviously appreciate your talents, here - as do I."

"Well, I don't care." Not-Johnny put down the mug and began placing armfuls of heavy equipment on the chairs in front of him. Finn couldn't help thinking his makeshift barricade would have looked a bit more daunting if the whole thing hadn't been mounted on castors.

Hitch leaned against the open door. "Oh, don't be like that. Anyway, you have to help me. This is official business."

"Yeah, right. You said that last time."

"No, but this one's sanctioned by Winchester herself."

"You said that, too."

"Oh, come on. Look, why else would I have a watcher with me?"

"I dunno. Restraining order? Conditions of parole?"

Hitch glanced at Finn. "Indulge him. He thinks he's a comedian."

For the first time, Not-Johnny glanced at Finn. "She doesn't look like a watchman."

"Not her, you great steaming dung-monkey." Hitch gestured into the corridor. "Him. Duggan. My new bodyguard."

As though conjured by the name, a muscular arm emerged from the corridor. Swiftly, it seized Hitch by the back of the neck and banged his head against the woodwork of the door.

"Oops," said Duggan, grinning as he pushed into the doorway. "Sorry *boss*, but I think what you might have meant to say there was 'babysitter'."

Not-Johnny looked unhappily at the watchman and pointed a wavering finger at Hitch. "He can't be serious?"

"Oh no," said Duggan. "The man's a joke. A sad, sad, quickly forgettable joke."

"Hey," said Hitch, rubbing at an ear. "Enough. Urgent official business - remember?"

Duggan conceded the point with a roll of his eyes. "There's a problem with the gates - a security problem. For reasons I'll never understand, they think this... *specimen* can help them with it."

Hitch grinned. "They asked me to put together a team."

Not-Johnny folded his arms. "Well the answer's still no."

"Look, I get it," said Duggan. "No one would actually want to work with him, I know, but he's right; Winchester's taking a personal interest in this. You've got no choice."

Not-Johnny shook his head so vigorously that he looked like he might shed his ears. "Doctor Rowan will never allow it. I'm indispensable."

Duggan sighed. "She's already signed the release."

The young man backed away. "I don't believe you."

Stepping forward, Hitch gave the swivel chairs a gentle push that sent them rolling to opposite ends of the lab. "True, I'm afraid, but, hey, cheer up; we're partners again. You and me. The old team... That's got to be good, eh?"

"No." He wagged a finger. "No. We are definitely *not* part..."

"I'm sorry, John," said Doctor Rowan, following Duggan and Cariola through the door. "Mr. Duggan's right. I don't like it one bit, but I have no choice. This goes over my head."

"You see," grinned Hitch, throwing an arm around the young man's shoulders. "Partners."

"Mr. Duggan," said Rowan, flatly. "You said something about needing some equipment. I'm going back now to whatever remains of my experiment, so I want this sorted out quickly. Get what you need and then, please..." Her expression darkened. "Get the festering *hell* out of my department."

"'Course, ma'am." Duggan nodded as she left the room then turned a predatory smile on Hitch. "Ladies: you're staying here. Dopey: you're coming with me."

Hitch grimaced. "*Dopey*. D'you know, I get no respect at all from that man. Here I am, saving the world..."

"Now, Frog-face." Duggan shoved him through the door.

"Oh, be nice Duggles, or you'll make me cross and we shan't be friends."

John/Not-Johnny sighed as the two men vanished into the corridor. "God, I hate that man," he said.

"Annoying, isn't he?" Finn perched herself on a table beside him.

"I *hate* him." It wasn't clear whether he'd heard her or whether he was just continuing a private soliloquy.

"I'm Finn. Hello."

He glanced sideways. "John Forster. Hi."

"Why does he call you Faustus?"

John sighed. "Oh, because I'm a genius... Apparently."

"Oh, well that'll be handy." Finn stayed silent for a moment but when her new friend seemed reluctant to add anything, she tried again. "You've got to admit, though, Johnny Faustus is a pretty cool name."

A half smile contended with his angry frown. "Mm. Well."

"Anyway, since you're all super-clever and everything, I suppose you could probably explain where those avatar people came from, couldn't you?"

"You want to know?"

"Well... briefly. Yes."

Johnny turned to face her. "How much d'you know about the Many Narratives Theory?"

Finn shuffled. "Well, imagine I knew nothing at all..."

"Alright. Um... so do you have a technical background?"

Finn gave a little wince. "English literature."

"Oh, right. Excellent." Johnny looked impressed, which surprised Finn. In her experience, it wasn't how most people tended to react. "Well, as you know, all realities are subjective. Narrative Theory states that every reality must be conceived and written by a higher level author, who, in turn, must be the creation of a still higher-level author. Layers and levels, yes? Possibly infinite; possibly toroidal."

"Okay..." Finn bit her lip. It looked like this might be heavy going.

"But, obviously, there's a barrier. Higher level authors can create people like us just as easily as we create fictions of our own, but we occupy different dimensions, don't we? Authors can't share space with the characters they create."

Finn brightened. "Ah. Except through this virtual reality thing that Doctor Rowan's doing."

"Exactly. Now, for the first time, it looks like we've got a way of communicating directly with higher level beings. We need to be careful about how we develop the relationship, of course, but if we do it right, we could question them about their world instead of just working by inference and extrapolation. It could change everything."

"Ah, right. Interesting."

"Interesting? It's amazing. Think of the mysteries we could solve; the resources we could harness. Imagine if you could get an author to *help* you; you could fix all the problems of the worlds. Crime, sickness, hunger - you name it - you could solve them all at a..." Johnny pursed his lips as the door burst open.

"Well, this is all quite lovely," said Hitch, setting a large, heavy-looking bag on the nearest table, "but everyone needs to come with me. There's a crazy person on the loose and the sooner we get going the better."

"He's right," said Duggan, following in behind. "We've..." He stopped as his reader sounded a sharp alert tone. Cariola's and Hitch's did the same.

"Oh dear," said Cariola. She'd been quietly poring over her reader for the last half hour but now she started swiping feverishly across its screen.

"Well, that's not good," said Hitch, glancing at his arm.

From around the building, Finn could hear pagers, phones and other devices chirping out alerts. Never one to fear the obvious question, she asked it: "What's going on?"

"It's Winchester," said Duggan. "She's vanished."

15. The C-Word

The gate was another alabaster rectangle, just like the one that had snatched her from her shop. Now, though, the surroundings were very different. Instead of the neutral white emptiness that had greeted her arrival, this room was filled with flustered Bureau technicians and hastily gathered equipment.

They were still in the E&P *Research and Publishing Centre*, but several storeys higher up, in a corner office with a balcony that overlooked the city. Through tinted windows, Finn could see the vast dome of the gate complex shining in the early evening sun.

"You really don't need to do this," said Cariola, squeezing Finn's shoulders.

"I know," she said. "But don't worry; I'll be fine."

"Course she will," said Duggan, shooing the counsellor back. "I'll be looking after things."

Nodding, Cariola backed away towards a quieter corner, offering supportive smiles and gestures all the way.

"Now," said Duggan, bending forward to look Finn closely in the eye. "D'you understand how this is going to work?"

"I think so," she said. "They've done something to my phone."

"Yeah; it's slaved to Snitch's reader." He nodded reluctantly in the direction of Hitch, who was busy annoying someone. "It means you go where he goes."

"And they said it's got a sort of automatic disguise function."

"Yeah. And you're going to leave that set on *automatic*, okay? You never touch that. You just follow our lead, stay close, and above all, don't talk to anyone."

"No, right. I understand. They told me we mustn't interf..."

"The most important thing," continued Duggan, "is that you mustn't interfere. I can't emphasise that enough."

"No right. I get that. In the briefing, they said I should nev..."

"Under no circumstances do you ever talk to anyone, touch anything, leave anything behind or get yourself noticed. Some of these could be live narratives; if you mess up there, only bad things are going to happen. Are we clear?"

Finn felt her forehead creasing. "Yeah. They told me. They..."

"I mean; interfere in any way at all and you could ruin it forever." He raised a finger. "Case in point: did you ever read Shakespeare's *King Arthur?* Or that other one: *Love's Labour's Won?*"

Finn shook her head. "No. They never existed."

"Right," said Duggan, tapping the side of his nose. "Precisely. And that, little lady, is why we don't mess."

Finn smiled thinly. "You've made that very clear."

"Good. I'm glad that's understood. And you..." The watchman clamped a heavy hand on Hitch's shoulder.

Glancing round, Hitch laid his own hand on top of it. "Yes, honey?" He batted his eyelashes.

Duggan snatched his arm away, his brow suddenly looking like a badly ploughed field. "I'm watching you. Try any stupid tricks and I'll shoot you in the balls."

Hitch returned a reassuring smile. "Right-ho, sweetie. And are we about ready to go, d'you think?"

Duggan glowered. "Born ready."

"Jolly good." Hitch raised himself onto tiptoe to peer over the heads of the technicians. "Oh Johnny?"

"What?" Their new cable spoke with the kind of seething resentment normally only witnessed by the parents of young teenagers.

"I think we're about ready for you, old fruit. Destination codename Shoreditch."

"Wait." Duggan squinted suspicion at him. "What's with the codes?"

With a furtive air, Hitch inclined his head towards the watchman. "You know what Winchester said. You can't be too careful who you trust."

"Huh. Well, just remember what I said." He pointed at an angular bulge in his jacket and then at the somewhat smaller bulge in Hitch's trousers. "Pistol. Nuts."

"Yes, yes. Rest assured that whenever I think of you, 'nuts' will be the very first word that springs to mind."

Duggan scowled. "You're a funny man, Hitch. You'll be even funnier as a eunuch."

"Ten seconds, everyone." Johnny spoke over the speaker system. "All non-essential staff please exit the room."

"Bye, Cathy." Cariola waved from amongst the departing crowd and, despite herself, Finn waved back.

"Remind me," said Duggan, looking down on her from a considerable height. "Aside from being his only friend, is there any actual reason he's bringing you with us?"

Finn drew herself erect and forced herself to meet his gaze. "Because you need me," she said firmly. "I run a small independent bookshop and I've got a master's degree in English literature."

"Oh. Well that's just tremendous," said Duggan, and this time, his reaction was much more the sort she was used to.

"Three, two, one..." said Johnny Faustus.

Hitch seized her wrist and suddenly she was walking through a wall.

Whoever designed the gate had really missed an opportunity to include some nifty special effects. Finn's transit from doorway to doorway involved no *Doctor Who*-style whooshing down interstellar tunnels; no kaleidoscopic passages or psychedelic patterns of colour. Instead, there was a moment of whiteness as her eyes met the surface of the stone and then she was stepping into the dining hall of a great Gothic castle. A moment ago, her heart had been pounding out a thumping dance track rhythm and now here she was, in an empty hall, her first outbound journey having passed in an instant. The architecture was all very grand and everything but, in truth, the journey itself had been a bit of an anti-climax.

"Here we are." Hitch gestured to the suits of armour and the vast hanging tapestries. "Be it ever so humble..."

Finn checked behind her to see if the control room was still visible. It wasn't. There was just a nine foot oaken door, locked shut and embellished with carvings of rampant lions.

"So what are we doing here?" Duggan had unholstered his weapon and was now training it along a wooden gallery that overlooked the hall.

"Put that away," said Hitch, his voice echoing. "You'll hurt someone."

"I asked you a question."

"We're here to find the Locksmith," said Hitch. "If we're going to understand what this sabotage thing is all about, we're going to need his help."

Duggan frowned. "You talking about *Professor* Locke? *The* Professor Locke?"

"I am. Now come on, keep up." Hitch turned towards a broad stone stairway at the far end of the room.

"Locke would never work with a lowlife like you. He's top drawer. Hell, he even knows Winchester."

Hitch glanced back. "Duggan, sweetheart; here's a suggestion: why not just let me get on with my job? See what happens, eh?"

Finn followed them nearly to the top of the stairs when a voice like sherry fruitcake called from a doorway to their left.

"I say, do I hear our friendly postman?"

"Hello Mae," replied Hitch. "I'm here with a friend. And a man called Duggan."

"Well, my dear, any friends of yours... and so on and so forth."

Finn reached the walkway just as a short and essentially spherical old woman pottered out from beneath a stone arch. Hitch hurried forward and hugged her.

"By heavens, Mae, you get lovelier by the day. If I were only twenty years younger..."

"Oh, get away with you." She gave his arm a playful punch. "But you're being very rude; you haven't introduced everyone properly."

Hitch nodded. "My apologies. Mae Rillington, this is Cathy Finn, a literary professional, a purveyor of fine books, and an expert in modern genre languages."

Mae nodded a smile. "Delighted. And this is?"

"Duggan," said Hitch. "A goon with a gun."

The watchman narrowed his eyes. "Sorry to bother you, ma'am, but we're looking for Professor Locke. You wouldn't know his whereabouts, would you?"

"Well, I'm his agent," smiled Mae. "I probably ought. Won't you come into my office?"

Mae was not the fastest of movers so their journey down the long, gas-lit corridor gave Finn a little time to enquire about the mysterious Locke.

"He's a Recurrent," murmured Hitch. "A kind of immortal."

"*Immortal?* How does that work?"

"Oh, it's all about demand. There's a lot of it for certain character types. You know the sort: wise-cracking action heroes, bent cops, recovering alcoholic cops, hard-bitten cops approaching retirement..." He looked at the carpet. "Actually, come to think of it, cops do seem to be a bit over-represented. But there are others, too: religious maniac serial killers, crooked attorneys, tragically orphaned Chosen Ones... You sold books; you know the kind of thing I mean."

"Sure, yeah: clichés."

Hitch flashed her a warning look. "Hey, easy now. You don't want to be dropping the C-word around people like this. *Very* touchy about their reputations..."

Finn pulled a face. "Okay. But go on; what makes them so different?"

Hitch sniffed. "Well, people like you and me, we come from just one story, don't we? We live and we die and that's it. Same as pretty much everyone else. But Recurrents don't belong to just one narrative; their characters get so well used - they crop up in so many different places - they end up becoming Aware and self-aware, if you see what I mean."

Finn shrugged. "Not really, no."

"I mean they recur so often that they start to *notice*. If they're killed off in one story, they'll just pop up again somewhere else. When they've done that often enough, they start to remember who they are and what lies beyond the story they're in. They realise they're never really going to die."

"Ancient and immortal..." Finn glanced again at the Gothic surroundings. "Don't you think they sound just a teensy bit like vampires?"

"Hah. I'll tell Locke you said that."

"Don't you dare."

Hitch looked away. "No, but actually, now you mention it, I suppose there *are* parallels."

Finn frowned. "Like what?"

"We'll, you know: never growing old; the constant drifting from land to land... I mean, don't forget, these people were shifting between stories long before there were any gates."

"Uh huh."

"And then of course there's that whole thing with the virgins and the blood-sucking."

"Well, naturally." Finn sent Hitch a wry smile. Maybe she was getting the measure of him now. "So you know quite a few of these Recurrents, do you?"

Hitch nodded. "All my best clients."

"And this Locke character is one of them. What's he like?"

Hitch smiled. "Ah, well, I suppose he's your all-round, general purpose expert. If you're writing a story and you need a crusty old expert on, oh - I don't know - Babylonian agriculture or something, he's your man. If you want the world's greatest living authority on the Holy Grail or alchemy or low-energy particle physics, then, hey, what d'you know, he's your man again. Basically, if it's distinguished and clever you want, Locke's probably going to be competing for the role."

"Competing?"

"Oh sure. There are others like him. They're fighting for parts all the time. That's why he's got Mae working for him. She gets him his jobs and manages all his appearances. Timelines don't mean a lot to these guys; he might be working three or four different narratives at once."

"Right. And remind me: why do we need him?"

"Well, he's experienced, isn't he? He's been around. Living that long gives you a chance to do some pretty useful learning. If we're going to figure out what's happening, we're going to need his brain."

"Well, I supp..."

"Here we are," announced Mae. "Do make yourselves comfy."

Her office was a grand, Victorian-style library, complete with towering mahogany shelves, endless rows of leather-bound tomes, and several of those wonderful wheeled ladders that Finn had always desperately coveted.

Around Mae's desk was a collection of plush wingback chairs and a brightly studded chaise longue. Finn settled herself down and soon had to fight a strong temptation to start valuing the works around her. Fortunately, she was spared any such madness by a new line of questioning by their host.

"When were you hoping to see the Professor?" Sitting before a book the size of a suitcase, she found a page and tutted. "He is very busy, I'm afraid. It's Gothic dramas until the fortieth, then ten days in Patagonia. After that, it could be another Da Vinci role. That one's still undecided, though, so we might possibly find a slot for you before the start of summer."

Duggan leaned forward in his chair. "Madam, I don't think you understand; this is a priority mission. Helen Winchester herself has sent us. We'll need to see him today."

Mae peered at him over glittering half-moon spectacles. "Oh, well that simply isn't possible."

Duggan rose. "Well I'm sorry ma'am, but you're going to have to *make* it possible."

"My good man..." Knitting her fingers, Mae sat back and stared at him with a face like an unhappy walnut. "One does not merely summon Professor Locke with a click of one's fingers."

Simmering quietly, Duggan reached into a pocket and set a paper down in front of her. "That's from Winchester," he said. "Full authority. It means I get exactly what I want, *when* I want it."

"What it means, young man..."

"Mae, sweetheart." Hitch gave her a little wave. "I'm sorry. Duggan's a boorish oaf. He'd be the first to admit it, I'm sure, but don't be fooled by his crass ways and unfortunate looks..."

Duggan turned and pointed at Hitch's trousers. "What did I say, Hitch? What did I say I'd do to you if you started giving me any trouble?"

Crossing his legs, Hitch flashed Mae a smile. "What he's trying to say, bless him, is that we know the Professor's a very busy man. We don't expect him to come running; we'll gladly go and find him, wherever he's working. That's right, isn't it, Duggy-dumps?"

Duggan made a pistol of his forefinger and thumb.

Hitch blinked innocently. "And we only really need a quick chat."

Mae pursed her lips and, for just a moment, she could have been Yoda in a blue rinse wig. "I see. Well, suppose for one moment that I were tell you he's already working on one of Helen's little projects, and has been for the last few days. What then?"

Duggan blinked. "Locke's already working for Winchester?"

Mae smiled tightly back. "All very hush-hush. And a considerable way above your security clearance, I'm afraid."

Sensing that this little battle wasn't destined to produce any winners, Finn cleared her throat. "Has the Professor heard about Winchester's disappearance?"

The old woman's eyebrows vanished into her hairline. "Her what?"

"I was just coming to that." Hitch flashed Finn a look of annoyance. "I'm afraid these are very troubled times, Mae."

She closed up her massive tome. "She's disappeared? When did this happen?"

"About an hour ago. A little less, maybe."

She held out her hands. "Well out with it, then. Details, boy. Details."

Hitch shrugged. "All we know is she went missing after a meeting of the Heads. The Watch is looking for her, of course. Some are even wondering whether she's behind all the recent problems."

"You mean the sabotage?" Mae scowled. "Not Helen. Ridiculous."

Hitch sighed. "Well, in any event, we need to get word to the Professor. If they can get to Winchester, they can get to anybody."

"True." Mae's expression hardened. "But I see no reason to involve you and a pair of strangers. I'm perfectly capable of sending him a message myself."

"Mae, if he's in-story now, it could be a long while before he gets that message. Someone needs to find him now."

"Hm. And why ought that to be you?"

Hitch rose to his feet. "Mae, sweetheart, this could only be an inside job; a betrayal of a long and greatly valued trust."

"Quite so..."

He gestured to his clothes. "Well, look at me; who's ever trusted me with anything?"

Mae flickered a grim smile. "You're a sweet boy, Hitch. Silly and misguided, but a decent sort. But what about these two? You'd vouch for them?"

"Oh, Finn's okay," said Hitch. "Straight and sneaky as they come."

"And this one?" Mae regarded the watchman as though he were a stain on a shirt.

Duggan darkened. "*I*, madam, am a watchman. Security is what I do."

"You see," smiled Hitch. "Three trusty messengers, all of impeccable character. So can I pass on any special messages for the Professor when we see him?"

Mae looked thoughtful. "Just tell him to get in touch as soon as he can. We're going to have to look at his diary."

16. Balls

Duggan spoke close by Finn's ear. "I thought we agreed you weren't going to do any talking."

Having garnered an address from Mae and left her cogitating in her office, they were now part way down a long side passage in a distant wing of the castle. As they walked, Hitch was busily assessing its various doors for whatever arcane quality lent itself to inter-diegetic travel. Finn had been watching him carefully, trying to figure out how he was using his reader, but now, stung by Duggan's question, she turned to face him.

"That was the agreement, yes," she said, "but that was before you started getting in the old girl's face. All this officious macho crap you go in for - it was getting us nowhere."

"Ha!" Hitch grinned back at his minder. "And you asked me why I invited her along!"

"Oh, getting nowhere, was I?" Duggan faked a laugh, rolling his head as though sharing the joke with bystanders. However, the only other faces in the corridor were on marble statues or fixed inside gilt frames, and none of them seemed especially ready to join in the merriment. "Well let me tell you something, my girl: you don't know the first thing about investigation."

"Huh."

"Actually," said Hitch, "you should both have kept quiet and let me do my thing."

"Rubbish," said Finn. "You were doing no better than he was."

"Oh, come on, that's not true. I was just getting my mojo going."

Finn and Duggan snorted together.

"I was. I've got hidden talents you could never understand."

This elicited two further snorts.

"It's true. I can be *powerfully* persuasive when I want to be." He waggled his fingers as though conjuring a spell. "A couple more minutes and I would have had her eating out of my hand."

Duggan sighed. "You were just going to slip her some biscuits, weren't you?"

Hitch opened his mouth to protest, then looked away. "That's... one of the tools I employ."

"Oh, just one? And what else you got, Toad-boy? What other genius pl..."

"Ah, this one will do." Hitch looked up and down a mahogany door frame. "You kids ready?"

"That depends," said Finn. "Where are we going?"

Hitch brushed an imaginary speck from his shoulder. "Why, we're going to a ball, my dear."

Finn was beginning to understand the rules. With a bit of preparation and a target address, you could open a gate into a narrative and freeze the action for about half a minute. That gave you time either to extract some unsuspecting victim, or to press on in and quickly take yourself somewhere quiet. After that first thirty seconds, things would start up again regardless, and for anyone still stuck inside the diegesis, that was when things could get tricky.

Stories, it seemed, were terrifyingly fragile things. Block up a burrow with an idly kicked rock and you might rob Alice of her Wonderland, leaving her only a drab anecdote about a glimpse of an albino rabbit. Nip into a newsagents for a quick bite to eat and poor Charlie Bucket might never get to enjoy his life-changing factory tour.

This next stop was going to be one of these dangerous live narratives. Hitch was keeping the address a secret for now and hadn't told either of them its name. This was ostensibly for security reasons, though Finn suspected he was really just doing it to annoy Duggan. All she knew for the moment was that it was an Unaware world; a place that might be forever ruined by a thoughtless act or word.

She knew things were getting serious now because even Hitch was beginning to fuss a little.

"Finn, you take my arm, okay?" He crooked an elbow. "Keep your head down and if anyone speaks to you, just make out you're feeling faint. Through here, that's like a standard, catch-all excuse."

"And listen," warned Duggan, "if we get separated and you see anywhere that looks grey and misty, back the hell up."

Finn gave him a wary look. "And do I want to know why?"

"It's called the Unimagined," said the watchman. "It's the boundary; it's as far as the author ever visualised things. Step beyond that and... poof! End of the story for you."

Hitch tapped his reader. "So, yeah, useful tips there - rule number one being: don't get separated."

Duggan made some final adjustments to his reader. "And if you're struggling to remember that, missy, just keep your mouth shut and follow my lead."

Finn ignored him.

"Here we go, then." Hitch hit the pad of his reader and, in response, her wrist felt a little buzz.

One step and a brief instant later, she and her two companions were dressed in elaborate finery and emerging into a silent waxworks. Caught in the amethyst glow of tall, stained glass windows, masked and gorgeously costumed dancers held impossible poses, frozen in their arabesques. To their flanks, cavorting beneath purple tapestries, jesters leered while courtiers made lustrous, arcing sculptures of poured wine.

"Alrighty then," said Hitch. "Follow me." Restricted by the crowd, he released Finn's arm and quickly threaded a path through a narrow maze of burgeoning silks and satins. He made towards to a side door and a stone-flagged corridor just visible beyond.

"Twenty-five seconds," said Duggan, following close behind. "Keep moving; we've got to be quicker than this."

Moments later, they were out of the lavender-lit dance chamber and hurrying down a long, closed passage where motionless servants tended braziers hung from heavy iron tripods. Finn feared her floor-length gown might catch a spark as she passed, but although she could see the movement of its folds and hear it swish in the strangely pregnant silence, the familiar touch of denim against her skin reminded her it was no more than a clever illusion.

Rounding a sharp turn in the passage, she half-collided with a blank-faced Pierrot, who'd evidently chosen this quiet corner to relieve himself into a pot. The impact should have been gentle enough - she'd only glanced him - but neither he nor his little golden stream wavered by so much as a millimetre. It was like sideswiping an armoured car.

"Bloody hell," she said, rubbing at her elbow.

"Yeah; they don't move till the story does," said Hitch.

"Ten seconds," panted Duggan. "What's your plan, Bug-eyes? We're running out of time."

"Just... Just..." A few metres ahead of her, standing with his back to another brazier and a deep green Gothic window, Hitch faced two dark doors. Waggling his fingers uncertainly like a demented game show contestant, he seemed to be struggling to make his choice. "This one," he decided.

As she and Duggan crowded around the door, he grasped the latch and waited.

Duggan consulted his reader, which had somehow assumed the appearance of a gentleman's snuffbox. "Three... two... one." He nodded.

Finn flinched as, all at once, a torrent of sound engulfed her. Music, laughter, the stomping of feet - an explosion of noise suddenly filled the air. In the same moment, Hitch threw open the door and Duggan bundled her inside.

The room beyond was more shadow than light. It was evidently a study of some kind, illuminated by a solitary candle at either end. Its windows revealed only mist and darkness outside.

The watchman set the door closed behind him and pointed accusingly at Hitch. "Alright. What did I say about your balls? If this is the wrong room..."

"I beg pardon?" In the far corner of the study, the shadows shifted and a young man's face loomed into the light of the candle.

Surprised, Duggan started so violently that he banged his head on the door behind him.

"Who goes there?" demanded the young man, raising his candlestick. "What do you mean by intruding thus upon the Prince's chambers?"

Duggan tried to gather himself. "Ah, yes. The Prince. Um. Well, funnily enough..."

Hitch sent Finn a worried look and began delving into the folds of his costume.

Finn sighed. Duggan couldn't have looked more out of place if he'd been standing there in a spacesuit, and Hitch clearly put far too much faith in biscuits. She thought back to the rooms she'd just passed and leaned in towards Hitch's ear. "This is Poe, isn't it?" she whispered. *"The Masque of the Red Death?"*

Hitch gave her a wary look, but nodded.

"Right." Ignoring Duggan's gruff stammering, she stepped forward with all the confidence she could summon. "That will do, Dugo." She didn't recall Poe's story having much dialogue in it but she hoped an ersatz Regency style might sound convincing enough.

For a moment, three pairs of eyes looked at her in confusion.

Committed now, she pressed on. "I had hoped to find my uncle here and yet I find his rooms occupied by another. And since that occupant is a stranger to me, I ought to ask him the very question he puts to me. Who are you, sir, that walks so freely within my uncle's chambers?"

"I am Dardano," said the man, advancing around a lacquered table. "And your uncle; who pray might he be?"

Finn squared her shoulders. "Why Prince Prospero, of course. Are you not a guest at his ball?"

Dardano paused. "I am."

Finn gestured blithely towards Hitch. "Then allow me to introduce my brother... Antonio - who is sadly mute - and his valet, Dugo."

Dardano narrowed his eyes. "His valet has an impertinent tongue, my lady."

"You are mistaken," said Finn. "Rough and ill-born he might be, but he has always proved himself loyal to our family."

Dardano was now close enough that the candlelight revealed some uncertainty in his expression. "But he spoke of, well... it scarcely becomes me to..."

Finn gave a testy sigh. "He spoke of my brother's midwinter ball and the New Year masquerade that I myself intend. He will have a hand in their planning."

"Oh, then forgive me. I misunderstood."

"The error is understandable. Balls have quite possessed his mind of late; such is his obsession, I fear they are now become the sole object of his thoughts."

"Of course. Of course." Caught between Finn's frosty glare and Duggan's thunderous demeanour, Dardano now had the look of someone seeking a more hospitable climate.

Raising her chin, Finn pitched her look somewhere between Ellen Ripley and Cruella De Vil. "Now, sir, will you detain us any longer, or might we prevail upon you to return to the revelries?"

Dardano cleared his throat and offered a shallow bow. "My lady."

Finn turned to Duggan. "Well, open the door, Dugo. Let the young man pass."

Through grinding teeth, Duggan managed a murmur of acquiescence and, relieving the young guest of his candle, closed the door upon him.

"Mute!" exclaimed Hitch as the latch clicked shut. "Why mute?"

Finn shrugged. "I didn't want you to start blathering on about digestives."

"That," said Duggan, pointing a finger at her, "was unacceptable."

"Look," said Finn, "I've seen how you work. You were either going to shoot him in the head or bore the guy to death. I thought of a better way to get rid of him."

"You took a *big* risk, there, missy."

"Oh God. Here we go. Another lecture."

"Actually, he's right," said Hitch. "That wasn't safe."

Finn snorted. "You said it was the *Red Death*, didn't you? Well, I know that one; I've read it."

Hitch took Duggan's candle and approached the desk. "You might know *one* of them."

"One?" Finn frowned. "And just how many are there?"

"More than twenty - and those are just the ones I know. Plays, screenplays, film scripts - they all produce new worlds. You just got lucky."

"Huh. So what was *your* clever solution going to be?" Finn shook her head. "Actually, you know what? Never mind." Furiously, she removed herself to the window.

"More importantly," said Duggan, "where's Locke?" He had joined Hitch at the desk and, as yet, neither of them seemed to have unearthed a hidden professor.

"Ah, well." Hitch produced an insufferably smug grin. "If you knew the old Lockster as well as I do, you'd know he always has a trick or two to play."

Duggan folded his arms. "Go on, then, Toad-features. Astound me."

Hitch took up a small, leather bound book from the desk. "Chaucer - and with a bookmark placed at... let me see. Ah, yes: *The Man of Law's Tale.*"

Duggan peered at it closely. "So what you saying? That's where Locke's gone?"

Hitch grinned. "Precisely. I don't suppose you've got any good codpieces stored in that reader of yours, have you?"

Duggan sniffed and tapped at his device, quickly transforming his garb into that of an improbably-endowed medieval nobleman. "Fancy enough for you?"

"Lovely," said Hitch, prodding away at his reader. "Very understated. I think I'll stay on automatic, though; I couldn't compete with that."

So saying, he strode back to the doorway and hit a button. Instantly, it spread a wavering film of light across the frame.

"Hey, Johnny, can you hear me?"

There was a pause. Then, from his reader came a petulant *'yes'*.

"Jolly good. Listen, I need a new gate: *The Man of Law's Tale*, original version. I'm guessing we're looking for the eponymous 'Sergeant of the Lawe.' Can you patch us through?"

"Still working to Shoreditch?"

"Yup, absolutely. How long do you think that'll take you, Mr. F?"

"Give me a minute."

Hitch beamed at his unhappy companions as they waited.

"Okay. Try it now."

"Thanks, Johnny. You're a wonder." Hitch tapped out a rapid pattern on the face of his reader and the light in the doorway flickered again. "Right," he said, stepping quickly forward. "If you'd like to follow me..."

"Hey, hey. Not so fast, Frog-boy." Duggan unholstered what now looked like a flintlock pistol and yanked the smaller man back. "I think I'll take the lead on this one, if you don't mind."

"Oh." Hitch gave a reluctant shrug. "If you like."

"Oh, I do," said Duggan, readying his weapon. "Now, same rules: let's go."

Finn watched him step through, though Hitch seemed in no hurry to follow. A moment later, the light in the doorway winked out.

Hitch smiled. "You still there, Johnny?"

"Still here."

"Ditched the dog. Nicely done."

"Hah! No problem." All his former resentment seemed suddenly to have dissipated.

Finn felt a slow grin spreading. "Wait. You two planned this, didn't you? *Shoreditch.* That was your plan to get rid of him."

"I did say Johnny and I made a good team." Hitch attempted an apologetic frown but his heart didn't seem to be in it. "He has a small share in my biscuit business, so we work a bit more closely than we were letting on back in the lab. Are you disappointed that we fibbed?"

"Quite the contrary." Finn looked him up and down. "I think I'm discovering a new faith in you."

"Oh. Well, good. And likewise, of course."

Finn blinked. "Really?"

"Oh sure." Hitch tapped a knuckle on the study door and stepped back.

The latch rose and Dardano's face appeared from the brightness of the passage. "Oh, hello again, Hitch. Was that alright for you?"

Ushering him through, Hitch closed the door and then set an arm over his shoulder. "A convincing performance, my young friend; one deserving of a rich reward."

Dardano shot him a hopeful glance. "Flapjack or digestive?"

Hitch produced a short tube from inside his conjured cloak. "After a show like that, Dano old chum, only the very best will do."

Taking the pack, the young man tore it open, took a deep sniff and rolled his eyes. "Oh, that's good. That's nice. Yeah, that's very nice."

Finn folded her arms and tried not to allow herself to be distracted by these oddly orgiastic noises. "So hang on. If you both knew... Was this all just a test?"

Hitch pursed his lips. "Well, not *just* a test. We got rid of Duggan, didn't we?"

"I suppose..."

"Well then. And now we know you can improvise in a tight spot. For someone in my line of work, that's a useful thing to know."

"Oh." Finn tried not to let her smile show. "And what about Duggan?"

Hitch tried again to look sorry. "Can't be too careful who you trust these days."

"That costume..." Finn gave a little wince. "I don't think they even wore codpieces in Chaucer's time, did they?"

Hitch shrugged. "No idea. I just thought it would be funny if he arrived back at E&P wearing something ridiculous."

"Oh. So you didn't send him back to *The Canterbury Tales*?"

"Heavens, no. That would have been irresponsible. If I'd wanted to be vindictive, there were many worse places I could have sent him. Dante's *Inferno* did cross my mind."

"He's going to be mad, you know."

He waved dismissively. "Oh, Duggan was quite mad already. Anyway, we'll be long gone by the time he finds his way back here."

Finn leaned against the wall. "So what next? Do we still need Professor Locke or was that just a ruse as well?"

"Oh, no, we definitely need the Lockster." Hitch ambled back to the desk. "But Mae's already told us where to look." He took a small notebook from under a sheet of vellum. "She said we had to look again at his diary. This will tell us exactly where to go."

17. Revelations

Trying to ignore onset of what was clearly going to be one bitch of a headache, Doctor Rowan gritted her teeth and knocked firmly on the office door.

It had been a shocking day. A vital experiment ruined, Winchester's disappearance, and now this - Max Roberts seeking to mire her in matters of security. What was he thinking? Why drag her all the way over here, to the very heart of the gate complex, for what could only ever amount to a brief and pointless conversation? He had the entire Watch network at his command; what help could she possibly offer to a man like that?

The door opened to frame a large and unfamiliar watchman.

"Francesca Rowan." She announced herself as tersely as she dared. "Max asked to see me."

"Please." The attendant - a tough, military sort - gestured for her to enter.

She'd never visited Max's office before, though to judge by its central location, she must often have passed close by. It was set on one of the higher levels of the dome and the entirety of its right hand wall was a window that looked out upon the Core. A little way below, in a huge, cable-strung void, the ancient engine hung, unsupported, like a frosted glass balloon. Measuring a fraction over three metres in diameter, it was encircled by movable walkways, gantries and cantilevered decks. Upon them swarmed an army of researchers and technicians.

Surrounding the little sphere at a radius of nearly twenty five metres, the dome's interior wall was a bright patchwork of windows and gadgetry. Behind every mirrored pane worked countless production staff, technical wizards, analysts and data gatherers, each group working hard to justify its privileged proximity. Rowan knew well the intensity of the competition; lying somewhere down to the right, some eight floors below her, was her own team's particular link-facility - a pokey little cupboard of a place, grandly titled *The Centre for Avatar Research*.

Annoyingly, Max's workplace was considerably larger than hers - a long, rectangular space boasting a gleaming conference table, antique bookshelves, and a veritable forest of potted ferns.

She wasn't its only occupant. In addition to the watchman, three powerfully built figures sat poring over reports at one end of the main desk. Its other end was concealed behind a curving bank of computer screens. There were more of them on the wall behind.

"Ah, Doctor Rowan." A wild-haired figure rose up from behind the arc of monitors. "Interesting outfit. Thanks for coming so quickly."

Chewing her cheek, she clasped her shirt over as much of her cleavage as she could. "It was essential to my research," she said. "You caught me at an inconvenient time."

"I can only imagine." He smiled and cocked his head. "I'm sorry. I'm sure you must be busy."

"Extremely. How can I be of help?"

"Well, these are challenging times, Doctor, as I'm sure you're aware. With Helen missing - and we're presuming she's been abducted - I'm trying to get a picture of what she's been doing of late; whether any of her recent projects might have exposed her to any unusual risks."

Rowan glanced again at the heavies in the room - men who looked as though they'd rather be hurling furniture than sitting on it. "Let us speak plainly, Max. Am I under suspicion of anything?"

The security chief shook his head. "Oh no. Not at all. In fact, I think I have a very good idea of the saboteur's identity. What no one really understands is his motive. That's why I asked you here. Your research... you're making good progress, I hear."

"I am. I give the Heads a weekly report. You'll have copies, I'm sure."

Max perched himself on the side of his desk. "Oh, I dare say, but I wondered, in light of Helen's disappearance, if there might be any more to it. Any recent results she might have asked you to... well, sit upon, perhaps; delay their publication until they could be corroborated."

Rowan shook her head. "No. My reports were unexpurgated. I've been entirely candid. I've said very clearly we've been getting close to a breakthrough - extremely close, in fact. For all practical purposes, the technology is now proven. It's just that, lately, we've had one or two irksome... setbacks."

Max nodded. "I see. So there's nothing Helen might have learned that would make a her a particular target?"

"No more than you or me." Dr. Rowan shifted uncomfortably. A medieval tart's blouse was hardly fitting attire for a conversation like this. Nevertheless, with a reputation as a professional badass to uphold, she couldn't afford to let it hamper her. "So what's this really about, Max? What aren't you telling me?"

Rising from the desk, Max nodded at a side door opposite the long window. "I think that's something more easily shown than explained. Would you mind?"

The three goons stood to let him pass. They looked strangely eager; not at all the usual watchman types.

Max raised his wrist and tapped in a code. The doorway shimmered as he approached.

She held out her hands. "I'm sorry; I came in a hurry. I don't have my reader with me." Crossing a threshold without a reader was against all protocol. Max of all people ought to...

Suddenly, she became aware that the watchman from the door was looming beside her.

"Don't worry," said Max, "it will only take a moment. And I give you my word: neither I nor Joshua here will leave your side."

"Madam." Joshua extended a calloused hand towards the door.

Rowan took a slow step forward. "Max, just what is it that you have to show me?"

Max pushed back his mane. "Only what I said, Francesca: I want to share what we know about the saboteur. I promise you, you'll find answers and friendly faces waiting on the other side." He held out an open palm. "Now, please..."

She didn't feel in the least bit comfortable about this, but these were unusual times and maybe she was just being paranoid. The reader thing was just a failsafe, after all, and where could she possibly be any more secure or carefully scrutinised than the heart of the gate complex; the Watch command centre itself? And besides, she had no choice.

She took Max's arm and allowed him to take her over the threshold.

Her next step took her onto a low hill at one edge of a broad, sandy plain. Below her stood a city-sized assembly of tents, troops, and armoured vehicles; an army that extended towards the horizon, far out into the wavering heat. Above it, military drones swarmed and darted in the dry, fume-filled air. Higher still, holding steady at a dizzying distance, the hazy shapes of vast interplanetary warships cast their shadows upon the clouds.

"What..?" was as far as she got before Joshua seized her free arm and spun her towards a cluster of low concrete bunkers.

"Now, don't worry." Max held her other arm tightly. "I'm a man of my word, Francesca. I promised you information about the saboteur - and you shall have it. It's me."

She writhed in his grasp. "Max, you miserable, skunk-sucking shit."

Joshua pushed down her head as they ducked into the nearest half-sunken building. Inside, two armed guards stood beside a cell.

"And, as promised, some friendly faces." Max gestured through the bars, where dim figures were slowly resolving as her eyes adjusted to the dark. "Helen Winchester you already know of course, and I dare say you've met Hector, too. As for the others... Well, you'll have plenty of time to get acquainted."

Professor Newton-Sharpe dabbed his brow with his neckerchief. A harsh Egyptian sun burned down upon his back, scarcely diminished by the advent of autumn, or his long, winding ascent into the hills.

He blew sand from the markings and wished to heaven that Descombey would hurry back with his kit. Where was the young scoundrel? Any fool could see the enigma here: writings neither Ptolemaic nor Phoenician, and all set upon the entrance to a lowly desert tomb whose elevated position made no sense whatever. It was the most curious thing he'd seen in years, but without his brushes or anything upon which to make a rubbing, he was all but powerless to investigate.

He looked back, down the ragged slope to his two khaki tents and the salvaged halftrack he'd managed to piece together after El Alamein.

"Valentin!" he shouted.

There was no sign of the man. What on earth could he be playing at?

Ah, there! A flicker of movement. From the larger of the tents, a lithe young figure emerged and waved an acknowledgement. But instead of hastening back to the path as he ought, he strode towards the vehicle. Had he left some vital tool in the driver's cabin?

There was a flash of sun against glass as the Frenchman slammed shut the door. A moment later, the rear wheels vanished amid a cloud of exhaust.

"What the devil!" Furiously, he waved his hat. "Descombey, you fool! What are you playing at, man?"

To call from such a distance was futile, particularly to a man who would be all but deafened by the roar and rattle of the motor. And yet what was he thinking, to place him in such an infernal predicament? What possible reason could he have for leaving him stranded upon this hill, with little more than flies for company and a sun hat and a water bottle to preserve him?

For half a minute, the halftrack hauled itself eastward, back the way it had come. Then, unaccountably, the engine eased back to a quarter-speed, its tone falling by more than an octave. Well, that was a curiosity: it was set on a descending path, yet it sounded to be rolling to a halt. Had his aide suffered a change of heart?

For a moment, the Professor could make no sense of it. Then, close by, in the corner of his vision, he glimpsed a movement. From the rocky wall beside him, a small, iridescent beetle - one of the *cicindelinae* - had taken flight. Its wings were beating a slow rhythm, far slower than the laws of aerodynamics demanded, and yet still it rose.

Ah. Now he understood. It was not the vehicle but time itself that was slowing.

Instantly, the tomb markings made sense, as did all of Winchester's earnest warnings. It was a trap. The thinly-veiled allusions to the She-Wolf legend etched into the rock - he should have seen them for what they so obviously were: bait to catch a man old enough to have known better.

Cursing his stupidity, he sloughed off the Newton-Sharpe persona. Until the narrative resumed - if indeed it ever did - there was little profit in adhering to the role.

He looked back at the carvings. What was this world into in which he'd blundered? An edited tale, bastardised in an effort to delay him? Or worse, was this further evidence to support Winchester's theory - that someone did indeed have the power to conjure new worlds, all carefully configured to serve their whims? It had happened once before, and it was only fortunate that the She-Wolf had treated her creations kindly. That such a singular occurrence might be repeated was a prospect few Recurrents had ever entertained. None at all would welcome it.

The tiger beetle's wings stilled altogether. By now, any diegetic character would be frozen into the narrative. As a Recurrent, he had at least the luxury of choice. He could settle back into the timeline and sleep while he awaited its resumption, or he could exit now and pursue a more productive line of enquiry. Of course, this was no choice at all for a man such as he. Indolence had always held a special horror for him. He had a busy schedule to maintain. If *Treasures of the Desert Fox* was to be put in mothballs, then he had better things to do than sit about twiddling his thumbs.

Stepping before the tomb entrance, he slipped a cigarette case from his jacket and opened it. A little keyboard and screen gleamed back at him.

The doorway flickered when he entered his code but, ominously, the faint membrane of light failed to materialise. His reader responded with an unhappy buzz.

Frowning, he tried again.

Again, it flickered. The evidence for his trap hypothesis was mounting steadily.

He brought the reader close to his face. "Mae, my dear. Can you hear me?"

Static was his only answer, but that was conclusive enough.

Well, damn it all! What a witless fool he'd been! Through his own impetuousness, he'd just condemned himself to a period of indefinite exile. Once his absence was known, there would be any number of eager pretenders yapping for his roles. How galling it would be to lose them! He'd had another juicy Mycroft to perform immediately after this little jaunt for Winchester, then a new take on Kepler which would have presented something of a diversion. Now, though, he might have to resign himself to the very dullest of waits.

His reader chirped.

He looked to the tomb doorway, which blinked as a pale film smeared itself across it.

Through the inbound gate stepped two figures in Bedouin dress.

"Hullo." He smiled and turned his hips slightly, hiding the hand that slid back towards his revolver.

The nearest pulled the covering from his face and beamed a familiar smile.

"Now then, Professor; what have I told you about loitering round doorways?" He peered into the sky with exaggerated concern. "I swear: one day, you're going to get yourself saucered."

Locke laughed. "Well, blow me; if it isn't the Postman!" He extended a hand. "My dear boy, you're a delight. You'll scarcely credit how uplifting it is to see you come for an old man like me."

The dark-eyed rogue returned his handshake and gestured to the dusky young woman at his side. "Professor, this is my colleague, Cathy Finn. Finn, this is Professor Locke - known in one or two more interesting circles as *The Locksmith.*"

Locke flicked back his hair for dramatic effect. "Oh, tush. Do forgive him, Miss Finn; he can be horribly theatrical. Please, call me Paul."

"What did you mean, 'saucered'?" asked Finn, sitting amongst the lengthening shadows of the rocky cleft.

Hitch produced a low, wavering whistle and, with one flat hand, mimed a spaceship lifting off.

Finn rewarded this little pantomime with a blank frown. "What's that? I don't understand."

"Yeah, you do. Imagine: you're a character in an Unaware world like this and you stumble onto an open gate. What you going to do? You're going to blab, aren't you? Only natural."

"Probably..."

"Well, E&P can't allow that, can they? It would be a disaster. So they send a team to extract you before you can do any damage."

Finn's eyes widened. "You're telling me they go about *abducting* people in flying saucers?"

Hitch shrugged. "Well when you say it like that, you make it sound sinister."

"You think?"

"Hey, it's not like they do it all the time. I mean, yeah, it's a bit of last resort but it's better than corrupting a whole narrative."

"But that's... We get alien abduction stories like that in *my* world. I never believed them for a moment."

"Well there you go." He folded his arms. "An effective solution to a tricky problem."

Finn opened her mouth but then paused. "Are you winding me up again?"

Hitch smiled and turned to watch the Professor doing something unfathomable with their readers. Connected by a nest of little wires, the paired devices were vibrating horribly and producing occasional puffs of smoke. It was oddly unnerving, like watching some weird electronic vivisection. She'd no idea what Locke was trying to do but she suspected the manufacturer's warranties weren't going to be worth very much after this.

The Professor had been at it a while now, largely because their arrival hadn't yielded quite the speedy extraction they'd hoped. When they'd tried to conjure an outbound gate, Hitch's reader had produced no more than a sad little burble and a fleeting light that caressed the tomb entrance like wisps of St Elmo's fire. Disappointed expressions had swiftly followed.

With some complex-looking tinkering, Locke was now attempting to open a communications channel back to E&P to see if Johnny Faustus could do any better. It was a tricky and time-consuming process, but he seemed happy to talk as he worked.

Feeling tired and thirsty, Finn cast her gaze over the desert. "Where are we, exactly, Paul?"

The Professor replied without turning his head. "About sixty miles south west of Alexandria."

"Egypt. Oh, wow."

"You've never been?"

She shook her head. "I flew over it once with my granny when I was little."

"Oh? She was an aviator?"

"No, no. She came over from Ethiopia in the seventies."

"The seventies. Oh, I see, so you're not exactly a child of the twentieth century?"

"Not exactly, no."

"So a straddler, then, eh?" A faint smirk appeared. "Well, let me see if I can recall the lingo. Um. 'Welcome to the crib, dog?' Is that the right sort of greeting?"

Finn shook her head. "Not really, no."

"Oh. Well, I'll get my tongue round your vernacular sooner or later. Do keep talking; you were telling me about your travels with your grandmother?"

"She was taking me back to see her old homeland. I don't remember it being so hot, though."

"Ah, yes, the heat. Not so bad in the Abyssinian highlands but a confounded nuisance here."

"Yeah, well anyway," said Hitch pointedly, "don't let us slow you up. Wouldn't want to distract you with too much talk."

The old man snorted. "Not at all; I'm rather partial to idle chat. It does no harm at all to widen one's circle; admit a new friend. Wouldn't you agree, Miss Finn?"

"Mm." Finn decided to change tack. She ran her hands over the shallow carvings in the face of the stone. "So, you were saying it was just these little symbols that brought you here?"

"Yes." He cast a rueful look at the sandy wall. "I was hoping Valentin would do a little rubbing for me but there's no chance of that now. He didn't understand, of course. The boy had a fine eye, but no conception of the layered worlds that surround us. He interpreted those little lupine figures as jackals, bless his little cheeks, but to anyone who's ever set an eye upon New Tybet, they're a clear allusion to the founding of the gates."

"But they're actually a trap?"

"Yes, and I was a fool. For hours, I'd been poking my nose into this poor Egyptian's entrance; I really ought to have grasped it sooner. With hindsight, these symbols are all much *too* obvious. I was unable to think it aloud in a live narrative - what with being the protagonist and all - but the similarities to the Origin myths are unmistakable."

"And now here we are stuck in a desert," said Hitch. "Never a big fan of deserts. Too hot in the daytime, too cold at night. I hope you've got some supplies down in those tents of yours."

"Naturally." Locke resumed his fiddling. "Two cosy little beds, blankets, food and water. Of course, that's always assuming young Valentin hasn't absconded with the lot."

Finn's eyes followed the track leading away from the tents. A thin haze was forming over it. Perhaps a dust storm was blowing up.

"So, anyway, about these comms, Lockster? How's it going?" Hitch peered over his shoulder.

"Well, not too badly, my boy, although it would go a lot quicker if you didn't keep thrusting yourself into my light."

Hitch took a small step to the side. "And when you say 'not too badly...'?"

Locke tutted. "Patience, dear chap. A few more minutes, and we should have you and your little Johnny all hooked up."

"Um..." Finn stood and peered more closely at the little encampment. "You remember Duggan talking about things going all grey and misty?"

Hitch picked at the remains of something lodged in his teeth. "Uh huh. The Unimagined."

"Yeah, well I think it might be coming this way."

Hitch examined a small nutty fragment on his fingernail. "Nah. The U never moves. It can't. Authors either imagine a setting or they don't. Places don't get unimagined."

"You sure?" She pointed down the hill. "What do you make of that?"

Hitch glanced up and followed the line of her finger. The haze above the desert was thickening to a white fog; the sky slowly paling to white.

"Ah," he said. "Well that's a bit unexpected."

"Mm," said Finn. "So just to be clear: that is the Unimagined, yes?"

"Um, yes."

"And it's coming this way."

"Yes. Yes it is."

"Despite the fact you said it couldn't."

"Mm."

"Didn't you also say something about it being completely and utterly fatal?"

Hitch pursed his lips. "I might have said something along those lines, yeah."

"There's a ready but unpalatable explanation," said Locke, still working at the readers. "We've been lured into a work in progress; a tale left deliberately unfinished, designed to swallow us up like an insect in amber."

Hitch struck a knuckle against his head. "Stupid! Stupid! Stupid! Rule number one, Finn: never, ever enter an unfinished narrative."

"You said rule number one was not to get separated."

"Yes, well, this is a different rule number one." He gestured at the vanishing hills and the eerie nothingness that was descending like a rolling fog. "Different situations, different rules."

Duggan's eyes blazed. "What d'you mean, I can't come in?"

Cariola looked back at him through the little window in the control room door. "He thinks you're going to be cross; that you might do something silly."

"Cross?" He banged a fist against the glass. "D'you know where he dumped me? In a frigging kindergarten! Surrounded by kids! Dressed like Henry the Eighth with a hard-on."

"Well, I'm sorry, but he swears it was an accident."

"Accident, my arse! Little Johnny's laughing his balls off in there, isn't he?"

"No, no." Cariola waved anxious denials. "I think he's actually rather frightened of you."

"And so he damned well should be. D'you know what those teachers did? They called the Watch; wanted to talk social services. I was nearly put on a bloody register."

"Well, I'm very sorry, Mr. Duggan, but he's working terribly hard. You see, we're having some bother with..."

"I don't care if Satan's in there bending him over a desk." He showed her his pistol. "You open this door now, or I swear I won't be held responsible for the consequences."

Cariola turned her head and muttered something that was lost in the woodwork of the door. When she turned back, it was with the look of a reluctant hostage negotiator. "He says there are some conditions."

"Uh huh." Duggan chambered a round and pointed his pistol at the door handle.

"Um, but I'm sure we can discuss those later." Cariola fumbled with the lock. A moment later, she was holding open the door.

He marched past her. "Where is the little scrote?"

"Over there, behind the..."

"Right, you." Duggan strode between banks of equipment nested within a coiled mess of cabling. "Just what the hell do you think...?"

Unbelievable. Sitting by a keyboard and gazing intently a monitor, the scrawny little twonk was pushing a headset to his ear and wafting him away like he was a wasp.

"You!" He tore the phones from his head. "I'm talking to you!"

Johnny's eyes flashed defiance. "Give those back! You've no idea what you're doing."

Well, that was a surprise; the boy had a bit of fight in him after all. Duggan bent down until his nose was just an inch from the young man's eyes. "I'll give you them back just as soon as..."

"Um, hullo? Is that Mr. Forster?" A voice crackled from an unseen speaker somewhere on the other side of the control room.

"It's the Professor!" Johnny leapt from his seat and rolled beneath a table. He rose on the other side to seize a peculiar metal device that looked like the unhappy progeny of a microwave oven and a Van de Graaff generator.

Duggan straightened. "*Locke?* That's Professor Locke?"

Ignoring him, Johnny stabbed at some controls. "Professor Locke? Can you hear me?"

"I can, Johnny. Good to hear your voice. I wonder, could you do us a rather urgent favour?"

18. Waif and Stray

"Boorman, you were the one who collared this 'Hitch' character. What do we know about him?"

"Permission to speak freely, sir?" Standing erect, Boorman glanced at the faces in Max Roberts' office. He didn't recognise them. He wondered about their security clearance and how they'd managed to rise so inconspicuously through the ranks.

Max nodded.

"He's a wriggly little bugger, sir. Small-time, but he's quick and clever, and he knows his way around. A proper pain in the arse."

Max looked ruefully at his desk. "Well, Boorman, small-time he might have been, but I think he might now be raising his sights. You'll recall that Winchester thought it a good idea to bring him on side?"

"Yes sir. I do."

"Mm. Well, I see from your expression that you share my views on the wisdom of that particular decision. In fact, I think our scepticism was well-founded."

"Sir?"

"We sent him to see what he could find out. Instead, he ditched his watchman at the first opportunity and made his way straight to Professor Locke - one of Winchester's most senior operatives. Why, we're not sure, but immediately afterwards, we got reports that Locke's reader had malfunctioned. He was very nearly cut off from us altogether."

Boorman felt his fists tightening. "You think this Hitch is the saboteur, sir?"

Max nodded. "I think he's one of them."

"And you want me to bring him in?"

"If you can, but don't take any risks. Notify the Watch. Tell them he could be dangerous. You say he's a tricky one, Boorman, so take no chances. You understand? No escapes. I want that threat eliminated. Use whatever measures are necessary."

Words as sweet as music. Boorman nodded. "And Locke?"

"A difficult one, that. The two of them have clearly got history, but we don't know whether he's being fed misinformation or if he's part of the conspiracy. Locke disappears a lot more often than I'd like; he could even be this Hitch's handler. And he's a Recurrent, of course, which presents problems of its own." Max knitted his fingers. "On the other hand, I don't want to make an enemy of the man without good cause. Track him down. Let's get him separated from this Postman and then off to a safe-house somewhere. If he's a threat, we'll contain him. If he's got nothing to hide, then a safe-house still makes good sense. He knows a great deal; he could easily be a target for another abduction."

"Yes sir." This was brilliant. Cases like this were the pathway to promotion and a flashy office.

"Oh, and Boorman." Max beckoned him closer. "When you do get your hands on the Professor, I want you both to disappear. You understand? Get to a safe-house - one of your own choosing - and tell no one but me. You understand the security problems we're having. We'll keep this just between the two of us."

"No, wait!"

Splosh.

"No. We aren't here to..."

Splosh.

"Just stop for a minute and let me exp..."

Splosh. Splosh. Splosh.

"Come back; I promise you, we're friendly."

Hitch laid a hand on her forearm. "Leave it, Finn. These things happen sometimes."

"Leave it?" She pointed at the five frantically swimming crewmen who'd just hurled themselves over the rail. "Don't be stupid; they'll drown."

"No they won't." He pointed over the stern towards a forested lump in the middle distance. "An island, see? It's fine."

"Fine? It's not fine. We've just scared five perfectly decent men off their own boat, and that's a very long swim. We've got to help them; turn this thing round."

"No, no, look; it's okay. It won't change the narrative. So long as we don't affect the main characters or the plot, everything will just re-set itself when we've gone."

"What?"

"Well, not immediately." He pointed his palms skyward. "What I mean is, this day is the day the author imagined. Whoever wrote this narrative didn't imagine those guys being here yesterday or tomorrow; they're only ever here today. There is no tomorrow for bit-parters like them; this little scene's like a sort of time bubble. Once we've gone, so long as we haven't messed up anything important, things will go back to how they were and they'll just keep reliving this day forever. Come the morning, they'll be back on this boat, doing exactly the same thing, and they'll never know we were here."

"Well that's great," said Finn, "but in the meantime, five innocent men are going to drown. Bit parts or not, they're people and they're scared."

Hitch sat on the rail. "You do know they're probably pirates, don't you?"

"Oh really? And what evidence have you got for that?"

"Well, okay, forget that; let's look at this from another perspective." He held up a finger. "Question number one: d'you actually know how to turn a boat like this around?"

"No..."

"No. Nor me. And question number two: does it look like they want you to go after them?"

"Well, no; obviously not, but that's 'cause we've just appeared in their cabin doorway and frightened the living crap out of them. Look, we're wasting time." She turned her attention to the Professor. "Paul: you must have sailed a bit in your time."

"Hm?" Locke was gazing intently at his snuff box. "Oh yes. Just did a three month stint as Captain Nemo."

"Good. So you'll know how to turn this thing around."

"Yes, but to be honest with you, my dear, I don't think we can afford the time to start filling the boat with seamen. I have some urgent concerns about our readers, and if I'm going to work on them, I'll need somewhere rather steadier and better equipped than a seventeenth century schooner. We must be off this vessel as quickly as we can."

Finn turned back to watch the sailors splashing their way into an admittedly very pretty Caribbean sunset. "Well fine, you worry about that; I'll worry about them." Taking note of precisely how much help Hitch wasn't offering, she grasped the ship's wheel and spun it.

Hitch himself stood and joined Locke by the cabin door. "So what's the problem, Lockster? Why the rush?"

The Professor dabbed at some buttons. "Well, it strikes me that while one faulty reader might be chalked up to misadventure, two failing on precisely the same spot does rather smack of malevolent intent."

Hitch leaned over to study the old man's efforts more closely. "You think someone was deliberately jamming us?"

Locke nodded grimly. "Which means time is not our friend. Young Mr. Forster did exceedingly well to slip us out - a random leap like that will cover our scent for a short while - but such an extreme measure will have set alarm bells ringing."

Hitch tapped his own wrist. "So whoever was trying to box you up in Egypt won't find it too hard to figure out where we've gone?"

"Quite so, darling boy. We need to beat a hasty retreat. Any suggestions?"

Hitch raised his eyebrows. "One or two."

"Agh!" cried Finn. This was now her eighth or ninth jump and, this time, she'd arrived on a stairwell landing. What had startled her was that to either side of the lift shaft door, the Unimagined was so close she could have stepped across and touched it.

"Don't worry; that's normal here," said Hitch. He had preceded her through the gate and was now peering suspiciously through the door behind her. It led into what looked like a hotel corridor.

"A textbook choice." Locke pressed the call button for the lift. "If someone's riding your tail, you do all you can to make it hard for them. Nicely done, Mr. Hitch; the closer we are to the Unimagined, the trickier it will be to track us."

"Right... and where exactly *is* this?" Finn found it horribly disconcerting to be standing between two insubstantial walls, just two paces from a cold, white oblivion.

"Just another story," breezed Hitch, stepping back onto the landing. "It's not important."

A bright ping sounded above her head. The lift doors opened to reveal a small, mirrored interior.

Reluctantly, she followed Locke in and leaned back against the handrail. Hitch followed, found the metal keypad and pressed zero.

The elevator descended to the sound of muted saxophones.

"You're being very cagey all of a sudden," she said. "What's going on?"

Hitch smiled thinly. "We'll be out in a minute."

"No, come on. What's the big deal? Just tell me."

Hitch sighed. "Alright. If you must know, it's erotic fiction. They always have plenty of U for shielding. Apart from the bedroom, the hotel foyer and wherever the main characters live and work, it's pretty much all Unimagined."

Finn looked around her and frowned. "Well, this lift seems real enough. Why d'you think it's..." She leapt from the rail as a vividly unpleasant thought struck her. "Oh God. Did they... you know? In here?"

Hitch looked appraisingly at the mirrored walls. "Yup. Very probably."

There was no doubting that each new world *felt* real. Light played convincingly on every surface and objects behaved exactly as they should. When the wind blew, Finn felt her hair move and sensed the cooling of her skin. When she studied things closely, the detail resolved itself just as it would have done at home. Aside from the occasional appearance of the U, there was nothing to distinguish the reality of her world from that of any other.

In this latest world, though, it seemed her unconscious mind was reasserting itself. Somewhere on her bookshop floor, or in the back of an ambulance perhaps, her mind was stirring. She knew that because when she'd stepped onto this dark, frozen hillside, it had triggered a strong sense of connection. She just wasn't sure yet what it was.

The night was intensely cold and snow blew almost horizontally across their path, yet bizarrely, the illusion of a simple woollen cloak seemed to be keeping her warm.

"The cold," shouted the Professor, fighting to be heard above the gusts that howled into her ears. "It isn't bothering you, is it?"

"No, no. I love it. Big fan of snow. Always was."

He nodded. "Oh, well then, you're in luck. You could see a good eight inches tonight."

She rolled her eyes. "You are aware that you speak entirely in double entendres, aren't you?"

"Really?" The Professor looked pained. "Oh, my dear, I *am* sorry. Is it so obvious? I try so hard to suppress it, you know."

Finn waggled her head and offered no comment.

Locke gave her an earnest look. "Please believe me when I say I mean no disrespect at all. The last thing I'd ever want to do would be to put you in an uncomfortable position. It's a sort of tic, you see, acquired after playing one too many Oxbridge dons. It's a condition peculiar to Recurrents: display a certain quirk a little too often and it begins to embed itself into one's psyche."

"Honestly, don't worry about it."

"No, but I'm most embarrassed, Ms. Finn; I hadn't realised my affliction was quite so evident."

Finn smiled. "I wasn't offended, Paul. Just curious."

The Professor seemed relieved. "Well, that's reassuring. Thank you. And if I do occasionally slip one in, please pay me no heed. At my age, the tongue is willing, but it's about the only organ that is."

She grinned. "Well, I did wonder whether a man of your age might struggle to keep it up."

"Ha!" Locke clapped his hands. "Capital! My dear, I can see that we shall get on famously."

"I'd like that." She nodded at Hitch, who was following the line of a dry stone wall a few metres ahead. "And actually, you're not even the weirdest man I've met lately."

"Ah, you mean young Mr. Hitch?"

"Yeah. Is he really as clever as he likes to make out?"

Locke nodded, seemingly relieved that the conversation was moving on. "Every bit. He's really an excellent guide. Tales and genres - they're bewilderingly complex, you know. They fork continuously, like the branches of a family tree - but in three dimensions, if you can picture such a thing."

Finn frowned. "So... like a tree, then?"

"Ah, yes." He chuckled. "Precisely so. And that young man is a living map. He has an amazing ability to navigate all these different branches, hopping between them wherever they cross or touch. It's a most singular mind he has; he can conceive of routes and shortcuts that would occur to no one else."

Finn tried to imagine what her route back home might look like and wondered whether she'd ever learn the trick of navigation. "So why do we need Johnny, then?"

"Ah, well, a reader can only be used to conjure a gate wherever two narratives are close; when there's some sort of generic or thematic connection between them. In the absence of such a link, we need the help of someone like Mr. Forster."

Finn squinted into the driving snow. "But if Johnny can just take us straight to wherever we want to go, why are we taking such a long route?"

"Caution, my dear. With a saboteur at large, we must rely on young Johnny only in extremis. The systems he uses can be infiltrated. For so long as we remain independent, we have a good chance of remaining undetected."

"Huh. Well, let's hope so. It'd be nice to make sense of all this before I come round."

"I'm sorry? What was that?"

"I said I hope so."

"Oh, don't worry, Miss Finn. The more gates we pass, the more the odds stack up against anyone finding us."

The lowing of a cow broke through the sound of the wind. Both she and Locke raised their heads to see Hitch waving them over.

Ahead, ringed by a wall and part-shielded by thrashing fir trees, a substantial farmhouse appeared from the darkness. It was built from heavy stones, strongly reinforced, and one wall bore a thick frosting of white. Around it stood a number of unlit outbuildings: a barn, a shed, a pigeon cote and others too distant to be properly made out.

That memory nagged again, and now, as she reached the outer wall, Finn's eyes lit up.

"Oh my God! I know where we are!" She gave a little dance. "I've been on these moors before! The school trip to Haworth! Oh, God, but I never thought I'd really see it!"

She saw Hitch and the Professor exchanging nervous glances.

"This is Mum's favourite book! Wuthering Heights! She *named* me after Catherine Earnshaw."

"*This* is her favourite book?" Hitch looked unimpressed.

"She loves it. We both do. It's brilliant."

"It's the sweaty imaginings of a tight-laced clergyman's daughter - that's what it is." Hitch angled his head towards what might have been a stable. "Anyway, come on. This is no time for literary criticism."

"No, but look!" She pointed up at a narrow, latticed casement. It looked just the way she'd always imagined it. "*That's* the window!"

Setting his hands on his hips, Hitch looked at her with all the enthusiasm of a Goth on a pogo stick. "What are you doing? What's got into you?"

Seized by an inexplicable feeling of abandon, Finn extended her arms and spun in the snow. "Oh, we're right here; *this* is where she says 'I've been a waif for twenty years.' It's like the song!"

"The song?" Locke frowned.

"Oh, you know..." She spun again and in her finest falsetto produced a couple of lines from the famous seventies hit.

"What in the name of..." Hitch stared at her.

"Yeah." She rubbed her nose. "Sorry. Those might not be quite the words. I know the novel better than the song."

Locke smiled uncertainly. "And that's, um... that's your natural voice, is it?"

Hitch leaned in close. "That's a polite way of saying you're a rubbish singer."

Finn laughed. "No, I was doing Kate Bush; she sang it like that."

Hitch pulled a worried face. "On purpose?"

"Look, don't spoil this." Finn pulled out her phone. Back in Egypt, she'd decided to start documenting her journey in case the photos produced any useful clues later on. "This is a big deal for me, okay? I grew up with this book. So just give me a second, alright? I want to... There!" Her phone flashed.

Hitch grabbed her arm. "Will you put that away! We're supposed to be on the run."

"Oh, that's torn it," said the Professor, pointing up at the upstairs window. "There's a light."

Hurrying into the lee of the whipping fir, Finn watched as a pale, candle-lit face peered out into the darkness.

"There you go," said Hitch, holding up his finger and thumb. "You got *this* close to ruining your mum's favourite book. Tell you what, why not go out and do another little song for him?"

Finn stared. "Woah. That must be Mr. Lockwood."

"And *that* is a gamekeeper with a shotgun," said the Professor, tugging at her shoulder.

She and Hitch turned together. Though he was still a good way distant, a heavy-coated figure was indeed approaching along the edge of the wall. It didn't look like he'd seen them yet.

Finn pressed herself against the tree. "I don't remember any gamekeepers. Not here."

"That's 'cause he's not a gamekeeper," said Hitch, dropping to a crouch. "He's wearing a reader."

19. Once Upon a Time in the West

our more doorways took them to a dusty side street that smelled strongly of manure and newly sawn wood. Long shadows told that it was late afternoon, but the air clung to her skin, hot and sticky as a microwaved pop-tart.

Hitch had refused to reveal the name of this particular work. He'd said only that it was vanishingly obscure and home to one of his hideouts. Quite why he was being so cagey was beyond her. Perhaps he feared that if she or Locke were to find themselves gazing at a vast trove of contraband biscuits, one of them might lose their cool. The man seemed to have a very peculiar sense of priority, but it didn't much matter. All they really needed was somewhere to rest safely and reassess their position.

Having disabled most of her phone settings in case they were somehow trackable, Finn was now obliged to take the arm of one of her companions every time they crossed a threshold. She did so reluctantly, not least because it made her feel more the dependent than ever. However, she consoled herself that she had a plan. She'd been watching Hitch intently as he'd conjured each gate. She hadn't yet figured out the art of using a reader, but the knowledge was coming, little by little. The clear memory kindled by her spell on the Yorkshire Moors had only strengthened her resolve to get home and warn her mum. Sooner or later, she meant to take her chance.

For the moment, though, her priority was to make sense of whatever challenge her mind was setting her - and that meant evading the saboteur. In that sense at least, they had a shared goal.

While Hitch went to check their surroundings, she waited for Locke to emerge through the gate; in this instance, the side entrance to a barber's shop. He appeared wearing a bowler hat, a smart black waistcoat and half-moon spectacles. These, together with her own plain calico dress and apron suggested that this latest world lay somewhere between *Pale Rider and Little House on the Prairie*. She just hoped it would be the sort of place where the blueberry muffins greatly outnumbered the gunslingers.

Locke regarded his attire as though it were something recently coughed up by a dog. "Oh, splendid," he said. "Another waistcoat. This confounded reader never puts me in an anything else. They're supposed to be personality-sensitive, you know. Why not see me all wrapped up in a nice pair of sturdy chaps? That would make a change, wouldn't it?"

Finn smiled. "Well, that would be my choice, obviously."

"But our friend isn't quite so fashion-conscious, I see."

Ahead of them, dressed in a pair of grimy jeans and a collarless white shirt, Hitch was inching toward the alley's junction with a broad, sandy street. He called back over his shoulder. "You know another word for *fashion,* Lockster?"

"My boy, I know sev..."

"Copying," said Hitch, firmly. "All it is. Plain and simple. No sane man should waste time thinking about it."

"Well, that's rather a jaund..." Locke was silenced by some furious hand-waving. Having just peered round the street corner, Hitch ducked quickly back into the shadows.

"Oh, those miserable, stinking fun-suckers," he said.

"What is it?" Paul joined him to survey the scene.

"The guys at the other end of the street."

Wide, rutted and trafficked by the obligatory ensemble of traders, grifters, drifters and drunks, the main thoroughfare could have been a film set for pretty much any western ever made. A stable, a saloon, a general store, and a sheriff's office fronted the main street, together with an undertaker's and a handful of rented rooms. Here, when the story's bad guys made their inevitable appearance, residents would doubtless peer nervously out between the curtains before flicking them smartly shut. It pretty much checked the entire Old West cliché list, right down to the bullet-holed trough outside the hotel. For an extra point, it might have featured a sombrero-clad Mexican sleeping by a saddler's storefront but that was the only notable absence. Perhaps they'd given him the day off.

The only real departure from the standard formula was also the reason for Hitch's outburst. Outside an assayer's office near the far end of the town, several dark-suited lawmen were holding back a handful of onlookers with stern looks, shouldered rifles, and a certain amount of unwarranted satisfaction. Some of them were loading crates and suitcases into a covered wagon. A four-horse team implied they'd come with the expectation of a sizeable haul.

Finn looked at Hitch. "Your secret hideout, I suppose?"

Hitch nodded, closed his eyes and rested his head back against the shop wall. He looked like a boy who'd just seem an ailing pet packed off on its final visit to the vets.

"Well, this won't do at all," said Locke. "It seems to me that we need to do rather less running away and rather more intelligence-gathering."

Hitch was too busy sulking to respond.

"No more running," said Finn. "I'm with you on that. I'm dead on my feet. Let's find ourselves somewhere to rest and have a proper think."

She glanced at Hitch but he was still doing the thing with the moody silence. Perhaps he was going for a *Fist Full of Dollars* vibe. If so, then he wasn't doing badly; he already had the stubble, and his clothes probably hadn't see a laundry in weeks.

"Then it's decided," said Locke, tapping at his wrist. "But first things first; radio silence. We must all disable our readers; dispense with everything but the disguises."

Silently, Hitch and Finn acquiesced.

"Good. Now let's try to get a better look. But be on your guard. If they're in league with the saboteurs, then they might well be on the lookout for us. Much as I enjoy being part of this brave little threesome, I suggest you two go on ahead. We'll be less conspicuous if you pass yourselves off as a couple."

Hitch sighed and held out his arm. "Alright. Come on then, wifey."

Finn raised an eyebrow. "Wife? I was thinking daughter. Niece, at best."

"The Professor's an odd one, isn't he?" said Finn as they made their way up the street.

"A bit fruity, you mean?"

"Yeah."

"Oh, don't worry. He's harmless."

"I wasn't worried. I was just wondering if all Recurrents were like that."

"No, no. That's just his... thing." He nodded at another shop. "Try that one."

Finn turned the handle, but it felt like the door was nailed shut. What was wrong with this place? They'd tried three different shops and not one of them had been open. It felt more like a film set than ever; the store fronts appeared to be no more than facades.

Hitch raised a hand to the glass and peered inside. "It's all Unimagined. None of these interiors feature in the narrative."

"So what do we do?" Finn eyed the lawmen ahead. "We're getting a bit close."

"Yeah, give me a minute. I'm trying to remember if there's anywhere else that only appears in one scene."

"Does that make it safe?"

"Uh huh. Once the scene's over, no one's coming back to it; you're pretty much free to do what you want with the place.

That's why I chose that, um..." Hitch nodded in the direction of his hideout.

"But those guys..." Finn eyed the lawmen, who seemed to be finishing their task. Some were already mounting up. "If this isn't part of the original story, what are they doing raiding it?"

Hitch pursed his lips. "I think that's the same question the Prof wants to answer."

"You reckon they're working with the saboteurs?"

Hitch shrugged. "Dunno. But somebody's definitely interfering."

Finn slowed her pace. "So how close do you think we should get?"

"Just close enough to..." Sharply, he turned his head towards the window, seized her elbow and steered her down an alleyway between the buildings. "Quick. Keep walking."

"What is it?"

"There's a guy there I recognise." He put his shoulder to the door of a large two-storey building. To Finn's relief, it swung inward. He pulled her inside.

It was a wheelwright's workshop, or a carter's - or whatever the correct term was for someone who fixed wooden wagons in the nineteenth-century. The place had a wagon in it, anyway, and one end rested on a pair of axle stands. More importantly, the building also had a pair of small, dusty windows that overlooked the main street. Hitch was already hurrying towards them.

"That's him. The big guy." He pointed at a man in a grey duster coat whose stature hinted at an unnatural encounter between a recent ancestor and a grizzly. Barging his way through the crowd like a human forklift, he was clearly no favourite amongst the townsfolk.

"Ugly fella," said Finn. "Where d'you know him from?"

"Well that's the worrying bit." Hitch looked her in the eye. "He's a watchman."

"But I thought they weren't supposed to be seen in a live narrative. Not supposed to interfere."

Hitch turned back to the window. "They're not. Only in the worst kind of emergency."

Finn was saved the bother of responding by an ominous click from behind them. It was the sort of sound that demanded an awkward silence and a slow turn of the head.

Slowly and awkwardly, Finn turned her head.

Grey eyes glinted from beneath the brim of a bowler as a figure advanced from the shadows. The twin barrels of a shotgun caught the light from the door.

He raised his head a little. "Stick ya hands up, ya bums."

"Do *what?*" Finn blinked in alarm. "I promise you, I'll do no such thing."

The figure shook his head. "No, no. I said 'stick ya hands up.'" He paused, emphasising the unspoken comma. "'Ya bums'."

Finn felt her eyes widening. "Oh. Right. Sorry, I thought... Well, it doesn't matter." She raised her hands.

Hitch caught her eye as he did the same. "Very slick."

"This here's my property," said the man. "You mind tellin' me what you're doin' here?"

Hitch cleared his throat before producing quite the worst Texan accent Finn had ever heard. "Oh, well, see, I was just moseyin' on over to the assayer's office, but then I saw all those men and, well, hey... I didn't come lookin' for no trouble." Towards the end, his accent had drifted somewhere south of Alice Springs; in a single sentence, John Wayne had become Kylie Minogue.

Finn shook her head. The next time this happened, she was going to revert to the mute brother tactic.

"Uh huh." The carter looked suitably unconvinced. "Well it looks to me like you're hidin' out. Like maybe you got somethin' you wanna keep from the law."

"Listen." Finn made no effort to feign an accent. "Those men out there aren't lawmen; they're criminals."

Her captor peered past her, watching the posse saddle up. "Well, I don't know about that ma'am, but I wasn't fixin' to take ya to them."

"Hoo-ee! Now that there's a fine lookin' woman!"

"Shut your mouth, Ezrah, or you know what you'll git." Sheriff Jackson gave them all a hard look before closing the door on them.

This unexpected turn in their journey had yielded both good news and bad. The good news was that Finn had been able to satisfy a long-standing curiosity about what the inside of a jail cell looked like. The bad news, of course, amounted to very much the same thing.

After the departure of the watchmen, Abe the carter had ushered them across the street, into the sheriff's office, and thence into the jail itself. Two cells were set against the back wall, separated from one another by a row of rusting bars. In one stood Finn and Hitch. In the other sat Ezrah, a man who seemed to be composed entirely of beard, food scraps, and acne. He was regarding Finn with an interest that looked as unhealthy as his complexion.

"So who's the little woman?" His grin showed that dentistry was still something of a developing science round these parts.

"My fiancée," said Hitch, slumping onto the cell's one rudimentary cot.

Ezra's unwholesome grin widened as his hand strayed southward. "Uh huh. You two *done* it yet?"

Hitch shrugged. "I have." He closed his eyes. "I don't know about her."

Ezra's eyebrows wandered in different directions. "Huh?"

Ignoring him, Finn sat beside her accomplice and yanked up his sleeve.

"Hey," said Hitch. "What you doing?"

"Checking you've still got this." She tapped the side of his reader. Like her phone, it was choosing to present itself as a leather wrist cuff. Thankfully, the sheriff hadn't removed them. He was probably erring on the side of leniency while he investigated their claims to be assistants to a prominent surgeon.

Hitch pushed down his sleeve. "Can't do much with it till the Professor shows up."

"Mm." Finn looked up at a small barred window and the swift-fallen darkness beyond. "Where is he, d'you think?"

"Hm. I wonder... A Wild West town with a saloon packed full of dancing girls and drunken cowboys. Where do *you* think he might be headed?"

"Oh. Right."

"Don't worry; he'll be along eventually."

"He can take as long as he likes." Finn closed her eyes. "I need to get some sleep."

"Hey, wake up." Hitch shook her shoulder.

Finn kept her eyes closed. "I haven't been to sleep yet. You keep shoving me with your elbow."

"Well, you keep leaning over onto my side. Anyway, listen, Lockster's arrived."

Finn opened an eye but the door to the sheriff's office was still shut; all she could see through its little barred window was the lantern-lit ceiling in the next room. Nevertheless, a conversation was taking place and she recognised the voice.

"... a geologist, yes."

"And you're sayin' that there couple - they're your assistants?"

"I am, Sheriff, for indeed they are."

"Huh. See, that's what I can't quite figure out, 'cause they told me you're a sawbones."

Finn and Hitch exchanged unsightly looks.

"Did they?" Locke's explanation continued with barely a pause. "Well, they're quite right, of course. Amongst other things, I'm a Fellow of the Royal College of Surgeons of Edinburgh."

"Is that right? So why'd you come in here saying you was an assayer; a geologist?"

"Well, because I am. I also have PhDs in mineralogy and geomorphology."

"Huh. Well, I mean no disrespect, Doctor, but can you prove any of this?"

"Um, well it's *Professor*, actually, but I'm sure I can oblige. Let's see." There was a pause and a sound of shuffling. "Well, proving one's geological expertise is a little tricky, but if it's of any interest to you, the walls of your jail are made predominantly from quaternary sandstone. And as for my medical credentials, I might start by pointing out that those red patches on your skin are known as spider angiomas. They could be a sign that you ought to cut back a smidge on the whiskey. Tell me, Sheriff, do you find you sometimes experience swelling on the palms of your hands?"

"Uh, sometimes, I guess."

"Occasional numbness or tingling?"

"Um. Yeah. Maybe."

"And what about gastritis? Upset stomach?"

"Gut ache, yeah. I sure get that."

"I see." Locke lowered his voice. "And what about downstairs? Have you noticed any shrinkage of the testicles? Any concerns about impot..."

"Okay. Alright, Doctor, that's... that's enough." There came the sound of chair legs scraping floorboards. "I reckon we've kept your assistants waiting long enough, ain't we?"

"Oh, right. Jolly good."

A half dozen footsteps later, the door swept open to reveal a beaming professor and a preoccupied-looking sheriff. He unlocked their cell with barely a word and quickly discharged them from the building.

"Have you really got all those qualifications?" said Finn as they stepped down into the moonlit street.

"I really have," said Locke, "but don't be misled. That was largely improvisation back there. I may have twenty three doctorates and a weighty satchel of professorships, but when I leave the narratives in which they were earned, most of the knowledge evaporates. I might have absorbed the odd factual nugget in my time, but in a place like this I'm little more than a jack of all trades."

"And hey, that's absolutely super," said Hitch, "but I've got a more pressing question. Is it safe to be out here?"

Locke started back towards the centre of town. "Oh, quite safe, I assure you. Come along."

"Where are we going?"

"To the saloon, dear boy. I found us food, drink, and a decent place to rest. I thought you might approve."

"I like all those things," conceded Hitch warily. "I'm tired and hungry and I need a drink, so a saloon would be an excellent choice."

Locke raised an eyebrow. "But..."

"Well, it's never that easy with you, is it? There's always a catch."

In the event, there were two catches, and both of them were watchmen. However, just as Locke had promised, they had already lost their battle with a bottle of something brown and imprudent. When Finn followed the Professor into the crowded saloon, she found one mumbling incoherently at his own hat, while the other sat with his forehead resting on the edge of his table - whether sleeping or dead, it was difficult to say. The marginally more conscious of the two had his back turned to the door and was presumably not adhering to anything approaching best practice in the field of covert surveillance.

"Those men are *heroically* drunk," announced Hitch, his voice registering something akin to admiration. "That anything to do with you?"

Locke smiled, raising his voice above what sounded like someone playing the piano with a pair of mallets. "I had a quiet word with the bartender and asked if he might keep my friends supplied with his strongest liquor."

"*Strongest?* In a town like this?" Hitch gave a low whistle. "Professor, you are a dangerously reckless man. Remind me never to upset you."

Locke accepted the compliment with a bow. "The barman assured me it was whiskey. Taking him for an authority on the subject, I merely trusted his word."

Hitch shook his head. "Never drink unfamiliar whiskey in an Old West town, Finn. That's rule number one."

"Well I certainly need *something* to drink." Finn's throat felt as dry as a sandpaper sunhat. There'd been water in the jail, but it had tasted like something dredged up from the trough outside. "You want anything?"

Hitch rolled his eyes. "Dear me, Finn. If you have to ask, you really don't know me at all."

"There'll be no fancy cocktails, that's for sure." Locke threaded his way towards the barman, who was polishing glasses with something the colour of a pizza topping. "I asked earlier if he could fix me up with a nice fruity matador and he looked at me as if I were mad."

"Maybe just get us some beers." Hitch attempted to summon the barman. "You two head up to the rooms and make yourselves inconspicuous."

"No, no," said Locke. "There's work to be done. We agreed to start gathering some intelligence."

"No we didn't." Hitch looked aggrieved. "That doesn't sound anything like the sort of plan I'd agree to."

"He means *we* agreed," said Finn. "Paul and me."

Hitch frowned. "Well that's hardly fair. I didn't bring you two along so you could start taking democratic decisions."

Finn shrugged. "Two against one."

Hitch raised a finger. "You remember what Aristotle said about democracy and despotism, don't you, Finn?"

"No."

"No. Well okay, no, neither do I, but you know... it's a slippery slope."

"Nevertheless..." began Locke.

"No, no. Not nevertheless." Hitch pointed at the two legless lawmen. "In case it's slipped your minds, those men over there are watchmen. They're drunk, they'll certainly be armed, and for some strange reason, they don't seem to like me very much. So hanging around here is not a clever survival strategy."

"Ah, but the fact that they're drunk works to our advantage," said Locke. "They've dropped their guard and they have absolutely no idea we're here. There's no better time to find out what the Dickens is going on."

"Okay, fine; you two get yourself killed if you want to." Hitch collected the first of his drinks and pointed to Locke when the bartender held out a hand for payment. "Food, booze, and bed - that's my mission for the night."

The Professor slid some coins across the bar. "Now Hitch, come along..."

He shook his head. "Nah ah."

"Oh, just leave him, Paul." Finn sent Hitch a disparaging look, but found it expertly ignored. "We'll do it without him. What's the plan?"

Sighing, Locke angled his head in the direction of the watchmen's table. "Our sleeping friend there has left his reader on the table."

"That silver tobacco case thing?"

"Quite so. And it strikes me that if we can get our hands on it, then we might be able to listen in on their colleagues."

"Okay. So what do you suggest?"

"Well, if I can somehow disguise myself, I thought I might inveigle my way to his table and start up a conversation." He sent her a conspiratorial wink. "Though I say so myself, I'm quite the interrogator. The more I pump him, the more I'm sure I can get him to spill."

"Mm." Finn winced at the image. "Or we could just do this..." With a deftness earned from five years of jostling around packed student union bars, she swiped a bottle from the bar and slipped into the crowd.

Working her way between close-packed tables, through the obligatory cast of cardsharps, drunkards, and moustachioed thugs, Finn soon reached the wasted watchmen. The nearer of the two still had his back to her and was oozing forward like a slowly melting waxwork. The reader lay on the table between him and his loudly snoring friend.

"Your beer, sir." In one smooth movement, she set the bottle down to the watchman's left, passed behind him and, as he turned to peer at this strangely materialised beverage, reached over his right shoulder to snatch up his reader.

It might have been an impressive move if she'd been able to march briskly away, but her escape route was suddenly blocked as a heavy set salesman backed towards her and inadvertently boxed her in. As she began to turn, she felt someone groping for her wrist.

"Hey, now, little lady." Though the watchman's eyes still seemed fixated on his newly acquired beer, his mouth and at least one of his hands still seemed to be responding to some sense of duty. "What's the hurry, huh?"

Finn's fist tightened as he blindly patted the side of her leg. Perhaps it wasn't duty that was driving him. Carefully, she grasped his sleeve, eased it away from her thigh and bent close to his ear.

"Hey, honey," she said, producing an accent that was barely any more convincing than Hitch's previous attempt, "if you wanna be friendly, why don't you set your hand right here?" So saying, she guided his fingers to the salesman's back pocket and then stepped smartly away.

"Hey! What you...?"

She kept walking as the cries of surprise quickly escalated. She'd got as far the next table by the time she heard the first bottle smash.

Nothing, it seemed, spread more quickly than a bar room brawl in the Wild West. In three paces, the fight had overtaken her and the whole room had erupted into a maelstrom of breaking chairs and flying glass.

Beside her, a wiry young cowboy drew back his arm for a punch and his elbow connected sharply with the side of her head. "Ow!" was her instinctive but not altogether inventive response.

"Oh, pardon me, ma'am!" The youth's apologetic frown quickly distorted as a fist the size of a watermelon met the side of his jaw.

To her left, a waistcoated gambler arced through the air before reducing a table to a fountain of cards and splinters. As Finn re-calculated her route back to the bar, a heavy weight fell against the back of her legs and pitched her forward to the floor.

This was considerably more physical than she'd expected. Now, as heavy boots leapt and danced around her outstretched hands, she rolled for cover under one of the few surviving tables. From that temporary refuge, she peered out the other side and saw Hitch watching the scramble from halfway up the stairs. When his gaze met hers, he raised a bottle in salutation, then continued up towards the landing.

"This ain't no place for a lady, ma'am." Behind her, a leather-faced labourer - quite possibly the same heavy weight whose fall had landed her here - passed her an empty bottle. He seemed to imagine she'd have some use for it.

"Um. Thanks." It seemed rude to refuse.

A gap in the crowd revealed an anxious-looking Locke who stood by the bar peering through the forest of thrashing limbs. The gap seemed as wide as any she was likely to see, so she shoved a chair out of the way, rose to her feet and hurried in the direction she'd last glimpsed him.

Nearing the edge of the brawl, she paused as a bearded drunk fell heavily from the chandelier. She sidestepped, then stumbled as an angry-looking dancing girl broke the remains of a chair across her back. Fortunately, she managed to keep her feet and was able to hurry forward as another gap appeared. By the time she reached the Professor, she was grinning and breathless.

"That," said Locke, "was inelegant and ill-judged. Are you hurt?"

"Well I took a couple of knocks when..." She paused. "Actually no; I'm not hurt at all. Why is that?"

Locke raised his eyebrows. "You're a non-diegetic in a lopey narrative."

Finn wondered whether she'd misheard. "In a what?"

"Low-P: Low Plausibility. Something rather more easily demonstrated than explained. May I?" Smiling, he took her bottle and lobbed it gently into the melee. Despite the absence of effort, it smashed spectacularly across the back of a man's shoulders and instantly laid him out.

"Aah. Right."

"Yes. In a place like this, gunfighters can neuter a gnat at thirty paces or render a man unconscious with little more than a stern look." Turning towards the stairs he crooked his elbow, inviting her to take his arm. "You secured the reader, I take it?"

20. Awakenings

Knock, knock.

Finn poked her head into Hitch's room and tapped again on the half open door. "Hey, sleepyhead. Wake up, it's morning."

A muffled grunt issued briefly from the darkness.

Finn herself had been a little disappointed to wake up in an Old West bedroom. She would have much preferred to find herself back in her bookshop, even at the price of a painful wound and a long stay in hospital. On the upside, at least she'd managed to get some rest. Now, having slept the sleep of the dead, she felt invigorated. Hoping to imbue her companion with that same spirit of verve and energy, she strode past his bed and threw back the curtain.

"Aagh. Umph!" Hitch rolled over and covered himself with his pillow. He couldn't have sounded more affronted if she'd just doused him with boiling tar.

"Come on, grumpy." She grabbed his foot through the blanket and waggled it.

"What d'you want? Go away."

"It's morning."

"What? What d'you mean?"

"Morning." Finn sat on the edge of the bed. "You know: sun-up; breakfast time."

"No. Still not with you."

"I'll give you five minutes. If you're not ready, I'll start singing Kate Bush again."

He groaned through his pillow. "You're beyond cruel. Why do you hate me so?"

"I don't hate you. It's just morning. Getting up is what people do."

"Oh, you don't want to listen to people. People are stupid. They watch television and do sports and, oh, I don't know... eat yogurt, probably. They have pointless routines. I choose not to follow their example." He curled into a tight ball. "Now go away and leave me alone."

"Shan't." She waggled his other foot.

"Oh, you're despicable. An awful, awful person." Removing the pillow, he shot her a resentful look. "This is no way to live. Mornings are for madmen."

"Don't be so melodramatic."

He sighed noisily. "Look, try to understand something, Finn: today's May the eighth, okay? It's always May the eighth in this town. It was May the eighth yesterday and it will be May the eighth tomorrow. You understand? This is a pass-through town; a one-day set. That carter we saw, he'll have forgotten all about us - the jailer and the bartender, too. That little fight you started downstairs - there won't be a trace of it. The only thing that's any different is that now all my stuff's been stolen."

"Uh huh. And your point is?"

"My point, honeybun, is that nobody here is going to care if I have a nice little lie in. The only person it matters to, apparently, is you."

"Well, me, the Professor, and whoever's still looking for us." She cast an eye to the window. "And you've got to wonder about that, haven't you? I mean, I'm sure you've got other hideouts; who's to say they're not out there now, looking for more of them?"

"I will not be manipulated, Finn." He closed his eyes, shuffled uncomfortably and then opened them again. "Anyway. Let's just say I did get up. What happens?"

"Well, Paul's been looking at the readers. We need to figure out..."

"No, no, no." He waved an arm aimlessly above his head. "I mean mornings. Mornings generally. What happens? What are they... for?"

Finn stood and returned to the door. "For getting dressed, having breakfast, and figuring out what the bad guys are up to."

Hitch pulled the pillow back over his face. "That's already the worst plan I've heard all day."

Finn and Hitch evidently had very different views about what constituted a proper breakfast. For Finn, it comprised a gritty, salty porridge - two parts oats to one part gravel - and a cup of coffee so strong it looked like it might actually be dissolving her spoon. Rather than eat downstairs and risk meeting some hung-over watchman, she'd nipped through a miraculously restored saloon and found her way to the kitchen. There, she'd asked for her order to be sent up, together with a plate of fried eggs for the Professor. Now, giving the grey mush in her bowl an exploratory prod, she was beginning to regret her decision.

Hitch seemed more content. His breakfast of choice was whiskey. Somehow, possibly through a furtive biscuit exchange some time the previous night, he'd managed to procure himself a bottle. He was already well into it when he emerged from his bedroom.

"What are you doing?" Finn watched as he sat across the table from her. "We've got stuff to do."

He avoided her gaze and downed another shot. "I'm making myself unusual," he said. "The Russians call it *ostranenie.*"

"You're unbelievable." Finn found her fists tightening. There were so many other places she needed to be. "You make it impossible for people to be nice to you; you know that, don't you?"

He shrugged. "I can't be held accountable for the misjudgement of others."

Finn flung back her chair and strode to the window. "You keep talking about narratives and all these different fictions. Well you know what? Characters like you are supposed to *redeem* themselves at some point, Hitch. That fight last night - you did nothing to help. Nothing at all. Didn't even cross your mind. Just wandered off to get drunk again."

Hitch wouldn't meet her eye. "Oh, I'm done with being the hero, Finn. Been there; turned out badly. This..." he held up his glass as he surveyed the room, "this is my retirement."

"So you're not going to help us figure out what to do next?"

"Do?" Hitch snorted. "We're not going to *do* anything. There's no point."

Locke had been fussing with their readers, but paused to share her weary look.

Hitch poured himself another shot. "No, no. Really, there isn't. If they got to Winchester, then this is way too big for me. I've done enough." He waved a limp hand in the Professor's direction. "I found you. That's it; mission accomplished. Now we leave it to your massive noggin to figure it all out."

Finn stared at him. "That was your plan? That's all there was?"

"What can I say? I'm a delicate soul; I react badly to confrontation."

"And that's it? You're giving up? Some nasty men broke your ickle hideout so you're just going to sulk; drink yourself into a coma?"

Hitch nodded. "Pretty much. Hadn't thought about the coma thing, but it's a nice touch."

"No. Not an option." Finn snatched his bottle from the table. "I'm relying on you, Hitch. I need to make sense of all this; I need you to help me get home."

He gazed dully at his glass. "None of us get home, Finn. Haven't you figured that out yet? If I knew a way back, don't you think I'd have taken it? You think *any* of us would be here? Nobody chooses this. It's hard and it's unfair but it's the truth. We've all been torn away from someone."

Finn glared, but for a moment she could say nothing at all. Hearing it from Cariola was bearable; hearing it from Hitch was something altogether different. When she did speak, her voice came out low and leaden. "So why did you ask me to come? What am I even doing here?"

"I don't know." Hitch pressed the glass to his forehead. "Maybe Duggan was right. Maybe I didn't have anyone else to ask. When you said you wanted to get back to your mum, maybe I saw something in you that... Well, it doesn't matter."

Finn felt her eyes pricking. She couldn't decide whether to hurl the bottle across the room or drink whatever was left inside it. She was still deliberating her choices when Locke spoke out.

"Well, this is all very character-building, I'm sure," he said, "but here's something rather interesting: you were both carrying tracking chips."

"What?" said Finn and Hitch together.

He slid the gutted carcase of Hitch's reader across the table. Finn's phone had been similarly exposed. On each screen rested a tiny black and gold wafer.

"Shit!" Finn peered out at the street. "So the bad guys know we're here?"

"Unlikely." The Professor picked up one of the chips. "They don't have the power to transmit continuously. Without my tools, I couldn't say precisely how often they send but I'd guess it could be no more than once every two or three hours. We turned our readers off soon after getting here, so unless we were exceptionally unlucky, we should be clear for the moment."

"Okay. Okay. Right." Hitch shook his head, then held up a finger. "So, two questions. Firstly and most importantly: can I have my whiskey back?"

Finn narrowed her eyes and weighed the bottle for balance. "No."

Hitch frowned, but was wise enough to concede. "I see. Question number two, then: who put the trackers in?"

"The Watch," said Locke. "Which is reasonable enough, given that they were sending you off on an important errand. They'll doubtless have wanted to keep an eye on you."

Hitch swilled his drink around his glass. "But then why wreck my hideout? If they were looking out for me, why steal all my stuff?"

"That," said Locke, "is the more interesting question. And quite frankly, none of the answers are looking very good."

Finn took a seat. "We picked up that watchman's reader. Did it tell you anything?"

"It did. They're using high-level encrypted channels." The Professor turned the stolen device over in his hand. "And the protocols can only mean their orders are coming from someone at the top."

"But Winchester herself sent us," said Hitch.

"And was abducted shortly thereafter," said Locke. "Which all has the unfortunate whiff of a coup about it. I know she had grave concerns about security. That was why she brought me in. We found that someone had been conducting secret research into the Origin myths; snooping around in various tales and then trying very hard to erase them from the system."

Finn chewed her way through another mouthful of coffee. "The Origin myths. These are the She-Wolf stories you keep talking about? Like the carvings we saw in Egypt?"

"Precisely so - and our little adventure in the land of the Pharaohs has convinced me of something more alarming still. Our saboteur has found a way of doing that which we had always held to be impossible. Either they've found a way to breach the Core, or they're communing with an author from a higher level. By one or the other means, they have found a way to create new narratives."

Finn realised the Professor was pausing for dramatic effect. "Oh, right. Wow...."

Locke chewed his lip. "You don't really grasp the significance of that, do you?"

"Um. Not really. No."

"It means they can create new worlds to serve their own ends. To trap or kill us, for example, or to build themselves an army."

Hitch blinked slowly. "An army."

Locke nodded. "I'm afraid so. All our missing winches were abducted in highly militarised narratives; history, science fiction, fantasy - the genres varied, but they all featured considerable firepower. And with the winchmen's readers lost, whoever took them can re-open the gates at will."

"But so what?" said Hitch. "The gates have never allowed weapons through. Unless you're a watchman, you'd struggle to get through with a gardening trowel."

The Professor nodded. "Quite so. Gates are set with strict limits, as a safeguard against just that sort of threat. But those limits might soon count for nothing if the saboteur has breached the Core."

Hitch snorted. "In which case, we've already lost. If someone's got into the Core, they can do anything. Literally anything. You'd be picking a fight with a god."

"Well, not quite." Locke rose and paced before the window, looking every inch the learned academic. "The fact that someone wants to prevent us from completing our mission tells us something, does it not?"

Finn was feeling the caffeine rush. "That you know something that threatens them, and they don't want it getting back to everyone in that dome."

"Precisely so. And if they are feeling threatened, then they are not yet invulnerable."

"So what *do* we know?" Finn was aware that the 'we' was stretching things a bit but she didn't want to feel left out.

"Firstly, that if the Core has not been breached, then our saboteur must be in league with a higher level power. And secondly, that New Tybet is the likely target for an invasion."

Hitch produced an unhappy sigh. "An invasion. You sure?"

Paul held out his hands. "A guess, I'll admit, but an educated one. Control of the gates rests in New Tybet and the city is the hub through which any army must pass. If there's to be an assault, it can be the only target."

Hitch sagged in his chair. "And let me guess: you want us to do something heroic to stop it."

"What I want is to send a warning." Locke held up the watchman's reader. "Once we've returned this to the saloon, we must take ourselves off to some new narrative; somewhere secure, whence we can contact Mr. Forster and make Gate Control aware of our concerns."

Hitch blinked. "So just sounding the alarm? No running around being shot at?"

"Merely sounding the alarm." The Professor pulled his spectacles down his nose and looked them each in the eye. "This could be very important. Are we clear? Do you both understand what I'm saying?"

Nodding firmly, Hitch balled a fist. "Something about armies and Johnny Faustus. Got it."

21. The Origin Myths

"Listen, scrote, just pack it in with the techno-babble, alright? I don't buy it for a minute."

The Forster kid looked up at him like he was a moron. God, he hated it when people did that.

"I told you," whined the brat. "It was untargeted." He pointed at his screen. "That's what all those E-values mean. *Error.* It means the system wasn't able to assign them a value."

Duggan narrowed his eyes. "Yeah, and like I said, I don't believe you. You two have got all these clever little secret codes and things, haven't you? You think you can just give it this..." - with one hand, he mimicked a pair of flapping jaws - "and I'll lap it up 'cause I'm just some stupid, gullible plod. That's what you think, isn't it?"

Forster rapped his knuckles against the monitor. "What else can I tell you? I mean, look. There's just no data on the system. No genre code, no narrative reference, no time stamp or anything. That's what *untargeted* means. Their gate was being jammed; any value we entered would have got scrambled. I gave them the only kind of exit I could."

"Right. So you want me to believe that you've literally no idea where they've gone? It's just one great big wonderful mystery?"

"You heard the Professor. He thinks someone's hunting him and he doesn't know who he can trust. He won't *want* to be found."

Duggan pointed a finger at the lad's temple. "If anything happens to him and I hear you could've done something to stop it..." He glared at him for a moment, but this was about as far as he could push it. Hell, maybe the kid was telling the truth.

"Oh, Mr. Duggan?" The dozy nursemaid waved at him from the door.

"What is it?"

"I think you have a visitor." She stepped back to allow another watchman to enter. It was Boorman, a careerist knob-polisher from Pursuit.

"Duggan." He nodded as he approached.

"Boorman."

"So this is the geek, then?" He eyed Forster, who shook his head unhappily.

"It is." Duggan stepped across Boorman's path. He'd be damned if he'd let Pursuit just waltz in and take over. "Anything I can help you with?"

Boorman stopped and sucked his teeth. "I've been told to get to this Hitch guy. Priority one. Collar or kill him; the boss isn't much fussed which."

"*Kill* him?" Duggan frowned. "What the hell for? He's on our side; he's helping Locke."

Boorman sneered, eager little shit that he was. "Oh no, my friend. No he's not. He's one of the sabs. I heard it from Max Roberts himself. We've got full authority to track him down - use kill teams if we have to."

Duggan shook his head. "That's crazy. Locke was in trouble and these two - Hitch and the lad - they got him out. If they hadn't, Locke would have been dead or abducted by now."

Another snide grin from Boorman. "Or maybe that's just what old Professor Perv wanted you to think. I mean, did you actually see any of it? Try to open a gate for him yourself?"

Forster stood up behind him. "No, but *I* did. They were stuck; the exit was being jammed. There'll be records on the system to prove it."

"Oh, there will?" Boorman took a step forward but stopped when Duggan raised a hand to the watchman's shoulder. Until he heard different, this was still his charge.

Boorman narrowed his eyes. "Careful, Duggan..."

Duggan shrugged. "The lad's an important witness; I'm keeping him safe. Got any problem with that?"

Boorman snorted and leaned in close. "Bit of friendly advice then. Stay on the right side of this. You hear anything - anything at all - and you sing out, yeah?" He smiled and stepped back. "Oh, and just so you remember: that's not a request. That comes straight from Command."

Silas stood in the hanger and studied its great gate. "So we're all shut down now, as far as the system is concerned?"

McDowell nodded. "Completely off grid, sir. Control has been patched through to your office. Only you will see it."

"And security?"

"All reassigned to higher priority tasks elsewhere. There'll be just the one night-watchman to keep it from powering down completely."

"And you're sure he's a lackwit?" Silas walked over to the control room door and peered in through a small rectangular window. There, in the semi-darkness, a young man sat playing some colourful game on his reader.

"That's right, sir. Couldn't open a cereal packet without an instruction manual."

"You're absolutely certain, Mr. McDowell?" Silas looked him in the eye. "There's much at stake. This is no posting for a thinker."

"He came from a romantic novel, sir. With a man's torso on the cover."

Silas raised an eyebrow. "A muscular, naked torso?"

McDowell nodded. "With a woman's hand across it, sir."

"Sounds promising. Go on."

McDowell tapped at his reader. "If I may, sir: he's described - and I'm quoting here - as a mysterious young yachtsman who sweeps the heroine off on an exotic Aegean journey; a voyage of self discovery, passion, and adventure." He smiled. "He's basically just blue eyes and biceps."

Silas nodded. "Possibly ideal, then. But people change, McDowell. Post-extraction, a mind can develop in unexpected directions. Are you sure he can be trusted not to think too hard? Ask too many questions?"

McDowell shook his head. "We've checked him out thoroughly. He's been here eight months since extraction and all he's done is watch reality television and join a few celebrity fan clubs. He tried a brief stint as a life model but he said he found it too challenging."

"I see. And what have you told him about the role we'd like him to perform?"

A smirk flickered across McDowell's face. "Sir, he thinks he's here to help with a top secret statistical project; to count people as they come through the gate."

"And presumably he has no experience at all of statistics?"

"None at all, sir, but he didn't think to question it. When I told him he was going to meet the head of security and he just nodded and said 'neat'."

"He actually used the word 'neat'?"

"Yes sir. He did."

"Well then, bring him through, Mr. McDowell. I think we've found our man."

McDowell tapped on the glass and beckoned for the young yachtsman to join them. There was a short delay as he contended with the complexities of the door handle, but eventually, he appeared with a grin.

"It's Brandon, isn't it?" Silas held out a hand.

"That's right. Good to meet you, Matt."

"The name is Max." Silas smiled thinly. The old *nomme de guerre* would suffice for now.

"Oh, yeah; sorry. Max it is." Firmly, the young man shook his hand, then tried to turn it into one of those awful shoulder-bump-and-back-slap affairs.

Silas hated him immediately. This was one of the reasons why it was so important that his plan succeed. Society was going to hell. It was not the meek who were inheriting the world but the asinine, the shallow, and the crass. The age was sore from an excess of stimulation and something had to be done. Something would be.

He gestured to the gate. "McDowell has explained your role, I understand?"

"Yeah, yeah." Brandon opened his other palm to reveal a small metal tally counter. "This button for humans; the other one for everything else."

"And he's impressed on you the need for complete secrecy?"

"Oh sure. Yeah." He pretended to run a zip across his mouth, then held up a thumb.

"Excellent," sighed Silas. "Well, then, the first arrivals will be a mixed group - humans, ogres and one or two others. They'll want food, water, and equipment."

McDowell pointed Brandon at several of the larger container units in the hanger. "Food and drink there; armour and stuff there."

"Armour?" Brandon offered him a quizzical smile.

McDowell waved a dismissal. "Yeah. Armour and some military re-enactment stuff; they're all coming for the arts and history festival." He caught Silas's eye. "I'm assuming you've heard of it?"

"Oh, yeah, yeah." The young man nodded vigorously. "Art and history; defo. Been looking forward to it. Sounds neat."

"Indeed," said Silas. "Well, then, let's begin, shall we?"

Finn really wished she could sneak a quick photo, but she could see it wasn't a good time. For one thing, there were far too many people in the carriage. For another, a twenty-first century smartphone had no business being wielded about on the Orient Express.

It was a pity, though. She was developing a collector's obsession for documenting her travels, and this would have made a wonderful addition to her portfolio. Here she was, clattering her way towards Constantinople, in a plush carriage of wingback chairs, gold curtained windows, and brightly polished brassware. Before her on the table sat an art deco lamp, together with a pair of wine bottles and four cut crystal glasses. Her fellow passengers were clad in the very height of nineteen-thirties fashion and everyone nodded polite greetings as they passed. It all felt very grand.

In keeping with the setting, her precious device had chosen to disguise itself as a paperback novel. Hitch had said the journey would take at least an hour, so she'd been trying to use the time to read the city guide that Cariola had installed for her. That had been the plan, at least, but her surroundings and the imposing Austrian countryside were all much too distracting, as were Hitch's frequent interruptions.

"If Johnny's been doing his job, then he'll have been laying some false trails," he murmured. "It's clever. You want to know how they work?"

"Not really." She guessed these little overtures were his attempt at an apology for his outburst back in the Old West, but she still hadn't quite forgiven him. *None of us get home*, he'd said. She was going to prove him wrong.

"Oh." He paused, then gestured to the table. "Hey, try the wine. The red's delicious."

"How would you know? You haven't opened it yet."

He shrugged. "I make this journey a lot. I must have drunk that bottle a hundred times."

"Eew." Finn wrinkled her nose. "Well, then, I certainly don't want it. You make it sound like it's been recycled."

"Suit yourself." Hitch waggled the bottle at the Professor, who sat in the opposite window seat. His offer was rewarded with a broad smile and a nod.

Finn glanced down the carriage. A middle-aged man with an elaborate moustache was making his way through the door.

She nudged Hitch. "Oh my God. Is that Poirot?"

Her companion gave her a withering look. "We're not on *that* Orient Express. Cuh. D'you know, I'm actually offended? Someone's trying to track us and you think I'd go for something as obvious at that?"

"Sorry." She returned to her book but couldn't concentrate. "So how long before we have to - you know - jump?"

Hitch leaned in towards the window and studied the mountainous skyline. "A while yet. When we start to come up on the castle, I'll tell you. Maybe read your book for a bit, eh?"

"I've been trying."

The guide's *welcome* section was as dull and predictable as Hitch had warned, full of glib phrases like 'unique utopian setting' and 'a chance to make a fresh new start.' At the third repetition of 'great opportunity' she decided to skip it altogether. Reading it had certainly produced no great feelings of comfort or satisfaction, except perhaps for the knowledge that New Tybet was a refuge for the dead, so plenty of marketing executives must once have been murder victims, too.

The same, cheesy, clichéd style persisted throughout, though a passage in the 'acclimatisation' section was a little more absorbing. It pointed out that the most common reaction to being newly extracted was to imagine it all a dream. This, it said, was healthy. It gave the mind the chance to adjust; insulated the newcomer from the immediate shock of arrival and permitted a slower, smoother transition. This would inevitably be aided by a growing sense of familiarity and the support of new friends.

Finn wasn't quite sure how to take this, but she decided that if she ever wanted to get home to save her grieving family, then developing friends and familiarity was probably a very bad idea.

She found her eye drawn to a new heading.

The History of New Tybet: The Origin Myths

One of the first questions that's bound to strike you as you take your first wondering steps out into this strange new metropolis is how it could possibly have started. Where did it come from? Who brought all these amazing technologies together? In what crazy kind of world could science and magic ever co-exist?

To answer such questions, we'll have to step back more than four hundred years, to a time of myth and legend, when the city was ruled by the mighty She-Wolf: the great wizard Damelyka.

There are countless tales of her courage and adventure but, in truth, little is known of this murky period of history. Though it's said to have been an era of demons, superstition, and savage battles, so much of the Origin Myths are now shrouded in the deepest mystery.

Finn shook her head. *Shrouded in the deepest mystery.* Bloody hell. This might as well have been headed 'Mythology for Morons.' The brochure-speak was terrible but, on the other hand, she needed to make herself inconspicuous, and reading was as good a tactic as any. Reluctantly, she pressed on.

According to the most popular legends, Damelyka was the foremost wizard of the city's Magical College. One day, venturing out on a brave expedition, she encountered a powerful demon who told her of a mystical, far-off gateway. Beyond it, said the demon, lay all the power of life, death, and creation, but none who had dared pass through it had ever returned alive.

At once, Damelyka applied all her powers and ingenuity to finding this gate. For years, she trekked tirelessly across the world until, at last, she found it. How she entered - and how she survived - are mysteries that are lost beneath the shifting sands of time, but what she discovered in that hidden place was a magic to rival anything that this or any other world had ever known.

The gate bestowed upon the She-Wolf such knowledge and power that she could conjure new worlds with no more than a thought, or build bridges between any fictions ever conceived. In just a few short years, she had created the gate complex and set at its heart the Core: the repository of all her secrets and magical energy.

For years, the city grew and its people prospered but, in time, Damelyka became reclusive. Some say she wearied of her role; some that she learned of an even greater mystery and devoted herself to its study. Others still believe that she was lured away by her demon lover and imprisoned in some distant realm where none might ever find her.

All that is truly known is that a little over four centuries ago, she departed this world and was never seen again.

The She-Wolf's fate is, of course, one of the great enigmas of the Origin Myths and it has spawned a plethora of theories, many of which have found their way into modern culture and traditions. Every neighbourhood has its own preferred explanation, and people of all kinds and cultures maintain the quest for knowledge. Some pore over historic records or explore archaeological sites in hopes of unearthing fragments of the truth. Others believe that the answers are to be found in the fabled 'Last Book' - said to be Damelyka's own written account of her life and work.

Meanwhile, thousands of professional researchers devote their careers to studying the secrets of the Core - hoping to shed new light on the greatest mysteries of creation.

If you'd like to explore the many academic and popular publications examining or dramatising this subject, please refer to...

"Hey, Finn." Hitch tapped her arm. "Time to go. You ready?"

Nodding, she put her reader away.

Locke had already taken up his hat and was shuffling along his seat.

"Until next time, sweetheart..." Hitch kissed the bottle and set it back on the table.

Finn rose to her feet. "How long have we got?"

Hitch inclined his head towards the window. "See those ruins on the hill? That's where we need to leave."

When they'd arrived on the train, popping out into an unoccupied sleeper carriage, it had already been travelling at full speed so Finn wasn't too worried about leaving it the same way. But she was a bit bothered about the timing. Hitch had said he was being especially cautious now and their next destination could only be reached from a moving gate. The window of opportunity was quite narrow. As they made their way down the aisle, offering polite apologies to other passengers, Finn quietly voiced her concern.

"Don't worry," was Hitch's less than helpful response. "It'll be fine."

"But what if we don't time it right? What if one of us misses the gate?"

Hitch peered again through the window and smiled. "With all these mountains? I suppose you'll make a very interesting fossil."

22. To Catch a Thief

The Mrs. Margulis Home for the Eminently Rum.

Boorman read the words and produced something resembling a smile.

Wreathed in ivy, the signboard was half hidden by the oaks and rhododendrons that overgrew the entrance to the estate. Wild and evidently untroubled by gardeners, they were slowly enveloping the masonry and the rusting ironwork.

His men leapt from the van and ran to the gates, a pair of bolt-cutters making short work of the padlocked chain. Throwing the remains into the undergrowth, they hauled the gates aside and hurried back.

It would have been easier to use the main entrance, but that would have meant intercoms and a porter's lodge. That could easily have given the game away. This way was better. This way, no well-meaning receptionist was going to warn the oily little turd that he was coming for him. Hitch had made one little mistake in trying to cover his tracks and one mistake was all that Boorman needed. Now, he was going to punish him for it.

With his team back on board, he lifted the clutch and sent his vehicle squealing and protesting between the untended brambles. The paintwork was somebody else's problem. His only concern was to bring the Postman in, and whether that was dead or alive didn't matter a tinker's damn.

Ducking and jolting over the potholed driveway, the van followed a serpentine route between choked ponds and moss-clad statuary. A hundred years or more past its prime, the estate looked dank and beaten by the years - a fitting place for Hitch to meet his end.

As he approached, the woods parted like curtains to reveal the western aspect of the old pile. It would once have been impressive, but there was no time to admire the architecture. He rolled to a halt, killed the engine and turned to look back over his seat.

"Jammers working?"

"Yes sir. If he's getting out, it's going to have to be on foot."

"Good. Let's go."

His men disembarked quickly, two going left towards the rear of the building where the old servants' quarters gave out onto a cobbled yard. Two more went right to keep any eye on the ground floor windows.

Boorman himself strode towards the main entrance, where a pair of pyjama-wearing inmates were sharing a cigarette. He ignored them. A clever disguise could only do so much and both men looked too hunched and frail to be the man he was after. Two bounds took him up the steps. A moment later, he was at the reception desk, where sat an old woman with thick glasses and the beginnings of a *bandito* moustache.

"The name's Boorman." He flashed her his ID.

The woman squinted and turned up her hearing aid. "I'm sorry, dear, what's that you say?"

He gritted his teeth. "I said, my name's Boorman." He held up the badge again.

"Hello, dear. My name's Edna." She peered over her spectacles. "What's that you've got?"

"It's my badge. I'm a watchman. I've come to..."

"Ooh, a watchman's badge. I've never seen one of those close up. Can I have a look?"

"Oh, for..." Boorman tossed it onto the desk. "Look, this is urgent. I've come to see one of your inm..."

"Ooh, it's heavy, isn't it? Do you have to carry it around all the time?"

Boorman snatched it back. "Listen, this is urgent. I've come to see one of your inmates. He's calling himself..."

"Residents, dear." She offered him a diazepam smile. "That's the term we like to use here. Nobody's a prisoner at Mrs. Margulis'."

He took a breath. "Right, whatever. He's calling himself Alfred Hitchcock - like the film director. Is he here?"

Edna beamed. "Oh, Mr. Hitchcock. Oh yes, he's here. One of my favourites."

"Right. And how long has he been here?"

"Ooh, a few months now."

Boorman frowned. Maybe Hitch had a stand-in or something. There were plenty of bored, under-employed Recurrents who'd happily play a role for the sake of a few hot meals and a warm place to sleep. "And he seems settled, does he? Not acting strangely?"

"Oh, happy as a lamb. He's got his crosswords and his little plot."

"Oh, very cosy. So he likes his gardening, does he?"

Edna shook her head. "No, no. He thinks he's planning a bank robbery, bless him."

"A robbery?" Boorman raised his reader, a finger poised by the communicator button. Comms had been getting a lot of disruption lately, but most of the Watch channels were still okay.

Edna wafted her hand. "Oh, all quite harmless; he's just a bit confused. He's like a lot of our residents; he finds it hard to separate his new life from the old one."

Boorman lowered his reader. He could still make this collar on his own.

"Oh, Mr. Hitchcock?" Edna opened the steam-room door and tapped on the glass. "You have a visitor."

Boorman could see only vapour and shadows inside, but that didn't matter. They were in the secure wing now. He'd had to check in his gun to pass through the detectors, but he could certainly handle one flabby, middle-aged crook. There were no other exits to the sauna so he'd got the little snot-gargler all nicely shut in.

He closed the door again and gestured to the handle. "Once I've gone in, bolt it behind me, okay, Edna?"

Edna frowned. "Bolt it, Mr. Boorman? I'm sorry, but we'd never put a lock on a sauna door."

"Wouldn't you?" That seemed odd. They always did that in the movies.

"Well, no." She looked at him strangely. "That would be very dangerous, wouldn't it? We'd never get our risk assessments passed with one of those."

"Well..." Boorman looked around. "I don't know; can't you slide a table up against it or something?"

Edna blinked. "At my age? With my arthritis?"

He frowned. "No, no. Obviously n... Hang on; I'll just call..." He tapped his reader, but it produced only an angry hiss of static. "Oh, for God's..." He looked about. "What about getting a couple of the other inm... residents to hold it shut?"

"Is that really necessary?" Edna shifted uncomfortably. "Mr. Hitchcock really is harmless, I assure you."

"Please, Ma'am, just do as I ask. I know what I'm doing."

"Oh, very well." She waved at a couple of likely-looking old gents who were herding a wayward library trolley down the hall. "Rupert; Sir Andrew; would you mind lending us a hand?"

Boorman nodded them an acknowledgement as they tottered up. "Thanks, gents. I'm going in to apprehend a suspect. There'll be some shouting but I don't want you to open this door until I give you the special knock, okay?"

The two old men exchanged wary looks but when he flashed them his badge they signalled their agreement.

"And Edna? Maybe keep everyone else away, eh? We don't want to upset anyone."

"Very well, Mr. Boorman. I'll do my best."

"Right, then. Let's do it."

Slowly, he opened the door, stepped inside and pulled it shut. Rupert and Sir Andrew shuffled up against it and gave him the thumbs-up.

He nodded, turned and called into the mist. "Right, Hitch, you sneaky old bugger; let's have you."

A voice issued from the far corner. "I'm sorry. Are you talking to me?"

He was putting on a silly accent but he had to know the game was up. Boorman began to close him in.

"Oh, I am, indeed, *Mr. Hitchcock.* And no more running, if you please; now your ass is mine."

"Who the devil are you? I'll box your impertinent ears."

"Hah! That's the spirit! I was hoping you weren't going to come quietly." Boorman moved forward until there formed the shadow of a seated man. He was keeping quite still. "Ah. Here we are. All cosy and quiet. There's a good boy - 'cause you so much as *flinch* and I swear I'll tear you a new one, my lad."

"How dare you?"

"Oh, believe me, I dare. And then when I'm done with you... Well, let's just say you'll be going down for a *very* long time."

"You sir, need to be taught some manners."

Boorman paused. Hitch was still doing the silly voice, but it had come not from the seated figure but from a little way to the left. He glanced aside and from that same direction came a metallic squeak, closely followed by the steam-blurred shape of an old, one-legged man in a wheelchair. He was tiny, but gnarly hands gripped the push bar behind him.

"Oh, wait." Boorman frowned. This couldn't be the man he'd...

"We don't take kindly to perverts," advised a deep voice from somewhere over his left shoulder. The seated man was also rising and, bloody hell, he was *big.*

"No, no. There's been a mistake." Boorman sidestepped right.

"Oh, you made a mistake alright," said the towel-clad behemoth. "And now we're going to show you why."

It was only as the men started to close in on him that Boorman remembered something important: he hadn't shown his special knock to the old guys waiting outside.

Finn emerged into a cold, very narrow space with a stone-flagged floor. To one side was a great masonry wall and to the other was a thick hanging tapestry.

Hitch was ahead of her, apparently dressed in chainmail. He put a finger to his lips. "Follow me," he whispered, "but keep quiet and don't touch the curtain."

"Where are we?" asked Finn. "What are we doing?"

"We're going to see Lonely. He's the only other guy who knows about this hide-out." Hitch flashed her a grin that cried out for heavy sedation, then turned away and began crabbing along the wall.

After only a few steps, Finn heard voices. On the other side of the heavy fabric, a man and a woman were arguing.

Finn tapped Hitch's shoulder. "Who's that?"

"Shh. Doesn't matter. The door's just here." He turned away again and disappeared left into a small alcove.

Finn shook her head but followed him. A few quiet side steps later, she found him shaking the hand of an old man. He wore a bloodstained satin gown and was clutching a large leather cushion.

"Hey, Lonely," he whispered. "You well?"

"I am." Lonely frowned at her. "But who comes here?"

"Oh, just a couple of friends."

Finn stepped forward and offered the old man a little wave.

He ignored the friendly overture. "And they are honest? You would vouch for them?"

Hitch gave a solemn nod. "You have my word as a knight."

Finn shuffled further into the alcove, making room for Locke to sidle in behind her. Beyond the tapestry, the argument was intensifying.

"This is Finn," said Hitch, "and I think you've probably met the Professor before, haven't you?"

The old man's tone became icy. "Oh. Hello, Locke."

The Professor smiled thinly. "What ho, Lonely, you old rat."

He sneered. *"What ho?"*

Locke grinned and pointed to the curtain. "That's your cue, old fruit: don't forget your lines."

Lonely looked suddenly startled. "Help, help, help!" he cried. He started beating his cushion against the tapestry.

Finn gasped, fearful that they'd just messed up a narrative. Had they been rumbled? She looked to Hitch for a clue but he just smiled and quietly opened the hidden door.

From beyond the curtain came a shout from the arguing man. "How now, a rat? Dead for a ducat, dead!"

Struck by the familiarity of the words, Finn turned back to stare at Lonely. A thin blade pierced the curtain and plunged into the cushion, which the old man held out like a matador's *muleta*.

Slumping the floor, he threw his makeshift shield to one side and directed one last contemptuous look at the Professor. "Oh, I am slain," he cried.

"Just perfectly dreadful," muttered Locke, shaking his head.

Curling his lip, Lonely flipped him the bird. It was his last act. A moment later, while the Prince and his mother argued in her chamber, his eyes momentarily flashed pale pink, then rolled back into his head.

"Come on, come on." Hitch ushered Finn through into the next room.

The Professor followed close behind, a smug smile on his face. "Such woeful delivery," he said, closing the door. "Did you hear him? *Help! Help! Help!* That wasn't the noble Danish lord; that was Andromeda chained before Cetus."

Hitch re-set the jammer on the door frame. "Yeah. I'd forgotten you two never got on."

Locke pouted. "Well, honestly, he's awful, isn't he?"

Finn was tired of playing catch-up. "That was Polonius, wasn't it? As in *Hamlet?* As in Shakespeare?"

Locke nodded. "A very poor rendering, but yes."

"And I suppose he's another Recurrent?"

"Yes, and by no means the greatest example of our kind. The man has all the poise and grace of a rutting rhinoceros. Now he's gone, he'll be straight off to ruin something else."

"Oh, right..." Finn felt a little better about that. "And I'm sensing you two have a bit of history?"

Locke shrugged and gestured to his robes. "Professional rivalry, really. Fusty old academic; fusty old duffer - we compete for a lot of the same parts."

"Hey," said Hitch, gesturing impatiently to the room. "Less talk, more awe, if you please. You're in Elsinore."

The Professor smiled and peered down at his Elizabethan dress. "Oh, but I'm *terribly* excited, dear boy. Can you not see? I've come in my finest hose."

Finn cocked her head. It wasn't Elsinore as she'd ever imagined it. Granted, the hall before her was very grand, built with elaborately carved stone arches and a wooden gallery above, but a keen-eyed historian might have adjudged the pool table a little out of place. A real stickler might also have taken issue with the office desk and the swivel chair, the long racks of vinyl records, and the great congregation of beer bottles that gathered round the foot of an unmade divan bed.

She nodded at the brightly coloured duvet cover. "Thomas the Tank Engine. Nice."

Hitch's brow folded into ridges. "Yeah, that's... I'm looking after that for someone."

Finn nodded. "Sure."

"And we're quite secure, here, are we?" asked Locke.

Hitch looked appraisingly round the chamber. "Yeah. I think the screenwriter imagined a scene here and then decided against it. It's never been used."

"Screenwriter?" Finn was fairly sure that *Hamlet* had been written a little before the age of cinema.

Hitch shrugged. "Sorry - didn't I say? It's an adaptation - a bit less attention-grabbing than the original."

"Oh." Finn wasn't too disappointed. After all, she was still standing in Elsinore castle; that was a whole world better than the school trip to Stratford.

Locke ambled off into the jumble of crates and suitcases. "So what have we got that might help us slip little Johnny a missive?"

Hitch indicated a desk. "There are some bits and pieces over there. Oh, and there's some space-tech stuff under the stairs in the corner. Can I leave you to crack on?"

Locke made for the desk. "Absolutely. You know me: always happy to stick my nose in someone else's drawers."

"Excellent."

"And what are we doing?" asked Finn.

"We're going to pick up my most valuable stuff," said Hitch, placing both hands against a large wooden box. "Like you said, if they got to my last place, they could find this one, too."

Finn helped him push. The crate slid back to reveal a trap door and, beneath it, a wooden stairway. Hitch bustled down. She was half way after him when he turned on a light. Where he was getting the electricity from was anyone's guess.

"Woah." Finn looked down into a tall, vaulted chamber that made Aladdin's cave look like the last hour at a car boot sale. Some of the chests had obviously been lifted straight from a pirate adventure; they were overflowing with the obligatory collection of doubloons, necklaces, jewels, and goblets. But alongside them were glowing swords, huge gemstones, and some of the most impressive statuary Finn had ever seen - including a Venus de Milo that still had both her arms.

Hitch sniffed. "Funny what you pick up on your travels, isn't it?"

Finn pointed at the topmost painting on a stack of gilded frames. "Is that the Mona Lisa?"

"Mm," said Hitch. "I've got four - every one an original."

Finn decided not to ask. Instead, she ventured happily into the maze of contraband. Each new turn offered up a surprise.

"From the Royal Library of Alexandria," advised Hitch when she paused by a large plastic tub filled with scrolls.

"And what's through there?" She eyed a heavy curtain.

"Wine collection. Plus a few nice dwarvish ales."

"This is amazing." She began to drift towards the far corner. "It must be worth an absolute..."

"Oh, wait - don't..."

"Oh." Finn stopped as she found herself gazing at what had to the multiverse's most exotic collection of pornography, all rendered in print, sculpture, engraving, and hologram. It was feisty stuff; she wasn't even sure what she was looking at in some cases - although that was almost certainly for the best.

"That's not mine," said Hitch. "Some of this stuff... It was there when I got here."

"Right." Finn quickly backtracked. "So what *are* we here for?"

"Oh, none of this." Hitch had started buckling a pair of bandoliers across his chest. The loops in them were huge, far too big to take shotgun cartridges; Finn was suddenly struck by a vision of him stepping out to do battle with some improbable grenade launcher.

She had to ask. "What are *those* for?"

"Patience." After a moment's fussing, he approached a bare section of wall, pulled on a rusting sconce, and put his shoulder to the stone. A metre-wide section of wall pivoted back on a greased rail.

"There's more?" Finn braced herself for some sort of mini-arsenal.

"Come in quick." Hitch beckoned. "Don't let the moisture in."

A light blinked on and revealed what looked like a wine cellar, except that in place of bottles, the racks were filled with cardboard boxes and stacks of gaudily painted tins.

"My life savings," sighed Hitch. In the cold air, his breath was a visible cloud of reverence.

"Biscuits?" Finn looked at him. "Seriously? What is it with you and biscuits?"

Hitch didn't seem quite able to tear his gaze away. "The most valued currency in all the worlds."

"Not - oh, I don't know - *money*, maybe? Gems? Gold bars?"

Hitch shook his head. "Nah. The worlds are swimming in those. I mean, think about it: one sci-fi author writes a story about a planet made entirely of diamond and the market's instantly saturated. And how many stories d'you think have been written about treasure and gold bullion? There's no shortage of any of that stuff, believe me."

"Yeah, but biscuits..." Finn watched him slipping carefully selected packets into his bandoliers. "Why not medicines or something?"

"Because these don't change the narrative." He gave her quite the maddest grin. "Bring a load of antibiotics into a world that doesn't have them and you'll change its history forever. Same goes for contraceptives, inoculations, and all that. Trust me, I've thought long and hard about this stuff. Biscuits don't change things and they don't leave any evidence."

"But they're not even rare. Anyone can make biscuits."

Hitch shook his head and started filling a shoulder bag. "Not like these. Have you ever had a biscuit from a children's story?"

Finn had to admit she hadn't.

"Very few people have. But once tasted..." Hitch grinned again and rubbed his hands.

"Oh, I see," said Finn. "You're basically a pusher."

Hitch turned up his nose. "Well, just for that, you don't get to try one."

Deep in the mustiest corner of Evidence Vault Eight, which was to say about as far from a career advancement opportunity as it was possible for a watchman to stand, two figures inspected a rack of metal shelves.

"Eww," said Parker. At arm's length, he held a clear plastic wallet full of photographic prints. According to the handwritten tag, they'd been picked up during a raid on a gang of off-world blackmailers. The photos themselves needed no explanation. They made it buttock-clenchingly apparent that the victim - the host of a popular prime-time radio show - had sleazed his way into some sort of honey trap. The silver-haired celeb was clearly visible in most of them - or bits of him were, at any rate; great orange hummocks of fake-tanned flesh rising up amongst all the leather straps and blancmange.

"Notice anything funny?" Lambert ran her fingers through her hair and sent him a worried look.

"You mean the school tie wrapped round the old...?"

"Not the goddamn photos. Put those down." Lambert gestured to the rest of the shelf. "Anything else?"

Parker craned his neck to double-check the top shelf. "There's nothing else here."

Parker chewed the inside of her cheek. "Mm. That's what I thought."

"I don't get..."

"The guns, you moron."

Parker hadn't checked the vault for weeks. He probably should have done - it was technically an obligation under Internal Security protocol - but things had got so stupidly busy that nobody bothered any more. Lambert was next up in the chain of command and since she was usually pretty cool, he decided to come clean. "What guns?"

Lambert sighed and took a dusty paper from the shelf. "Well, let's see, shall we? Thirty-two semi-automatic pistols, three revolvers, six assault rifles, eight submachine guns, eleven shotguns, two RPGs and a surface-to-air missile."

"Woah. That is a lot of guns, isn't it?" Parker looked again at the empty shelving. "Still... a lot of the Pursuit teams are off-world at the moment - more than I've ever seen. You think maybe they've taken off with them?"

Lambert gave him a deadpan look. "You think we've run short of pistols so we've started handing out grenade launchers?"

"Well no, obviously... but so many IS and Pursuit teams have been sent away, I thought maybe..."

Silencing him with a shake of her head, she took a step back and cast a furtive eye into the corridor. "You know *why* I came to check?"

Parker shrugged.

"I got a call from DiStephano. He said he'd been down to their EVs and they were missing three crates of plasma rifles. He asked me if we'd lost anything, too."

"Three cr... *Jeez*. When d'you guess they were taken?"

"Within the last hour." Lambert sniffed and rolled up her sleeve. With a tap on her reader, she brought up a grainy screen-grab from a Watch security camera. Two men: one with an eye patch, the other with a spider-web tattooed across his face. "There you go. Recognise either of them?"

Parker shook his head. "Who are they?"

"The guy with the patch, that's Viktor. A bomber; a murderer. Exiled about eight years back. Haven't got a match for the other one yet."

"They're *exiles?*" Parker felt his scalp crawl. "They escaped? And they've been here?"

She nodded. "Must have. I came here, found this lot gone and then called DiStephano straight back."

"And? What did he say?"

She shrugged. "He didn't. He's vanished. His comms are down and no one's seen him since we spoke. Seems he went off to report it and then..."

"Then what?"

"Well, that's the thing: I don't know." She flashed him a dark look. "But one thing I do know: this isn't something that's going to be good for anyone's career. I plan to make myself very busy somewhere else. I suggest you do, too."

Finn returned up the stairs to find Locke gazing intently into a large wooden chest. "What you looking for?" she asked.

The Professor frowned. "An excellent question, my dear. I'm trying to remember."

"Trouble?" Hitch set down a heavy shoulder bag.

Locke rubbed his temples. "A head full of memories is all very well, but it's locating the little blighters that's so often the challenge."

Hitch peered over the edge of the chest. "What d'you need?"

"Something to boost a signal; someone's jamming communications with New Tybet."

"Ah... nuts." Hitch slumped. "So you were right. Someone's planning something nasty."

"I'm afraid it's beyond doubt."

Hitch shook his head. "Hardship and peril. I said so right from the start."

Abandoning his hunt, Locke smiled. "There is some useful news, though."

"Yeah?"

"Yes." The Professor inclined his head towards a shallow silver bowl on Hitch's desk. "In lieu of anything more reliable, I had to resort to hydromancy. It's horribly limited but it's the only channel that hasn't been completely shut down."

Finn glanced at the bowl. "And? Did you manage to warn Johnny?"

Locke shook his head. "I can't access any communications networks. I've only been able to access parts of my own database. But from there, I've been able to interrogate some gate control records and one or two news channels."

Hitch turned and peered into the bowl. "So what do we know?"

"Well, a couple of points of note: firstly, we can be sure the saboteur wasn't Hector."

"Can we?"

"Yes, because he's gone missing as well. Signs of a struggle in his office, apparently."

Hitch pulled a face. "Winchester *and* Hector. Wow. And the other thing?"

Locke smiled. "Ah, well that's even more interesting."

Hitch narrowed his eyes. "Interesting good, or interesting bad?"

The Professor waggled his head. "A little of both. How do you feel about making the city's *most wanted* list? Apparently, you're both a saboteur and a kidnapper."

"A saboteur and a kidnapper." Hitch blinked, paced away, then stopped. "Right. Okay. So just a small point: who am I supposed to have kidnapped?"

Locke pursed his lips. "My name was mentioned."

"Ah. And remind me: why is this *interesting* as opposed to, say, appallingly bad and unfair?"

Locke shrugged. "Because it substantially narrows the number of people that the real saboteur could be. It takes top level authority to issue a kill notice, especially when at least some in the Watch must know you to be innocent."

Hitch's face turned a colour most commonly associated with kitchen appliances. "*Kill notice?* As in..." His eyes and eyebrows did unconnected things. "As in... *Kill notice?*"

"I'm afraid so."

"But..."

Finn eyed the hall's many doors. "So what now? How safe are we here?"

Locke sent Hitch a meaningful look. "It's a very good question. What do you think?"

"Not safe enough," said Hitch. "Mobilise enough watchmen and you can track anyone down."

Finn nodded. "Okay. So we've got to give them a reason to stop looking, haven't we? Show people that we haven't been abducted."

"Well that's fine," said Hitch, "but how? There isn't a transmitter within a million miles of New Tybet that hasn't been jammed."

Locke narrowed his eyes. "Then we must look further afield. Then it merely becomes a matter of signal strength. We can do something about that."

"We can?"

"Of course we can. But we're going to need a bigger gate."

23. Discovery

"Mr. Duggan, please. I really do think..." Standing by the thick, soundproofed windows of the corner office, Cariola looked anxiously down at the peculiar scene playing out in the plaza below. She tried again to catch the watchman's attention but her exertions attracted no more notice than a housefly clearing its throat.

"Try that other channel," he said, craning over John Forster's shoulder. "The one you got before with that sort of flashing thing..."

"No, it's gone." The younger man leaned closer to the screen, his hands in his hair.

"Well, what about..."

"Look, this isn't the way," said Johnny. "I've got it scanning automatically; if there's anything there, it'll find it much quicker than we ever will."

"Well we've got to try," said Duggan. "You heard what Boorman said. They're out to *kill* him. I mean, don't get me wrong: I don't like the little scrote any more than I like syphilis, but it was my job to protect him. I'm not having that shin-kissing slimeball from Pursuit coming in and carting him off like a trophy."

"No, sure," said Johnny, "but like I said, this isn't the way. Everything's jammed. That can only be deliberate. We've got to think our way around this."

Cariola tried again. "Mr. Duggan. Will you please just come here and take a look at...?"

She was silenced by a tremor in the building. Fire alarms sounded on the lower levels.

Duggan's eyes flashed. "What is it *now*?"

Cariola met his gaze, though she felt herself reddening. "Um. I can see ogres running around the plaza with machine guns."

Duggan's shoulders slumped. He clearly believed none of it, but he began at least to thread his way towards her through the tangled web of electronics. "I swear, if this is just some protestor in a big jumper..."

"If he's a protestor, Mr. Duggan, then he's a very angry one. He just threw a grenade at the main doors."

Duggan stopped. "That was a grenade?"

Cariola nodded and turned again to the window. Her view was partly obscured by the outcropping balcony but she could certainly make out a squad of variously armed humanoids rushing towards the foot of the E&P *Research and Publishing Centre*. Neither research nor publishing looked to be chief amongst their interests.

Further away, in the direction of Gate Control, smoke was beginning to rise from a number of buildings. Around the base of the great dome itself, flashes that might have been gunfire flecked the shadows beneath the trees.

Duggan had seen it too. He jabbed aggressively at his reader. "Why the hell is none of this on the news?"

Without turning his head, Johnny grabbed a remote control and pointed it at a monitor high on the wall. An instant later, the tangerine tan of Larry Spangles was glowing back at them from behind a news desk. His customarily fluorescent grin was no more than a grim slit, half hidden behind a handful of handwritten notes.

"I can't hear him," said Duggan. "Turn it up."

"... following the actions of the protestors and the off-world refugees," said the lurid host. *"Official sources confirm that no one has been hurt, but citizens are advised to remain indoors until..."*

"Is that a gun?" Cariola pointed to the edge of the screen, where a dark rod-like object intruded periodically into shot.

Duggan approached the monitor more closely, raising himself on tiptoes to get a better look. "It bloody is!" he said. "Someone's got a gun on him."

"So what in heaven's name is going on?" said Cariola, satisfied that her concerns were at last being taken with the seriousness they deserved.

"I have absol..."

"A signal!" shouted Johnny, still staring at his screen. "Someone's trying to..."

"...should probably do it," said the distant voice of Professor Locke.

A moment later, a pair of faces emerged from a dark storm of static.

"Hitch!" shouted Johnny, recognising the other. "Where are you?"

Cariola hurried over to get a better view of the screen.

"Oh, hi Johnny." Hitch glanced over his shoulder into what looked like the interior of a spacecraft. Behind him, Cathy Finn was gazing through a window. "Probably best not to say; you never know who's listening in."

Johnny adjusted the brightness on the screen. "Is that... is that *Jupiter* I can see outside?"

Hitch raised his palms. "Shh. Look, we have important news."

"My God," breathed Cathy, her eyes still fixed on something in the darkness. "It really is full of stars."

"The point is," said Locke, "you're in danger. We think New Tybet might be under threat of attack."

"It might be happening already," agreed Johnny. "We've got ogres running about downstairs and the comms are all jammed - even the Watch channels."

"And half the Watch has been sent off-world," said Duggan. "Some of them to hunt you lot down."

"Well, look," said Locke, "the first thing to do is to get word to Gate Control and whoever's still in command; tell them to lock down the inbound gates. We think someone's planning to take over the..."

From somewhere beyond the office door came a splintering crash; the sort of sound that hinted at burly intruders and fiercely contested insurance claims.

"What's happening?" Duggan drew his firearm and moved towards the door.

"Say again?" said Locke.

Johnny rose anxiously from his seat. "Someone's breaking in."

"Then get yourselves out," urged Locke. "Get out immediately. We need you operational. Go anywhere you like - just don't let them take you. We'll find a way to rendezv..."

The screen flickered as another great crash sounded nearby. Cariola ducked. These were meant to be secure offices, but then the building's security specifications probably hadn't been developed with ogres and explosives in mind. It certainly sounded as though the architecture was fighting a losing battle.

"You two," barked Duggan. "With me." He pointed to an internal door and began tapping his reader.

Johnny followed. Cariola hurried along behind.

"Johnny, Johnny!" shouted Hitch.

"What?"

"*Mornington.* Codename *Mornington.*"

"Right. Got..."

His reply was cut short by an ear-bursting explosion that threw Cariola forward and sent chunks of ceiling sailing over her head. Tables fell, equipment shattered, health and safety posters burned. A web-work of sparking cables wrapped itself about her legs.

"Cariola!" When she looked up, Johnny was reaching for her. At the same time, Duggan was pulling him roughly back. Brawn won the battle. A moment later, the watchman bundled him through the newly conjured gate.

A pistol shot cracked and Duggan ducked for cover as a bullet buried itself in the wall by his head. "Stay low!" he shouted, reaching out. "Take my hand."

Cariola kicked against the wires entangling her ankles but succeeded only in losing a shoe. "I can't," she said. "I'm..."

"You! Stop there!" The sound wasn't human; Cariola couldn't see the speaker, hidden as he was behind a jumble of crackling equipment and overturned desks, but his voice spoke of fangs and a too-wide throat contending with unfamiliar consonants. She could also hear the wind outside; it seemed that the explosion had cost the office more than just its door.

Still crouching, Duggan raised his pistol and fired a shot towards the intruder. "Come on," he hissed, but he was too far from her to take her hand.

Cariola shook her head. "Go! I can't move."

Two more shots from the former doorway left conical craters in the wall by Duggan's still-active gate. He looked at her in desperation. They both knew he could get no closer.

"We'll come back," he said. "I promise."

Cariola nodded and watched him roll away through the gate.

"You! Stand up!" said the alien voice as the smear of gate-light winked out.

"I can't," said Cariola. "I'm stuck."

"Cariola?" The voice was Cathy's; distant, tinny and electronic but filled with concern.

A moment later, strong hands grasped her elbows and drew her to her feet. She wiped plaster dust from her eyes and found herself standing eye-to-nipple with a great grey-skinned horror.

Cathy's voice crackled from the monitor. "Leave her alone, you grisly shit!"

Slowly, the ogre turned and lifted the screen in one gnarled hand. The plastic casing creaked as its knuckles tensed.

"Put that down," said a man. "Gently, too; I would see that face."

Cariola leaned to one side, but found it difficult to peer around a creature that would make a silverback gorilla look frail. Only when her captor lifted her and sat her doll-like on a desk did she recognise the newcomer.

Max Roberts, head of security and leader of all the Watch stood bent over the desk, smiling at Cathy Finn as she glared back at him from the monitor. Beside her, Hitch had disguised himself with the aid of a paper bag and two crudely torn holes.

The Professor was off screen, but had evidently thought to reposition the camera to make their location less obvious.

"Well bravo," said Max. "A woman of rare enterprise. Might I ask of you your name?"

"You can ask," said Finn.

"I see. And you have a companion. Has he the same defiant spark?"

"Oh, he has," said Hitch, speaking gruffly beneath his mask. "And there are many of us. Here at my command, I have legions of..."

Max leaned in. "I'm sorry; is that you, Hitch? Mr. Quick, our trusty postman?"

The bag crumpled slightly.

Max smiled. "It was the bag that betrayed you. It says 'chocolate chip' at the bottom."

The bag shook in vehement denial. "I don't know what you mean."

Max found a swivel chair and sat upon it. "And might I conjecture that Professor Locke accompanies you? I would speak to him if I may."

The camera's view spun and now Locke's face filled the screen. He smiled indulgently. "Well, Max, you've surprised me. I hadn't guessed it before, but you're quite the hothead, aren't you? Every inch the thrusting young buck."

"Hello Paul." Max set his heels upon the desk. "Come back to the city, won't you? We are not men for the sweat and toil of the vulgar chase."

"Chase?" Locke produced a pantomime expression of bemusement. "Do you mean to arrest us, Max? Would you like me to assume the position?"

Max knitted his fingers across his stomach. "Let us not fence with words, Professor. I have much to do. Bring yourselves in or I shall be forced to have my men do so, and they will not be gentle."

Locke shrugged. "Shan't. You're a clever boy, Max, but you know me; I'm more than happy to play rough."

Max nodded in thought. "You helped our postman to escape, did you not?"

"I might have had a hand in his exit, yes."

"And the woman?"

Locke shrugged. "She needed an experienced escort; I was delighted to give her one."

"Hmm. So tell me, Professor, how roughly do they wish to play? As a Recurrent, you enjoy certain advantages - a certain robustness - but this one life is all they have. Bring them in and I give you my word they shall come to no harm. Fail, and their fate shall rest with you alone."

Locke cocked his head. "Why are you doing this, Max? You know this is wrong. I'd never pegged you as a ruffian; one for mindless destruction."

"Mindless?" Max gave a quiet snort. "The first defence of weak minds is to recriminate, Paul. You know that. What I do now, it will be my masterwork - a thing of virtue and of rare beauty. A reformation, if you will."

"Tush. You're talking like a fanatic, Max. You're educated enough to know where fanaticism leads: to pain, death and injustice."

Max held out his hands. "Needs must, my friend. You must have seen it yourself. There is unsoundness in the state. I mean to see it cleansed."

Locke's face grew stormy. "*Cleansed.* Listen to what you're saying, Max! For God's sake, get a hold of yourself. Listen to common sense; listen to your conscience."

Max threw back a tangle of hair and chuckled. "Yet what is conscience but superstition's dream?"

Locke began to speak but turned as Cathy placed a hand over the microphone. Her face wasn't visible but he frowned at whatever she was saying.

"What now?" said Max, angrily. "Do you weary of my conversation? Am I grown too dull?"

Locke nodded to his off-screen friend and then returned his attention to the camera. "An interesting choice of words, Max. But not exactly your own, are they?"

"*What?*" Max's transformation was startling. In an instant, he was up from his chair and grasping the sides of the monitor as if he sought to strangle it. "What do you say?"

Locke reached off to the left of the camera. "We'll be in touch, Max. In the meantime, try not to do anything too regrettable."

The screen flicked off, leaving Max staring at his reflection and a hissing swarm of static. "Find them," he said quietly. "Find out who that woman is. Focus on Hitch: use every algorithm, every wizard, every psychic in the city; use whatever you need, but track them down and bring her to me."

"Alive?" said a henchman.

Slowly, Max released the monitor. "If you can, Joshua, but don't feel unduly constrained."

"What's that you're humming?" asked Locke.

"Huh?" Finn looked up. She'd been studying Hitch as he'd conjured a succession of gates, all the time plotting further routes and choices with his reader. Besides an abiding concern over Cariola's fate, she hadn't been aware of much else.

"You were humming." Locke repeated the opening bars.

"Oh, right." She gave a sheepish grin. "*Daisy, Daisy...* My mum used to sing that to me at bedtime. Don't know why it's just popped into my head."

"I rather like it." Locke spoke seriously now, all theatricality shed. "But I was hoping we could discuss your observation about Max."

"I'm not sure what else I can tell you. He was quoting somebody; a writer - a poet maybe. I just can't remember who."

"A pity. He seemed transformed; his patterns of speech strangely mangled; a syntactic smorgasbord, if you will. A good philologist would have a field day with him. It might only be an affectation, of course, but if he's under somebody else's influence, it would be enormously helpful to know whose."

Finn pulled a face. "I'm sorry. I know the phrase rang a bell - that thing about conscience being superstition's dream - but God knows where I heard it. It just won't come back to me."

"Then we must get thee to a library."

"Or somewhere with a decent internet connection."

"Ugh. The internet." Locke shook his head. "What is this strange bond between young people and their electronics?"

Finn shrugged. "They're handy. I'm guessing you prefer proper books?"

"Naturally, but there's much less call for them these days." He rolled his eyes. "Now, it's all plastics, Wi-Fi, and wretched databases. The learned librarian is giving way to mere software. It's a dreadful state of affairs, quite alien to one such as me; certainly a far cry from my old Oxbridge days."

"Oxbridge." Finn smiled at how easily she could imagine him lounging in a punt. "I'm guessing you studied at both?"

"Studied. Taught. Thrice murdered. Even rowed on occasion." The Professor's eyes glittered. "I'll remember the nineteen-twelve race especially fondly. Trailing at Barnes Bridge, yet winning by a whisker... Tossing our cox in the Thames... Hah! Now that was an unforgettable day."

Finn glanced back at Hitch. "Well, I suppose I'm a bit of a traditionalist too - books-wise - but it's speed that matters now. A search engine's going to be a better bet."

"Ah, yes, the inexorable march of progress." Locke set a hand on Hitch's shoulder. "What say you, Mr. Postman? Can you get us somewhere a little more twenty-first century?"

Hitch kept his eyes on his little screen and wafted the interruption away. "I'm doing my best." His interview with Max had left him visibly unsettled and a succession of hasty gate-jumps hadn't done anything to improve his mood.

Conscious of the risks of pursuit, they hadn't stopped since they'd ended their transmission. Now, they were making their way down a narrow, tubular lounge in some gaudy interstellar limousine. Along both walls, long fur-draped sofas converged upon a pair of drinks cabinets framing a round door. Windows mimicking ancient portholes punctuated the curving interior, each looking out into a vast metal cavern filled with ships and eclectic engineering. There must have been a thousand vessels at dock amongst the hangar's endless shadows and gantries but, focused only on his reader and the door ahead, Hitch seemed oblivious to it all.

"What's so difficult?" asked Finn. Deciding that Locke was much more likely to produce a proper explanation, she directed the question at him.

Locke sighed. "He's trying to outsmart Max."

"He's closed half the gates down," said Hitch, his attention still fixed on his screen. "Just leaving the obvious ones that shepherd us back to Tybet."

"But I thought we could go anywhere," said Finn. "So long as there was some sort of connection between stories?"

"Yes, but it's a question of speed," said Locke. "Here, we're out in the Obscure, where there are fewer connections; fewer overlaps; fewer options. Closer to the Core, things are much more tightly packed. One can move faster on the inside lanes and Max knows that. Our challenge is to find a route back to the centre without crossing paths with anyone he's sent to find us."

Hitch nodded. "We're slower than he is but he doesn't know which way we'll go. Once he does, he'll try to come up our inside."

"Though he'd have to ask very politely, of course..." The Professor smirked, then looked suddenly aghast. "Oh, I am sorry. I do apologise; I think my old affliction returned for just a moment."

"Don't worry about it." Finn decided it was time to regain some control over her subconscious. "So let me see if I've got this. We're hiding out in a not very popular sci-fi story but we need to get ourselves back to something more mainstream. Is that about right?"

"Without going anywhere obvious," said Hitch, "and without walking into any blind alleys. Max is closing gates fast; he'll try to isolate us if he can."

"Hang on then," said Finn. "If this is sci-fi, couldn't we just enlist a bunch of superheroes to help us out? You know: get Superman or something?"

"No, no," said Hitch quietly. He continued tapping at his screen.

She frowned. "Well, why not? There must be loads of characters like that, surely? Couldn't we track down a few of them and..."

"Impossible." Hitch shook his head. He muttered something else but the only words she thought she gathered were 'copyright infringement.'

"Fundamentally," said Locke, pacing, "you're going to have to keep your options open. Somewhere with lots of doors is always a good bet. Keep your opponents guessing."

Finn frowned suspiciously. "You've started saying *you*, not *we*. What's going on?"

"Ah, well..." He winced. "I'm afraid young Johnny and his friends won't be able to sound the alarm after all, and with the city falling into such a pickle, I do think someone ought to nip back in there and see what can be done. Rescue a few captives, mobilise something of a resistance."

"You're going to leave us?" Finn reached for his hand. "To find Cariola and the others?"

"Someone needs to try."

"But... on your own?"

Locke smiled. "Oh, don't worry, my dear. I can be a cunning little creature when I need to be. I have more than a few friends in the city and I'm certainly no stranger to a tradesman's entrance."

"He'll be fine," said Hitch. "He's immortal. It's us we've got to worry about."

Locke peered over at Hitch's wrist. "And how worried ought we to be?"

Hitch sniffed. "Some very suspicious activity on at least six of the routes I've looked at. I don't know how many people he's got working for him but there must be hundreds at least. I think they're using personality-attuned prediction algorithms, too."

"What routes have you tried?" asked Locke.

"Oh, all sorts. I'm still hoping we can go from sci-fi dystopia over to fantasy dystopia; or corporate sci-fi over to corporate thrillers - they should all have plenty of tower blocks and doors. I mean, we're not short of options - there are plenty of good hubs to aim for - but it's getting there that's the problem. All the obvious routes are either closed down or they're likely set up for an ambush." He glanced up. "This is no fun at all."

"What about cartoons?" said Finn.

Hitch frowned. "I thought you were a literature buff - all about the classics."

Finn shrugged. "I can like cartoons, too."

"No." Hitch jabbed grumpily at his reader. "I don't do illustrated stuff." He made it sound like a perversion.

"Why not?"

"It's just a... Just a *thing* of mine, alright?"

"Surely it's got to be worth a look," said Finn. "Under the circumstances."

"Too dangerous." It was difficult to tell whether Hitch was arguing or sulking. "I don't know cartoons. We'd be sitting ducks."

Finn smiled. "Not with me you wouldn't."

Hitch harrumphed.

"She could be right," said Locke. "Especially since those algorithms will be attuned to your personality, not hers. And if things are closing down as fast as you say, then we haven't got much time." He set his reader and took a step towards the exit. "For which reason, I really must be away. Do what you can to catch up with wee Johnny. If all goes well, we'll rendezvous in Potter's Bar."

"Mm." As goodbyes went, Hitch's grudging nod wasn't the most effusive.

"Good luck, Paul." Finn gave the Professor a quick hug. "Take care."

"You too, my dear Ms. Finn." His smile seemed almost the last thing to vanish through the gate.

"I don't like this," said Hitch in the silence that followed. "Just so you know. From this point on, expect to hear frequent use of the phrase 'I told you so.'"

"Noted," said Finn. "But to be absolutely clear, any connection will do, will it? Between stories, I mean?"

"In theory."

"Good," said Finn, smiling. "Well, then, I think I've got a plan."

24. Fight and Flight

Cariola had been in something like this situation before. Tied to a chair and facing a sadistic monster, she wondered why her lives seemed to keep taking familiar turns.

"The name of the story or I break your arms," growled the ogre. Two oversized fangs protruded from its lower jaw. It ran them gently up her tear-wet cheeks.

"I told you," she said, recoiling from its weapons-grade halitosis. "I never knew it. I'm new to all this. It's my first week." She was ashamed of the tremor in her voice, but glad of the tears; they might yet convince her captor of her ignorance.

"Well, then, let's start with a little finger, shall we?" With an unwholesome grin, the creature glanced down at her tightly bound forearms.

"No! No." She thrust herself further back into the chair. "I'm telling you; Reception's been a mess for months. It's chaos. Nobody's had time to do anything properly. The one you need to be talking to is Joe Reed; *he* extracted her. I just read her the induction notes."

The ogre snorted. "Reed?"

"A winch. One of your people captured him - the narrative was called Resolution's Brink. Is he still alive? If he is - if you can find out - you could..."

"Shut your mouth!" A raised hand was all it took for Cariola to acquiesce. "I asked you where the woman came from. So you're going to tell me or..."

"That's enough." Max strode back into the shattered office, his second following close behind. "We have the intelligence we need."

The ogre ground his teeth, an action that nearly cost him an eye. "But I haven't..."

"And nor shall you," said Max. His attention seemed to be on something outside; something approaching from above. "There are yet battles to be won; I need soldiers, not gaolers. Get you gone."

The monster bristled. It directed one last narrow-eyed glare at Cariola and then went stomping off towards the blasted doorway.

"And you," smiled Max, turning his face to her. "Ms. Finn seemed concerned for your safety. That's interesting, isn't it?"

Cariola sniffed and shook her head. "I was her counsellor; that's all."

"Yet you claimed not to recall her tale of origin. That's also somewhat unusual, wouldn't you agree?"

"It's my first week."

"I see. Well let me kindle the spark of memory. *A Young Wolf's Cry*. Do you recall that?"

Cariola shrugged. "Perhaps. It's like I was telling your..."

Max walked slowly towards her, his arms behind his back. "And you yourself; you hail from a classic tale of man-turned-wolf, is that not so?"

She refused to meet his eye. She couldn't tell where this was leading.

"You see," said Max, "this touches upon a particular passion of mine. You know of the legends, I take it? Of the She-Wolf and the Signs she left? Of her Gatekeeper and the path to the Last Book?"

"I never paid much heed to myths."

Max squatted down before her; lifted her chin with a finger. "You would have me believe the woman is nothing more than a common evacuee? Just another unfortunate raised from a mad mire of words?"

Cariola swallowed. "I've only known her a day. You should talk to Joe Reed. *He* extracted her; he researched her; he's the one who knows her best."

Max blinked. "Joe Reed? Well, now there's a curious coincidence. I might do that very thing."

Cariola took a sharp breath. "He's alive, then? He's okay?"

"He's alive and... well, fit enough to answer some questions, certainly. You have feelings for the man, don't you?" He raised an eyebrow. "That's interesting, too."

Cariola felt her cheeks flushing; she hadn't meant to give her captors any leverage. "Don't hurt him. Don't hurt either of them."

Max marched to the window as a mini-flyer settled noisily alongside the balcony rail, its pilot waving from the open canopy. "Oh, don't worry, Cariola. No one will harm Cathy Finn. Truly, my first concern is to bring her safely to the city."

"And Joe Reed?" She couldn't help herself.

Sliding back the door, Max paused by the fractured glass. "Joshua will ask you some further questions. For so long as you are honest with him, you may be sure of Mr. Reed's wellbeing."

"But how will I know? How can I be sure you'll...?" Cariola cut short her own question. Max had already stepped aboard the flyer. A moment later, it dipped its nose and slid away into the air.

"Well?" said Finn. "How was that?"

Standing in the drawing room of a stately home, back in what looked and felt much more like a realer world, Finn was feeling rather pleased with herself. She knew she'd impressed Hitch with her encyclopaedic knowledge of the world of animation; her ability to suggest appropriate episodes with barely a pause to think. He wasn't admitting it, but there was no doubting they'd made a fast and efficient team. In quick succession, they'd passed from a NASA space shuttle to Alcatraz, then on via a performing arts camp and a haunted hotel to wind up eventually at the Burns mansion. From there, it had been an easy step to a more literary mansion of Hitch's own choosing.

"That," said Hitch, looking at his hands, "was hateful. My skin went yellow. What was that about?"

Finn smiled. "It's how they draw people. But we didn't get caught, did we? Admit it: it was a good way of getting about."

Rather than concede the point, Hitch pretended to be preoccupied with something on his reader. "The writers kept themselves busy; I'll give them that."

Deciding this was probably as much of an acknowledgement as she'd ever wring from him, she checked her phone. "So where next? We still need an internet connection."

Hitch shook his head. "All the gates in that direction looked closed or trapped. We'll have to do it the old fashioned way."

Finn frowned a question at him.

"You know..." He tapped a new destination into his reader. "A library."

"That'll be an awful lot slower."

Hitch nodded. "True, but it's sometimes easier to read stuff if people aren't shooting at you."

Again, her wrist gave a little buzz as her companion spread a new gate across a pair of polished oak doors. She glanced at him. "Any clues on where we're headed?"

"Wartime England. The Prof said he thought Max might have been here a couple of times."

"Max?"

"Don't worry; that was months ago." Hitch patted his biscuit bandoliers. "That said... if you see any kids about, let me do the talking."

The gate transported them not to a library as such, but rather a connected series of domestic rooms whose walls were lined with books, many of them clearly very ancient. The rooms, with their high ceilings, great cast iron radiators and ornate plaster coving, seemed to be part of some grand country house. Even accounting for the silence of these first time-stopped seconds, the place had an air of emptiness and age.

"Looks clear," said Hitch. "I'll check the landing; you check that door."

Finn crept to the entrance of an almost identical chamber. Quietly, she called back. "How many of these rooms are there?"

"I forget. Four, I think. They loop back to the landing."

Pressing on, scanning the corners and shadows of the room, Finn found she was getting accustomed to these intra-diegetic leaps. When the narrative re-started and the air suddenly filled with the sound of rain lashing against glass, she didn't jump at all. Blithely, she continued her search and advanced to the next door.

Reaching the last of the reading rooms, she discovered two things. Firstly, Hitch was right about the layout. She stepped into it just as he appeared in the doorway to her left. Beyond him she could see a polished wooden balustrade and the gloom of an unlit stairwell.

The other discovery was a simply dressed, middle-aged woman who leapt from her chair, recoiling from Finn as though she were an ogre with an assault rifle.

"W..." she began, pointing an accusing finger.

"Hey, hey... Ivy," said Hitch, spreading out his arms. "It's just me. Just me and a friend."

Ivy whirled, squinting suspicion and annoyance at him. "You. I might've known. What the 'ell are you doin' 'ere? You lot treat this place like it's some sort of..."

Hitch held up a hand. "Now come on, Ivy; we're old friends, you and me. Don't be like that."

"Friends?" Ivy set her hands on her hips. "I'm no more to you than a housekeeper's dogsbody. I should run and tell the master o' the house at once."

Hitch produced a packet of biscuits from under his coat. "You're a friend, Ivy. A dear, dear friend. Why else would I have brought you these?"

The servant woman eyed the packet with a curious expression. "What are these, then? They'll 'ave to be good, considerin' the trouble you give me."

"Good?" Hitch feigned deep offence. "My dear lady, they're the finest in all the worlds."

"Oh yeah?" Ivy looked unconvinced. "Are they Blyton?"

Hitch waggled his head. "Blytonesque."

"Give 'em 'ere." She held out a hand and Hitch obliged. Within seconds of the exchange, she was rolling her eyes and making sounds that wouldn't have sounded out of place in an adult video.

"Friends?" smiled Hitch.

"Uh huh," agreed Ivy though a mouthful of crumbs.

Finn cleared her throat. "Um. What did you mean, *you lot?* Has someone else been here?"

"A watchman," said Ivy. "Big mop of hair 'e 'ad. Called 'imself... oh, now what was it?"

"Max?" offered Hitch.

"No. Something a bit fancy..." She took another bite from her biscuit. "Silas. That was the name."

Finn and Hitch traded dubious looks.

"D'you know what he came for?" asked Finn.

"I know 'e made a mess." She gestured for the others to follow her into the next room. "Left it in a right tip. And him a watchman, too; you'd think 'e'd know better than to go messin' up other people's narratives."

"Ivy's another Recurrent," whispered Hitch as they circled behind a small desk and a studded leather chaise longue.

"Left a big stack of these books piled up, 'e did." Ivy gestured at the shelf. "Didn't apologise, either; just said 'e was doin' important research and left me to clear it all up."

Finn withdrew an old leather-bound tome. "These books?"

"That's right. An' some from that shelf above."

"Coleridge and Southey," said Finn, opening the first. *"The Fall of Robespierre.* I think I read that once; maybe that's where..."

"Shh." Hitch glanced towards the door. "Someone's coming. Ivy - go see who it is, would you?"

"Hah!" Ivy looked to Finn for sympathy. "That's a fine way to treat a friend, isn't it? 'Go see who it is, Ivy. Run and fetch, Ivy.'"

"Please, Ivy." Hitch ducked behind the sofa and tugged Finn's sleeve, urging her down. "We don't want to cause you any trouble."

"Cuh, I don't know." Ivy sighed and shuffled away. "Supposed to be a classic, this is. But you lot treat it like it's no more than a railway platform."

"What's going on?" whispered Finn as she settled beside Hitch.

"Probably just the kids. Let's listen."

After a moment, Ivy produced a startled squeak, then came backing into the room. "And who the 'ell are *you*?" she demanded.

Finn lay flat. Between the legs of the chaise longue, she could see two pairs of feet - one Ivy's, the other a man's.

"My name is Joshua," said the newcomer. "I'm a watchman."

"Well what do you want? You'll 'ave to be quick. We've got a scene 'ere shortly. It's pivotal."

"I seek three fugitives. Criminals of rare cunning and devilish conceit. Two men and a woman, brim-full of foulest intent. I have good intelligence that they came this way."

With eyes fixed on the dark floorboards, Hitch pulled a worried face.

"Well I ain't seen nobody," said Ivy. "If anyone's been 'ere, I ain't seen 'em."

Finn watched the man's boots step closer to Ivy's. "You have crumbs on your shawl, ma'am. Might I ask why?"

Ivy stood her ground. "Biscuits. I 'ad a couple of biscuits with me tea. Is that a crime now?"

"Perhaps not." Joshua paused and seemed to reflect a moment; then he turned and paced back into the doorway, where he stopped. "If you have business elsewhere, ma'am, then please attend to it. If you see any strangers, then please report it at once."

"Right," said Ivy in a tone that failed to register as enthusiasm. "And like I say, we've got a scene 'ere in a minute or two. You'll need to make yerself scarce, too."

"Goodbye, ma'am." Joshua's farewell was expressed more as an instruction than a pleasantry, but it produced its intended effect. With a final snort of reluctance, Ivy headed in the direction of the stairs.

"What now?" mouthed Finn.

Hitch held up a hand. "Just... wait."

Across the other side of the room, Joshua started pacing by the window. His reader made faint noises, half masked by the sound of the rain.

"Joshua," said an electronically rendered voice. *"Is that you?"*

"Aye. It is. I must speak to Silas on a matter of great import."

"He is busy."

"He will find time for this. Tell him I follow the She-Wolf's Gatekeeper and her trail is yet warm."

"One moment."

Finn caught Hitch's eye. "Gatekeeper? Does he mean me?"

Hitch frowned and looked away, which didn't help very much at all.

"Joshua, my friend." The voice from the reader was unmistakably Max's.

"Silas. I have found her trail. She may yet be within these walls."

"Then contain her; how many men have you?"

"One man of the Watch. No more."

"Then be vigilant and wait but a moment. You shall have all the reinforcements you need."

"Thank you. I await their arrival."

Joshua's reader emitted a short tone as the transmission ended.

"We've no time," whispered Finn. "There'll be more of them coming. We've got to do something now."

Hitch shook his head. "Like what? He'll have a gun."

"Your nuts," said Finn, opening a hand. "Gimme."

Bravely resisting the opportunity to capitalise on a cheap pun, Hitch scowled and reached into a pocket. "What for? What you doing?"

Finn mimed throwing a nut into the next room. "A distraction," she whispered. "We throw one in there, he turns around and we run for the other door."

Hitch's eyes blazed. "This is no time to start going all protagonist on me. That's a ridiculous plan. It'll get us both killed. Wait..." He peered around the edge of the sofa as Joshua stepped back into the doorway. "He's moving."

Joshua's reader chimed again. "Mr. Boorman," he said, "please join me in the reading room. Support is on the way."

"Boorman." Hitch looked even gloomier. "Should've guessed that charmless old rag-weasel would show up."

"Okay then, look." Finn pointed to a long wooden pole-hook leaning against the bookcase. "I'll get his attention, then you creep up behind him with that and..."

Hitch looked indignant. "And what? I'm not going to fight him. I'd very obviously lose. What would be the point of that?"

Finn felt her own fists balling. "Reed would have fought him."

"Oh please. Reed's an action hero. For people like that, fighting's just another way of showing off."

"Well, we've got to do something."

"I don't get into fights. I made my mum a solemn promise."

"Great. So what do you suggest?" Finn peeped over the chaise longue. Joshua hadn't gone far, but he still had his back to her.

Hitch glanced nervously at the other door and shifted his position. "I don't know, but I'm..." As he rolled, there came an ominous sound; the sound of expensive biscuits crumbling under his chest.

Spinning in the doorway, Joshua caught Finn's eye. She was reminded suddenly of that moment in the coffee shop when she'd seen the killer on the pavement. This time, however, there was no interposing glass; no van driver pulling at the other's arm.

"Run!" shouted Finn, scrambling towards the other door.

"Aaaaagh!" Hitch rose and ran at Joshua with his improvised pole-hook spear.

"Agh!" agreed Finn, skidding to a halt as a battered-looking Boorman appeared in the door ahead. She stopped, turned and saw Joshua deflect the weapon with an easy swipe of his forearm. He followed it with a fierce punch to the side of Hitch's jaw.

Hitch stopped, blinked twice and then turned slowly to send her an accusing look. "You see," he said, "this is precisely why..." He stopped there. His knees gave way and he slumped chin-first onto the sofa.

"Miss Finn," said Joshua, straightening his sleeve. "A pleasure to meet the famous Gatekeeper at last."

"What are you talking about?" said Finn, conscious that Joshua now had reinforcements. Behind him stood another burly watchman sporting a rather clichéd ensemble of raincoat and broad-brimmed hat. If escape was now out of the question, then she planned at least to learn something from her captors.

"Oh come," smiled Joshua. "Pray, let us not..."

Rather to everyone's surprise, not least Joshua's own, he ended his prayer there. Chiefly, this was because the watchman behind him had just clubbed him over the head with the butt of his pistol. With a quizzical expression, Joshua fell forward to join Hitch in the Land of Nod.

"Drop it, skid-mark!" The raincoated watchman now levelled his firearm at Boorman, who dropped his own weapon and raised his hands with an expression of disbelief.

"Duggan, are you crazy?"

"Duggan?" Finn peered into the shadows of the hat. "My God. How did you...?"

"Time for that later." Duggan kept his weapon trained on the other. "Boorman, I don't like you; I never have. You're a brown-nosing bum-rag with all the charm of a tapeworm, but I need back-up and I need you to listen."

"Listen to *you*?" Boorman sneered. "You've just pissed your career away. Why would anyone..."

"Shut it. You're gonna listen because you've been sold a lie that's tearing the city apart." He gave a malicious smile. "And because I'll shoot you in the balls if you don't."

Boorman snorted and looked to the window.

"Listen. Max has taken control of the city; he's brought in an army of off-world thugs and he's declared martial law."

"Like hell he has."

"This is one of his men. You ever seen him before?" Duggan rolled Joshua over with his foot, then tossed a pair of handcuffs to Finn. "Cuff him, sweetheart. I'm going to want to ask this crud muppet some questions later."

Bristling at the 'sweetheart' but more than happy to neutralise the worrisome Joshua, Finn knelt on his back and manacled his wrists. She took his reader for good measure.

"It's the new immigrants; they're the ones behind this," said Boorman. "We got reports of organised riots and mobs storming the gates."

"It's all lies," said Duggan. "Max made it up. He's been jamming comms and closing the gates so we can't get back to stop him from taking control. Why else d'you think he sent so many of us away? Internal Security was down to a quarter strength when the attack came."

Boorman shook his head. "Bullshit."

"Look at your reader, man. The gates are shutting down all over."

"To stop the immigrants," repeated Boorman. "They've got themselves organised."

"Oh, for God's sake..." Duggan glanced at Finn. "Can you wake Frog-face? We've got to get moving."

She shook Hitch's shoulder, but succeeded only in eliciting a drowsy groan.

"I can't carry both of them," said Duggan. Kneeling beside Joshua, he kept his pistol trained on his fellow watchman. "You're going to have to do something."

"Hitch," said Finn. She shook him more forcefully, then ventured a gentle slap.

"If I agree to get up," said Hitch, his eyes still closed, "will everyone promise to stop hitting me?"

"Stop wasting time." Duggan hauled Joshua to an upright position. "Help me move him; we've got to go."

Hitch sat up. "I've just been very heroic and badly beaten. I'm in no shape to start carrying people."

"You," said Duggan, waggling his weapon at Boorman. "You're so keen on your new governor; you help carry him, too."

Cursing quietly, Boorman crossed the room and put his head under his boss's arm. Together, he and Hitch took the man's weight and preceded Duggan through the door.

Following on behind, Finn didn't see whatever it was that made the others shout, but the fact that they dropped Joshua, turned and ran back towards her didn't augur very well. A moment later, a colossal spear buried itself in the side of a bookshelf just beside Boorman's head.

"Run!" suggested Boorman, a sudden convert to Duggan's cause.

Finn didn't wait. Now leading the little group, she sped through to the next reading room and across to the left hand door just as Boorman let out a pained yell. Glancing aside, she saw what looked like the back end of a crossbow bolt protruding from his arm.

"Out, out, out!" shouted Duggan.

Out was very much where Finn intended to be. An instant later, she was tearing along the landing and heading for another door.

"Good thinking," panted Hitch from somewhere behind.

Finn wasn't sure that thinking had played much of a part in her choice, but she barged through anyway and darted immediately left, allowing the others to follow.

"It's empty!" said Boorman, bundling in behind. "No bloody doors!"

He was right. The room was bare and unfurnished save for a large mirrored wardrobe. However, as her three companions slammed the door and pressed themselves hard against it, she had an idea. She still had Joshua's reader and, if she was right, a fair idea of how to use it. She ran to the wardrobe, flung open the doors and stabbed quickly at the keypad.

As she did, the door to the landing gave a tremendous crunch. It sounded as though a small family saloon had just driven into it.

"D'you know what you're doing?" Hitch and the others winced with the effort of keeping the door closed.

In answer, Finn hit the activation button. A familiar sheen appeared across the wardrobe. A second later, her heart racing, she dived through.

25. Potter's Bar

"Where are we?" demanded Duggan. They'd stepped into a large, empty, unlit bedroom in the middle of the night.

Finn looked down at Joshua's reader. "One of the Austen novels, I think; I didn't know where we were before. I just went for one with another country house setting."

Duggan nodded. "It'll do. We won't be staying."

"You didn't know where we were?" Hitch sounded disappointed.

Finn shrugged. "No - you just said it was something in wartime Britain. That could have been anything."

"So why did you go straight for the wardrobe?"

"We were boxed in; that was all there was in the..." Finn paused. It was something about the way he'd said 'wardrobe'. She peered at him as a thought struck her. "Wait. *The* wardrobe? The Wardrobe? As in lions and...?"

Hitch nodded. "That's why I thought you were being clever. A big magical wardrobe like that; the interference will have played havoc with anyone who tried to follow us. Chances are they won't be able to track our gate at all - if they go in, they'll just come out on the other side."

"Hang on." In the darkness, Duggan's frown somehow made itself audible. "You're saying we've just sent a murderous dwarf and a bloody great minotaur into another narrative?"

"Well..." Hitch waved a dismissal. "Maybe they had creatures like that there already."

Duggan stepped closer. "Now listen to me, Toad-boy: we don't go around sending mythical monsters into Unaware worlds. I'm a watchman, for God's sake."

Hitch shrugged. "No harm done. I mean, you know the story; maybe that's how they got there in the first place. Who's to say?"

"That was a *minotaur?"* Finn could stay silent no longer. "Seriously? That was what all the noise was about?"

Hitch nodded. "You didn't see it?"

"No." She felt strangely disappointed by that. Another missed photo opportunity.

"Well anyway," said Duggan, "we know one thing: Max is running low on people he can trust. Looks like he's having to raid the Subways for extra muscle."

"Oi!" said Boorman. "Case you lot hadn't noticed, I've got a bloody great arrow sticking out my arm. Hurts like a bitch. Are we just going to sit here chatting or...?"

"Alright, alright." Duggan produced a small torch and shone it at him. "Bloody hell, Boorman; you're a mess, aren't you? Arm all shot up and... what happened to your face?"

Boorman's nose was crossed by a narrow plaster and one eye was black. The other cast an accusing glance at Hitch. "Someone set me up. I went to see a guy called Hitchcock but it turns out it was the wrong bloke. That ring any bells with you, Postman?"

"Um..." Hitch edged back into the shadows.

"Well anyway," said Duggan, "we've got to get you to a hospital. Question is, where? Where's safe?"

"How did you find us in the first place?" said Finn.

Duggan rubbed his chin. "That Forster boy. Clever little bugger. Said if we can't track you, why not track Joshua instead? Figured he'd lead us to you eventually."

"A bright lad," agreed Hitch, "but that's a point; we need to trash Joshua's reader. Wardrobes or no, that's not a safe thing to have around."

Finn handed it over. It felt like losing a lifeline to home but she couldn't really argue the sense of it. With a few deft movements, Hitch removed what looked like a battery and a memory chip.

"I'll take those." Duggan snatched them away. "I'm not having you raffling them off later."

"So *anyway*..." said Boorman, "about this bleedin' arrow?"

Hitch turned to the window with a thoughtful smile. "I can't think of anywhere completely safe but you know what?"

"Amaze me," said Duggan.

"I think we should go straight back to the city."

Waiting for his call to connect, Silas sat at his desk, eyes scanning the workers as they repositioned the gantries around the Core. Despite the necessity of appointing replacement labour, good progress had been made in the great chamber.

His screen brightened to reveal the face of a young officer of the Watch. She sat erect, papers readied in her hands.

"Sir?"

"You were going to seal things up, Kincaid. How are you getting on?"

"Almost finished, sir. Transport's down and the last of the Parallels are being shut off now. If the insurgents have gone into hiding, they'll have a hard time regrouping."

"Good work. Once that's done, I want you and your teams to pull back to Gate Control. You understand? We need a tight cordon on the perimeter. Guards on every entrance. I want to keep GC safe against all threats - infiltration and surprise attacks."

"Sir. Give us five more minutes and we should be done here."

"Good. GC out."

Silas looked across at the conference table, at the four holographic ghosts that sat thereabout. Two starship commanders, a nameless wizard and, strangest of them all, an avatar of an AI consciousness he'd plucked from a burning station. A motherless creation of artifice, a thing born of cold wires and circuitry, it sat silent, still and devoid of human physiognomy. A faceless doll, it betrayed nothing of its inscrutable puppeteer.

The AI's caution was understandable. All owed their lives or liberty to him; each had pledged him their loyalty; yet forging an equivalent trust between them would be a challenge. For the now, they sat, a wary company of strangers.

"Forgive the inelegance of my language," he began, gesturing at his screens. "We live in an inelegant age."

"Immaterial," said the avatar, though lips and tongue were absent. "Proceed."

"Very well." Silas rose from his desk. He'd dispute that assertion: immaterial. Any inhabitant of an Aware world knew that language was a defining characteristic; a mark of one's origins; something one bore like the colour of one's eyes or skin. Yet these naive, newly-penned creations knew nothing of authors and narratives; still believed in the immutable reality of their freshly conjured worlds. That they shared a common tongue and style was a sure sign of their common origin - that all had issued from the same quill - but that was a secret that must be kept a little longer.

He drew out a chair. "We are gathered because we are each assailed by frightful forces. We know what it is to suffer the attentions of fiends and tyrants. Is that not so?"

Three holographic heads nodded. One did not.

"A presumption," intoned the avatar. "We can only know what forces have assailed us individually; we cannot..."

"No, no. Quite so." Silas resolved that henceforth, in the face of such determined pedantry, he would excise all rhetoric from his address. "But none here would doubt we have suffered; that our foes have inflicted needless deaths; that as individual forces, we have struggled to prevent abhorrent loss."

A silence implied assent.

"And you know already that I would see us banded together in a brave and just fellowship, compounding our efforts to strike back at those that would wield the whip."

"We do. We know this, Silas." Commander Sabatini steepled insubstantial fingers. "You came to our aid and we each vouchsafed our loyalty. Be not over-gentle in your address. Who is to be our quarry?"

Silas nodded a smile. "The man wears names like ribbons; vainglorious titles bought with the blood of others. This is what we know of him." He directed their attention to the main monitor as he tapped at his reader, the details already cued up for display.

Data scrolled slowly up the screen, interspersed with graphs, charts and illustrations; the villain's home planet; his hilltop palace; the distinctive scar upon his brow.

"You each have a reader," said Silas. "Through them, I share with you all this intelligence and more; the full weight of evidence of his atrocities, his wilful hurt of the unfortunate. Read it, digest it, and have no doubts, my friends; this man is the most base of monsters, a devil who takes unholy delight in transforming worlds into sepulchres."

Captain Boniface shook an airy fist. "And like five hammers striking singly upon a nail, our gathered forces shall drive him swift into the dirt."

"A flawed analogy," observed the avatar. "Logically, five hammers could not..."

"No, no, but nevertheless." Silas quickly brought his battle scheme upon the screen. The AI might be invaluable in countering their enemy's digital weaponry but its companionship would all too soon become insufferable. He had not foreseen such troubles. Creation was a business fraught with complexity. With the unwitting aid of his muse and master, Silas had all but conjured the creature from empty air, yet that same delicate mechanism that gave it life also gave it quirks and powers that resisted his control. Accordingly, the AI made an imperfect ally. But that could be remedied in time.

Silas highlighted a zone at the outer edge of the villain's planetary system. "His chief defences are stationed here. Sabatini; they shall be your target."

"Aye. Understood."

Silas adjusted the view; now it showed only the home planet, ringed by concentric shells of patrol craft, mines, and drones. "Boniface, penetrating these defences falls to you, and the task of landing our ground troops here." A square patch of ground swelled to fill the screen.

"Aye."

"Remember: this is a man well used to the methods of modern war. Chemical, biological and high energy weapons - all these he will expect, but never has he encountered the forces of magic. These, together with the collapse of his communications, shall render the bulk of his defences impotent. Victory is then assured. All that is required of us is the will to work together."

"Inaccurate," said the avatar. "What is required is more than will. What is req..."

"Yes. Indeed," interjected Silas. "Any questions?"

Three holographic heads shook. One remained resolutely still. Not a one spoke.

"Good. Then all that remains is for us each to study our plan and await the opening of the gates."

"An incomplete assessment," said the avatar. "The tasks that remain..."

With a sharp stab at his reader, Silas dismissed the assembly.

Returning to his desk, he found his screen displaying a long queue of waiting calls. The fourth in line was the one he'd been awaiting.

"Joshua," he said, tapping it through. "You have good news, I trust."

"No. Regrettably not."

He frowned but kept his voice level. "Explain."

"We had her - Boorman and myself - but we were attacked; taken by surprise. I could not inform you until I had secured a new reader."

"An attack?"

"From behind. I know not how many aided her. Now Boorman is disappeared, as are the first of the reinforcements you sent to aid me. All are vanished quite."

"Where did she go?"

"She's a demon, Silas; a cunning..."

"You will remember to call me by my proper name when using these channels, Joshua, if you please."

"Forgive me... Max, but the woman; she left no trail at all. I would swear she is more than she seems."

"We know her to be the Gatekeeper, Joshua. She is without any doubt a great deal more than she seems. That is why it must be our utmost priority to bring her here. She is become the very keystone of our strategy."

"Aye."

He peered closely at the screen. "In which of the reading rooms did you find her?"

Joshua rotated his wrist to afford a clearer view. "In here."

Silas exhaled slowly. "Then this is the worst of news. She may have guessed the object of my search; with help, she may yet discover more. Apply every effort, Joshua every man, every resource. Find her and bring her to me, no matter the cost. I need her in this city."

Returning to New Tybet was proving more challenging than Finn had expected. For one thing, no one was willing to risk exposing Johnny Faustus by making any unnecessary contact. For another, the routes Hitch would normally have taken looked either to be dead or guarded. As a result, Finn and the two watchmen were now sitting amongst the stone arches of a Roman catacomb while Hitch prodded glumly at his reader.

"You know, it's funny," said Finn, watching him work. "I see a lot of the same titles cropping up on those destination lists. Why is that?"

Hitch flinched at the question. He turned the screen away. "Like what? What d'you mean?"

"Well, when I had Joshua's reader, *A Young Wolf's Cry* came up. My story. It's on yours, too, and I keep seeing *L. Woodsmeade*. That's not Little Woodsmeade, is it? Little Woodsmeade in-the-Dale?"

Hitch shrugged. "Dunno. How's Boorman?"

"He's okay. Duggan's with him." She couldn't help smiling. "Oh, but do you remember the Woodsmeade Tales? My sister and I used to *adore* them. Fred Bear and Quickory Hitchpost... I just loved that squirrel. That was our favourite bedtime reading; the stuff of my childhood."

"Uh huh. So Boorman; he's not getting feverish or anything?"

Finn cocked her head. "You seem very interested in Boorman's health all of a sudden. What's going on?"

Hitch sighed. "Look, I don't actually give a figure-skating toss about him, but if you start talking about his poorly shoulder, then it's a lot easier for me to switch off. I can happily ignore you and concentrate on getting us safely home."

"Oh. I see. I'm distracting you."

"Yes. Yes you are." Hitch waggled his device. "So d'you mind if I, you know... get on?"

Less than an hour later, and despite Hitch's assurances that the next jump would take them straight back to the city, Finn emerged into a narrow cobbled street wearing what appeared to be little more than rags and an old cloak. She seriously hoped the smell wasn't coming from her.

To either side, ramshackle half-timber houses teetered over her. The upper storeys widened as they rose, rough plaster walls almost meeting overhead. The sun shone somewhere above them, but barely penetrated this precarious tunnel of masonry and soot-black wood; it manifested only as a thin, straggling line of light. Down at the road level, the place was a pit of shadows, broken sporadically by the orange glow of torch-lit doorways and chain-hung lanterns.

"This isn't Tybet," she concluded.

"It is," said Hitch. "We're just in the Subway."

"The what?"

"The Subway. Parallel world technology." He gestured at a dwarfish maid scrubbing clothes on her doorstep. "Not everyone's comfortable living in a big space-aged city. Some people toddle off-world to find some place that feels familiar; others come here."

"And it's still Tybet?" Finn stepped to one side as a moustachioed barbarian strode by, half a hog slung over his shoulder.

"One of many Parallels," said Hitch. "They share the same space, all layered on top of each other. This one's all fantasy and magic."

"And the others?"

Hitch shrugged. "Some are more sci-fi; some are dressed up like different sorts of afterlife - Valhalla, Elysium - all that kind of thing. Others go for a bit more historical accuracy."

"And Max is controlling all of them?"

"Probably not. He won't need to. The dome exists in every Parallel, so once he's got control of the gate complex, he just has to bolt the doors and shut down the Subway system. That pretty much locks everybody out."

Dressed in what looked like leather armour and scraps of chainmail, Duggan leaned in from behind. "But he'll still have his spies out, so keep your bloody voices down."

"Fair point," said Hitch. "Oh, it's left here."

"Where are we going?" asked Finn.

"Tavern district." Hitch produced a wide and worrying grin.

"Taverns?" Boorman flashed him an evil scowl. "I need a surgeon, not a bloody barmaid."

Hitch sighed. "I haven't forgotten. But this is where we'll get you the help you need. See, here you go."

Around the corner, the street dipped between two opposing rows of tall, gaudily lit inns and hostels. Interspersed among them sat several other establishments, which, if their sign boards were anything to go by, served either as brothels or dormitories for especially friendly contortionists.

"The Brontës?" Finn read the name of the nearest tavern. Below the painted lettering, exhausted revellers spilled out onto the steps through a pair of great gilded doors. Not all of them were landing on their feet.

"Yeah." Hitch put a hand to her shoulder and steered her away. "And you really don't want to go wandering off in there, believe me. It can get pretty wild."

"Wild? Then why *The Brontës?* They were hardly the most..."

Hitch held up his hands. "Hey. Characters can change after they've been scooped. Some of them can *really* change - especially the tight-laced ones. Anyway, come on, that's not where we're headed."

"Paul said he'd meet us at Potter's Bar. What's...?"

"*In* Potter's Bar. There." Hitch pointed at a narrow tavern wedged uncomfortably between a dirty-looking hotel and what could only be a fetishist's outfitters. Lit by wall-hung torches, the sign above the door bore the image of a wand and a pair of round-framed spectacles.

Finn shook her head. "Surely that isn't..."

Hitch grinned. "Lot of people died in that world. Most of them wound up here." He stopped to admire the irregular masonry and a pair of carved boars' heads that frowned above the entrance.

"Wait here," said Duggan, pushing open the door. "I'll check the place out."

Finn stopped and took a moment to look around, wondering what fresh weirdness her unconscious mind might next throw at her.

"You!" Sitting against the front wall like a pile of unwanted laundry, a goggle-eyed loon pointed a thin, wavering arm at her. "It is you. The Chosen One!"

"Get lost," advised Boorman.

Finn flashed Hitch a worried look. *"Chosen One?"*

Hitch shook his head. "Forget it; it's a scam - they say it to everyone. Been doing it for years."

"Oh. Right."

In the doorway, Duggan reappeared and signalled them inside.

Hitch shambled in first. Finn came close behind. Boorman, cradling his arm, came last through the door.

"Hey, Postman." A woman in a tight leather bustier pushed her way towards them through a noisy crowd.

"Oh, hi." Hitch raised his head a fraction.

"Scumbag." She slapped him sharply across the face, then turned and walked briskly away.

Finn smiled."You two have got a bit of history, I take it?"

Hitch rubbed at his cheek. "Seems that way."

"But you don't remember what that was for?"

"Not clearly, no. Unless..." He squinted. "I might once have tasered her dog."

He was interrupted in mid-reminisce as a large hand grabbed his lapel. Something big and spotty thrust itself cackling into his face. "Hey, Party-Pooper! Looking for a laundry?"

Hitch shrugged him off. "Hey, you know that's not fair. That was food poisoning. I was actually very ill that night."

"Yeah; we saw. Ha, ha!" Pointing at him lest any of his friends had missed the object of his tremendous joke, Mr. Zits produced another loud guffaw.

"Over there." Duggan barged the happy comedian out of his way. "Grab a seat." He nodded towards a wizard in a huge conical hat, who sat at a dark corner table with a pipe clenched beneath his teeth. Though his face was obscured by shadow, he had a certain air of power about him; the tavern's many patrons were choosing to give him more than his fair measure of personal space.

Quietly, Finn pushed her way through the throng until she emerged into the halo of bare floor that surrounded the mysterious stranger's spot.

"Hello, Ms. Finn." The ridiculously oversized brim lifted and grand-wizard Paul Locke was suddenly beaming back at her.

26. The Quick and the Dead

"**P**aul!" Finn hurried forward to hug him.

"Now, now," said Locke, returning the embrace, "this isn't doing my mystique any good at all."

"Bugger the mystique. How are you? What's been happening?"

"All in good time, my dear. But dear me, look at your friend; he's injured."

By now, her three companions had assembled behind her. None of them seemed ready to join with her display of affection.

Pale and sweating, Boorman took a seat on the end of the bench. "Arrow wound," he explained. "Left it in till I could get help."

Locke dipped his brim. "I take it you've heard there's no moving between the Parallels?"

"Closed off," nodded Boorman. "They said it's Max Roberts. That true?"

"Yes," said Locke. "I've alerted as many of the remaining Watch as I could but they're thinly spread. As for medical care, I fear you'll have to take your chances here."

"Healing magic?" Boorman looked as if he'd rather mud-wrestle an anaconda.

"Oh come now, it's not as bad as people say."

Boorman jerked a thumb over in the direction of the bar. "The innkeeper's got one eye and a hook for a hand."

"And I'm sure he's delighted with the impression they make." Locke took Boorman's good arm and tapped an address onto the screen of his reader. "Now, you find this young lady and tell her I sent you. She's a healer and a masseuse. She's a wonder; always done marvels for me whenever I've felt any stiffness."

Boorman chewed his cheek for a moment. "Alright. I'll get this fixed up, then I'll do what I can to catch up with you."

Locke smiled. "Excellent. They do say you can't keep a good man down."

Turning to Duggan, Boorman pointed to his reader. "You keep me informed, okay? You know how to contact me."

Duggan nodded an acknowledgement as the wounded watchman left.

Hitch adjusted his cowl as he took Boorman's place at the table. "I feel like we're on show," he said. "Why is everyone giving us such funny looks?"

"Ah, that," said Locke. "A misapprehension. I think the landlady might have allowed a rumour to spread concerning my being a master of the dark arts. I only said I wanted a table but the darling girl's so eager to please. Always has been. She'll let me slip in the back door on even the busiest of nights."

"Well that's fascinating," said Duggan without the merest shadow of sincerity, "but we need to debrief."

The Professor smirked but said nothing.

"I'll start," said Finn quietly. "We think it's Coleridge; Max's muse or whatever we're calling it. And he's started going by the name of Silas. Bit weird, don't you think?"

"*Coleridge?*" said Locke. "That's odd. I've met a couple of versions of the man but he never struck me as one to incite a war. Far from it." He paused, thinking. "And Silas, you say?"

Hitch nodded. "That's what that Joshua bloke called him - before we knocked him out."

"Oh, *we* knocked him out, did we?" Duggan raised an eyebrow.

Hitch breezed that away. "We: the team."

Locke ruminated for a moment. "And remind me, what was he calling himself when he abducted Mr. Reed?"

"Oh, hang on, I know this..." Finn raised her eyes to the ceiling. "It was, um..."

"Tomkyn," said Duggan, checking notes on his reader. "Commander Tomkyn. That's assuming it was the same guy."

"Okay, but where's this leading?" said Hitch. "And why is no one offering me a drink?"

"Wait," said Finn. "I remember this... Those names. Something about an alias: Silas Tomkyn... something."

"Silas Tomkyn Comberbache." Locke gave her an approving smile. "STC. The initials of our poet. Samuel Taylor Coleridge once used the name when he sought to enlist."

Finn blinked as the memory returned. "That's it. Yeah."

"So he's using an alias. So what?" Hitch leaned back in his seat, opened his mouth and lobbed a hazelnut into his hair.

"Yeah. Why does any of this matter?" said Duggan. "How's it going to help us take back control?"

Locke smiled. "Because, my dear boy, it might point us to his Achilles heel. I've come to suspect that Max is communing with a higher level power - an author or a poet - and now we might just have identified who that is."

"Communing with...." Duggan snorted. "No one can do that. They've had researchers working on it for centuries."

"Well I hope you're right." Locke tapped at his unlit pipe. "But I've been using my time here to retrace Max's movements. And though he's tried hard to cover his tracks, I'm now certain he's intent on breaching the Core."

"It's not possible," protested Duggan. "It just isn't."

"If one has the help of a higher level author, then it might be," said Locke. "But whether he has it or not, that isn't his only stratagem. Almost all his movements in the last few years indicate a growing obsession with the legend of the Last Book - the She-Wolf's account of how she secured narrative power."

"Then he's chasing whispers and rainbows," said Duggan. "The Book doesn't exist."

"Max Roberts believes otherwise," said Locke. "It may only be a delusion, but he's bent on finding a figure known as the Gatekeeper."

"The..." said Finn. "Oh bugger."

Under his massive hat, the Professor blinked at her. "I beg pardon?"

Finn felt her scalp tingling. "He thinks it's me. We heard him talking to Joshua on his reader-radio thing. He thinks I'm the Gatekeeper."

Locke closed his eyes for a long moment. "It fits, I suppose. The Gatekeeper is said to be hidden in a tale of wolves. For months, Max has been secretly scouring narratives with wolves, jackals and foxes in them. That's probably why your tale was bumped up the schedule for extraction - along with hundreds of others."

"But who is this Gatekeeper?" Finn felt suddenly conscious of her distinct lack of superpowers. "What can she actually do?"

Locke steepled his fingers. "The Gatekeeper is another part of the myth. A servant of Damelyka the She-Wolf; the keeper of the Last Book, and thus the key to the Core. If Max believes the legends - and we can surely deduce that he does - then finding the Gatekeeper represents the final phase of his plan."

"But why single out Finn?" said Hitch. "Just because she sold books?"

"His attitude underwent a quite singular change when we pointed out that his quote wasn't original. That seems to have been the crux. Before that, he was paying Ms. Finn no heed at all - only you and me."

Finn pursed her lips. "D'you think he guessed we'd made the Coleridge connection...?"

"Possibly."

Duggan leaned forward. "Okay, okay, but where's this weakness of his?" He looked like he'd be a lot happier if he could only shoot at something. "Talking's all very well, but we need to take action. Time's passing. Where's this going? What do we actually *do*?"

"Two things," said Locke. "First, we must protect Ms. Finn. Gatekeeper or not, she's fallen directly into Max's sights."

"Protection." Here was a language Duggan understood. "I can do that."

"Second, we must test our hypothesis: that Max has been creating new narratives; readying new armies with the help of some fictional off-world Coleridge."

Hitch gave him a weary look. "Right. And in all the worlds, how many versions of a massively famous poet do you think there are?"

The Professor shrugged. "A good number, certainly. A better question would be how many of them Max himself has visited. He believes he's hidden his tracks but now that we know what we're looking for, I doubt he'll be a match for the talents of our young friend Mr. Forster."

"I can contact the boy." Duggan swiped a thumb across his reader. "Give me a minute."

"So what next?" said Finn. "Where do we start?"

"Wait." Hitch's heavy-lidded gaze exuded all the joy and promise of a melting snowman. "Call me Fanny Faintheart if you will, but doesn't all this sound just a tiny bit, you know... suicidally dangerous? I mean, sure, I'm all for stopping Max and everything, but what say we think about a Plan B, just to be on the safe side?" He raised a finger. "For example: how would it be if Duggsy here went and gave exactly the same plan to all his brave friends in the Watch? You know... if we just let the professionals handle it?"

"Then we'd lose any last shred of security or surprise," said Locke shortly. "Word would quickly get back to Max, together with a very useful approximation of our whereabouts and intentions. The rest, I'm sure you can imagine."

Hitch looked down at his fingernails. "Well, yeah. That's what I thought, too. I mean that *particular* Plan B is obviously no good but the principle I was getting at..."

"Shut it Frog-features." Duggan was busy texting and didn't bother to look up. "We are where we are. We suck it up and we deal with it."

"Quite so, Mr. Duggan." Locke shuffled to the edge of the bench. "To that, I should also add the recommendation that we visit an acquaintance of mine who has been preparing a rather cunning masking device. It won't be foolproof, but it should hamper Max's efforts to follow us."

With varying degrees of enthusiasm, Finn and the others rose and followed him to the door.

Outside in the street, little had changed, except that a large crowd of miserable, anxious-looking people seemed to have chosen to gather around a freestanding stone arch.

"A Subway portal," explained Hitch. "They're all over the city - and they're all shut."

"Ah. Okay." Finn pointed at the narrow street ahead, where a stampede of peasants, merchants, and labourers was thundering towards them. "And what's this lot doing?"

"That I don't know." Hitch glanced ahead at Locke whose giant hat no longer seemed to be commanding its former sense of awe. Panicking people jostled him as they hurried by.

Unholstering his pistol, Duggan pointed back towards the taverns. "Ogres! Run!"

Finn ran. It seemed like good advice. As she did, a blue bolt of light shot past her ear and caught a portly soothsayer in the back of the head. Finn braced herself for some grisly explosion but, when it came, the result seemed somehow worse. Without sound, warning or saving throw, the poor man was instantly transformed into a beetle the size of a two-seater sofa.

"Agh!" All she could do was jump over him and run on.

"Wizards, too," gasped Hitch. "They've got wands. Find a door; any door."

Finn glanced back at a scene of unhappy chaos. Hitch had already fallen behind and the Professor was further back still, though to make himself less of a target in the milling crowd, he'd wisely elected to shed his hat. Duggan was keeping pace with him, helping him along while loosing off occasional rounds at the muscle-bound monsters that pursued them.

Stopping at the entrance to an ink-black side alley, Finn ducked in and made a savage grab at Hitch's wrist. The sudden yank caught his attention, but his momentum took him past the junction; he had to fight against the flow of bodies to make his way back. By the time he reached her, Locke and Duggan had joined them.

"They've seen us!" Hitch flung his arm in the direction of the darkness. "Go!"

Another something flew past Finn's head. This time, it looked alarmingly like Hitch's reader.

"Grab it! Grab it!" Hitch pushed them forward.

Blindly, Finn swept for the fallen device and quickly found something smooth, hard and covered in what she hoped was mud. Turning it over, she caught a flash of faintly illuminated lettering. "Got it!"

"Quick, give it back!" shouted Hitch, though now Locke and Duggan were both in the way as they jostled together down the tiny alleyway.

"There isn't time," cried Locke. "Finn, you'll have to do it yourself. Take the first door you find."

Lacking the chance to plan anything remotely cunning, Finn simply stabbed at the keypad, scrolled across the screen and hit the first green gate link that appeared.

The reader, it seemed, could cope better with the darkness than she could because within three steps, a blue sheen had spread itself across an unlit doorway that she would never otherwise have noticed.

"Go! Go!" shouted Duggan.

Finn barged through and instantly found herself emerging through the side entrance to a bedroom. Faint light shone beneath a wooden door by the head of the bed. It revealed the shadowed form of a man frozen in a moment of sleep.

"Go - the door!" Hauling the Professor after him, Duggan pointed.

Finn reached it just as Hitch leapt, gasping into the room.

"Wait! It's okay," He took two steps, then bent forward and set his hands on his knees. "It was too... it was too narrow for the ogres... They stopped. They couldn't..." Unable to breathe, he made calming gestures with one hand. "Give me my reader. We should be... we should be alright for a couple of m..."

From the gate came a loud crack and another fleeting blue wand-spark. It shot over Hitch's shoulder, struck the sleeping man under the chin and promptly transformed him into a giant bug. It had Finn's friends up and running in under a second.

"Here!" With practised fluidity, Duggan conjured a new gate. He plunged through it. Finn didn't hesitate to follow.

A moment later, she wished she had.

Bursting into a gloomy urban street, she stopped at the roadside beside a burned and windowless Mercedes. As she did, a stifling sense of wrongness settled about her. The place had clearly once been a modern metropolis of tower blocks and asphalt, but now it lay decaying, lightless and unpopulated. She knew it at once for a sepulchre. No street lamps resisted the advance of night. The vehicles in the road were abandoned, rusting and dusted with ash. Thin weeds grew between the paving slabs. Not a single building was lit.

"Get round here!" Urging them behind the ruined saloon, Duggan crouched, aiming his pistol back at the door.

Finn ducked beside him, watching the building as her friends took similar positions. The doorway had once been the entrance to a high-end fashion boutique, to judge by the paper-thin mannequins laid out behind the shattered glass, but now the store's wares were mouldering to rags.

After a long moment of nothing very dramatic, Hitch grasped the side of the car and hauled himself upright. "Okay. So they aren't coming," he said.

"I don't think they will," agreed the Professor, straightening. "Magic doesn't work in this narrative. Wizards would be powerless."

"But they'll be sending others," said Duggan. "We've got to move."

Finn looked up at the empty buildings. "So where are we? This place is a morgue."

"And more importantly, where's my reader?" Hitch snatched it back with a frown. "My whole life is in this thing. It's... Oh, great. Look; you broke the strap."

"Sorry," said Finn. "It was in that crowd. I was trying to..."

"We're in New York," said Duggan. "And not one of the nicer versions."

Finn glanced at the fast-darkening sky. "No? And do I want to know you mean by that?"

Hitch examined his injured device. "Probably not."

"Well, in any event," said Locke, "we need a plan. Our options are narrowing all the time; running blindly from gate to gate will only hasten our return into Max's lap."

"True," said Hitch, attempting a hasty repair, "but let's find somewhere safer to do it. I don't think this is the place to be planning anything."

As if to underscore the sentiment, the world around them stirred. Not into life, exactly - there seemed a dearth of that - but into the sounds and movement of a restless, sombre wind.

"Shit! There!" Duggan pointed back at the boutique.

Finn turned to see a white, emaciated figure shuffling from the darkness of the interior. Hairless and nearly naked, it might once have been a woman, but now it stood stranded somewhere beyond death. One arm hung uselessly at her side, the other stretched out towards them in what could have been a gesture of entreaty. Her hand was a shrunken claw, her body a travesty of taut skin and fleshless bone.

"Oh, hell no." Finn felt her own skin tighten as the abomination stumbled out over the threshold. Weirdly, it occurred to her that death had moulded the creature into the only shape that might actually have fitted the overpriced garments behind her, but she shook the mad thought away. This was unquestionably a zombie; the one thing in all the worlds she most feared.

"Shoot it!" hissed Hitch.

"No. Back up." Duggan indicated the crossroads immediately to their left. "It's slow. Any noise will just attract more of them."

"More?" A cold flush of panic suffused Finn's blood. Crossing her arms tight across her chest, she scanned the streets for signs of life, death, or anything in between. Until this moment, doorways had always promised opportunity and escape but, abruptly and unnoticed, they had changed their character. Now, like dark mouths agape, they spoke only of awaiting horror.

"Quietly and calmly over there," said Locke. He pointed left, to a grand, stone-fronted building done out in the classical style. "Good stout frames on those doors. They should take us anywhere we need to..."

"Run!" shouted Hitch.

He didn't need to point. Buildings all along the street were suddenly disgorging their dead. Ahead, behind and to their right, bone-white forms fell out into the road, some crawling, some walking, some of them lurching forward at a shambling run. All were converging upon them, and that left only one way to go.

Finn fought to keep control of her thoughts. Part of her wanted very badly to scream at the sheer clichéd stupidity of it all; to ask why so many crappy, herd-following hacks insisted on populating their worlds with the same hideous creations. Zombies were no more than a sick celebration of decay and lovelessness; why in anyone's hell did they remain so insanely popular?

A more pragmatic part of her agreed in principle with all this but suggested that it might be a sentiment better expressed from somewhere much further away. To lend weight to its argument, it began flooding her legs with adrenaline.

The street to the left would once have been a thriving place. The architecture hinted at townhouses, hotels, and embassies. But smashed windows and derelict vehicles told that it had also been the scene of some dreadful conflict. Riot, weathering, and seasons of neglect had left it a ruin.

"Over here!" cried the Professor, making for a double door in the stone facade.

"No wait!" Duggan threw out an arm to seize the old man as the doors swung open. A tall, gaunt monster with empty eyes took a step towards them, then stopped and crumpled as Duggan's bullet tore open the back of its head.

"Keep going! This way!" Casting fearful glances over his shoulder, Hitch stooped to pick up a long-discarded bicycle. The chain was broken and the child-sized frame much too small for him, but he mounted it anyway and with great strides began propelling himself along the street.

Finn ran after him, keeping doggedly to the middle of the road. It was a maze of debris and broken vehicles but sharp, rusting metal held fewer terrors than the prospect of being leapt upon by an unreasonably spritely corpse.

Behind her, with Duggan's help, Professor Locke was making better progress than she would have expected.

Another shot broke the unnatural stillness as Duggan felled another of their pursuers. For all its numbers, the ungodly horde was making almost no sound at all; only the thump of feet against pavement and the quiet rustle of rotting cloth and skin. She kept running. With the possible exception of a pre-teen beauty pageant, Finn couldn't imagine anywhere more wretched or unnatural than this.

The street was over a hundred metres long but, thankfully, nothing more terrifying than an expensive shoe shop appeared ahead of them. Perhaps they were entering a district that the undead considered unfashionable or unaffordable, or perhaps they were just running into some dreadful final ambush but, for now, Finn was content just not to have her brains chewed.

The street opened into a T-junction, where the lofty city seemed briefly to defer to the natural world. To left and right stretched a long, three-lane avenue, all strewn with abandoned cars and buses. Ahead lay a wooded park. Its trees were withered and rooted in ash but it was a park nonetheless. Instinctively, Finn felt drawn to it.

"Try that one?" Striding furiously on his little velocipede, Hitch had outdistanced their dead-yet-surprisingly-quick pursuers and now he pointed across to a wide brick building set some way back from the road.

"That could be worth..." Duggan was interrupted by the roar of an engine.

Finn turned to see an armoured vehicle ploughing through the rear of the zombie ranks, its windows covered by welded grilles. "People!" she shouted.

"Or Max's thugs." Hitch hurled aside his bike and tapped his reader. "Keep running."

She followed him between low gateposts and down a flight of steps, but the building ahead proved no more hospitable than the others. Its doors, set between Gothic looking towers, opened as they approached. The failing light made it impossible to see what waited beyond but, with no more than an exchange of glances, she and Hitch agreed not to enquire.

"Down!" yelled Duggan.

Finn didn't throw herself to the floor as cinematic convention demanded. Being pursued by zombies had given her a healthy regard for staying on her feet. She merely flinched and ducked her head to one side, but it was enough. From the direction of the armoured car came a streak of orange and a harsh whooshing sound that reminded her of upsetting news reports from hot and dangerously religious countries. It arced overhead and crashed through the building's doors in a bright eruption of flame.

"This way! This way!" Hitch hadn't stopped running. He'd turned left across the front of the building and now ducked sharply to the right.

Finn ran on again. Another explosion lit the trees for an instant but, behind her, she could still hear Locke and Duggan urging her on.

Rounding the corner, she saw Hitch approaching the rear of a rusting pickup. On it, the words *Central Park Zoo* could still clearly be read. Panting and stabbing at his reader, he scampered down a low flight of steps towards an arched door in the side of the building.

Finn turned to crouch by the remains of an iron gate and was relieved to see the Professor puffing his way towards her. Duggan was just behind, emptying his pistol in the direction of the road.

"It's open!" Hitch pointed at the faint glow that had appeared across the doors.

"Go, go!" The watchman waved fiercely.

Hitch dived through. Finn grasped Locke's arm and helped him down the steps.

Three strides, two strides from the gate. Finn glanced back.

Duggan was at the top of the steps, aiming his weapon back the way they'd come. When he pulled the trigger, it produced only a click. A moment later, his eyes went wide. "Grenade!" he yelled.

With one last step, Finn and the Professor were across the threshold and tumbling down a narrow flight of stairs.

27. Fields of Green

"Where's Duggan?" Kneeling over her in a drab basement full of dented filing cabinets and stale air, Hitch grabbed her shoulders.

Finn blinked. "He's right beh..."

As she looked up, an incandescent cloud burst through the gate, together with assorted debris and a silhouetted something that might have been a man. It hit the staircase with a jarring crack that sent the whole wooden assembly crashing to the ground.

"Jam it!" cried the shape. Or perhaps "damn it." In all the noise and confusion it was hard to tell.

The single light bulb in the ceiling flickered.

Hurrying to the wall, Hitch dug in an inside pocket and reached up to place a small device at the foot of the doorway. "It won't give us more than a couple of minutes," he said.

With a disgruntled-sounding *pink*, the light bulb fizzled out entirely.

"Is everyone alright?" Hearing the Professor's wheezing voice provided a kind of reassurance, though Finn guessed it would be some time yet before her imagination would stop trying to populate the newly fallen darkness with images of the shambling dead.

"I'm fine," she said. "Where are we?"

"Some... some local authority storage facility." Hitch was still struggling for breath. "And now we've got less than two minutes."

"There's another door at the back." Duggan's face was lit by the glow of his reader. "But we've got to clear this lot before we go." He produced a torch and shone it at the floor.

"You want to *tidy up*?" Hitch shot him an incredulous look. "Did you see what was after us?"

"This is an Unaware narrative," said Duggan flatly. "And I'm a watchman. So we clean up."

"He's right," said Locke, stooping. "There's no telling what harm we might do."

"Just grab what you can and bin it," said Duggan. With his boot, he began sweeping together fragments of burned paper and broken wing mirror.

Finn picked up a rectangle of curiously warm metal. "Any suggestions?" she said, waving it.

Duggan's torchlight dazzled her. "What is it?"

Squinting, she turned over the little sign. "It says *Beware of the Leopard*."

"Just stick it in one of the drawers over there." He pointed to an old toilet cubicle and a filing cabinet that all but filled it. "Quick as you can. We've got to go."

Moments later, she was following her companions through the door and out into the brightness of a summer meadow.

"What d'you go and land us in the bleedin' countryside for?" An early morning walk in rural England seemed to have put Duggan in the foulest of moods. It had also very nearly exhausted Professor Locke.

"We need time to think," said Hitch. "Open countryside means no doors - and no doors means no sudden ambushes."

Duggan sneered. "Time to think? You mean you're running scared."

"Yes. I am." Hitch stopped, set his forearms upon a moss green gate and gazed out across a misty hollow. "Running because people are trying to kill me. And scared for much the same reason. That's not unreasonable, is it?"

Duggan curled a lip. "So what happened to all this brave talk about stopping Max and taking back the gates?"

Hitch looked over his shoulder. "That was you, you great... clod. I said we should hand it all over to the Watch. I didn't ask for any of this." He stared at the watchman for a moment, but couldn't hold his gaze. Instead, he sighed and turned back to stare at the distant treetops. "I'm tired. All I ever wanted was to go home."

"Well, tough." Duggan began reloading his pistol. "You said you knew Max's weakness. You said if we could get to this poet bloke, we could stop him. So that's what we're going to do."

Silently Hitch shook his head. What little fight he'd had in him had gone. With all the resentment he could convey, he slumped upon the gate and watched a peculiar-looking donkey grazing amongst tatters of mist.

Finn cleared her throat. "Maybe he's right about needing some time. We need to figure out..."

"Oh, he's *right,* is he?" Now Duggan turned his ire on her. "Well now there's a surprise. Little Miss Bookworm agrees with Bug-eyes. Don't you think you've done enough thinking for one day, Missy?"

Finn blinked. "What the hell? Where's all this coming from?"

He snorted. "Oh, don't think I've forgotten what happened back in the city. You get your hands on a reader just once, and what's the first thing you do?" He looked about, once again looking as though he were playing to some hidden audience. "You drop us right into an Unaware narrative, and some poor sod winds up turned into a giant friggin' beetle. Have you not had enough of messing up other people's worlds?"

"We were being attacked," said Hitch. "Don't take it out on her."

"She..." said Duggan, a finger stabbing the air, "needs to understand that actions have consequences. You can't go leaping about in other worlds like they're your own personal playground. People in worlds like this - they don't know they're a fiction."

"Hey," said Finn fiercely, "I never..."

"A fiction? Is this all a fiction?" Raising its head from the damp grass and thistles, the old grey donkey scanned its field unhappily. It turned a doleful eye upon Duggan. "Oh dear, oh dear. Well that is a gloomy thought."

Vinson waited nervously in his chair. He knew he should be rehearsing the phrasing of his report, but his attention kept flitting between Max and the construction work going on beyond the long glass wall of his office. One of the panels had been removed since his last visit, replaced with a heavy steel frame. That meant Max could use it as a conventional door - to a newly emplaced gantry running across to the Core wall - or as a gate big enough to take an armoured car.

Not that anyone would have much use for an armoured car, here in what was still only an office on one of the upper levels of the Gate Control complex, but Max would doubtless have his reasons. What they were was anyone's guess; like so many of the man's schemes and motivations, he was keeping them very much to himself. He'd started to talk very strangely, too.

Standing against a background of frenetic building work and bright blue bursts from the welding torches, he was the very paradigm of efficient multi-tasking. Beside him, a bank of monitors presented a steady stream of intelligence from his off-world agents, allies and lieutenants, and these he consulted as he conversed with his aides.

"You have acquainted yourself with our first target, Joshua." Max gestured at one of the screens.

"Indeed. An uncultured fiend; he will make a fine first conquest."

"Over eighteen billion dead." Max leaned back against his desk. "The man has been industrious in his time."

Joshua shrugged. "Industrious. Murderous. Remorseless. He has laid waste to three star systems. Few shall lament his passing."

"And you share my belief? That we have sufficient advantage?" Max ran his fingers through his hair. "After all, appearances are everything, Joshua; the unsuspecting worlds have never seen our like; we must announce ourselves with only the most spectacular of victories."

Joshua grinned. "And that we shall. Our advantage is more than sufficient. I have witnessed the power of our awaiting fleets. One would be enough. Now we have four awaiting your command."

Max nodded. "Then when the gates are ready, send them all. Leave naught but atoms of our foe. And record it all, Joshua. Let others know what we can do. Show them that our reign, our power, is absolute. Let tyrants quail; let them see what befalls those who dare to stand against our brave new regime."

"The commanders stand ready upon your order," said Joshua. "All that remains is to unbar the gates. How goes it with the Gatekeeper?"

At this, Max turned his attention to Vinson. "Not so well as we had hoped, Joshua. We tracked her as far as some grim, life-in-death apocalypse, but Vinson lost her."

Vinson swallowed. Now he knew for certain that his rehearsals had been inadequate. Under the scrutiny of the two men, his carefully prepared report, with all its detailed explanations of signal jamming and garbled transmissions, dispersed into a puff of unconnected syllables. He didn't even bother to open his mouth.

Joshua turned his back upon him and leaned in close to Max.

After a moment, Max muttered something back. The only phrases he caught were *live ammunition* and *rocket propelled grenades*. These were accompanied by ominous shakes of the head.

"Vinson," said Joshua, turning.

"Yes, sir." He was relieved to find he hadn't entirely lost his command of the language.

"Come with me."

"Yes, sir." Rising, Vinson followed him to the side door of the office. When Joshua tapped his reader, it became a gate.

"After you, Vinson."

He felt a surge of dread. A gate could take him anywhere. In recent history, New Tybet had been civilised and peaceful. Though loosely controlled, it had never been reliant on the strict hierarchies of authority that so easily lent themselves to abuse elsewhere. No corrupt, self-serving demagogues had risen to power in the years since the foundation of the Core, and never before had the gates been used as an inventive form of punishment. Criminals were sometime banished, but to worlds chosen for their remoteness, not their hostility.

Now, though, Max was overturning that order, and his fixation on the Gatekeeper woman was absolute. Vinson had relayed his orders faithfully - told his teams to bring her back alive and unharmed - but Max's jamming protocols had interfered with communications. Accordingly, his men had gone after her with all guns blazing. He could only be thankful they hadn't killed her. Had they done so, his punishment might be considerably worse than whatever lay beyond this gate.

"Now, Vinson, if you please." Joshua set a heavy hand on his shoulder.

Swallowing, he crossed the threshold.

He blinked. Now, he stood on spongy grass, on an implausible, yet strangely familiar landscape of rolling hillocks, tall pines, and daffodils. Rabbits hopped happily about and a bright, yolk-yellow sun beamed down from a cloudless sky.

"You let us down, Vinson. Your reader, if you'd be so kind."

He turned to see Joshua standing in the entrance to the prettiest little flower-framed grotto. He was pointing a gun at him.

Vinson stepped back. "What? No, you don't understand; the signals were jammed. I gave my men exactly the right comm..."

"Now, Vinson." He cocked the pistol.

Slowly, he peeled back the strap and handed the reader over. "This isn't fair. I didn't..."

"Thank you," said Joshua. "Now step away."

Vinson looked around. "What is this place? How long are you going to leave me here?"

"How long?" Joshua smiled as he backed towards the gate. "You failed in your duty, Vinson. You put all our plans at risk. You must not expect to return at all."

"But what...?" He stopped. He was addressing empty air.

A small sound made him turn.

"Oh God." In a moment of dawning terror, he recognised the thing coming out of the woods towards him; big glassy eyes, a covering of bright blue felt. Suddenly, a childhood of memories flooded his consciousness. He knew why the landscape looked so familiar.

"Whassis?" simpered the creature. Its voice was a squeaking, lisping affront to his ears.

Vinson backed up. "No. Get away. Get away from me, you freak."

"Wantsasong?" Grinning inanely, the creature cocked its head.

"Oh, hell no." That was it. Now he remembered. That was the very worst thing about this, the very worst world that children's television had ever conjured. *The Puffleboos* were gibberish-spouting merchandise monsters who communicated in only two ways: in nonsensical baby-talk that made you want to stick hot needles through your ears, or in song. And, oh great merciful God, the songs were horrible.

"Ewantsasong," decided the abomination.

"Asong? Wantsasong?" Now another of them was closing in from his left.

Vinson whirled. From out of the trees lumbered yet more primary-coloured horrors, all dead eyes and vacuous smiles. He looked about for a fallen branch - anything to beat the bastards away - but the grass was as short and manicured as a bowling green.

Vinson slumped against the grotto entrance and considered braining himself against the rocks. The Puffleboos had encircled him and now they were preparing to sing.

"Bloody hell," said Finn, waving the remains of a digestive. "You weren't kidding about these biscuits. They're fantastic."

She sat on a warm, grassy slope overlooking the sort of countryside that only children's story characters ever seemed to inhabit. Here, the fields were bordered with wooden fences rather than lengths of rusty barbed wire. Sparrows fluttered in the hedgerows instead of wind-blown scraps of polythene. Every inch of arable was a demonstration of precision ploughing, every other field a polkadot spread of rich grass and cloud-white lambs.

Better yet, there wasn't a building anywhere in sight, so unless Max's forces had equipped themselves with a heat-seeking missile, she and her friends could feel considerably safer than they had in quite a while. Accordingly, sensing an opportunity for an impromptu picnic, Finn had pestered Hitch for a couple of biscuits and, eventually, he'd relented. What he produced was cracked and broken, and had certainly not benefited from its many hours of storage close to his armpit, but it was still quite possibly the most delicious thing Finn had ever tasted.

"Will you get up off your arses and move!" Duggan, as ever, was failing to read the mood.

"There's really little point," said Locke.

"*Professor...*" Duggan shook his head. "I'm disappointed. I never thought I'd hear you say die."

"And I, sir, will thank you not to put your inferences in my mouth. What I said, quite correctly, was that there's little point in moving."

"I don't understand."

"No," said Locke. "And nor do any of us, which is the first of two excellent reasons why we should pause and take stock."

Duggan scowled. "What's the other reason?"

"The gates are all shut." Hitch lay in the grass, eyes closed, hands laced behind his head. "Even if Johnny's figured out where this poet guy's supposed to be, there's no way we can get to him. The only places left open are Tybet and our own TOOs."

"Maybe the Forster kid could help." Duggan started pacing. "He's bright, that lad. I wouldn't be surprised."

"I suppose we ought to contact him, at least," said Locke. "If he has news, we need to hear it."

"We'd need a comms channel," said Duggan. "Are they all down, too?"

"Down, but not out," said Locke. "They're being jammed but I could likely find us a way through. We'd have to get ourselves close to a door, though."

Hitch propped himself up on his elbows. "Wait. No. Hang on. Does this mean you want us to start moving again?"

Duggan grinned. "Uh huh."

He slumped back. "Oh... But I like it here. I haven't been punched or shot at once."

"Well, if it helps," said Duggan amiably, "I can kick you around a bit till you decide."

Wearily, the Professor rose to his feet. "Where do you have in mind to go, Mr. Duggan?"

The watchman consulted his wrist. "There's a storage building about quarter of a mile west of here."

"Then we must think as we walk." Locke started trudging in the direction of Duggan's outstretched hand.

Finn caught up to him and lent him her arm. "It's getting a bit tough, isn't it? You think there's still a chance we can find this fictional Coleridge?"

Duggan followed close behind. "I was going to ask the same thing. What else do we know about this Achilles heel of his?"

"No more than conjecture," said Locke, "but my guess is that he's an autobiographical construct - a creation of the original Coleridge. In his memoirs, the man often wrote of a 'friend' who offered good counsel whenever there were tricky decisions to be made. It's commonly held that this friend never really existed; that he was a fictional device - useful for expressing a contrary point or explaining a change of heart."

"So what makes him so useful to Max?" said Duggan. "We're all dreamed up by someone. This imaginary chum of his should have no more power to create worlds than I do."

"Indeed not," said Locke. "But that isn't what I meant. The fictional Coleridge isn't the *source* of Max's power. He's a conduit; the means by which Max is able to influence the poet himself."

Duggan's facial muscles did unusual things. "How the hell can a fictional character influence his own creator?"

"Delusion?" offered Finn. "Coleridge was addicted to laudanum. Maybe the drugs mess up his understanding of what's real."

"I wondered the same thing," said the Professor. "When they're lost in their reveries, the two poets may be of one mind."

"Huh. So we're thinking that Max is getting this 'friend' to influence what the real Coleridge writes?" Duggan couldn't have looked less convinced if the Professor had been wearing a tinfoil hat and issuing earnest warnings about mind control. "Is that all we're pinning this on?"

"I said it was conjecture," said Locke, "but it would explain how Max has been able to create new narratives. If we're right, then separating Max from this fictional friend would rob him of his most powerful asset."

Finn looked ahead. As they rounded the shoulder of the hill, the roof of a small stone structure encroached slowly upon the skyline. Facing the prospect of a jump to yet another world, she found herself wondering about the wisdom of it.

"So where do I fit in?" she said. "If Max thinks I'm the Gatekeeper, what's my role in all this?"

Locke sighed. "Max believes that if he can get to you, he won't need Coleridge. He'll be able to do what only the She-Wolf has ever done before: breach the core and secure ultimate narrative power."

Finn bit her lip. Ultimate narrative power sounded handy - like just the sort of thing that could help her to get home. She leaned in closer to Locke. "And when you say ultimate...?"

"I mean exactly that, my dear; the power of life, death, and all creation."

Finn nodded. "Okay. Wow."

"Which means you'll be very much his principal target, of course."

"Mm. I hadn't forgotten."

Locke lowered his voice. "But if you truly are the Gatekeeper, then there are other implications, too. Most importantly, it means your world was never really the result of a published work."

"I don't understand." This was one of those occasions where honesty felt like the best policy.

Locke squeezed her hand. "It means you're different, Ms. Finn. We all came from elsewhere. *You*, I suspect, came from something in the She-Wolf's original tale; perhaps even from the Core itself. It means you were written for a purpose."

Finn gave an unenthusiastic shrug. "Okay, but so what? Am I supposed to get x-ray vision or something? I mean, what difference would it actually make?"

"Well, for one thing, it would raise some very interesting questions about your relationship with your narrator."

Finn snorted. "Interesting questions; no useful answers. I get a lot of that."

"The answers will come." Locke smiled and set his eyes on the horizon. "Authors do love that sense of destiny and revelation. And cheer up; it could easily work in your favour."

"Yeah? How?"

"Well, consider this - and bear in mind it may be something that has not yet occurred to Max. If you were not created by an external author - if you were created from within the original She-Wolf narrative - then that would make you an extension to Damelyka's own tale."

Finn grimaced. "Oh great. You're making me sound like a sequel."

"Oh, good heavens, no. Perish the very notion. But consider it; as the creation of the She-Wolf herself, you would stand as the instrument of the most powerful force in all the worlds." He held her with his glittering eye. "You would be that which New Tybet has lacked for over four centuries: a protagonist."

Finn gave a quiet snort. "Well that settles it: I'm definitely not the Gatekeeper. I wasn't even the protagonist of my own story, let alone something like this. If this She-Wolf woman picked me for a hero then she made a colossal mista..."

"Heads up!" Duggan pointed back the way they'd come. "What are those?"

Finn turned to see a pair of small airborne objects glinting in the sun. Darting back and forth across the skyline like heavily armoured hoverflies, they were a long way distant, but there was something unmistakably predatory about them.

"Hunter drones," murmured Locke. "Stay low, keep quiet, and let's get to that shed as quickly as we can."

Still holding the Professor's arm, Finn helped him over the last hundred metres to the little stone building. Then, pressing herself to the stone, she glanced back around the sheltering wall. As yet, they seem to have gone undetected.

"Hitch," said Locke, "might I trouble you for your reader? I'll need both if we're going to get through to young Mr. Forster."

Hitch squatted beside him and handed over the device. "Johnny's going to have to do something pretty spectacular if he's going to find us an exit before those drones get to us."

"The boy's clever," said Duggan. "And what choice do we have?"

"We could give ourselves up," said Hitch. "We've only got one exit left and I'm pretty sure that'll take us straight through to a prison cell."

Finn frowned. "No, hang on. Back there, you said there was something else; somewhere else we could go. I didn't understand what you said but there was the city and our own... something."

"Oh." Hitch shook his head. "No, just our TOOs."

"Our what?"

"It doesn't matter; we can't use them."

"But what...?"

"Tales Of Origin," said Duggan. "Where we came from; it's a private thing."

"But why can't we...?"

"Because we're already dead there." Glumly, Hitch popped a walnut in his mouth. "You can't erase it from your reader - the connection's always there - but it's not an escape route."

"Huh." Finn sat against the wall. "So that's why the title of my story kept coming up on your..."

She paused. She blinked. She started looking very intently at Hitch.

Glancing uncomfortably at her, he leaned away. "What?"

She continued to stare at him. Surely not. He couldn't be.

"Stop it," he said. "You're being weird. I don't like it."

"*Little Woodsmeade in-the-Dale*," she said. "That keeps coming up on your reader. Why?"

"Over there," hissed Duggan, pointing. "Troops - coming out the woods. How are we doing with the comms, Professor?"

"Got him!" cried Locke, bringing his reader close to his face. "Johnny, my dear, do please come in."

The reply was audible, but swamped in static. *"Professor? Is that you?"*

"Ah, my boy, it's dashed good to hear your voice. Did you find the poet's location?"

"I'm sending you the details now, but it's no good Professor. The gates are all shut down."

Hitch snatched back his reader. "Johnny, we're in big trouble. We've got armed goons coming at us and we've got no exit; they'll be here any time."

"I'm sorry Hitch, there's literally nothing I can do. It's all shut down. Every last narrative."

"Every one?" Hitch looked like a cornered animal; like a fretful, oversized, nut-munching squirrel. "You sure?"

"Every single record. Everything the system's ever crawled. It's all been completely locked down. But listen, I've been thinking. If we - the winds howl, loud the waves roar, thunderclaps rend the air..."

Hitch squinted at his reader. "Johnny? Who's that singing? Where are you?"

"Sorry, sorry." The Professor adjusted something on his screen. "We'll have him back in a..."

"...if I can only get through to her databanks."

"No, no, we lost you." Hitch grimaced at Locke. "Say again."

"Rowan's avatar research," said Johnny. *"It's password-protected but there are some artificial narratives in there. If I can access them, I might be able to gate you into one of those. It'll only be a buffer; a stepping stone, but..."*

"How long, Johnny? We're running out of time."

"An hour, maybe; I'd have to hard-wire..."

"No. That's no good." Hitch shook his head. "We've got minutes at most."

Finn took out her phone. "I've got an idea. Johnny? Are new stories still coming onto the system?"

"Yes; all the time. But they're all queued up; it takes time to crawl everything. Until a story's been indexed, we have no idea what's in there."

"But if someone we knew wrote us a story, could you find it? Could we use it?"

"You mean before the system crawled it? We wouldn't know anything about it. It would be incredibly dangerous."

"Johnny," said Hitch. "We've got about a hundred very enthusiastic killers approaching us right now and our only defence is a winning smile. Can you do it or not?"

"If I knew at least something about it, maybe: the title, the genre - the more data I've got the better. But the whole thing's moot; there's absolutely no way of knowing when a higher level author's going to publish something, or what it will be."

Finn grabbed Hitch's wrist. "Johnny, how did you get hold of those avatars you brought to Rowan's lab? What did you do to reach them?"

"Dr. Rowan hacked into a VR gaming system - the fictional environment it generated; we could talk to the players so long as they were online and their software was running."

"Could you do it again?"

"Yeah. It's a separate system; it's running all the time at this end. I'd just have to..."

"Can you, I don't know, hook us up? Log me in? I don't know the right words, but can we...?"

"Your readers will carry a comms signal, yes. Just give me a... okay, I'm logging you in now; I'm monitoring you. What do we want to do?"

Finn started dialling a number. "Well, let's start by hoping this works."

28. The Watcher of Roth

[Mulder96] I'm telling you man its aliens. For real

[RiddickMcN] I don't know what it was but there's noting on the web about it

[Mulder96] Wont be on there. Dark web maybe. If it really was an Abdullah

[RiddickMcN] What?

[Mulder96] abduction. Fracking autocomplete. What did jez reckon

[RiddickMcN] He's no sure. Says keep quiet till we know more. Wait... Phone. BRB

"Yello..." Neil pushed away the keyboard and tilted back his chair.

"Is that Neil?" A woman's voice crackled through his headphones. It didn't sound like a telesales call.

"Um. Yeah?"

"Hi, wow. I didn't think this would work. Look I don't know if you remember me, but it's Finn. Cathy Finn. We met online, on that VR demo?"

"Yeah. Wow, yeah." He sat upright in his chair. "The games tester. The Bagpuss girl."

"The what? Sorry, this line's a bit..."

"Bagpuss. You said you dropped him down a well."

"Bloody hell, you remember that?"

"I remember all of it. It was the weirdest thing ever. Did you...?"

"Look, sorry Neil, but it's got even weirder. I need your help. Will you help me?"

"Well, yeah, sure, of course."

"You said you write fantasy fiction. Have you got anything you could put online?"

"What, like writers' groups - forums and stuff?" He wrinkled his nose. "I don't know. I'm not sure if it's good enough, really."

The line sounded muffled for a moment.

"Yeah, yeah. A writers' forum would be fine. Can you pop something on - just a short story, even?"

In the background, there was sudden loud crack, like a pistol shot.

"What was that?"

"Nothing. Well, not... Look, I know it's weird and sudden but could you post it, like, incredibly quickly?"

"Thanks, but I'm really not sure it's any good. It's a bit...."

"Oh, no, I'm sure it's great, Neil. What's it about?"

"Oh, it's just an idea. It's not finished. I've had it for ages, but it wasn't coming together. But then I went back to it after you said you might be interested..."

"Oh wow. So our little chat inspired you. That's great."

"Well, I don't know. I'm not really..."

"Neil, please. If you could help me, I'd be so grateful. You'd be a life-saver."

"Shit, I'm hit! I'm hit!" A second voice. A man's.

Neil recoiled from the phone. "Who... who was that?"

Down the line came the muffled sounds of movement. He flinched as another pistol shot rang out.

"Cathy..? Finn? What's happening?"

"Neil? You still there?"

"Still here, yeah. What's happening?"

"Just having to move someone. Look - can you upload something now? I mean, like, actually now? This minute? I can't explain, but if you can do this for me, Neil..."

"Okay. I'm doing it, I'm doing it."

"Great. This is... great. Really appreciate it. So what's it called? Where are you sending it?"

"Um, do you know the Authoscribe forum? It's not a big..."

"No, but I'm sure I can find it."

Bang. Another shot cracked in his earpiece.

"Got the bastard!" The man's voice again.

A mechanical whine preceded the crump of an impact. It sounded like a car crash.

"Cathy? Are you okay? It's uploading now."

"Yeah, yeah. Still here. And the name? What's the name of it?"

"Um, well, it's called 'The Watcher of Roth' but that's just like a working title. I mean don't expect too much; it's not really..."

"Look, Neil, don't worry about that. The main thing is..."

"Duggan's down," said a new man's voice. *"Sleep dart."*

"Grab his pistol!" That sounded like Cathy.

"You grab his pistol. I don't want it."

"Just grab it, you wuss; you don't have to use it!"

"No. I made a promise."

"Oh, for f... Neil, how's it going? Is it uploaded yet?"

Neil peered at the screen. "Chapter one's up now. I'm just doing chapter two."

"Hang on." The line went quiet again. *"No, that's fine, Neil. One chapter's enough. I think we can work with that. Neil, you're a star. I really can't thank..."*

There was a brief burst of static, then only a steady electronic tone.

Slowly and carefully, Neil replaced the receiver. He looked back at his monitor and minimised the forum website. His in-game chat window was still there blinking at him.

[Mulder96] what's happening bro
[Mulder96] seriously Ridd-man what you doing
[Mulder96] you there.... hello???

[Mulder96] ok frack this Neil

...

Frowning, Neil put his fingers to the keyboard.
[RiddickMcN] BAK. U still there?
[Mulder96] WTF?
[RiddickMcN] Sorry Keith. The craziest thig just hapened

"Well, I didn't enjoy that at all." Hitch threw open the door of a long-abandoned hovel. "And look at this place; it's even worse."

Finn gave him a hard push that sent him staggering into a muddy forest clearing. "I can't believe you left Duggan behind! You're unbelievably selfish."

"Hey." Through a holographic suit of armour, Hitch rubbed his shoulder. "That hurt. And it's not my fault. He's a big guy. He was unconscious. There's no way I was going to be able to lift him."

"You didn't even try."

"What can I say? I know my limitations." He backed away. "And besides, Max's men were right on top of us; I had no choice. If I'd stopped, they'd have got me too."

Finn shook her head. "You're pathetic. You didn't even get his gun, did you?"

"I told you, I never touch anything like that. I made a solemn promise."

"Oh yeah, of course. You and your promises." She peered up into the trees, angry enough to cast delicacy aside. "I figured it out, you know. I know who you are."

"What?" She was pleased to hear the little tremor in his voice.

"I didn't believe it at first, but then I kept thinking back to all those little quirks of yours. The nuts, the constant hoarding, all those solemn promises to your mum." She looked him in the eye. "And then there's the name, isn't there? *Hitch the Postman.* Mr. Quick. Not the subtlest of changes, was it?"

Hitch turned away. "We haven't got time for this."

She grasped his shoulder. "Admit it. You were Quickory Hitchpost, weren't you? You were a bloody squirrel."

Casting his eyes to the forest floor, Hitch shook his head. "My past is nobody's business but my own."

"But I'm right, aren't I? I grew up with those stories. And bloody hell, I loved them, Hitch. I mean... you were the cutest, bravest, sweetest creature ever written. What happened to you?" She loosened her grip; waggled his sleeve. "How did you become... *this?"*

He shook his head, a new look in his eyes; a look that spoke of feelings she knew too well. "Things were taken from me, Finn. Family, friends; important things. I don't want to discuss it."

Finn smoothed his sleeve. "Come on. You have to. What happened?"

"I told you; it's private." He shrugged away, back towards the door, where Locke was busy pulling at one of the frame's mouldering uprights.

"Give me a hand with this," said the Professor. "If we can pull this apart, we can stop anyone using it to follow us. And then perhaps then we can figure out exactly where we are."

"You look weary, Col." Silas crouched beside the young poet in his parlour and laid a hand upon his wrist. Finding him alone, he'd had to light the candles himself. How long the man might have sat in darkness he dare not guess.

Oh, but the worlds were unfair! This poor tormented man; this colossus of the intellect; this living image of his own creator - he sat slumped into his chair as though all the weight of the worlds were upon him. What a kindness it would be to take him away from all this.

"You do not meet me at my best, Silas." The poet flickered a weak but playful smile.

He sighed. "Then we shall pursue none of our usual diversions today. They may wait for another time."

"I fear they must." The young man stirred a little, righting his position. "But you discomfit me, Silas. The more I reflect, the more it seems your thoughts have tended lately to violence and revolution. These are troubled times, I know, but you must be careful, dear friend."

Silas smiled. "Always, Col. But you are right. The times *are* troubled; perhaps more so than you know." He stood and slowly paced the little room. "We are become a weak, fractious, fearful people, made numb and stupid by the pursuit of empty pleasures. Couched in comfort, stimulated to excess, we forget the horrors of which men and nations are capable. The public spirit turns mean and insular; reproachful; dangerous. Surely, any civilisation worthy of the name must aspire to greater heights than this!"

Col produced another weak smile. "Ever the pantisocrat."

"But of course. For I have seen the new world and all that it could be." He gestured to the window. "I have stood there, Col, upon its very earth. Its rivers, its gardens, the great dome in their midst - they would amaze you. I have seen what an Elysium it might be; how it might outshine this old, tired England." He set his hands against the window frame. "But wherever men walk, the same sins and suspicions persist; aimless in a half-governed land, they stray. What is wanted is a firm, governing hand. Give me but the chance and I should see them shocked from their stupor; made bright and brave and whole again."

"Silas." Col raised a wavering hand; squeezed shut his eyes as though trying to shake off a mental fug. "Your energy and conviction do you credit, but this passion... it disposes me to believe there... there is more to..." He put a hand to his temple, seemingly unable to continue.

Silas returned to his chair-side. "Please, don't trouble yourself, my friend. Forgive my outburst. I did not mean... Sleep if you must. I am here."

The young man nodded, but kept his eyes closed.

Silas' wrist buzzed. It startled him. Covering his reader with his palm, he returned quietly to the window, fitting an earpiece as he went.

"Joshua, this is not a good time."

"My apologies, but the woman escaped."

Frowning, he strode into the darkened hallway. "But we had her. How, when every gate is shut?"

"I have yet no explanation. We are making every effort to know the truth. I thought you would want to know on the instant."

"Of course. You did right." Turning in the doorway, Silas saw the poet sleeping fitfully in his chair and knew it was time to act. "I shall return presently, Joshua. And I shall be bringing a guest."

"Johnny was right, you know." Hitch kicked and thrashed his way through the thinning undergrowth like a knight errant in a steaming sulk. "This is incredibly dangerous. What if this geek friend of yours decides to edit the story while we're in it? What if he starts writing us *into* it? We'll never get out."

Finn prodded her phone. "I've tried calling him again but the line's dead."

"That's because the system hasn't parsed the narrative." Locke had taken up a fallen branch for a staff and now had every appearance of an elder wizard. "Until it does, we won't be able to talk with anyone except Mr. Forster - and even that might be difficult."

Hitch jerked a thumb skyward. "Did you at least tell your old mate not to re-write anything while we're in here?"

Finn smiled thinly. "D'you know, there really wasn't a lot of time, what with all the drones and poison darts and gunfire and everything."

"Besides, it would hardly have been wise to reveal our intentions," agreed Locke. "Under the circumstances, you did exceedingly well, Ms. Finn. And I ought to congratulate you. You've accomplished something of a first. Establishing such a dialogue with a higher level author is without precedent in the whole hist... "

"Oh... *Trumpton.*" Hitch's shoulders sagged as he cleared the forest's edge.

Finn and Locke caught him up in two strides. "What's the matter?"

"Look at that."

The woods ended abruptly at the top of a barren slope of red earth. To the left, a track led down to a rickety timber bridge, beneath which flowed a river of lava that spat with all the frequency of an angry teenager. Beyond it lay a standard-issue medieval village comprising a church, a tavern and a sullen cluster of thatched roofs. Quite how the bridge or the thatch survived their proximity to the lava was anyone's guess but perhaps logic wasn't too much of a constraining force round here. That would certainly explain the geologically unlikely spire of rock that rose immediately behind the settlement, and the great turreted castle perched atop it.

"Geeks," said Hitch gloomily. "Always the same. It'll be fire-breathing dragons next, just you wait."

"It's not ideal, I'll grant you," said the Professor, "but, still, we need a door. I suggest we hurry along."

Finn had reached the midpoint of the bridge when the mountains popped up. They did so without sound or fanfare. One moment, the castle was set against a darkening sky; the next, it was flanked by a horizon-spanning ridge of jagged peaks.

"Woah," said Finn. "Look at that."

Hitch had been peering down into a fiery chasm at the time and hadn't noticed the arrival of an eighty mile-long mountain range. When he saw it, he agreed.

"Woah," he said.

"Woe indeed," said the Professor with a dark look. "It's as we feared; our writer friend is re-imagining his tale."

"Ah. Well that's not good." Finn felt she was finally getting a handle on things.

Locke gave them both a gentle push in their backs. "We must find a door at once."

Hurrying across into the main street, Finn found the place deserted. If fantasy villages were supposed to be populated by droves of rosy-cheeked peasants, no one appeared to have told Neil. Every door was barred shut and covered in blood-red runes. She wasn't great on runic alphabets but Finn could gather their meaning well enough: strangers probably shouldn't expect too much in the way of fruit baskets or welcoming floral garlands.

"Try that one." Locke pointed his staff at the nearest door.

Finn turned to take her first step just as the street widened noiselessly beneath her feet. She staggered, nearly falling as the cobbles spread and divided. When she looked up, the village was considerably enlarged and newly ringed by a great stone wall. The buildings themselves were sturdier now; masonry stood in place of timber; thatch had given way to slate and tile. All of which lessened the fire hazard, admittedly, but with the whole settlement shifting uncomfortably about her like a dragon with a threadworm infestation, it came as little consolation.

"This is not good at all." Hitch swiped at his reader. "The doors keep changing. I can't fix on any of them."

Leaning on his staff, the great wizard Locke rose unsteadily to his feet. He pointed along what still appeared to be the main street. "The church. It hasn't changed. It might be more clearly imagined than the rest."

Finn took his arm and hurried on. "How can Neil be re-writing things so fast?"

"Not re-writing," said Locke. "Re-imagining. When a published draft is parsed by the Core, that fixes the narrative - makes it safe and stable for the likes of us. Until then, any new idea will manifest as an immediate change in the diegesis."

"So absolutely anything could happen?"

Locke nodded ruefully.

"Okay," said Finn. "Well, let's crack on."

Closer to the centre, the buildings grew taller. That is to say, the individual structures rose visibly around them as they approached. Some sprang, plant-like from the ground while others sprouted new storeys from their upper levels. It was a little like walking amongst some animated construction toy advertisement, except that the experience induced a deeply unpleasant sense of motion sickness.

"Ah... nuts." Hitch pointed to the church's entrance. The doors had been burned from their hinges. A wide crack had split one side of the stone arch.

"Inside, then," said Locke. "There must be something we can use."

Finn helped the old man up the steps into the warmly glowing interior.

At once, Finn was struck by the unusualness of the building. Partly, it was the architecture: a queasy blend of Ancient Greek and twisting, organic-looking forms that wouldn't have looked uncomfortable in a painting by HR Giger. Partly, too, it was its emptiness: its pews, altars and tapestries had all been reduced to lines and scatterings of ash. Mainly though, what really did it was the great blazing hoop of stone fixed upright in the centre of the floor - that, and the three-metre tall warrior who stood before it, silent and still, with his eyes set unwaveringly upon the flames.

Not unnaturally, Finn paused. There was something vaguely odd about it all, or - to be more precise - a certain oddness remained even when one looked beyond all the other nonsense that was going on. Here, after all, was an oversized knight, standing before a poorly disguised stargate, in a ruined church at the centre of a frankly not very realistic medieval village. There was a fair degree of weirdness associated with every part of that, but it wasn't any of these things that nagged at her.

Then she saw it: the stance. The great warrior hadn't moved, despite their unheralded appearance, and there he stood, shoulders squared to the portal, with the tip of a decidedly unwieldy broadsword resting between his feet. She'd seen that stance, that image somewhere before, in some superhero movie franchise. She couldn't recall its name but the whole feel of the scene was suspiciously familiar.

On the other hand, the familiarity wasn't very important. This was Neil's story and now really wasn't the time to get all cynical and litigious. If there was any plagiarism afoot, she was determined to overlook it.

"Um. Hello?" ventured the Professor.

"Who intrudes upon the Watcher of Roth?" boomed the creature. Its voice was loud enough to set the crows flying, except that Neil didn't seem to have imagined any.

The Professor edged forward. "My name's Locke. We're looking for a door; a way out."

The great warrior didn't turn his head. "Choose another," it advised, still evidently convinced that booming was the only way to go.

Finn glanced at Hitch. It seemed like a reasonable suggestion. Of all the doors and archways available to them, there really wasn't any good reason to choose one that led directly into a furnace - and that was always supposing that 'furnace' wasn't an unduly optimistic description. Given the tale's fantastical setting, it seemed quite possible she might glimpse the occasional cloven hoof or pitchfork amongst the flames.

"He makes a good point," said Hitch.

"Be gone and leave the Watcher to his vigil." Thus far, all the evidence suggested that booming was his only mode of discourse. "Here lies only pain and darkness."

"Right-ho. Well we certainly don't want any of that." Hitch popped a peanut in his mouth and turned to examine the soot-blackened masonry. "I mean, this whole fiery portal thing; we're not wedded to it at all. We'll be happy to try somewhere else if you can just point us in the right direction."

The Watcher ignored him.

Hitch looked back over his shoulder. "I mean, *quid pro quo*, obviously. If there's something you'd like..? A chair perhaps? Something to sit on?"

"The Watcher needs no *chair*." There was just a hint of testiness mixed in with all the booming.

Hitch shrugged. "Alright. Okay. Just a thought."

"Come over here." Locke had returned to the broken door.

Finn joined him.

"Our author friend seems to have finished his re-imagining." The Professor indicated the static and largely well behaved properties surrounding them. "I think now would be a good time to leave."

Finn took a breath. "Any suggestions?"

"The tavern," said Locke, pointing across the square. "My eyes aren't what they were but that doorway looks to be set beside a rather splendid statue."

Finn nodded. "And if he's gone to the trouble of thinking it up, he's not so likely to unimagine it."

"You're learning quickly." Locke smiled benignly. "You know, that's one of the great pleasures of being an educator: one gets to touch so many young people. If I've rubbed off on you, Ms. Finn, I would consider our little adventure a success."

"Hold on." Hitch had made it halfway down the steps. "Wait. There's something funny about that statue."

Finn followed him. "Like what?"

"Well..." He wrinkled his nose. "It's you."

"Oh dear," said Locke from a little way behind.

"What do you mean, it's me?" said Finn. "There's no way... Oh."

Now midway across the square, standing beside a dry, but recently materialised fountain, she could see the detail of the statue outside the inn. It depicted a woman in unnecessarily revealing leather armour, equipped with a bow, a long dagger and a cleavage that could securely park a bicycle. The face above it had pointy elfin ears, but it was unmistakably hers.

Finn shook her head. What was it with boys and leather thongs?

"Oh dear," repeated the Professor as he caught her up. "This could be very bad news indeed. We must hurry, Hitch."

"Working on it." Hitch leaned against one of the statue's inadequately clad thighs and began fussing with his reader.

Finn felt a growing unease; a tightening in her chest. "What's the problem?"

Locke shook his head. "If your writer friend imagines you too vividly into this tale then I'm afraid you could become anchored to it. You would acquire a second Tale of Origin. It could change you; bind you here."

She shook her head. "Neil wouldn't do that. I mean, why me? He'd have to be completely obsessed..."

She stopped. Locke was frowning at the carvings on the fountain. They were moving as she watched; transforming themselves into the shapes of handmaidens, mermaids and dryads. On every figure, the face was hers.

The tightening in her chest increased. She looked down at her outfit. Beneath her holographic hunter's cloak and the equally illusory leather breastplate, something was shifting; pressing; *expanding*. It wasn't just her eyes that were getting bigger.

"Are you alright, my dear?" Locke regarded her with concern.

"Oh my God." She pressed her hands to her chest. "He's... My... Look, you're right; we've *really* got to get out of here."

"Back up! Back up!" Hitch turned and began running. "Back to the church!"

"Wh...?" Finn cut short her own question. The tavern was fading to a mist. She felt Locke tugging at her arm.

"Hurry, my dear. It's changing again."

To the left and right, the village was losing its colour and substance; fading to the whiteness of a blank page. Only the church ahead of her retained any solidity at all, but even that looked vulnerable. Its spire was already paling.

"Hitch," cried the Professor. "We must raise Johnny at once."

Together, they bundled back into the fire-lit church.

Hitch stabbed frantically at his wrist. "Comms are dead. What about yours?"

Locke consulted his reader. "Likewise. I'm afraid..."

Finn's phone crackled into life.

"Finn, it's me," said the voice of Johnny Faustus. *"I'm so sorry. They tracked the signal; they found me."*

29. The Unimagined

"*Be cheerful, Miss Finn.*" The face of Max Roberts appeared on her phone. "*The chase is ended, but it ends well. I pray you, return to the city and let me lay out my scheme for your inspection; let me prove to you I am no iron-souled despot.*"

Finn offered him a tired smile, the kind she normally reserved for doorstep evangelists. "And I suppose this is the bit where you reveal your dastardly plan, is it?"

"*My dear lady, hasten not to judge. Your flight robbed me of the chance to explain myself. I beg you, before you name me dastard, understand me at least.*"

"Oh, I don't know, Max; I think I know enough." She sighed. "Lies, abduction, murder..."

Max shook his head. "*A half-crazed tyrant who glories in the howl of maniac uproar. Is that how you should paint me?*"

Finn nodded. "Pretty much. Not sure about the half."

"*Then, truly, you misjudge. Please, Miss Finn; return to the city. You shall see the rightness of my intent: to rid the world of its vacuity; to reinstate the law of all moral and rational beings.*"

"And if I say no?" She was conscious that Locke was now a reassuring presence at her shoulder. "What then?"

In answer, Max nodded to an off-screen aide. An instant later, the Watcher of Roth produced a great melancholy sigh and, turning, ended his not-quite-so-ceaseless vigil over the burning gate. He hefted his great sword and took a deliberate, menacing step towards her.

"Finn!" Hitch interposed himself, flinging out his arms, but as the giant moved, so its form lost substance. In two more paces, it had vanished entirely from the church.

"*You see,*" continued Max. *"Your tale is now mine to alter as I please, but I offer no threat, only an honest welcome. Believe me, Miss Finn, no one wishes you more safely returned than I."*

"To serve your own lunatic ends!" cried Locke, leaning in to the screen. "To serve you in your insane demagoguery!"

"Insane!" Max produced a laugh that rather made the Professor's point for him. *"My dear Professor, you misapprehend. I gather my armies and what do you conclude? That my motives be selfish and malign; that I seek no grander prize than my own elevation. You are wrong, my learned friend. Surely you must see; when the world is grown so sick as this, one must needs find a cure."*

Locke snorted. "An impressive dictum, Max, but I won't have you ramming it down my throat. An old fool I may be, but I've heard too many madmen try to justify their wars with noble-sounding words."

"But is it not oftentimes right to fight, Professor? When faced with a manifest wrong, is it not a good man's duty to stand against it?" Max gestured to the room around him. *"For too long our world has grown weak and stupid, ailing under the idle gaze of its narrator. Our celebrated She-Wolf - she won her power, but to what purpose did she put it? Why, to none at all. She looks on aloof as our culture runs to waste; as our people - spoiled by too much comfort - turn to greed and meanness."*

"More fine words," said Locke. "But let us speak plainly, Max. You want power - absolute power - and I dare say you're not so far gone that you've forgotten the old adage about that."

"Power to do something worthy of our culture, Paul. You have seen how things are shaping: the decline of intellect; how

jealously the common man protects his empty, cosseted little world. The age grows uglier. Our people have forgotten history - you must see it. They seek again to throw up walls and fences; to cast out all that is new and unfamiliar. Through spitefulness and fear, they would see our nation made a fortress - a fortress that would make prisoners of us all."

"He's stalling." Hitch tapped his reader. "What is it you're really up to, Max?"

"Ah, Mr. Quick. Ever the cynic. Is it so hard to believe that I would have this matter peacefully resolved?"

Hitch sniffed. "Frankly, yes."

"Then consider: you stand on stones I could at any instant turn to searing coals, yet I forbear. I could conjure demons from the mist and have them bring you here by force, yet I forbear. Do you not question why?"

"Well, at the risk of messing up your soliloquy..."

"To prove I am not urged to this by hate or madness; that I hold courage and intelligence in high esteem; that I would have you as a willing ally."

"An ally?" Hitch snorted. "To you? A man who hounds me, takes my things, sends his thugs after me with guns?"

"Ah yes, your precious things." Max smiled. *"Your worldly goods; your contraband, and your little... biscuits. You have made a career of trade and negotiation; let me then offer terms a man like you should understand."*

Hitch glowered, but said nothing.

"I present you with a choice, Mr. Postman. And an easy one, I think, for one such as you." Max flashed him a businessman's smile, wide and easy. *"Open the gate and lead your companions to safety. Do so and you may name your own reward. Refuse and you force me to more brutish measures."*

So saying, he reached to the side of the screen and touched some unseen control. The church's vaulted roof vanished like a mist. Its walls tumbled away, fading into a dull white silence. All at once, the building was a raft of stone, alone and adrift on an Unimagined sea.

"You have nowhere left to run," said Max. *"So come now; the city awaits; bring yourself home."*

Slowly, Hitch shook his head. He looked away, seemingly rapt by the whiteness all about. "If you knew anything at all about me you'd understand: Tybet was never my home."

Max made a quick, dismissive gesture. *"Then make a new one of your own choosing. Help me now and, upon my honour, I shall reward you with all you could ever wish."*

When Hitch turned back, his eyes were dark; wild like the fires blazing in the gate. "I *had* all I could ever wish. Don't you understand? I *had* it once, but it was stolen from me. My author made me old overnight; stole my childhood; snatched away my parents and my friends. And you people, you didn't let me die there; you extracted me; took me away from everything I'd ever loved." He gestured at his chest. "You gave me this body and you sent me off to live again, somewhere cold, and harsh, and stupid. You 'saved' me but you never once thought to ask me if it was what I wanted."

Max shot him a perplexed frown. *"Then... then that too may be remedied. You understand the prize I seek. Deliver Miss Finn and I shall have the wherewithal to make full and proper restitution. You yearn so for your former life - then help me and let me reinstate it. What say you? Should you be your old self again; walking in your old world amongst those whom once you loved?"*

Hitch gazed for a long moment at the screen, but at last he shook his head. "See, it's a nice offer, Max, but it all sounds just a bit needy, you know? I just can't bring myself to believe you."

"Hitch!" Max leaned forward into the screen. *"You cannot doubt how important this is to me; how fervent my wish to see our world renewed. My eyes and spirit are set high; I feel no urge to spite or petty vengeance. And think: when this is done, what should it cost me to reward you? I speak of simple reciprocity. Do you not comprehend?"*

"Reciprocity." Hitch gave his chin a theatrical rub. "Um. Could you maybe use it in a sentence?"

Max threw himself back into his chair, his face pained. *"This shabby defiance - this aimless futility. My patience erodes every moment. I will send in my soldiers if I must, but as an honourable man, I ask you once more: spare yourselves the hurt, the ignominy. Accept what is inevitable and for reason's sake, bring yourselves home."*

"Hitch," said Locke, looking up from his wrist. "You were right; he's stalling. He's using your reader to scan the gate."

"Oh, no you don't." Hitch hit a sequence of buttons on his reader and unwrapped it from his wrist.

"Hitch!" Max came so close to the camera that the edges of his face escaped the bounds of Finn's screen. *"What are you doing? This is suicide!"*

"Finn, point that thing at me." Hitch strode to the centre of the floor. "Here's your answer, you cheap, dog-bothering turdling." With a look of furious rebellion, he hurled his reader into the Unimagined. In a heartbeat, it had paled to nothing.

As if in sympathy, Finn's phone winked out.

A quiet moment passed.

"Has he gone?" asked Hitch.

Finn raised her eyes and nodded.

He nodded. "Right. Well that's something, anyway."

"Hitch..." The Professor's face was sombre.

"Hmm?"

"Do you understand what you've...?"

"Uh huh." He attempted a brave face. "Lost my reader. Chucked it away. Probably not very sensible, really."

Finn held out a hand. "You said your whole life was on there."

He shook his head. "Not my real life. Not the one I wanted."

Locke cleared his throat. "Hitch; we only have one reader now. I can probably get Ms. Finn's phone slaved to this one, but even so... Max has locked everything; only two of us can leave."

Hitch gazed at the flames beyond the circle of stone. "Yeah. I know that. I knew that. It's just... I'm *tired,* you know? Of all this. It was never really me." He glanced at Finn. "You asked me how I became this. Truth is, I don't really know."

She put a hand on his arm. Her mind raced.

He smiled weakly. "Well anyway, it's done. And while Max was busy boring us all to death, I think I figured out how you two could get away." He nodded to Locke's reader. "I'm guessing he'll have a much harder time hacking yours than he did mine?"

Shrugging, the Professor tinkered with his settings. "They call me the Locksmith for a reason. Max will be an older man than I before he finds his way into this."

Hitch nodded. "Okay. Good. So you get Finn's phone hooked up to that, and then we dial up my TOO."

Locke shook his head. "But my boy..."

"Yeah, yeah; I know. Only two of us can leave." He looked again at the emptiness surrounding them. "But listen, Prof; it's the only way. You know that. We can't send Finn back to her origin, and you don't even have one. Besides, I want this; all I ever wanted was to go home. You want to know the last time I was really happy?"

Locke smiled. "I'll hazard a guess at *Quickory to the Rescue*. The last in the series before *Quickory's Last Tale*. I read them all, you know."

Hitch grinned, even as a tear welled in his heavy-lidded eye. "You read them? I didn't know that."

"I did, though I didn't much care for the last. Hastily written and poorly conceived. If you ask me, deathbed scenes have no place in a child's tale."

Hitch took a steadying breath. "Well, it's where I want to go. Where I should have ended it a long time ago."

Handing over his reader, Locke clapped a hand on his shoulder. "It's a commendable plan, Mr. Hitchpost. I'm sure your mother and father would have been very proud of you. But brave as it is, it will require one small modification if it's to work."

"Yeah? What's that?"

"I must be the one to remain here."

Hitch shook his head. "No. No, because..."

"My boy; you know very well the gate command can only be entered by the one who..."

Finn laid down her phone and watched the debate unfold, each man arguing why he should make the sacrifice. Slowly, she walked to the edge of the floor, where gently undulating waves of white nibbled away at the stone.

She looked back at their little stone stage; two fictional figures in a fictional tale, each trying to do their best. She was a long way from home, but it was strange how things repeated themselves. Here with her stood the two dearest people in this world, and their discussion was taking a predictable turn. They'd do their best to save her, but that was no longer what really mattered.

Things would be different now. She was going to make this *her* story.

"Finn! Stop! Be careful." Hitch turned, realising at last how close she stood to the Unimagined.

"It's alright," said Finn. "It's fine. I appreciate everything you've both done, but these worlds are where you belong, not me."

"Now, now." Locke took a step towards her, one arm extended like a hand outreaching from a lifeboat. "Let's just be rational for a moment."

"We *are* being rational," said Finn. "All of us. Rational and selfless and brave - like proper heroes. And you know what heroes do, Professor? Sometimes they take an unexpected step."

"My dear, please believe me: the Unimagined is not the place to do it."

"You said if I was the Gatekeeper, then that would make me the She-Wolf's creation; her protagonist. If that's true..."

"I said *might*, Cathy!" Locke's eyes were bright with alarm. "It was conjecture - nothing more."

Her raised palm warned him back. "I trust your instincts, Paul. Maybe this will give you two the chance to pull something amazing out of the bag. Maybe it will get me home. Either way, it's worth a try."

"Don't do it, Finn." Hitch shook his head. "It's just stupid."

She smiled. "You're not a great one for parting words, are you?"

"Finn, I..."

"Never mind. Now go and be geniuses and stop that madman."

Without waiting for a reply, she stepped backward into the mist.

30. The Return

What strange reverie was this? Sounds and images danced like sprites at play.

"... walls and towers manned, sir."

A glimpse of the ice white dome of which Silas spoke so fondly.

"... forces standing by the Alpha rivergate."

Soft foliage brushed his face; a flash of green, then silver light.

"... would know more of the woman. All there is." That one voice was familiar; his friend Silas.

"...a father lost; a sister surviving her..." The words drifted.

"...Ethiopia?" Silas again.

"... Abyssinia. Maternal ancestry. Little is said of her father's side..."

And now a half-glimpsed cavern; a miracle of invention, rigged with ropes and hawsers that shone like silver. And within it an orb, floating midway like a thing of frosted air.

"... no incubus; nothing of the demon. Not a word."

"... what other option..."

"...Woods... in the Dale... but where she sets the gate..."

"... prevent it... five miles about..."

Firm hands set him gently in a chair. Words and strains of music swam. Blessed sleep once more reclaimed him.

Finn could sense the voices - not hear them, exactly, but process them somehow, like words read from a page. A man's thoughts, for sure, but confused and fractured, like those of some wanderer in a crowd who snatches fragments of conversations as he goes. And in amongst them, the name of Silas, together with oblique references to herself.

That she could sense anything at all was unexpected. It meant she was still alive.

Instinctively, she'd closed her eyes as she'd stepped back off the church floor. Now, opening them, she could see her body standing beneath her and a small circle of ground, all closely bounded by the enclosing whiteness. The world seemed to be filling itself in around her as she moved. The church steps reappeared beneath her feet; so too the cracked stone arch of the door. The Unimagined hung tight around her, yet she hadn't vanished as she'd expected; it hadn't annihilated her or sent her back to her bookshop floor. Instead, it seemed to recoil from her. It shrank from her touch like a timorous animal.

Which was all a bit awkward, actually. A rather fundamental element of making a grand sacrificial gesture was that you didn't just reappear a moment or two later, as though you'd only popped out to bring in the milk. Returning unscathed did rather take the gloss off it.

But what choice did she have? With no reader, she couldn't go anywhere else. That meant she could either return to her friends or wander forever around a poorly formed fantasy world with just her own, uncomfortably inflated breasts for company.

Bemused and a little disappointed that the role of protagonist wasn't easier, she plodded up the steps and back into the church.

"Finn!" Expressions of disbelief lit the ashen faces of both Hitch and Locke.

"Hi. Hi." She offered them a bashful wave.

"But what..? How did..?" Locke rushed forward to hug her, uncharacteristically bereft of words.

Hitch scowled. "Don't you ever do anything like that again. We thought you'd..."

"It just kept budging out of my way," said Finn, hoping that an explanation might steer the conversation in a less awkward direction.

Locke released her shoulders, but took her hands tightly in his. "Then it's just as I said! The story followed you in! After more than four hundred years, New Tybet has a protagonist again!"

"Well, I don't know about that..."

"My dear; you absolutely must return to the city now. Hitch has a plan."

"No, I haven't," said Hitch. "Not one that doesn't get you killed."

"I fear the time for debate is ended, sweet boy." Locke nodded at the edge of the floor, where the Unimagined was now steadily encroaching. "It seems Max is attempting to force our hand."

"Shit." Finn shuffled towards the gate. "How long have we got?"

"No more than two or three minutes," said Locke. "So let us look simply at the facts. I have no origin and yours, Cathy, is more than a little doubtful in its provenance. That only leaves yours Hitch, so if we don't wish to deliver ourselves straight into Max's hands, the only viable exit is Little Woodsmeade in-the-Dale."

"Yeah, but..."

"And if we are to use that, then you, Hitch, must go through."

"No, that's..."

"You must. It's your origin; if it were otherwise, the gate simply wouldn't work." Locke handed Finn her phone, together with his reader. "Moreover, it's clearly crucial that Ms. Finn goes with you."

Hitch shook his head. "I'm not leaving you, Locke."

The Professor gave a quiet smile. "Once you activate the gate, Max will be able to send his men the other way. If you hurry, I can give myself up to them."

"Or you two could go," said Finn. "We know the U won't touch me; I'll be safe hiding there."

The Professor shook his head. "The plan won't work without you."

"Why? What plan?"

"You use my old extraction gate," said Hitch. "The one they used to scoop me from my original story. We wind your arrival time back as far as we can. You get yourself close to my old house - it'll be the deathbed scene - then you wait for the winch team to take me through. After that, I reckon you've probably got a window of about five to ten seconds before it closes for good. If you can get to it, you should be fine. It'll take you through to the Dome, but not anywhere Max will be expecting."

"And you must take Hitch with you, of course," said Locke. "If you're quick enough getting through to the city, there's every chance he'll revive. Then you simply create a new gate and pay a visit to our friend Mr. Coleridge." He pointed at his reader. "Johnny sent me the location; with Hitch's help, you should be able to reach it from within the Dome itself."

"But you said Hitch would be dead if we went back."

"Inert," said Hitch, glumly. "The original me will be there in the story, and no one can have their consciousness in two places at once. You'd have to carry me till we're out the other end. If you're too slow... well, then you're on your own."

Finn looked dubiously at Hitch's tubby frame. She didn't have to say anything.

"He'll revert to his original form," said Locke.

The U was only a few short metres from her now, but Finn couldn't help smiling. "What, you mean I actually get to cuddle Quickory Hitchpost?"

Hitch narrowed his eyes. "Carry. No one said anything about cuddling."

Finn held up her hands. "Okay. Boundaries. I accept that."

Hitch looked uncomfortably at Locke. "You sure about the shape thing?"

Locke shrugged. "It's an assumption based on some old reports."

"What sort of reports?"

"It isn't important."

"What *sort* of reports?"

"Oh alright; suicide investigations, if you really must know. People occasionally... do that."

Hitch nodded. "Suicide. Right."

"So anyway..." said Finn, edging ever closer to the gate. "Once the old you - I mean your younger self - once he's been taken through, you'll wake up again? You'll be okay? Back with us, all bright-eyed and... well, you know?"

"No idea," said Hitch. "This isn't something I do very often."

Finn frowned. "Alright, but that still doesn't explain why it has to be me. It sounds like the plan would work just as well with you two."

"You once told me you enjoyed cross-country running." Locke cast an anxious look towards the U. Less than a third of the floor remained. "I inferred you were something of an athlete."

"I do a bit of fell running with a club, but I'm hardly..."

"Five miles in forty-five minutes." He gave her a stern look. "Could you do it?"

"That's what? Eight k?" She waggled her head. "It depends on the terrain. Certainly not in these shoes."

"Do it barefoot." Hitch shrugged off his bandoliers. "It's all soft, rolling hillsides where I'm from. Spongy grass and not a thorn or a sharp rock anywhere."

"Well, yeah, I suppose I could probably do that, then, but..."

"Well that's excellent," said Locke. "So we're agreed: you step through, pick up our sleeping squirrel and then run like the blazes to his home. D'you know where that is?"

She smiled again. "I grew up with those books. I'd know it anywhere."

"Good. But remember: timing and discretion will be essential. All the usual rules of non-intervention apply. Any interaction and you risk ruining the tale and erasing it from history - together with our frowning friend here."

Finn nodded. "No, right; I understand. I'll sneak into the village - I'll come in past the churchyard - and then I've just got to wait for the last winchman to leave through the gate. Once he's gone, I should have a few seconds to follow him through."

"You can buy yourself a few more seconds by pressing these." Hitch indicated a pair of buttons on Locke's reader. "That stops everything."

"Well bravo," beamed Locke. "We have a plan, though precious little time to implement it. I suggest you get to it."

"Hitch shook his head. "And you're going to let Max's men take you?"

"I dare say they'll be keen to probe me if they can."

"And what if they don't get here in time?"

Locke batted that away. "Oh tush. I'm a Recurrent, dear boy. Such a trifling thing as death doesn't faze me."

"But this is the U." Hitch gestured to the blankness all around. "That's different."

"And time is pressing," said Locke. "The longer we debate, the slimmer my chances."

"You absolutely sure?"

"Please, Hitch. Just go."

Finn squeezed the Professor's hand as Hitch took the reader and entered the key. "Don't you dare get yourself killed."

He gave her a paternal smile. "I wouldn't dream of it, my dear."

"Ready," said Hitch, taking Finn's arm. "Oh, and this might come in handy for... well, you know." He passed her a bandolier with its convenient, squirrel-sized loops.

Finn allowed herself to be led into the gate. She ignored the flames; instead she kept her eyes on Locke, watching him as long as she could. She felt the tug of Hitch's arm and stepped forward.

As she crossed the threshold, she thought she glimpsed the Professor beginning to turn away in the direction of the Unimagined.

31. Through Wood and Dale

It should have been so much nicer than this.

After all, here lay Little Woodsmeade in-the-Dale, the place of a thousand imagined adventures, and it looked exactly as she had always envisaged it. There, on the side of Cock Robin Hill, Bluebell Brook came meandering through the woods, turning the wheel of Fred Bear's woollen mill before wending its way down into the valley bottom. The fields were their old familiar patchwork of colour and, ahead, not far distant, rose the crooked spire of the village church. Not a thing looked out of place, yet she felt anything but comfortable.

Hitch had slumped forward the instant he'd made the crossing, hitting the spongy turf in the form of a little red squirrel, its whiskers all curled and greying with age. He fitted well enough into the bandolier she now wore across her mercifully reduced chest, but his little body kept sagging and slipping as she ran. The knowledge of her responsibility weighed heavily on her, as did her uncertainty about the fates of Locke, Duggan, Cariola and the rest. They'd all fallen in this race to stop the psychotic Max, and now she was running alone.

And then there was the heat. The air was thick and close - cosy as a child's bedroom - and that made running a bugger and a half.

Quickory's Last Tale had never been her favourite - as an adult, she recognised the signs of an ageing author cashing in with a sentimental, cartoon-friendly finale to the series. Winnie-the-Pooh had managed to go out with class, but Hitch's creator - the matronly Edith Braxton - had evidently just sold out. Perhaps hoping to win some long-coveted literary prize for mawkishness, she'd taken every opportunity to pile on the symbolism and the schmaltz. Now, as the pivotal scene approached, the sun hung low on the horizon like a half-closed lid. The sky shone a garish red, as though viewed through a television set with the saturation turned up too high.

The ruddy twilight at least afforded her some cover. When she'd told Locke of her running times, she hadn't considered that she'd have to be discreet. Twice she'd had to duck behind a pathside bush as a furry figure passed close by, and the interruptions played hell with her rhythm.

At last however, panting, barefoot and wet with sweat, she arrived undetected at the churchyard wall. Its grey, oval stones looked just as they had on the posters she'd once pinned to her bedroom wall.

And there, beyond the far boundary of the enclosure, set a little way back from the well in the village green, was the scarlet-fronted Post Office - home to Quickory Hitchpost himself.

She'd expected a village of Lilliputian scale but for some reason known only to the imagination of the estimable Ms. Braxton, the buildings were not much smaller than those of any historic village. Quite how a diminutive squirrel was supposed to operate a five-foot door was anyone's guess, but Finn supposed it worked to her advantage. Sneaking around a model village would have been an exercise in futility. Some good sized cottages meant plenty of cover and a manageable approach to her destination: Quickory's bedroom window.

She crept her way to the back garden. Bounded by a low wall, it had a little rustic gate that led out into the surrounding fields and woods. Now, stepping over it to avoid those famous squeaking hinges, she crossed between the burgeoning flower beds and, crouching, pressed herself against the brightly painted plaster wall.

Pausing for a moment, she reflected that she probably cut a rather sinister figure - panting, sweating, and lurking furtively below a window with a squirrel's corpse dangling from her belt. It really wasn't the sort of image you were supposed to encounter in a picture book tale like this.

The sooner she could move on the better.

Carefully, she peered over the painted window ledge. The lantern-lit scene was just as it had always been depicted, except that the original drawings had been imagined from the perspective of the doorway rather than that of a would-be peeping-tom.

There lay Quickory, surrounded by his friends, giving his long deathbed speech about the importance of family, courage and always doing one's best. She wondered exactly where he was up to. She could remember the other eleven books almost word for word but she'd tended to skip this one whenever she'd been offered the choice. The window was ajar but the dear old squirrel was weak and tired, and his entourage of friends and grandchildren made a furry little wall that his words simply couldn't escape.

"But Grandfather," said a dewy-eyed kit, "what must we do when you are gone?"

Why, my dear one, you must love one another. Finn didn't need to hear the words to remember his much-quoted answer.

And bloody hell, that was it, wasn't it? Those were his dying...

At once, the scene froze and a pair of giant squirrels in loose-fitting fur ducked clumsily into the room.

Finn blinked. The costumes couldn't possibly hide the fact that there were human beings inside them, but to be fair, they were very well put together. The extraction teams obviously used to be a lot better resourced than they were today.

How strange it was to see someone else responding to a winch team with the same sense of bafflement and alarm that had once crashed over her. Granted, when her turn had come, she hadn't had to contend with the appearance of two giant, talking rodents, but then perhaps that was helping to cushion the shock for the ailing Mr, Hitchpost. At first, he stirred under his sheets and pressed himself fearfully back against the wooden headboard but, at length, he took the hand that was offered to him.

Thinking back, she realised this must be protocol. Winches didn't just seize you and march you off. Forcible abduction might be an easier option but they seemed to wait for you to make that first critical choice. Slipping back into her shoes, she wondered what happened when characters refused to be extracted. Surely that must happen sometimes? She decided she'd ask someone if Hitch's little scheme ever actually worked.

"Fifteen seconds." An electronic voice spoke out from somewhere beneath a fluffy shoulder.

Finn stood and waited. With the story stopped, there was no risk of any villagers spotting a scarlet-faced squirrel-slayer loitering around the back door of the Post Office, and she doubted the winchmen could see anything much at all underneath so much thick polyester.

Slowly, the three figures - two large, one tiny - walked hand in hand towards the door, the diminutive Mr. Hitchpost looking a good deal meeker and calmer than she'd ever have imagined. And then, just as he reached the gateway, he cast a final backward glance at his home, taking in those familiar painted walls, the gentle faces of his family and the view through the window to his beloved old gard...

Shit. Finn ducked back. Had he seen her? Was that a flicker of a smile that had crossed his face?

"Ten sec..." The voice of the cable ended abruptly.

Enough wondering. It was time to go. Finn yanked on the handle of the back door, but nothing happened. It didn't budge; didn't so much as creak. It was like trying to pull open a fresco on a marble wall.

Nine, eight...

Crap. Doors didn't move when the story was stopped. Nothing did. How stupid she'd been. Could she get in through the window instead?

Seven.

No; the gap was too narrow. She have to try the front door. That was famously always open.

Six. Five. She vaulted the side wall and turned.

Four. Three. She rounded the next corner and there was the front door, overhung by its brightly painted canopy.

She wasn't going to make it.

Locke's reader. Hitch had said it could freeze narrative time. She doubted he'd ever have tried something like this before, but she was out of options.

Two. She hit the pair of buttons.

One.

Nothing changed. But then that didn't really tell her anything.

Zero. She burst in through the doorway, half crouching to avoid the wooden beams above.

Zero and a half. Maybe she'd miscounted. Only the sound of her own footsteps disturbed the silence. She pressed on, around the counter and into the tiny hall.

Zero a bit more. There was the open bedroom door, Quickory's family still fixed in time beyond it. But no film of light stretched across it. Had it already blinked out? Was it only visible from one side? If you came at it from the wrong side, did it send you off somewhere else?

She didn't pause. Her tired legs made the decision for her. She ducked under the doorway, caught one perfect glimpse of the scene she knew so well, then spun around to find the gate-light still flickering before her.

Slipping Quickory from her bandolier, she stepped into the gate.

And bloody hell. She was doing it. This was it.

This is what it was to be a hero.

32. Revolution

She stepped into a resolute darkness - a cold, echoing void that spoke of marble floors and an absence of furniture. An extraction room, probably, and an unattended one at that.

The dark wasn't a problem. She didn't have to see anything more than Locke's reader and, by its dim glow, the gate from which she'd just emerged.

On screen, the coordinates of Max's fictional poet blinked slowly back at her, prompting another landslide of uncertainty. She hadn't had time to ask all the questions she'd meant to. Was Max only jamming the gates outside the Dome, or would they be shut here, too? And what was she supposed to do if she couldn't get a new exit? And this whole thing about having gone back to the point of Quickory's extraction; did that mean she'd just gone back in time? If she'd just taken him back several years into his own past, did that mean she'd have to put his body into storage until the calendar caught up with him again? Did she have minutes to make this work, or years?

And why the hell was Hitch still a squirrel - all useless and inert? She'd been counting on him for help but he wasn't waking.

She wasn't even sure if he was alive. She hoped to God she wasn't supposed to be giving him mouth-to-mouth.

Hellfire, this heroism business was difficult. Why did protagonists always end up having to face the most important challenges of their lives with no friends, no plan, and almost no information whatever? If she did ever get to meet her own narrator, some frank views were going to be exchanged.

In the meantime, all she had were blind faith, a staunch disregard for plausibility, and the distinct suspicion that none of this was in the least bit real. She tapped the activation controls on her wrist and waited.

"Hey, watch it!" Boorman rubbed his bicep as another hastily armed citizen jostled past in the direction of the barricades. It could have been worse. Locke's masseuse had actually fixed his arm up pretty well - her weird combination of potions and spells closing the wound a lot quicker than he'd have believed possible. He was supposed to be resting it, but to hell with that. He had work to do. Max had corrupted the Watch and that was unforgivable. He'd make sure he got what was coming to him.

But it wasn't going to be easy. Even getting here had meant taking a gamble. Only one dumb minotaur had seen him with Duggan and the rest, and now it was gone; vanished through a magic cabinet to some place it was never going to come back from. With any luck Max would still think Boorman an ally. It was a risk, sure, but a good man didn't just sit on his arse when the world was going to hell. So he'd caught up with a watchman in the Subway - some bland-faced ape who'd swallowed the whole story about an organised rebellion - and told him he had an urgent report for Max. As soon as he'd shown him the codes to return to Control, the guy had met with an unfortunate fist-related accident. Boorman had taken his gun and his reader. Now, he needed to get back inside the Dome.

Trouble was, Max was being cautious. He'd told all the news channels that the insurgence was the work of newly arrived migrants planning a big take-over; that Control had only barely managed to restore order; that only a quick decision to bring in some off-world volunteers had saved the city from catastrophe. It was a back-door way of introducing martial law, but people were buying it. No one was asking who these volunteers were, or where they'd come from, or even where the insurgents had gone. If anyone had thought to wonder why the same ogres and thugs who'd been shooting the place up were now organising the civil defences, they were keeping their concerns to themselves.

Most people didn't seem to be wondering very much at all. They just seemed happy to have someone to blame; a convenient enemy they could dump their frustrations on. Pick any individual in the crowd and you soon found that no one had seen anything of the rebels since that first attack. But it wasn't dampening anyone's enthusiasm. All around the bullet-pitted walls of the Dome, righteous citizens were gathering with every garden tool and every pokey stick they could muster. Looking increasingly wild-eyed and uncharitable as their numbers grew, they were starting to accost passers-by with something more than an enthusiastic sense of civic duty.

A watchman's badge had got him through most of it, but some heavy-duty thugs were stationed round the doors. They didn't look like they'd be so easily impressed. Anyone approaching the nearest entrance was being turned away by an ogre in a greatcoat, and he didn't seem to care very much what badges or papers were pushed his way. Accompanying him was a man Boorman was sure he'd once put away for life. Now, armed with a pistol and a megaphone, he was standing on a makeshift stage, doing his best to whip up some good old-fashioned nationalistic fury. The usual fans of outrage and xenophobia were cheering him on whenever he paused for breath.

Well shit. This was going to be harder than he'd thought. Here was the third door he'd tried and they'd all been blocked. Frowning down at his reader, he was just wondering about an alternative approach when an unexpected jerk interrupted him. His name was Randolph, an over-chummy nobody from the junior ranks, and he announced his arrival by clapping him on the shoulder with a heavy hand. It was a good job it wasn't his injured arm; someone would have ended up getting shot.

"Boorman!" Randolph was one of those blokes who thought that hard slaps and crushing handshakes were the true measures of a man. A prize dick, in other words. He pointed a thumb at the Dome behind him. "I thought you'd be on the Alpha gate. That's where the rest of your unit is."

"Is it?" Boorman nodded grimly. "I've been out of contact."

"Well you won't get in now. Everyone's been sent to man the perimeter. No one's getting in or out."

"I've got to. I've got to report to Max."

Randolph grinned like a turd with teeth. "No chance. He's cleared everyone off his floor; got 'em to lock all the doors; seal off the Core in case this attack gets serious."

Boorman cocked his head. "So what you saying? He's all on his own up there?"

"That's what they say; the whole inner section's been evacuated. If you want to report anything, you'll have to give it to his new second in command."

"Joshua's back?"

Randolph shrugged. "Shouldn't he be?"

Boorman looked up at the Dome. "Oh, sure. Just surprised he made it back so fast. He was with me when we were attacked."

"Oh, right." Randolph gave a sardonic smile - the sort that might easily be improved with the aid of a baseball bat. "So you're seeing action with the bigwigs, are you?"

"Yeah," said Boorman. "So... Joshua: where do I find him?"

"He's off-world right now."

Boorman narrowed his eyes. "Where?"

Coleridge's lodgings at Nether Stowey were full of surprises. The first was the cold, electric brightness of the interior, which swept a long, crisp shadow from Finn's feet all the way across the parlour floor. The second was the absence of an interior wall.

Where any traditionally-minded structural engineer would have chosen to separate hall and parlour with a sturdy brick partition, someone here had decided to set an oversized intra-diegetic gate instead. The architect of this unusual and somewhat anachronistic feature for a late eighteenth century cottage was, in all likelihood, the same wild-haired man who now stood in the office on the other side of it, pointing an enormous pistol at her.

"Miss Finn," smiled Max. "Please, do come through."

Finn had had a few weapons aimed at her in recent times - certainly far more than her usual monthly quota - but it wasn't an experience to which she was getting any more accustomed. Looking down the business end of a barrel still produced a disco heartbeat and a readiness to comply with the wielder's demands. With few other options left to consider, she stepped grudgingly across the threshold. She did so with a scowl on her face, but that was about as far as her newfound heroism would extend.

The office design was ordinary enough - corporate poseur blended with hotel foyer chic - all enlivened with a collection of potted plants, piped muzak, and enough CCTV monitors to keep visiting employees in a state of perpetual paranoia. What distinguished it, however, was the fact that it boasted three fewer walls than the accepted norm, and a Romantic poet.

The man sitting beside Max was undoubtedly Samuel Taylor Coleridge; his portrait adorned the cover of one of the books that would still be sitting on Finn's fireside shelf at home. Granted, this particular version of the man was now laid back, tripping his tits off in an electric wheelchair, but the face was unmistakable.

To the right of the pair was a glass wall and, beyond it, an enormous spherical chamber. At its centre hung a globe made of something like ice or frosted glass. A metal gantry extended from its near edge up into Max's office, passing through a wide metal frame set into the glazing. The Core - because this certainly had to be it - looked as though it should be the focus of tremendous activity, but the cavern was devoid of life. Abandoned tools and materials gave the impression that people had evacuated in a hurry.

Max motioned toward the other wall; the one to her left. "As you see, I was expecting you." You could say what you liked about the man; he'd certainly read all the manuals when it came to spouting villainous clichés.

Finn's eyes followed his gesture. Where the wall should have been, a gate now stood, and through it she saw the interior of her beloved bookshop. She let out a small gasp.

The threshold was as wide as the one from Coleridge's cottage - far broader than anything she'd previously seen - and it ran the full width of her shop-front. The scene was frozen and just as she'd remembered it, only now she was seeing it from behind. There stood Marcus, motionless, with his arm extended towards her winter-coated shade; a dead-eyed facsimile waiting patiently to take three bullets to the chest.

The gate itself held steady. Unless Max had been determinedly resetting it every thirty seconds in the hope of making a dramatic first impression, he must have found a way of creating a perpetual link between worlds. To test the theory, she glanced behind her. The view of the poet's parlour was still there.

"No words, Miss Finn?" Impatience and a continuing desire to gloat seemed to be vying for control of his tone.

She ignored him. Her familiar bookshop - there before her at last, visible in all of its three dear little dimensions - seemed to pull at her. Somewhere in that world lived her sister and her mum. She took two short steps towards it.

"Have a care, Miss Finn." Max pointed at the smart-suited assassin, from whose pistol an orange-grey floret of smoke and flame had begun to bloom. "The extraction team has just this instant left. The clock begins again at your first footfall - and that should leave you, what? A scant five or ten seconds to live?"

Finn paused and looked again at Marcus. She hadn't realised how bald he was; viewed from behind, he was a veritable Friar Tuck.

"You keep a most valuable book," said Max. "In a moment, you will point it out to me. But first, I would ask you to remove your...?" He waggled his firearm at her bandolier; at the lifeless red pelt that hung from it.

Finn removed it and laid it gently on the floor.

"A brave endeavour." Max attempted an expression of regret. "And a surprisingly gallant end for one so fixed on his own comforts. That final dramatic moment of redemption; it is always a thing to behold, is it not?"

Finn refused to be drawn on that. Too many people were dead or missing. Even to think about them would be to lose all focus. Instead, she let her eyes settle on the Core. "What's this about, Max? You said this was all part of some grand scheme; some clever plan to put the world to rights. You said you wanted me to understand you. So... I'm here. Go ahead and explain."

"Oh, Miss Finn, please." Max shook his head. "You persist in regarding me as your antagonist; some scheming tyrant who must be thwarted at the last. That is not to be our tale."

"No? And yet here you are, building an army." She looked him up and down. "You've killed people, Max. Now you're holding a gun on me."

Max ran his free hand through his hair. "What I do, I do in the name of honest progress; in pursuit of the greater good. Have you not heard it said? One must sometimes be terrible to prevent the people from being so."

Finn gave a snort. "If it's a quote, it's not your best."

Max's face hardened as he pointed at his sleep-murmuring companion. "No man was ever yet a great poet without being at the same time a profound philosopher. That man; he is the truest genius of his age. His eyes make pictures when they are shut, Miss Finn, and I - his Opus Maximum, his greatest work - mean to see the realisation of his dreams."

"Huh." Finn looked appraisingly at the troubled young man. "So this particular Coleridge; he's a big fan of killing is he? It's funny, that, 'cause that's not how he came across in the history books."

Max glared. "Do not mock me, Miss Finn. You have not seen so much of this city, but I'll hazard you've grasped something of its vacuity. Culture and intellect are in decline; knowledge and reason forsaken. People are become children again, clapping for the noise and colour of the most tawdry entertainments."

She sighed. "Well, that's not really so unusual, is it?"

"It is dangerous!" Max whirled an arm in what was presumably the direction of the city. "When the populace is grown so sick and weak as this, it takes a mere nothing for despotism to rise. It is not a difficult thing to make a fool fear; to make a fool hate; to make a fool ready to wage war."

"And you're doing just that." She pointed at the monitors; some showed seething crowds; others showed improbably vast war-fleets waiting at their gates. "All this talk of migrants and rebellion; it's a smokescreen, isn't it? You just want to sign people up to your damned army."

"The willing conscripts, yes." Max gave a quick nod. "And I have an honest use for them. Have you witnessed the atrocities perpetrated beyond our gates? All the horrors that authors inflict daily upon their creations?"

Finn shrugged.

"It is a true reign of terror, Miss Finn. Believe me, I have seen it. And once we had a narrator who seemed ready to prevent it; to stand against such wilful cruelty." He let slip a flicker of a sneer. "But where is she now? Gone! Neglectful, uncaring, indolent or overpowered - I know not which - but though she had the power to end this tyranny, she failed us. Now, in consequence, horrors grow upon the hour, dwarfing our efforts to save the innocent, and all the while our people descend into the most vile and ignoble lethargy."

Finn nodded. "And so now you want to be narrator instead. You want all that power for yourself so you can get a bit more... what? Proactive?"

Max pointed again at her bookshop. "Is that so wrong? To intervene in an unjust world? Why the prohibition, Miss Finn? Where is the wisdom in it, when tales so oft contain naught but the direst malice?" Casually, he aimed his pistol at the back of Marcus' head. "Consider it. What if some little action might prevent your murder and see your tale forever changed?" His eyes glittered. "What if you could go home, Miss Finn? What if we could all go home?"

Home. Finn blinked. The implied offer had a siren charm but some instinct within her resisted. Max was a liar; surely experience had taught her that? And what did she really know about what it meant to change a tale? Could a story be altered as he suggested, or would the slightest interference corrupt it and delete it forever?

Conscious that any decent Gatekeeper probably ought to be a lot better informed than this, she played for time. "Let me see if I understand you, Max. You're saying you want to declare war on all of literature?"

At this, he grinned. "No, no, Miss Finn. Upon chosen foes; in tales in which we might save billions of innocent lives. That is my goal, truly, and I have gathered already the forces to see it achieved." He gestured again at the monitors. "All I require now is your help."

"But you're talking about *wars,*" said Finn. "Huge, huge wars."

"Waged by people who would never have lived, were it not for my own efforts and interventions. Waged by devoted allies and the willing portion of our own people."

"Many of whom are going to die."

"Aye, upon a vast stage of horrors - one that shall shock our people from their stupor; drive them back into the embrace of rationality - to an appreciation of reason, equality, and responsibility."

"This is just madness." She pointed incredulously to the restless Coleridge. "Death and war, Max. That's not any vision your precious creator would embrace."

Her captor turned away to stare at the screens by his desk. "I was a winchman for many years, Miss Finn. I have known horror. I have seen madness. You must believe me when I say I have no enthusiasm for either of them. But I have given this the most sober consideration." He indicated a monitor showing a feed from a high-mounted camera that panned slowly across the mob outside. "Ill feeling has been rising in this city for decades now. The tempest gathers. People are grown jealous of their cosseted lives; it shall not be so very long before that anger finds its release in brutishness. Left unmanaged, it shall turn to the persecution of blameless strangers. Logic demands it be managed, and I mean to do exactly that; direct it against a more deserving foe than a few impoverished refugees."

Finn wandered slowly to the gateway to her shop and ran a hand down the frame. "So you're saying a conflict's inevitable; you're just a nice, reasonable guy trying to make the best of things?"

Max perched himself on the corner of his desk. "It is no poor thing to show people to what bloody ends their hatred leads them. That alone is a goal worthy of the endeavour. But to dash evil upon evil, Miss Finn - just think of it; if we succeed, we shall achieve more than could our extraction crews in a thousand, thousand lifetimes."

"Well, look," said Finn, leaning against the frame, "I can see this project has got you all very excited but, I mean, obviously, there's no way I'm going to help you start a war. I'm sorry, but... it's just not me."

Nodding, Max swept a remote control up from his desk and pointed it at one of the larger monitors.

"I did, of course, imagine you might say as much." He clicked a button.

On screen appeared a number of faces crowded together in what looked very much like a prison cell.

"You recognise the two here, I take it?" Max pointed towards the shadows at the edge.

It took Finn a moment to recognise the frightened faces of Cariola and Johnny Faustus. "I see," she said. "And this is the bit where you tell me they'll be fine so long as I do exactly as you say." She raised an eyebrow. "And all the while, you're still the good guy in all of this."

Max turned. "I am an instrument of a great man's vision, Miss Finn. I have seen how the worlds must change and here, with you, that transformation begins."

Finn shook her head. "Oh come on. What do you want from me? You don't honestly believe there's some big magic book, do you?"

Max smiled. "You are the Gatekeeper, Miss Finn. That is for you to tell me."

"Well then fine. That's easy. There isn't one."

Max's finger hovered over a button on his keypad. "Then I fear you leave me bereft of choice."

"Wait. What d'you...?"

Max tapped the button. "Joshua, are you there?"

The on-screen view swivelled until a familiar face filled two thirds of it. *"Here and waiting on your command."*

"Take the nursemaid outside and begin a count of ten. Should you receive no further instruction before its end, shoot her."

Crack.

Joshua's video feed hissed and fractured into pixels, then whirled and fell to the ground. For a moment, all it revealed was a close-up of particles of grit, blurring in and out as the autofocus struggled to fix. What it found at last was the grimly smiling face of Watchman Boorman.

"Hello, Chief." The view shifted to reveal a pistol pressed to the side of Joshua's temple. In the shadowed background, figures hurried out through the cell door. Johnny Faustus was amongst them.

"Boorman!" cried Max. "What possesses you to... agh!"

From somewhere to Finn's right, a streak of orange brown arced through the air. It connected with Max's trousers and hung there, twisting and wriggling like an angry sporran.

Finn's eyes went wide. "Hitch! No! Be care..."

"Damned creature!" Max slapped away the squirrel and pointed his weapon as it scurried for cover behind the potted ferns.

"Run!" squeaked a tiny voice.

Max fired twice. Finn's ears rang with the noise.

Spinning, Max changed his aim. "The book, Miss Finn. Give it to me now."

Finn's hands shook, but at least half of that was anger. "I don't have it," she said. "And even if I did, I'd sooner die than give it to you."

"I assure you, M..."

Finn denied him the chance to say any more. She had a plan of sorts - a desperate, half-thought thing - but if it was going to work, then she had to keep him angry. She sneered. "And if I'm going to die, you wordy little shit, then I'll bloody well do it at home."

So saying, she leapt sideways through the gate and back into the most familiar place she knew.

33. The Core

Eight seconds left. That was her best guess. Max would be only a moment behind.

Dodging past Marcus, she barged aside her shade.

Seven.

She ran on towards the back of the shop.

"Stop!" roared Max as he leapt across the threshold.

Six.

She dropped behind an old desk and a display of Christmas best-sellers. In the leg-space between the two stacks of drawers sat a cardboard box full of unsorted works that she'd picked up at a car boot sale. She grabbed the topmost title; some nonsensical thing about avocadoes.

Five.

"Get out!" There was a desperate edge to Max's warning. "Miss Finn, you must..."

Four.

Finn rose from behind her shelter, holding the battered paperback like a talisman. Her plan was probably a very poor one, but she'd be dead in just a few seconds anyway. At this point, there was a limit to how badly things could go wrong.

Three.

"Is this what you want?" With a malicious smile, she tore off the cover and, with it, the book's first few pages.

"No!" With an anguished shout, Max surged forward - closer to where she needed him, but not quite there yet.

Two.

A flash like soundless lightning illuminated her shop. It came and went in an instant, its source somehow imperceptible. Reflexively, she squinted. As her eyes refocused, she saw Max moving impossibly slowly towards her. He was running - that much was still true - but at a pace that would have made a tortoise chuckle. Neither of his boots was currently in contact with the ground and though his leading foot was gradually converging upon its shadow, it would be seconds yet before it landed.

And on the subject of seconds, *one.* Surely one. Perhaps even zero. She'd lost any measure of time.

She glanced around. That peculiar silence had settled again, like that first frozen moment in her shop, or when she'd stepped out into the Unimagined and found it no more than a dull cocoon.

She blinked and took a breath, mainly because she could; because she wasn't caught in the same bubble of time that slowed Max's movements almost to a stop. What was happening? Was this it? Was this what happened when your time ran out?

She looked down at herself to see whether she might be fading out, or perhaps falling victim to some spectacular special effect.

She wasn't. Things were much as before, except that a hairline of light now connected her injured book to the Core. Unwavering and slowly thickening, it extended over her floor, over her fallen shade, past Max and Marcus, across the threshold and beyond. Holding steady like a laser, it spanned the office and the gantry until, at last, it came to rest on the upper edge of the frost-white sphere.

With the connection came a strange sense of roundedness; of purpose - the very opposite of that queasy wrenching sensation that had accompanied her first taking Reed's outstretched hand. Somehow and at last, she felt like she belonged in her own tale.

But why? And why was this randomly chosen book the catalyst?

She looked at its ruined cover and realised her mistake. The tattered paperback was incidental; the light passed through it, not damaging it but simply ignoring it, as if it wasn't there. The beam emerged through the half torn pages and continued on, into the very centre of her chest.

The Core had connected with *her*.

The narrow beam produced no physical change in her but, with the kind of clarity that can only come when a narrator is really rooting for you, it delivered an epiphany. This really was her story. Not just the bookshop and *A Young Wolf's Cry*, not even the extraction that had followed it, but all of this: New Tybet, the Core, and everything and everyone connected to it. She stood at the centre of a web - a complex tangle of words and ideas; a multiply-connected construct of arcs and obstructions, amendments and erasures. She saw the whole of it at once; its shape, its convergence upon a moment, and she saw herself at the heart of it. Locke had been right. This was what it meant to be the protagonist: the worlds filled themselves in around you as you moved.

And Max had been wrong. There was no magical book that was going to open the Core for him. That power lay only with the unseen narrator - and now perhaps with her. If Max thought...

Max. She stopped. The balance had changed. She didn't need him now to fall for her desperate ploy. She had an author's power behind her; she could settle this a different, more peaceable way. He didn't need to die.

Instinctively, she stepped towards him. The heel of his front foot was now grounding, giving him the appearance of a statue, improbably balanced, with wild eyes set upon her book.

Behind him, the grey floret in the barrel of Marcus's pistol bulged and coloured. A slow shockwave rippled up the fabric of his suit towards his collar and that incongruously affable smile. And from the end of the weapon, a fleck of dark silver pushed out from the glowing bloom, riding its own little pressure wave towards her.

Towards Max. Her plan was working - of course it was. Didn't it always, when the hero was forced into one last desperate gamble? In his single-minded pursuit of the fabled book, Max had put himself into the path of a bullet intended for her. In just a moment, that evil glinting scrap would tear into his back.

Gauging the distances, Finn flung aside the book and lowered her shoulder in readiness for a charge. As she did, a worrying thought struck her: she had no idea how forces from different time-streams might work. Right now, she could outpace a bullet - which made an interesting addition to her CV - but if she tackled him at that speed, what then? She might very well break him in half. On the other hand, if she did nothing, he'd be shot and it would be her fault. What choice did she have?

Bang.

None at all, as it turned out. Her umbilical connection to the Core snapped and vanished. Her little bubble of time burst to the crack of a pistol and a cry of pain.

A spray of red fanned from Max's shoulder.

Bang. A second shot caught him as he fell.

Shit. Finn stopped and threw herself backwards as a stunned-looking Marcus saw her and adjusted his aim. His next shot missed her, but it sounded as though it had done some lasting damage to the Religion and Spirituality section behind her. It could have been worse, she supposed.

Bang. Bang. Bang. Damn it all; she wished people would stop shooting up her bookshop. From the floor, just out of sight, a wounded Max was evidently returning fire. A heavy thump told that at least one of his shots had found its mark.

A moment passed. Then came Max's voice, strained and breathless.

"Is this the book?"

Trembling, Finn peered over a little wall of celebrity autobiographies. Max was kneeling with the ragged paperback held tight against his chest; against a dark halo that was inching across his shirt. His still-smoking pistol was aimed at her.

He rose painfully to a crouch. "Is *this* the book?"

"There is no book," said Finn quietly.

"You lie." Max backed slowly and awkwardly away, his weapon demanding that she stay exactly where she was.

Finn stayed exactly where she was.

Weakly, Max stepped back, past her counter and her toppled shade. Behind him, Marcus lay face down on the floorboards, his body moated by blood. With difficulty, Max stepped over him, keeping his gun trained on Finn as though he expected her at any moment to sprout demonic horns and fly at him.

That was a thought. Maybe she had superpowers now. Maybe the narrator was the sort who liked that kind of thing.

Finn tensed her muscles and urged some magical transformation, but her body stubbornly refused. That was a shame. Changing tack, she tried to slow time again but the facility seemed to have deserted her. She was still resolutely ordinary. What was a hero supposed to do in a situation like this?

"Max, stop," said a man's voice. "This is wrong. You know it is."

Max turned stiffly and aimed his pistol with a shaking hand.

Beyond him, a scruffy figure in a heavy coat stood at the end of the gantry between the office and the Core. He leaned against the handrail, blocking Max's way.

Finn watched, aghast. What did he think he was doing?

"Brave," croaked Max, stumbling back into his office, "but do not hope to dissuade me, Postman. I know what must be done."

"No," said Hitch. "You don't. You think you've met your creator; that he's given you some divine inspiration. But he hasn't. He's just another fiction - like me, like all of us. Like you... Maximilien." He gave deliberate emphasis to the name.

"What?" Max steadied his aim. "What do you know about me?"

Cautiously, Finn rose and took a step towards the gate. What was Hitch doing?

Hitch held up a book. "It was in your desk drawer. *The Fall of Robespierre.* I thought I'd seen it somewhere before. So I had a look inside and there you were. Max Roberts; Maximilien Robespierre... it didn't take a lot of figuring out."

"Step aside." Max coughed into the crook of his elbow. "I am no villain; I do only what I must, but conscience shall not deflect me now."

"I can't do it, Max."

"Hitch!" Finn called from the threshold of her old familiar world. "Don't be stupid. Get out of the way. That book he's got; it's nothing. It's not the key."

Hitch shook his head and backed down the gantry. "Sorry, Finn. I don't know if I believe that."

Bang. The glass wall shattered as Max fired a warning shot. High above the Core, a pipe ruptured with a scream. A silver-white cataract of supercooled gas surged into the great chamber, clouding and spreading as it fell.

"Step aside," said Max, advancing.

Still shaking his head, Hitch retreated until the backs of his legs met the curved upper edge of the Core.

Bang. A shot ricocheted off the handrail only a metre from where he stood.

Shit, shit, shit. What could she do? The plan had been for Max to fall here in her shop. He wasn't supposed to get up and go staggering back out again. She'd been prepared to die here, too, in her own simple world of books and British drizzle, but that hadn't worked out either. If she was going to have any chance of stopping him, it looked like she'd have to abandon her home once again.

Grimly, she stepped back into Max's office, where a sleepy-eyed Coleridge sat enraptured by the falling spray. Max clearly revered the man and though she could perhaps threaten to push him, wheelchair and all, into the great void below, Max would see it for an obvious bluff. She'd have to do better than that.

"Max," she shouted. He was halfway across the gantry now and seemed inclined to ignore her. The sloping metal deck was wet with blood.

"Max!" From the edge of the broken window, she tried again. "The book's not the key."

By way of response, and without bothering to turn his head, he fired a shot over his shoulder. Somewhere far above her head, glass fractured.

"The book's not the key," she repeated. "I am."

That stopped him. Slowly, painfully, he turned. Under that wild squall of hair, his face was grey.

Standing beneath the frame at the walkway's end, she shrugged. "I'm sorry; this is my story, Max, not yours."

"Yours?" He squinted, as though peering through a fog. "But you are the Gatekeeper; my key; my challenge. A chapter; nothing more."

She shook her head. He was obviously dying. To gloat would only be cruel. "It's mine. I can feel the story in me. I think I even see how it's going to end."

"No!" Max fired twice more.

Finn didn't move; didn't even flinch as the bullets sped by. Standing this close to the Core, she could feel the pace and progress of the narrative; knew for certain that her tale wouldn't be ending here.

"You can't kill me, Max. That's not the way the story goes." She stepped out onto the gantry.

Click. Click. Max pulled uselessly at the trigger.

"I am no villain. I am a hero; a man of vision and of action." He dropped to his knees, his voice now strangely plaintive. "The task is mine: to blast the despot's pride and liberate the world."

Looking past him, Finn was surprised to see Hitch still standing fixedly against the Core. As she smiled, he slumped, drawing a red smear down across the white.

"Hitch!" Ignoring Max's attempt to stop her, she ran and leapt over to her fallen friend. That filthy coat had hidden all sign of his injury, but as he sat looking up at her, she could see his face was ashen; his lips and those heavy eyelids slowly paling to blue.

"Hello Finn." He smiled weakly. "Well, that didn't go very well, did it? Hit with his very first shot."

"Shh. Shh." She knelt at his side and pulled away enough of his coat to inspect the wound. The clothes underneath were sodden.

"I did say, didn't I?" He looked down at his chest. "Never get into fights. Just look what happens."

Finn ignored that. She needed to get him up; to get him to a hospital before he bled to death. She slipped an arm around his back. "Can you get up if I help you?"

Hitch frowned. "Don't be silly. I've been heroic enough already." He blinked slowly at her. "It's been an adventure, Finn, but now I'd really like to rest."

"No. No, Hitch, come on." Fighting back the anger and the desperation, she made futile preparations to lift him. He was too heavy for her, and probably too far gone, but she bent her back anyway and set her free hand against the Core.

As she did, something changed. Beneath her bloody fingers, the surface felt cold, smooth and substantial, just as she'd expected, but it seemed to respond altogether differently to Hitch. It softened around him, oozing around his body like a pool of tar.

Hitch glanced sideways, taken by a passive curiosity. "Well, this is new."

"No!" wailed Max from somewhere behind her. "Not one so unworthy. Not he."

Finn took Hitch's hand, but it felt cold; cold and strangely hard. His face, his skin, his clothes - all were losing their colour; taking on the texture of frosted glass.

"Hitch, wait."

"I think you've got to let me go." His words occurred to her now more as thoughts than sounds in the air.

"No, Hitch, you can't..." Finn stopped. The surface of the Core bulged and gently swallowed him. His hand was the last of him to go.

From behind her rose a bitter laugh.

"Fate," croaked Max. "Was there ever a more mischievous creature?"

Finn glared back at him. Hitch was gone. Kindness had gone with him.

"Do you not see the joke?" Max gave a sickly grin. "You bereft of friendship. I bereft of life. The Core opens to the most unworthy of us. Tragedies all - and yet my quest is won. The revolution begins. My creator lives, and by your bloody hand the gates are stirred to life. Soon his words shall spread to every corner of every tale, and fleets and armies from every era will gather to realise his glorious prophesy of war."

Wearily, Finn shook her head and sat back against the Core.

"You forget," she said. "I know this story. I've skipped on ahead." She pointed back to the office. "In just a moment, Boorman, Duggan, Reed and a bunch of others are going to come bursting through that gate. I wish I could tell you they get here in time to save you, but..."

Max coughed, no longer able to hold up his head. "Your Watchmen friends cannot prevent this. The greatest powers in all this realm could not..."

"No, no, I get that." Finn waved his words aside. "It's all in the hands of a higher power now, isn't it? Another Coleridge from another level; the one who shares his dreams with your puppet friend."

"*The* Coleridge," insisted Max. "The true poet. The man himself."

"Oh, I wouldn't be so sure about that." Slowly, Finn stood. "Writers create writers, layer upon layer, but characters like you and me will never really know how far it goes. To see those higher levels, or to do anything to change them, well..." She patted the Core. "I reckon you'd probably need all the powers of creation."

Max's eyes flicked towards the sphere; to the bloodstained patch where once had stood a man. His forehead furrowed.

Finn stepped over him and walked away in the direction of home. The Watch would arrive shortly, finding him with that same uncertain look fixed forever upon his face.

34. Paul Locke

B*uzz, buzz. Buzz, buzz.*
Finn smiled an apology at her customer, who departed the shop wearing a faint frown of disapproval. That was the problem with leaving your phone on vibrate. If you sat it on the shelf by the wrapping paper, it did rather give the impression that you'd got a sex toy hidden under the counter.

She reached for it and swiped the screen. Her sister's profile picture appeared beside a little text balloon.

[ChrisSis:] Hey you. Saw you in the news again.

As ever, this was followed by a little yellow smiley-face.
Chewing her lip, Finn texted back.

[Me:] Oh God. Really? Where now?
[ChrisSis:] BBC. Mum sent me the link. She's on FB now. Can you believe it?
[Me:] I know. She's turned into a proper little toast-poster.
[ChrisSis:] Toast...?

[Me:] You know; posts absolutely everything - what she had for breakfast...

[ChrisSis F:] Oh right. And what an amazing daughter she's got, of course.

[Me:] Daughters. Plural. And it'll pass. I dug up one old manuscript. That's it; my 15 minutes of fame right there.

[ChrisSis:] And you're turning into a bit of a talent-spotter...

[Me:] One young poet. Not exactly an empire.

[ChrisSis:] From little acorns...

[Me:] Yeah, right.

[ChrisSis:] Oh, got to go, hun. Meeting's starting. Love you. X

Finn set the phone down on the shelf again. She felt a little guilty about Chrissie - as though she'd snatched something away from her. This was supposed to have been her story, after all. Now there was no telling how things would play out. She certainly wouldn't be settling down with some handsome young detective any time soon.

Of course, Chrissie would never have resented the way things had worked out, but Finn couldn't help feeling that she'd left her - and the whole world with her - somehow rudderless and adrift. No one was in charge; no one plotting out their fates, and perhaps that should have been exciting. For the moment, she could only feel a little numb and displaced.

That was probably why she'd taken one or two uncharacteristic risks. Accompanying the young Coleridge back to his little chapter of remembered time, she'd seen his lonely little cottage for what it was: a prison. Written into existence by some higher level version of the man, he lived out the same miserable episode, day upon day, with no hope of company, recovery, or escape. Extracting him had been an act of compassion. Late in the evening, when his author could have no more possible use for him, she'd stolen him away, back through the chaos of the gate complex, into her own free and fateless world.

That was unequivocally against the rules. But as a wise man had once said, rules were... well, they were stupid. That was why she'd also taken the opportunity to grab a sheaf of papers from the poet's desk. Most were hastily sketched plans for tales that Max must surely have prompted - embattled star fleets and warriors from dystopian futures - but one was altogether different: a poem never before seen by the world of modern academia. With the author's permission, she'd subsequently 'discovered' the virgin verses in the pages of some unlikely old tome and presented them to researchers at her old university. The find - taken in conjunction with the recent shooting - had put her little bookshop on the map. There was talk of an auction some time in the spring.

Business had picked up markedly since then, but it came with a challenge: she had to account for the sudden presence of a strangely charismatic young man who had entered into her life with no verifiable past or documentation. A homeless amnesiac was her not-very-plausible explanation, and for the moment, that seemed to be enough. His distracted, otherworldly air lent some credibility to the claim, as had his recent emergence from a five-week addiction recovery programme.

For his part, the poet himself was still utterly in awe of the strange new world into which he'd been transplanted, and he professed himself perfectly content to play the role of an eccentric while Finn assumed the mantle of friend and patron. Already, the revitalised Col was producing some quite startling works - poems, essays and critiques - and the literary world had not been slow to notice. Extravagant deals had been mooted, and though Finn herself was still debating her fitness to assume the role of agent or publisher, the artist - now styling himself Cole Taylor - was adamant that they should forge a close and steady working partnership.

Success, then, seemed to be coming suspiciously easily. On occasion, she couldn't help wondering whether someone out there might not be landing her a hand.

As she mused, the bell sounded above her door. A smart, late middle-aged man strode in, a newspaper tucked under one arm, a furled umbrella held in the other like a cane.

Finn glanced towards the rear of the shop where Col was evidently absorbed in his ongoing literary analysis of *Ulysses*. He had his latte and his laptop; he seemed entirely happy.

Turning back, she smiled her shopkeeper's smile. "Hello. Can I help you?"

"Miss Finn?" said the gentleman. "The proprietor?"

"Yes. And you are?"

"Oh, I'm sorry, my name's Latch. Paul Latch. I'm a criminologist with Thames Valley."

Terrific. Another interview. She'd played host to dozens of police officers and forensic specialists throughout the latter half of December, but it had been weeks since the last of them had packed their cases and left.

"Oh right," she said. "I thought you might all be done with me by now."

Standing tall and erect, he reached across the counter and shook her hand. "Sadly no, my dear; I still have one or two questions. I know all those eager young detectives must have exhausted you, but I trust you won't mind if I pump you a little more?" His eyes glittered just a smidgen.

Finn felt a suspicious frown forming. "And you're a criminologist, you say?"

He shrugged. "A professor of criminology, in point of fact."

Finn suppressed a smile. "No kidding. So you're Professor Paul Latch, are you? And when you say you'd like to *pump* me a little more...?"

Latch's eyes went wide. "Oh, I'm so dreadfully sorry. These inadvertent innuendos; they're an affliction of mine. Please forgive me; I do sometimes slip one in."

"Paul Locke." Rounding the counter, she grinned and held out her arms. "You're alive, you wily old bugger."

"Miss Finn." Setting down his brolly and his paper, he hugged her tightly. "Oh, I must say, I'm inexpressibly pleased to see you again."

"Well, let me look at you." She stepped back. His face and frame were new, but there was something unmistakable in his smile. "Looks like I'm not the only one who can survive a spell in the Unimagined."

"So it would seem." He dropped his voice as he noticed the writer sitting at the rear of her shop.

She looked back too. "Ah. You recognise my protégé, I take it?"

"Of course, though I doubt my face will be familiar to him." Locke's expression grew conspiratorial. "I had heard he was here. But I wonder, Miss Finn; might we have a word in private?"

Finn wafted a hand. "Oh, don't worry about Col. He'll be completely lost in his work. What did you want to talk about?"

Casting a cautious glance over his shoulder, Locke tapped his newspaper. "Have you seen today's *Times*?"

"No." Breakfast had been spent explaining to Col the rudiments of thermostatic radiator valves.

Locke turned to an inside page. "I thought you might find it amusing. Doubtless there will be more in the *Literary Supplement* later in the week."

She gestured to Col. "Is he in it again?"

"No, no. Not him. Look here." Locke tapped a fingernail on an item in the lower right corner. *Finds Shed Doubt on the Braxton Legacy*, declared the heading.

Finn had already begun to read when the Professor volunteered his précis.

"The National Trust has lately been restoring the east wing of the Channingsborough estate." He spoke with barely suppressed glee. "As fate would have it, conservators discovered a crate full of documents hidden behind an attic partition. The results were... well, surprising."

"Channingsborough," said Finn. "Where Braxton wrote all the Little Woodsmeade Tales?"

Locke beamed. "The same. And might I tempt you to make a guess as to the contents of said crate?"

Finn shrugged. "Letters? More stories?"

"Ha! A veritable treasure trove, my dear. Dozens upon dozens of new tales." He clapped with such unalloyed delight that even Col briefly turned his head.

Finn felt her eyes widening. "And Hitch - is he in any of them?"

Holding onto his punchline for as long as he could, Locke looked as if he might burst. "He's in *all* of them," he ejaculated at last.

"No! Really?" Finn found she was grinning as widely as Locke. "So... so what does that mean? He can go back home? Even though he's supposed to have...?"

Locke laughed. "Yes, but that's not the whole of it. Look. Look here, at the last paragraph. *The new works, together with Mrs. Braxton's handwritten notes for an unfinished final chapter, inevitably cast doubt on the authenticity of the twelfth tale in her celebrated oeuvre."* He shot her a delighted smile. "Do you not see, Ms. Finn? He's escaped his deathbed scene altogether! The twelfth's a fake! He needn't die at all!"

Finn gazed at the letters on the page. She'd glimpsed something of this when the Core had connected with her, but that had been almost two months ago. Since then, the long wet weeks of an English winter had eroded her certainty; she'd seen nothing to confirm that Hitch had survived his encounter, let alone any evidence that he was now the most powerful force in all of creation. She had only vague and unsorted suspicions.

"You think he's still out there, then?" she said, at length. "Being a big powerful author and all that?"

Locke shrugged. "I suspect he's already found everything he ever wanted. And as narrators go, he might well prove to be the best of them, for perhaps he won't interfere at all."

"And that's good, you think?"

"I would say so." Locke looked around her shop. "Doesn't it feel good to be free of another's influence? To be living out a story you're writing for yourself?"

Finn pursed her lips. "I suppose it does, but that's the thing: I don't know if that's what I'm really doing. Things are going so well here; I can't help wondering if it's all a bit too neatly tied up."

"Ah." Locke glanced up at the ceiling. "You think our friend might be nudging the narrative in a happier direction?"

"Maybe. I mean, look at me - and now you, safely returned. Even New Tybet's getting back to normal."

"Ah. So you still visit from time to time?"

"To see friends; only that."

"But no plans to settle there? You are the city's long-awaited protagonist, after all."

Finn shook her head. "I think people put too much emphasis on protagonists. It's people that make a world, not heroes."

Locke smiled. "Some would say there are always roles for heroes too. You're wise enough to know we can never take the future for granted, Ms. Finn; I trust you'll keep in touch, just in case you're needed."

"Yeah. Like I say, I've got friends there now." She sighed. "But d'you see what I mean? It's so tidy. Reed's alive and well; the extraction teams are working again; the bad guys have been sent home; even the angry mobs sound a bit chastened now. Doesn't it feel a bit too 'happy ever after'? Like an Edith Braxton ending?"

Locke chuckled. "I'm not really one to talk about endings. I'm a Recurrent, Ms. Finn - as I suspect are you, though you might not know it yet. Tales end and we move on in search of new adventures. That gives us a peculiar perspective on endings; I'd advise you to pay them very little heed."

Finn chose to ignore at least part of that. She had enough to occupy her mind already. "You've still not answered me," she said. "Doesn't it feel like he's been helping out?"

Locke smiled. "Actually, I think it almost certain. Those awaiting armies never came. The gates never opened to admit Max's forces of war. The higher Coleridge was communing with your young friend there, and yet something happened. Whatever new fiction was supposed to have thrown open the gates, it was never finished. It was interrupted. Someone at a higher level intervened."

"I told Max he'd do it," said Finn. "It was the last thing I said to him. I don't know if it was something the Core had shown me or whether I just wanted to believe it, but I told him Hitch would stop him."

Locke nodded and folded up his newspaper. "Well I for one shall choose to believe that he did."

Finn smiled. "Me too. I just wish I could have been around to see it."

Scowling at the downpour, Hitch angled the hand-written page to catch the light of a timorous sun. It shrank into the clouds as though abashed at its own discovery. Milky white washed the page for an instant, then faded.

It was the right place. He tucked the paper back into his coat and considered the farmhouse opposite. A fat, drab curmudgeon of a building - an uninspired assemblage of slate and sandstone - it huddled resentfully against the long onslaught of a dismal English summer. A curtain behind an upstairs window flapped idly in the damp coastal breeze, but nothing in the first floor rooms concerned him. He wouldn't need to intrude so far.

He gave a theatrical sigh. He hadn't come dressed for this. This was definitely and absolutely the very last time he'd be doing anyone any favours.

Standing in the dripping doorway of the barn, he thought about adjusting the weather. After all, it was within his power and England really was the worst of all possible locations. The incessant rain was one of the many things he hated about the place. Cold, dark, and sodden: why would anyone choose to make it their home? If, as it was said, the country had been the original model for Little Woodsmeade, then someone had conveniently chosen to overlook the climate.

Somewhere round the side of the house, a dog barked. Quickly, Hitch stepped back into the cover of his doorway and gave himself another moment to evaluate the scene. He needn't fear anything now, but it was sometimes easy to forget that. Mistrust was a long-established habit, one that had mostly served him well. Unwarranted or not, it was an animal instinct; something that kicked in whenever he broke cover, and with one last job to do, it was time to move.

The dog growled itself into silence and the gentle hiss of the rain died away. Hitch allowed himself a small smile of satisfaction. The wet summer had left the farmyard a mire, but he drew his coat tight about him and crossed the potholed patch without incident. Narrators never got their feet wet if they could help it.

He rapped out his little three-two-four tattoo upon the door, more out of habit than anything else. The farm was a lonely place and visitors would be few. He waited.

After a long moment came footsteps. The bolt rattled.

"Just a moment." It was a man's voice. Refined; perhaps a little uncertain.

Thumbs set deep in his waistcoat pockets, Hitch gazed at the wooden door and said nothing. He'd decided that standing there rock-still with the dark, pewter-coloured waters of the Bristol Channel behind him might make him look a little bit cool or mysterious. In fact, maybe those waves were going to be a bit wild and white-headed, too; maybe there should be something of a storm rising back there. A fitting fanfare.

Behind him, the weather obliged.

The door opened. Hitch resisted the urge to have a flash of lightning lend the moment some drama. You could overdo these things, after all.

"Good afternoon." The young occupant stood blinking at the lightness of the day. He looked tired and distracted, much as he had in Max's office. There too was that same look of febrile intensity. Nevertheless, politeness and an instinctive good nature seemed be governing his response. He smiled. "Can I help you?"

Affably, Hitch shook his head. He'd been practising this bit. "No, no. Actually, I'm here with an offer from Paul Locke - a matter of business."

The poet looked perplexed. "Indeed? What manner of business?"

Hitch smiled. He only had to keep the man talking for a while, and he'd come well equipped for that. He reached into a pocket and produced a brightly painted tin cylinder. "I'm in the confectionery trade, Mr. Coleridge. My name's Hitchpost."

"Oh, then I'm pleased to meet you, Mr. Hitchpost." His host stepped forward. "And when you say 'confectionery'..?"

"I mean biscuits." Hitch opened the tin and waggled it at him. "Please: take one. They're really rather good."

The End

Acknowledgements

With thanks to the legion of kind friends who reviewed this book while it was still a young and profoundly troubled work in progress. Special thanks to everyone at the 'Comedy Literature Only Group', to Rob Wingfield at the INCA Project, to Ray Holland, Mark Roman, and Lucinda Elliot. And to Justine, of course, and all the fine inhabitants of Mirror World.

About the Author

Rob Gregson spent much of his youth reading fantasy novels, immersing himself in role playing games and generally doing everything possible to avoid the realities of life in the late 1980s. In his defence, we're talking about a time when ridiculous hair, hateful pop, and soaring unemployment were all very popular so it wasn't altogether a bad decision but nor was it without its ramifications. Had he abandoned the realms of elves and wizardry at an earlier age, he might have developed one or two useful life skills and he would almost certainly have found it easier to get a girlfriend.

Since that time, he and reality have developed a grudging tolerance of one another, although their relationship still goes through the occasional bad patch. This book, and his first two novels - *Unreliable Histories* and *The Endless Land* - are all evidence of that.

To learn more about our authors and our current projects visit: www.mirrorworldpublishing.com, follow @MirrorWorldPub or like us at www.facebook.com/mirrorworldpublishing

Or keep reading for a sneak peek at:

Unreachable Skies II: Exile

By Karen McCreedy

One

"If you go through the Deadlands, you will all die."

As I picked my way between strewn belongings, and smouldering campfires that did little to warm the icy dawn, it was the voice of Shaya, the Chief Hunter, which carried to me above the sound of breaking waves, whimpering younglings, and complaining females. Just two days ago, every wingless youngling, and every female who had produced one, had been sent into exile by our Prime, Kalis, urged on by his favourite adviser, Fazak. Yet already the arguments had started!

My nose alerted me to the stink of a shallow waste-pit and I edged around it, stepping over a broken beaker, and continued on toward the squabbling voices. As Kalis' Fate-seer I was expected to return to my dwelling on the *Spirax* peninsula, a few nines of wingbeats across the bay, but a Vision had shown me that my future lay with the exiles and, after visiting my Dream-cave, I had flown to their makeshift encampment.

The females, their wings broken by Kalis' new Elite Guard, had been netted over the river along with their younglings, and had been left on the claw of reed-tufted sand that jutted into the ocean from the Manybend estuary's north shore. As I'd circled over the nines of fires, their spiralling layout had shown that someone had taken charge of setting the camp properly, and my sole concern had been finding somewhere to land without being seen. In the end I had set down on the beach to the north, wetting my feet as I landed at the edge of the incoming tide. Taking care to make sure I would not leave any traces of my approach, I had walked along the tideline till I reached the promontory at daybreak. I had intended to find my friend Doran and make myself known to her, but the sound of raised voices had drawn my attention, and I had instead made my way across the camp to the ridge of snow-covered ground that separated the hook of sand from the mud of the Deadlands. I smelled cooking – branmeal bubbling in a pot to my left, meat patties warming in a pan to my right. My stomachs rumbled a protest that I was not stopping to eat, but my attention was on the group at the foot of the slope where Shaya stood, and the arguments that I could now hear more clearly.

"The Deadlands are frozen, Shaya, just like everywhere else. I don't see why we can't walk straight across them to the Ambit river. We can head for the Eye, or even the river upstream from there where it narrows and will be easier to cross."

I didn't recognise the speaker, though I knew from her copper tunic that she was an Artisan. As Shaya set her ears to a more aggressive angle and began to explain the dangers of the Deadlands – the thin ice masking mud that was deep enough to drown in, brambletrap that would feed on any creature living or dead – I spotted Doran's russet fur and green-and-black Healer's tunic amid the crowd. Forgetting that I had changed my appearance by dyeing my fur and changing my tunic from Fate-seer black to Trader blue, I made my way over to her and said, "Doran, what's going on?"

She twisted an ear my way, gave me a sniff, and looked me up and down. "I'm sorry, do I know you?"

I took a quick look round. Nineties of females were attending to their younglings, cooking meals, or still rolled in blankets, sleeping. Those in the group surrounding Shaya had their attention on what she was saying. Only Doran had an ear twisted my way. "It's me," I hissed, "Zarda. I promised I would join you, didn't I?"

"But you're," she said as she waved a paw from the neck of my tunic to my feet, "you look so different." She sounded disappointed. "I've been waiting for you to come. I thought that having Zarda the Fate-seer join us would help all these drax to face what lies ahead. But if they don't know it's you…"

It had not occurred to me that I might help anyone's morale. "I came because I Saw that I should," I said, "and because Kalis no longer listens to me. Besides, if Dru is to fulfil his destiny and defeat the Koth, he'll need help and guidance from a Fate-seer, especially—" No. Only members of the council knew that Dru had the Sight, and we had agreed to keep it secret for the moment. Doran had no need to know – not yet. I dismissed what I'd been about to say with a flick of an ear that told Doran it was of no importance, and spiralled a paw across the front of my tunic. "I can't be Zarda here. I know Kalis isn't interested in anything I have to say, but he is a stickler for tradition. I've left him without a Fate-seer and he won't be happy. He'll send the Guardflight to look for me – maybe even his new Elite Guard. And I think we can both guess what will happen to me if they find me." As I finished talking, I turned my head to indicate the pathetic figure huddled in a blanket, sitting alone in the shadows beyond the encampment fires.

Doran flicked an ear in sympathy – the other was still turned toward Shaya and the ongoing argument – and ran a paw over her tunic. "I never liked Varna, but to lose her wings like that…" She shuddered, then leaned toward me to confide, "She howled through the entire first day. Only subsided to a whimper when Limar threatened to bind her mouth shut. Dru kept taking her beakers of soup from Limar's cauldron, and showed her things he'd found on the beach, but she snapped and snarled every time he went near her. In the end, he stayed by the fire over there with Limar." Turning back to face me, she waggled an ear in apology. "I suppose you're right, you can't be seen to have joined us. Not yet, anyway. I just hoped," she said, indicating the group arguing with Shaya. "Perhaps if the Fate-seer had been able to step in, these silly females wouldn't be proposing to cross the Deadlands on foot."

I turned my gaze from Doran to the arguing group and then down to the laden carry-pouch that was still strapped to my shoulders. My black tunic was in there, buried at the bottom beneath cold patties, jars of healing herbs, bags of avalox for tea, a second blue tunic, a blanket, several beakers, knives, spoons, and a bag of precious spirelles which I had found in the Fate-seer's dwelling a few ninedays ago. Could I – should I – pull out the tunic and join my voice to Shaya's? As I hesitated, she climbed part way up the slope, sending snow and sand tumbling beneath her feet as she took the high ground in typical hunter fashion. As she turned to face the crowd again, I saw that there were five other hunters with her, standing at the foot of the slope. All of them had a defiant set to their ears and one wing apiece half-extended while they joined their arguments to their chief's – "the ice is thin," – "there will be quickmud," – "there will be nowhere you can rest in safety."

Shaya raised her arms and her voice once again: "And if none of that worries you, then the brambletrap should. Just because there's snow on the branches doesn't mean it's safe."

I eased my pouch to the ground, still uncertain what I should do. As I straightened up and rolled my shoulders, I almost forgot that I was supposed to have a damaged wing and started to give them both a stretch. Only when they were partly-extended did I remember. Giving what I hoped was a convincing yelp of pain, I winced and pulled one wing in.

No-one noticed. All attention was now on the females who wanted to leave the main group. They had heard all the arguments, all the reasons why they should not try to cross the Deadlands. A few moved away, ears drooping and muttering to each other as they shuffled back towards the campfires. But a female in the brown tunic of a farmer stood her ground and I recognised her as Colex, one of the first females I'd attended, along with my teacher Vizan, when her youngling hatched without wings. She had been stubborn and angry then, and sounded equally stubborn and angry now as she barked: "We'll all die if we go the way you are proposing. So the beach runs north – so what? There are dunes and rocks and cliffs before you even reach the Cleft Rocks. And you can't stay on the coast much beyond them, because the Ambit peninsular juts east, and if you go east, there is nowhere left to go except to turn and head back along the estuary. Even if your wings have healed by then, it will be difficult to carry all the younglings over the water there. Much better surely to go north and west through the Deadlands, and make for the narrower stretch of the Ambit west of the Eye."

The Eye was a small, vine-strewn islet that divided the Ambit's flow in two for a few spans, giving the river the appearance from above of looking back at you as you flew over it.

"That's a long way upstream from the estuary," Doran murmured. "We were west of that, I think, when we flew to the Forest that day, remember?"

"I'll never forget it," I replied, my voice low. "You were bitten by a vine-serpent, and I nearly got eaten by a mouldworm." I also remembered that it had taken us the best part of a day to fly there. How long would such a journey take us on foot? Especially if we took the longer but safer route along the coast and over the peninsula? Kalis had set no deadline for us to reach the Forest, but I was sure that he would not wish us to linger in his territory any longer than we had to. "It is a long way," I said, answering Doran's original point, "but at least by going along the coast there's a chance of reaching it. Anyone going through the Deadlands has no chance at all."

I twisted my ears back in Shaya's direction as I heard her make the same point. "At least wait a few days—"

"What for?" Colex extended a paw in the direction of the encampment as she spoke. "We haven't moved since the guardflight netted us here. I say we move now, and quickly, so that we can cross the Deadlands while they are still frozen." She turned in a slow circle, ears alert, nose busy sniffing for support from those surrounding her. "I'm leaving now, with Lexon," she added, placing a paw on the wingless shoulders of her offspring. "Get your carry-pouches if you're coming with us."

Doran gave me a sideways look and another quick sniff. "Are you going to say anything?"

I looked again at the carry-pouch in which I had buried my Fate-seer's tunic. Lexon had hatched before most of the other wingless emerged from their eggs. Only Colex's stubbornness had kept him alive when everyone else was urging that she left him in the foothills for the Koth to take. Back then, before it became clear that every female who had recovered from the Sickness would produce such offspring, even Vizan had suggested that the hatchling would be better off dead. He'd actually brewed a deadly mixture of zenox powder and rotberry juice, but Colex had knocked the beaker out of his paw. She had refused to listen to him, just as she was not listening to Shaya. "Colex won't heed anyone's advice," I said. "She certainly won't listen to me."

"Some of the others might," Doran retorted, indicating the group of several nines who were collecting their carry-pouches and their younglings. "They'll die if they go into the Deadlands. You know that, Zarda."

I did know it, but a glance round at the still-whimpering Varna reminded me again of what awaited me if Kalis found his errant Fate-seer. My wing struts developed an itch at the mere thought, but still I sniffed the air to discern how Colex's supporters truly felt. There was not so much as a whiff of doubt among them – only determination and a degree of sorrow. I looked around at the nines surrounding us, listened to the shouts of their younglings, and smelled their fright, pain, and doubt. I saw Dru, my reason for joining this exile, bound across to Shaya's side and heard him try to reason with Colex. "I'm not a Fate-seer," he shouted, his ears erect, and his white mane blowing in the breeze, "but I have the Sight. Shaya is right. If you try to cross the Deadlands, you'll die!"

Colex snorted. "I'm not going to stand here and listen to a pup tell stories. Get along with you, before I nip your snout, young Dru. It's your fault we're out here at all – don't pretend you can know what will happen to us when you couldn't even See what would happen to you on the Night of the Two Moons."

"That's not fair!" Limar, a pink-clad, fluffed up bundle of indignation, pushed her way to the front of the crowd, brandishing a ladle from the branmeal she had been preparing a few spans away. "None of this was Dru's fault, he did exactly what he was supposed to at the Two Moons ritual. It was Fazak finding some ancient scratching that said everyone had to be airborne that spoiled everything."

"Doesn't have the Sight, though, does he?"

And for that, Limar had no answer. Though she was Dru's half-sibling and nest-nurse, she had not been told that a visit to the Dream-cave with me had awakened his talent. Of those within earshot, only Shaya, Varna, and myself knew he was speaking the truth. Shaya had been on the council when it was agreed to keep Dru's abilities secret, and whatever had happened since then, I was sure she would not betray that trust. As for Varna – well, she was in no fit state to do anything, and was certainly not about to rise to her pup's defence.

Nor could I, not without revealing who I was.

As I'd flown south during the night, the Great Spiral itself had parted the clouds to send me a sign that my decision to join the exiles was correct. Those same clouds, edged with pale gold in the east, now hid the Spiral from view, but I sent a prayer skyward anyway: *"Tell me what I should do!"*

This time, there was no answer, no sign – just a memory of my own Vision of crossing the Ambit's mudflats with the wingless. The mudflats lay to the north, along the coast on the far side of the Ambit peninsula. If I was to cross them, I had to survive to travel with Shaya and the nineties with her. I couldn't risk putting on my black tunic. Even if no-one betrayed me when Kalis sent the Guardflight to look for me – and he would – we were just a short flight from the *Spirax* where the Elite Guard now flew. It was unlikely they would spot one single black tunic amid the myriad colours that surrounded me, but it was not impossible.

The scent of Doran's disappointment was overwhelming, and I looked up from my carry-pouch to see her ears and whiskers twitch with disapproval.

"I can't save them, Doran." My voice sounded hollow. "But if you want me to try – if you want me to risk my wings by speaking up – then tell everyone right now who I am, and hope that no-one betrays me when the Guardflight come. Because come they will, I guarantee it."

She half-turned away from me, getting as far as opening her mouth to call to Shaya and the others before I scented uncertainty. She looked back at me, then at the set of Colex's ears as the farmer picked up her carry-pouch and set her snout north-west. "I can't be responsible for you losing your wings," she said.

"Come on. We're supposed to have nine round each fire, but with all this upset no-one will worry about an extra one sitting at ours." Turning away from the sight of a line of females and younglings scrambling up the sandy, snow-lined ridge to set out across the Deadlands, she led me through the encampment to a warm fire where her youngling, Cavel, was stirring a pot of hot branmeal. "I suppose we'd better think of something else to call you," she said.

#escapewithus

Why Mirror World?

We publish escapism fiction for all ages. Our novels are imaginative and character-driven and our goal is to give our readers a glimpse into other worlds, times, and versions of reality that parallel our own, giving them an experience they can't get anywhere else!

We offer free delivery within Windsor-Essex in Canada, an all-you-can-read membership program, blind-dates with books, and you can order our novels from our <u>online store,</u> or from your favorite major book retailer.

We appreciate every like, tweet, facebook post, and review and we love to hear from you. Please consider leaving us your comments online or sending your thoughts or questions to info@mirrorworldpublishing.com

Thank you.